St. Raven

Also by Jo Beverley in Large Print:

An Arranged Marriage
The Stanforth Secrets
The Stolen Bride
Hazard
The Devil's Heiress
The Dragon's Bride
Devilish
Lord Wraybourne's Betrothed
Something Wicked
An Unwilling Bride

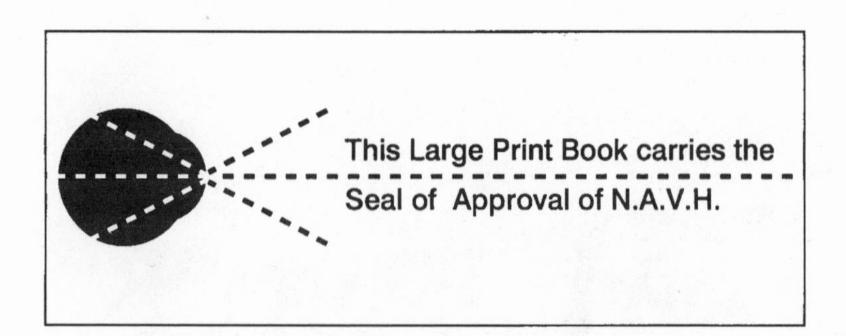

St. Raven

JO BEVERLEY

Published in 2003 by arrangement with NAL Signet,
a member of Penguin Group (USA) Inc.

Wheeler Large Print Romance Series.

The text of this Large Print edition is unabridged.
Other aspects of the book may vary from the original edition.

Set in 16 pt. Plantin by Minnie B. Raven.

Printed in the United States on permanent paper.

Library of Congress Cataloging-in-Publication Data

Beverley, Jo.
St. Raven / Jo Beverley.
p. cm.
ISBN 1-58724-425-X (lg. print : hc : alk. paper)
1. Inheritance and succession — Fiction. 2. Kidnapping victims — Fiction. 3. Large type books. I. Title: Saint Raven. II. Title.
PR9199.3.B424S7 2003

2003042266

St. Raven

Acknowledgments

Thank you as always to my wonderful editor, Audrey LaFehr, and to my supportive agent, Meg Ruley. You smooth my path.

I am blessed with many on-line friends and groups who are always ready to brainstorm, or supply information or act as a sounding board. I am equally blessed with a fun and supportive local romance writers group and critique group. Thank you, everyone.

I often go to the internet for spot research. For this book Rosemary Sachdev, whom I know through Dunnettry, found the names of a pair of Indian lovers for me, and also just the right term for a partner in such exercises. Fellow author Margaret Evans Porter helped me with the value of gemstones. If I have made any errors, they are entirely my own.

And thank you to all my readers. I could write for myself, but it wouldn't be nearly as much fun!

Chapter One

Summer 1816. North of London

Still as a statue in the full moon's light the highwayman watched the road. He controlled his mount without effort and without bit, and when the horse stirred, tossing its head, no jingle broke the quiet of the night woods.

His clothing was dark as the shadows, his face concealed behind a black mask and a delicate beard and mustache in the style of Charles I. He would be invisible if not for the splash of a sweeping white plume on his broad Cavalier hat.

That plume was the signature of Le Corbeau, the bold French rascal who called himself the Crow and claimed the right to peck at those who traveled the night roads north from London.

Though no one else could be seen, the Crow did not fly alone. He had men stationed north and south to warn of danger and of approaching prey. He waited for their signals in stillness except for the stirring of his feather in the breeze.

Then, at last, an owl hoot with a strange pattern at the end floated from the south. A victim approached. A suitable one. Not the well-armed mail coach or poor pickings on a swaybacked horse or in a cart. What came from the south was undefended but worth the effort, and would be here soon.

He listened until he heard the pounding of fast horses. With a sharp whistle of his own, he surged out of the trees and down the road head-on to the coach and pair.

The startled coachman dragged on his reins. By the time the coach stopped, Tristan Tregallows, Duke of St. Raven, commanded the two people in the coach with his cocked pistol, and two colleagues kept guard nearby.

Heart pounding in a way both alarming and pleasurable, Tris thought this was almost as good as sex. Pity this was his first and last night for the game.

"Monsieur, madame," he greeted with a slight inclination of his head. He continued in the French-accented English of the real Le Corbeau. "Pleeze to step out of ze carriage."

As he spoke, he assessed his victims as best he could, given the dim interior.

Perfect.

Terror or threatened apoplexy might have driven him off, but he had a fashionable young couple at gunpoint. The lady sat closest to his side of the coach, and she seemed more furious than frightened. Her mouth was set, and her direct, pale eyes showed outrage at his attack.

"Damn your eyes, you gallows bait!" the man snarled. The voice confirmed him well-born, which was excellent. He would not miss half his money.

"Zat is in ze hands of *le Bon Dieu* and ze magistrates, *monsieur*. You, on ze other hand, are in mine. *Sortez!* You know my reputation. I will neither kill you nor take your all — unless," Tris added, trying for silky menace, "you continue to disobey me."

"Oh, get out and let's get this over with," ordered the man, shoving the woman so hard that she banged against the inside of the coach.

Her head snapped toward her partner as if she'd blister him, but then she turned back to open the door, head bowed, apparently meek as milk.

As Tris backed Caesar a few steps to make sure he couldn't be jumped, his mind danced with curiosity. The man was a cur. It seemed the woman might think the same, yet she obeyed. It could be an unhappy marriage, but such wives rarely rebelled over little things.

He tried to shut off curiosity. He didn't have time for a mystery. Even so late, on a night with a good moon another vehicle could appear at any time.

The woman climbed down the steps, one hand holding her pale skirt out of the way, the other using the open door for balance. Half an eye on the man, St. Raven still made a number of instant assessments.

She tended to roundness rather than slender elegance.

She was graceful in this awkward situation.

She was dressed in a fine evening gown under a light shawl. Unusual for traveling. Damn. Perhaps they were called away to a deathbed.

She had a neat ankle.

When she arrived on the road and looked up at him, he noted a heart-shaped face fringed with dark curls frothing out along the front edge of a fashionable evening turban of striped cloth. She wore pearls at her neck and ears.

Modest pearls, however. He wished she showed signs of fabulous wealth. He supposed he'd have to take them, or at least part of them. Damnation. Would returning them destroy the purpose of this enterprise?

He turned his full attention to the stocky man who followed her. His top boots, breeches, jacket, and beaver hat might seem casual to some, but Tris recognized the height of fashion for a certain sort — a sporting Corinthian. The striped waistcoat, the flamboyant cravat, and the cut of the coat confirmed it and sent a warning: The man's heavy build would be all muscle.

Then the moon shone full on the man's sneering face — chunky, wide in the jaw, and with a nose that looked to have been broken more than once.

Crofton.

Viscount Crofton, a man in his early thirties of moderate wealth and expensive tastes, especially in women. Or rather, in quantity of women. He was a bruising rider and pugilist who was generally to be found at any event promising sport — with men or women — and with a preference for the rough.

Crofton had attended a gentlemen's party at Tris's house once. It had been made clear that he would never be welcome again. It would be a personal pleasure to distress Crofton, but the man was dangerous, and needed watching.

Tris reminded himself not to be distracted, but some detail niggled. Something that might be relevant here.

He brushed it aside. He had a simple task in hand — to stage a holdup so that the man in jail as Le Corbeau would be proved innocent.

"Your purses, pleeze," he said, but couldn't resist another glance at the woman. Crofton wasn't married, but dress, demeanor, and jewelry spoke of a lady, not a whore. Did he have a sister?

Crofton pulled a handful of banknotes out of his pocket and tossed them onto the ground, where they fluttered in the breeze. "Grovel for them like the pig you are."

"Crow," Tris corrected, tempted to force the man to pick them up with his teeth. *"Madame?"*

"I have no purse."

A cool, educated voice. A lady for sure, and the moonlight painted her features with white marble purity.

"Then it will have to be your earrings, *chérie*." Instinct clamored that something was wrong, and he couldn't ride away with this mystery unsolved. The thought of a well-bred lady in Crofton's clutches revolted him.

He glanced at the woman, but she wasn't looking at him. She was gazing at the moonlit countryside, denying his existence even as she took the pearl drops from her ears and tossed them down by the money.

Then she looked at him, eyes narrowed, lips tight. The mysterious lady wasn't frightened. She was furious.

She had to be with Crofton by choice to be so angry at the interruption. On the other hand, he couldn't forget the way Crofton had shoved her and her instinctive, outraged reaction.

And then, the elusive detail came to him.

A week or two ago, Crofton had won a property in a game of cards. Stokeley Manor in Cambridgeshire. To celebrate, he was throwing a party — an orgy, to be precise. Tris had received a presumptuous invitation, and unless he was mistaken, the event began tomorrow night.

So, Crofton was on his way there, and he wouldn't be taking his sister with him, or any other respectable lady. Unlikely as it seemed, the moonlit madonna had to be a high-priced whore. Not all whores were sluts, and some used a ladylike appearance as part of their stock-in-trade.

Experience and instinct, however, told Tris that this woman was no such thing. There was one way to try her out.

Le Corbeau was a foolish, romantic sort of highwayman, and he sometimes offered to return his loot for a kiss. A lot could be learned from the way a woman kissed.

Tris smiled at her. "Since my wages have so unfortunately fallen in ze dirt, *ma belle,* I must ask you to pick zem up for me."

He thought she was going to refuse. The moonlight did not show color, but he knew a flush of anger heated those rounded cheeks — anger that tightened her lips and confirmed his fears. It was the sort of cold, righteous anger no whore he'd known would ever permit herself.

"Do it," Crofton snapped, "and get rid of the cur."

She flinched under the order, but again she submitted, walking forward and then dipping down to pick up the money and earrings. She didn't walk like a whore, either.

Tris didn't like it. He didn't like it at all.

He'd heard that Crofton's entertainments leaned to the crude and that he had a taste for debauching virgins — the less willing, the better. Might he have found a way to force a well-bred virgin to be the centerpiece of his celebration?

The woman straightened and approached the horse, holding out the money and jewelry.

He looked down into steady, despising eyes. Who the devil did she think she was? Joan of Arc? She was on her way to an orgy with Crofton, and she'd be wiser to be looking for help than treating a possible rescuer like a slug.

He moved Caesar forward a step. The woman flinched back, her stony composure breaking for a moment. Afraid of horses? When her lips relaxed, however, they showed a temptingly full bow. Kissing her wouldn't be any sacrifice at all.

He remembered to check on Crofton. Damn stupid to have been distracted. The man seemed to be simply observing, amused. A bad sign. Tris moved Caesar forward another step, and again she backed away.

"If you keep retreating, *chérie*, we will be here all night."

Her lips tightened again. "Good. Then someone will come along and arrest you."

"Not in time. Ze money?"

She set her chin and stepped forward, holding the money and earrings up and out, coming no closer than she had to. The contrast between her bravado and her obvious fear of Caesar touched his heart.

He took the loot, and she hastily backed away. He separated the banknotes roughly in half and tossed part back on the ground. "I beggar no man."

Crofton laughed. "That amount wouldn't beggar me, cur. Are we done, then?"

Tris looked at the woman again. "I will return ze rest and your earrings for a kiss, *chérie*."

She took another step back, but Crofton pushed her forward. "Go on, *Cherry*, kiss him. I'll let you keep the blunt if it's a good one."

Tris saw her inhale a long, angry breath, sensed fire behind her eyes, but again she did not protest. What hold did Crofton have over her?

"Well?" he asked.

"If I must," she replied so coldly that he felt he should shiver. He suppressed a grin. He liked her spirit.

He extended his gloved hand. "I cannot risk dismounting, *chérie*, so you must come up."

Panic staggered her then. "On the *horse?*"

"On the horse."

Cressida Mandeville stared up at the costumed madman on the huge horse, knowing she had finally reached her breaking point. She had struck a loathsome deal with Lord Crofton, she had set out to be his mistress for a week, she had endured some pawing in the carriage without throwing up. She would not, however, could not get up on a horse.

"Keep the money," she snapped.

"Kiss him!" Crofton snarled.

Frozen by that, she did not react in time when the highwayman holstered his pistol, moved the horse forward, and leaned to snatch her up into the saddle in front of him.

She swallowed a scream because she wouldn't show that sort of fear, but when she landed on the horse and it sidled beneath her, she clutched the enemy's jacket, her eyes tight shut, and prayed.

"Zere, zere, *petite,* I assure you it is not so bad up here."

The amusement in his voice stung her pride, and indeed, now she was up and the horse was still, it didn't seem too bad — as long as she had the robber's big, solid body to hang on to.

She made herself crack her eyes open. All she could see was dark clothing. Her head was buried against warmth and wool, surprisingly surrounded by the smell of clean clothing and spice.

Sandalwood.

A strange crow, indeed.

Since pride was all she had left, Cressida made herself release her clutch and straighten her spine. Having achieved that, she turned her head to see what Crofton was doing.

Nothing, because another highwayman had the area covered by two pistols. Not a careless crow, but Crofton wouldn't interfere, anyway. He must be finding this amusing.

Cressida remembered attending the theater in London some months ago and seeing a play that featured this rascally highwayman. There he turned out to be the hero. Reality, of course, was very different.

All the same, given the choice between the two men . . .

The highwayman seemed to have moved back on the horse so that she was sideways on the saddle in front of him, but even so, she was crushed against his body. He chuckled, and she felt it.

Jupiter! She was nestled against him in the most intimate way. Her bottom was . . . well . . . between his thighs, her legs over one of them. She felt, in a most extraordinary way, the movements of his legs that caused the huge horse to begin to back, swaying beneath her.

She clutched again. "What are you doing?" It was almost a screech.

"Putting a little more distance between us and your so gallant escort, *chérie*. If I am to pay you due attention, I do not want him quite so close."

The words "gallant escort" bit with sarcasm.

She fixed her eyes on his jacket and not on the world moving around them. "You have no cause to sneer at him. You are a thief."

"So ardent in his defense."

She had to look. They were almost in the trees. She glanced back. They were five yards or more from the coach. "Stop!"

"So imperious. I adore a commanding woman."

He rolled the *r* in a way that seemed to shiver through her. She couldn't do this. She couldn't *kiss* this man! She had to do something to escape. But what?

Le Corbeau had holstered his pistol to control her. If she were a true heroine, wouldn't she grasp that opportunity?

And do what?

Hit him? A fine lot of good that would do. He'd scooped her up like a child.

And what was she going to save herself from?

From a kiss.

Only a kiss.

A mere nothing compared with the fate she'd accepted. All London talked of Le Corbeau, and some ladies drove up and down these roads hoping for an encounter and a rascal's kiss.

A kiss was nothing. . . . But then the horse sidled, and she choked back a cry. She had to kiss him on a *horse?*

If her imagination had ever stretched so far, this would have been the most impossible, most intolerable thing ever expected of her. She saw no choice, however. Given that, she would not be a coward.

She swallowed, then turned her head up to the masked and bearded face. "May we have done with this, sir, so I can proceed with my journey?"

She saw him smile and realized that he might be handsome. His lips were certainly firm, yet in a mysterious way, sensual. Like a painting of a god of pleasure.

Those lips lowered, and she almost went cross-eyed, trying to keep the danger in sight before it reached her. Shutting her eyes, she felt his lips press against hers.

His face hair tickled.

She tried to pull back, but his hand slid behind her head, confining her. His lips parted, and his tongue touched wetly against her.

Trapped by his strong arms and his controlling hand, she was helpless and she hated it. What's more, this was no sort of kiss she had ever imagined. This was nothing to do with tenderness or affection. It was a contest between two vile men, and she wished them both to Hades.

As his lips moved against hers, she sat perfectly still. She would give neither of them the satisfaction of seeing her struggle. If she admitted the truth, she was also still because any sudden movement might upset the monstrous beast beneath her.

The man chuckled, then licked her lips. She jerked back, then stilled again, but her hands became fists. Oh, but she longed to fight, to pummel, to claw at the monstrous beast who assaulted her.

But then he moved back and looked at her.

Thoughtfully. Questioningly.

And Cressida knew she had made a mistake.

She stared back. What had she done? Could she correct it?

He looked at Crofton. Then he pushed the forgotten earrings and banknotes down the low front of her gown. Before she could express her shock at that, he gave a sharp whistle, turned the horse, and rode into the woods, taking her with him.

Shock upon shock stole her voice for a moment, but then she screamed, "Stop it! What are you doing? *Help!*"

He pressed her face hard to his chest so she could hardly breathe, never mind shout, as the beast pounded beneath her, carrying her away. Now she fought, with arms and legs, trying to find a place to scratch, to hurt. She'd rather fall off the horse than be stolen away like this.

And her plan.

Dear heaven, her plan!

She heard the man curse, and the horse stopped, sidling and jerking. She freed a hand and yanked the highwayman's beard as hard as she could.

It half ripped off in her hand.

"Damnation!" He grabbed her hands. "Stay still, woman!"

She flailed and kicked as best she could. "Let me go!"

The horse began to rear and was forced down. The man's grip on her wrists tightened to the point of pain. She tried to land a solid kick on the horse.

Her ankles were caught by two strong hands.

"Have your hands full, have you?" drawled a fashionable voice.

"Stop laughing and think of something to tie her up with." Le Corbeau's spoke in the same aristocratic English accent.

That and awareness of a new enemy stunned Cressida to stillness, but then "tie her up" sank in, and she struggled again. She opened her mouth to shriek, and a gloved hand covered it.

"Know when you're beaten, you fool. I wish you no harm. In fact, I'm saving you from a fate worse than death. You'll thank me when you come to your senses."

She glared up at him, longing to scream her opinion of his interfering arrogance, but all she could manage was a growl.

Despite all her kicking and squirming, her evening shoes were snatched away, her garters — her *garters!* — untied, and her silk stockings stripped off. Then her ankles were tied. Moments later, her wrists were bound, as well.

"We need to blindfold her," her infernal captor said.

She tried to fight, but the bonds and despair turned her feeble. Tears stung at her eyes as they were covered by a cloth tied behind her head.

Oh Lord — oh Lord, to be safe home again as she had been until so recently, with no deeper concern than the choice of jam for breakfast.

"Think that counted as a holdup?" asked the other man, still sounding amused.

"It'll damn well have to. I'm not doing this again."

"Perhaps you should mind what you say, the lady not having anything blocking her ears as yet."

"Damn it all to Hades. . . ."

"Perhaps you should mind your *language*." The second man sounded as if he was laughing.

"Stubble it."

Then the horse jolted, and they were off again. Her mouth was free and she could have screamed, but for the moment she didn't dare. She couldn't even clutch now. She was entirely dependent on her captor's strong arms.

"Where?" asked the other man.

"The house. That's why she's blindfolded."

A house. A house that mustn't be seen.

Fear turned her cold. Le Corbeau was not a Frenchman, but an Englishman. A well-born Englishman. He'd do anything to save himself from the hangman. Killing her would be a mere nothing.

Lord, save me. Lord, save me. Lord, save me, she prayed with every sickening jolt of the horse beneath her, with every crush of her captor's body. He was her terror now, not the horse.

She was powerless, helpless, completely at the mercy of this mass of muscle and power.

She was going to vomit.

Would it choke her?

Would anyone care? . . .

The horse stopped.

Cressida shuddered and gave thanks, trying to swallow the taste of bile. The man moved, taking the pressure from her, settling her to sit sideways on the smooth and slippery saddle.

Then he was gone.

She was *alone* — blind, bound, and unbalanced in the cold air. The horse moved.

She fell!

Even as she screamed, strong hands caught her waist. She cried out again, this time in thanks for the strong arms beneath her, then for the strong body she was held against.

The monstrous beast again, but this one was solid and safe — and two-legged.

From her right the other man said, "Dear lady, please don't be afraid." He sounded sincerely concerned.

But it was the highwayman who held her, carried her. To where? To what? New fears should be boiling up, but it was as if terror was exhausted. She could only pray.

No. She could *think*. "Knowledge is power," Sir Francis Bacon had said, and she needed any power she could grasp.

She could hear, so she sorted through sounds. They'd left the horses behind, and the men must be walking on soft earth, because there was no sound of boots.

She could smell. No smell of horse, either, but a slight whiff that might be a pigsty not very far away. A farm? And sandalwood, of course, so common to her nostrils now that she hardly noticed it.

Then the men's feet made a crunching noise. Gravel? No farm had a gravel driveway. They were approaching a house of substance.

She was blindfolded *because* of the house, so she wouldn't recognize it. No, so she wouldn't recognize it again if she returned with the magistrates. That did suggest that they expected to let her go eventually.

After they'd had their wicked way with her?

She'd thought such things the stuff of Minerva novels!

They stopped. She heard a click. A latch?

Yes. The door didn't squeak, but it made a slight sound as it opened, and she was moved from outside to in. No breeze. Staler air. Polish. Faint memories of a meal. The steady tick of a large clock and wood floors beneath boots.

Fear trembled back into life. She didn't want

to be inside, inside his house. “Please . . . ,” she said.

“Hush. Make noise and I’ll gag you. I’ll put her in my room.”

The other man must still be there. Did that offer more safety or more danger?

With a shift of balance, Le Corbeau began to carry her upstairs.

To his room.

To his *bedroom.*

Cressida prayed. With Crofton it would have been vile, but it would have been her choice and for her purpose. Was she to lose her virtue to a thief’s whim?

Another door opening. Carpet under boots. A stronger smell of sandalwood.

His bedroom.

She was lowered onto something soft.

Onto his bed.

Chapter Two

Cressida's heart had been racing forever, it seemed, but now it settled to a deep, fretful thud as she waited for the worst.

For moments she heard only her heartbeats, as if she were alone, but with some deep and ancient instinct she knew he was there. It made silence more terrifying than shouting. She turned her head this way and that as if she might detect him.

Then he said — the highwayman said, "No one's going to hurt you. Please believe that."

Strangely, she did. Her frantic heartbeats slowed.

"I have things I need to do," he said, "so I must leave you bound here for a while. I'm sorry for it, but no one will hurt you." He spoke from closer by. "However, I need to tie you up a bit more."

"No."

He ignored her, lifted her, wrapped something around her at elbow level, and knotted it. Then he moved away, boots on carpet. She heard the door open and close.

Now, she was alone.

She wasn't sure whether to give thanks or vent rage. The scoundrel had wrenched her from her place and purpose, and now he had abandoned her here, bound and blindfolded. She raised her hands to push off the blindfold and realized why he'd tied her around her arms. She could not raise her hands high enough.

She wriggled her head on the pillow but couldn't dislodge the cloth. She stopped. The cloth was tied over the back of her turban, and that was held in place with hairpins that dug and pulled at every movement.

"Go hang yourself," she muttered to the absent villain, a useful phrase she'd found in Shakespeare. With any luck, he'd be caught and end up at Tyburn doing the hangman's jig.

For some reason, that image did not particularly satisfy her. She supposed that thus far he hadn't deserved death.

And he had blindfolded her for a reason. So she wouldn't see.

So he wouldn't have to murder her?

It was a warm summer's night, but a chill crept through her, and tears trickled beneath the blindfolding cloth.

Tris ran downstairs and found Caradoc Lyne waiting for him in the parlor, sipping cognac. Cary was a strapping blond Adonis who generally shared Tris's carefree attitudes and sense of mischief. Now he disapproved.

"I couldn't let her go with Crofton," Tris said.

"I'd think not, but why tie her up?"

Tris grabbed the decanter and poured himself some brandy. Smuggled brandy. A reward of another jape, but one that had gone a great deal more smoothly than this.

"I should leave her free to wander the house or to run off?"

"You could explain . . ." But then Cary pulled a face. "I suppose not."

"Quite. She'll keep, and we still have a coach to hold up."

"You said that would do."

"On consideration, it won't. Crofton, damn him, is hardly likely to complain to the nearest magistrate." Tris drained the glass. "Come on."

"Bollocks. If we have to try again, can I hold up the coach?"

"No. I claim right of rank."

"Spoilsport."

They left the room, debating the honor, heading for the stables and fresh horses.

"I could fit into the Crow's disguise," Cary argued.

"And how long would it take to darken your hair and stick on this damn face hair?" Tris touched his beard and realized that one side still hung loose. "Damn that ungrateful harpy."

Glue would take too long for his limited patience. While his long-suffering groom was readying fresh horses, he used a bit of sticky emollient to tack the edge back. Then the three of them set out again to play the High Toby.

Cressida finally realized one reason her prison seemed eerie. There was no clock. She was accustomed to a bedroom clock. Occasionally she heard a distant chiming — two quarters, then one o'clock — but here was only silence and her own anxious breathing. What was going to happen when the man returned?

She'd set out on this journey prepared for terrible things, but not this. She'd been prepared to give herself to Crofton, but she'd had a plan to avoid that, a plan that now lay in pieces, damn Le Corbeau!

She supposed she should be terrified, but she seemed to have moved beyond that to mild insanity.

Since arriving in London, she'd written frequent letters to her best friends back in Matlock, entertaining them with her observations of the capital and the ton. What a shame she'd not be able to write about this.

Witty phrases popped into her mind to do with Le Corbeau and the *haute volée,* which meant the high flyers of society — the dandies, dukes, and Patronesses of Almack's, who had all failed to notice the arrival amongst them of ordinary Cressida Mandeville. They'd notice if this scandal ever became known!

She wasn't particularly uncomfortable, but she was furious at how those men had handled her. Her wrists were tied with her *garters,* and she suspected her ankles were bound with her very expensive silk stockings. Which some man had removed, the knave!

Malmsey-nosed knave, she borrowed from Shakespeare, hoping that indeed her captor had the swollen red nose of the drunkard.

Strange that a person could be frustrated, bored, frightened, and furious all at the same time.

She turned her mind to planning. She must escape this captor, continue to Stokeley Manor, and complete her mission. . . .

It was very late, though, and she'd hardly slept recently for dread of this journey, so, wandering amid wilder and wilder plans, she drifted off to sleep.

She woke with a start.

Darkness? . . . No, blindfold! This wasn't a nightmare, then.

It was reality, and *he* was back.

She'd been waked by sounds — things being moved some distance away. If only she could see! Faint light around the edge of the blindfold told her a candle was lit.

He was back, presumably with time now to *do* things. Shivers ran through her, and her teeth threatened to chatter. She clenched them, but it didn't work. He'd hear, and he'd . . . do what?

Water. Splashing.

The mundane picture was shockingly clear.

He was pouring water from a ewer into a washing bowl. A slight splashing told her he was washing. It leached the terror out of her, leaving her limp and dazed. A vile rapist might well wash before attacking her, but it seemed so unlikely.

The sound of water awakened thirst. Her throat turned tight and dry enough to choke her.

"May I have a drink of water?" she managed.

Abrupt silence. "I thought you were asleep. Wait a moment."

She worked her tongue around her mouth to moisten it, all the while following sounds. Water pouring. Footsteps again, coming closer. She only flinched a little when he touched her face.

"Water," he said, clearly to diffuse her fear. What a strange villain this was.

She didn't resist when his arm pushed under her and raised her. When cool glass pressed against her bottom lip, she opened her mouth. He tilted the glass, and blessed water filled her mouth. She swallowed; he poured. A strange union — his hands, her mouth, working together as if practiced by familiarity. . . .

But then the synchrony broke. He tilted too fast or she swallowed too slow. She jerked, almost choked.

"Sorry." The glass was removed. She felt him stroke the dribble from her chin, and she smelled sandalwood again, stronger now. He'd just used sandalwood soap on his hands.

Soap, horse, leather, man. She had never noticed such things before, and she didn't want to now. They created a weakening sense of intimacy. She needed to see! To see a malmsey-nosed villain.

"Don't. Please —"

"Hush." He laid her back down, settling her head last and carefully. A new foolish distress attacked. She could imagine what she looked like, lying here in her tilted turban and crushed, disordered finery.

He walked back across the room, and she heard a strange sound. A soft tearing. A muttered curse.

His false beard and mustache!

What would he look like without them? More important, would she know him? She'd lived among the *haute volée* these past months. On the edges of the fashionable world, but still there. If she did recognize him, she must not show a hint of it!

A new worry stirred. Would *he* recognize *her?*

That would be disaster. She was merely the daughter of Sir Arthur Mandeville, however, minor nabob. She doubted most of the ton were aware of her existence. And anyway, a man desperate enough to become a highwayman would hardly have been dancing at London balls.

More washing. Two thumps that were probably his boots. Her hearing was so sensitized by then, so frantic for detail, that she heard his stockinged footsteps as he came back to the bed.

Now. Now it would happen. Fighting might be useless, but she'd fight anyway. When a hand grabbed her foot, she kicked.

Something cold touched her ankle. She felt a sharp tug.

Her legs were suddenly free, and she used them to try to push away from him.

"Don't be afraid."

"Why not? You're a criminal!"

"But of the more gallant variety."

She could tell he was coming no closer, so she stilled.

"You really didn't want to go on with Lord Crofton, you know."

"Oh, yes, I did." She wished he'd take off the blindfold, but then didn't. She mustn't see his face.

Silence, but then a weight settled on the bed

not far from her feet. She flinched. She couldn't help it.

"Why?"

"Why what?"

"Why were you going willingly with Crofton?"

"That, sir, is none of your business. Now kindly return me."

"You think he'll be waiting for you by the road?"

The lazy amusement made her want to scream with frustration. She *had* thought that, and it was ridiculous.

"Of course not. You can take me to Stokeley Manor."

"Whereupon he will have me arrested."

"Take me close, then. I will manage on my own from there."

"I don't doubt it." After a moment, he asked, "Who are you?"

Now what? He must assume that she was a light-skirt, so why the question? What answer would get her on her way? Everything, *everything,* hinged on getting to Stokeley Manor.

He seemed to think he was rescuing her. So he'd let her go only if he believed her to be a hardened harlot.

"Who am I, sir?" she replied in as bold and brittle a tone as she could. "Your captive, and yes, Crofton's whore."

The bed moved again. Oh, Lord. He was lying down. Not touching her, but lying beside her . . .

A hand brushed down the front of her gown. She flinched but managed to silence a protest. Presumably a whore wouldn't mind.

Would he feel her desperate heartbeats?

That hand stroked up again, lightly past her breasts, shockingly against the bare skin of her chest, and then over her throat, trapping breath there. She stretched back, desperate to escape.

"I won't hurt you, my lovely one, but if you're willing to serve Crofton, why not serve me for the night?"

He suddenly rolled on her, pressed on her, hot, hard, huge.

"No!" she screamed, trying helplessly to fend him off with her bound hands and skirt-tangled legs.

He captured her wrists, and she felt lips on her fingers.

He was *kissing* them?

"Why not?" Such a light voice, as if she were not fighting at all. "I'll pay your usual fee. I'll pay double."

How would a whore react?

"I'm very expensive."

"I'm very rich."

"And selective. I don't go to just any man with guineas in his hands."

He chuckled. "I'm not just any man, sweet nymph of the night. You know, I've never had a whore refuse me before."

She recognized her mistake this time. Probably a whore never did refuse a man with guineas in his hands.

Whore. She'd set off on this adventure prepared to be that, but only because she believed she could avoid it. Now here she was, assaulted, helpless, pressed upon by this vile man's body and his will.

Should she let him do what men do so he'd help her complete her journey? Bile rose at the thought, but she would let him, if it would work. It wouldn't. He'd find out she was a virgin, and heaven alone knew what would happen then.

Something brushed her lip — a thumb, she thought, and tossed her head to escape it. He overwhelmed her, his big body pinning her, pinning her hands between them, as his hands confined her head and his lips pressed to hers.

She heard her own stifled sob and prayed he'd take it for protest not terror.

"I've never forced a woman," he whispered against her lips, "and I won't start with you. But can't I persuade you? It would be delightful for both of us, and you know, you must know, how a man's blood heats after action and danger."

"No! I mean, *don't!* Lord Crofton hired me. I consider myself his at the moment."

"Honor among sinners?" He was laughing at her. "Come on, my pretty. He'd do the same if our situations were reversed."

He moved. His weight lifted off her. For a moment she hoped, but then his knee pressed down between her legs, parting them. Pressed up! . . .

"Stop. *Please!*"

He stopped, but he did not free her. She lay there, breathless, pinned, pressed. . . .

"Who are you?" he asked again, and at last she understood.

He didn't believe her. For whatever reason, he didn't believe she was a courtesan, and he was prepared to force the truth from her. He wouldn't stop until she gave in.

Bitterly, she accepted the inevitable. She was on his territory in matters physical and metaphysical. In this, he was the victor. What name, though? Not her own.

The first name to pop into her mind was that of the curate's wife in Matlock. "Jane Wemworthy."

"Whore?" he demanded.

Breath came now, a deep breath of anger. "No."

Then he was gone. Gone from her body, gone from the bed.

She fought when he grabbed her hands, but then she felt cool metal again. A moment later her hands were free. She reached up to shove the horrible blindfold from her face, almost taking her turban with it until pins caught her hair. She worked the cloth over it, sitting up, searching the room for information, for anything that might help her.

She was in a modest bedroom lit by a branch of three candles. Ivory wallpaper, mahogany armoire and washing stand, rust-brown curtains and bed-hangings.

And the man standing at the end of the four-poster bed was the gloriously handsome Duke of St. Raven. She felt as if her eyes were expanding with shock, and tried desperately not to show that she had recognized him.

How could she not?

Everyone knew St. Raven. He was the elusive star of society, the glorious prize. He'd inherited the dukedom from his uncle last year just after Waterloo and promptly fled the country. Cressida didn't know if he'd fled or taken the new opportunity to travel, but people had spoken of it in that way. He had, after all, instantly become the prime quarry in the marriage hunt.

A young, handsome, unmarried duke.

When he'd returned a few months ago and begun to attend society events, the steam of frenetic fervor had been enough to drive an engine. Cressida couldn't count the number of times she'd been in the ladies' room at a ball or soirée and heard young women gasping about *seeing!* him, *speaking!* to him, and sometimes even *dancing!* with him.

Most ladies held no hopes of becoming his duchess, but a few were contenders. Diana Rolleston-Stowe, toast and duke's granddaughter, had burned with ambition. The beautiful Phoebe Swinamer had assumed an almost proprietary air toward him. Cressida looked at the man before her and wondered how Miss Swinamer dared.

He was tall, but that wasn't what made him so formidable. Nor was his rank. In a simple shirt, open at the neck, and black leather breeches, St. Raven filled the room. He took up more space than his size explained. And he was as handsome close to as from a distance.

Though big and strong, he possessed a fine-boned elegance, along with the drama of dark hair and deep blue eyes. As she'd noticed before, his lips suggested things a lady should not even think about.

"You recognize me." It was not a question.

Too late, too late, she saw her danger. "Yes."

Would they hang a duke for playing highwayman? Surely they'd have to do something if she identified him. She slid a glance at the long, sharp knife on the table by the bed. She could almost feel it slicing into her throat. . . .

"More water, Miss Wemworthy?"

In her terror, the offer and the name confused her, so she stared at him. Then she managed, "Yes, please, Your Grace."

Surely not even the most deranged criminal and murderer would behave like this.

Or laugh, as he did now. "I think we've progressed beyond such formality. Call me St. Raven. I intend to call you Jane."

"Even if I object?"

He gave her the filled glass. "Miss Wemworthy is such a mouthful, and sounds so stern, as well. Like the sort of woman who disapproves of amusements, or writes improving tracts."

Cressida concentrated on drinking, trying to stifle her reaction. He had Mrs. Wemworthy exactly. Surely everyone didn't suit their names?

St. Raven did have something of the predator about him, but Mandeville was all wrong for her. Centuries ago, Sir John Mandeville had written of his travels to wild lands full of dragons and creatures who were half-man, half-beast. She loved the stories, but had never wanted to travel beyond the safe and ordinary herself.

Safe and ordinary? She was on the Duke of St. Raven's bed! She couldn't help thinking of the hundreds of young women who would swoon at the thought.

Surely she was safe from rape. Compromise a young lady whom he then might have to marry? She was surprised he hadn't already tossed her back on the King's Highway.

"More water?" he asked, as if her thirst were the prime concern.

"No, thank you." She had other needs, however, and refused to be missish about them. "I will soon need a chamber pot, Your Grace, and privacy to use it."

"Of course," he said, equally unembarrassed. Cressida realized that she'd hoped to put him out. "Give me your word that you won't try to run away before we talk again, and I'll provide you with a private room and all comforts."

She blinked at him. "You'd accept my word?"

"It is not binding?"

She wanted to rap out, *Of course,* but she wasn't quite sure. No one had ever asked her for it before, and being practical . . .

"Clearly not," he remarked, brows rising.

"If you were a villain, Your Grace, and I could escape by giving you my word, I'm afraid I would do it."

He smiled. "Clever and honest."

Her heart did a somersault. He was definitely the sort of man who drove women to make fools of themselves, and it wasn't entirely because of his rank.

Not her, she resolved. Not her.

"So," he said, "you must decide if I am a villain or not."

Suddenly irked by her position, she scrambled off the bed. "You are a highwayman," she pointed out, empowered by being vertical.

"Not true."

"How can you say 'not true'? You just held up a coach and kidnapped me!"

"Very well, somewhat true."

Improperly, he sat while she was standing, sat on the bed, leaning back against one of the carved bedposts, his right arm around his raised knee. She didn't think she'd ever in her life been with a man so casually — casually dressed, casually arranged, casually mannered.

And this was a duke! The Duke of St. Raven. She'd think she must be dreaming except that she could never conjure up anything so outrageous.

"But I was only playing at it for the one night."

She remembered now that he was said to be wild. "You find being a thief amusing?"

"After a fashion. This consequence, after all, is certainly novel."

"I think you're mad."

His lips twitched. "I wouldn't if I were you. Quite alarming to be in the power of a madman." He let that sink in for a moment, then added, "To return to the matter of your parole, I cannot allow you to go to Lord Crofton's, so unless I'm sure that you will be here in the morning, I'll have to take steps. Tie you up, perhaps. Or," he added, "tie you to me."

Those eyes swept to her breasts. She glanced down. Her too-large-for-fashion bosom was rising and falling with her agitated breaths. In the low evening dress that Crofton had insisted upon, they were highly exposed. She remembered the duke putting her earrings and the money down there. She raised her hand there to shield herself and felt the notes crackle.

She swallowed and met his eyes. "I am barefoot and heaven alone knows where, Your Grace. I will not leave until tomorrow."

"It *is* tomorrow. You will not leave until we have breakfasted and discussed matters."

She hated to be given orders, but she said, "Very well."

"Your word of honor?"

She hesitated again, but only in awe of being asked for it. "My word of honor."

"Come, then." He stood, took his branch of candles, and led the way out of the room to the one next door. It was only then, eye-to-back, that Cressida realized that he might have sat down to give her the height advantage.

Could she believe he'd do something so understanding, so thoughtful?

Chapter Three

The new bedroom was identical to his except that the hangings were a dull blue. Her sense of the house was that it was a modest country manor — strange for a duke. Borrowed for villainy?

He lit the single candle there. "The servants are all asleep. I'll bring you what's left of my washing water. The bed has not been aired, but it is summer."

She almost giggled at his concern about these housewifely matters. For her part, she didn't care. Sleep was creeping over her like an invader, dragging down her lids. "It will do."

"I'm next door if you require anything."

That was not housewifely. A quirk of mouth and brow gave it a naughty spice.

A rake, she remembered when alone. The Duke of St. Raven had the reputation not only of being wild, but of being a promiscuous lover, as well. Her friend Lavinia had a brother who gossiped to her, and of course, Lavinia shared the juicy stories.

The duke held wild parties. Parties for gentlemen and whores. Apparently there were Cyprian balls, and he was a notable attendee.

When he returned with his water jug and

towel, she watched his every move. But he simply put the items down and returned to the door.

Ah well, she was hardly the sort to drive men wild with lust, and anyway, as she'd thought, the last thing the duke would do would be to assault a decent woman.

He paused at the door. "My servants are discreet, but not saints. What will happen if word gets out that you stayed the night here?"

Sheer mischief made her say, "We'd have to marry?"

She saw his eyes grow wary, and felt a barrier rise between them.

"I'm sorry. I assure you, I have no wish to trap you into marriage, Your Grace. In fact, the name I gave you is false, so there is no danger."

The barrier thinned. "Wise woman. All the same, stay out of sight. I'll bring your breakfast — giving due warning so you can dress, of course. Which reminds me . . ."

He left again. She waited, hugging herself against the special chill that comes in a sleepless night.

He returned and tossed a crimson-and-gold garment on the bed. "Sleep well, Miss Nymph. We'll talk in the morning."

The door closed, leaving her in the silent room lit only by the one, wavering candle. A key stuck out of the lock on her side of the door, but she resisted the urge to turn it. A locked door wouldn't keep him out, and she was sure he wouldn't invade.

She picked up the garment — heavy, sinuous silk. A man's robe in a rich paisley pattern. She brought it to her face and smelled sandalwood again. She thought that sandalwood would remind her of this night all her life.

Now, alone, Cressida found it impossible to simply climb into the impersonal bed. Despite weariness itching at her eyes and aching in her joints, how could she surrender to sleep here in the rakish duke's house? She was practical, however, and prided herself on it. Thus she must sleep so that tomorrow she would have all her wits and be able to find a way to fulfill her mission.

She pulled back the covers to expose clean linen, which drew her like a magnet. Perhaps sleep wasn't impossible after all.

She pulled out the hairpins that held her turban in place and lifted it off, false curls and all. The fashion was for bubbling curls around the face, but she'd refused to have her long hair cut at the front. Anyway, her hair was heavy and straight and would need constant use of curling irons to achieve the look.

She dug out more pins, and her coiled hair slithered down her back. She didn't have the energy to plait it for the night. She wanted only to collapse into the bed.

Then she found that she couldn't unfasten her dress no matter how she stretched and twisted. Even if she managed that, she'd never get the corset off. With a sigh, she climbed into the bed as she was. She was surely tired enough to sleep anyway.

She tried. She tossed this way and that, seeking a comfortable position, but the bones of her corset dug into her, the shoulder straps bound, and her skirts tangled and trapped around her legs.

She rolled out of the bed and writhed again to get at the hooks. Impossible. There was nothing else for it. Huffing out a breath, she stalked out of her room and into his —

He turned from his wardrobe, naked from the waist up, breeches unfastened.

She had never seen a man's body before, and stared at lean muscle and visible strength. Her eyes drifted down to lock on his undone buttons. . . .

He moved. He refastened those buttons while walking toward her. "You should pay a forfeit for that, Miss Wemworthy."

Through guilt or simple bedazzlement, Cressida didn't fight when he pulled her into his arms. Perhaps some vague notion of struggle occurred, because she put her hands between them, but that only meant that they ended up pressed to his hot skin, to the muscles that moved as he lowered his head to meet her unresisting lips.

Honesty compelled her to accept that since their earlier conflicted kiss, she'd been longing for this, to have those fascinatingly tempting lips playing with hers, to taste that fire with leisure to absorb it.

And absorb it she did, or was absorbed. Encircled in strong arms, flesh to flesh, mouth to mouth, heat to heat.

Melted.

Swirled softly in sandalwood into delicious oblivion.

Only taste. Only touch. Only smell.

Blindfolded now by her own closed lids . . .

His lips left hers. The press of his body on her hands eased.

She blinked her eyes open to find him looking at her almost blankly. "Can I hope that you are a nymph of the night after all, come to pleasure me?"

His wonderful chest was rising and falling under her hands. She could feel his pounding heart.

To her astonishment, she said, "I wish I were."

He laughed and rested his head against hers for a moment. But then he stepped back, though he kept his hands on her shoulders. "If you didn't return to carry me to heaven, sweetheart, what brought you?"

The gap between them seemed chill, but she managed a slight, apologetic smile. "I'm sorry. I'm too tired to think. But I can't get out of my dress and corset. Since you said the servants are asleep . . ."

"And all male." He turned her and unhooked her dress. "This is Nun's Chase, by the way," he said as he parted the gown and began on the strings of her corset.

"Nun's Chase?" she echoed, holding her dress up at the front. She couldn't believe she was here doing this!

"Built on the site of a convent back in the sixteenth century. I'm sure the Chase refers innocently enough to hunting land, but it was too suggestive to resist."

Her wanton mind was fixed on his suggestive

hands pulling the laces loose bottom to top, on the general loosening of that familiar constraint around her body. She felt as if more was loosening than mere laces. . . .

"I hold gentlemen's parties here," he said, as if discussing the weather. "I don't keep female servants, in case a guest is tempted to misbehave. There you are."

She sensed him step back, and turned, aware of her clothes slipping from her skin. "You're a rake." She realized too late that she really shouldn't fill her sight with him like this.

"What is a rake? I don't drink to excess or game for disastrous stakes. I don't rape serving wenches — or ladies, for that matter. But I enjoy women, both their company and their bodies." His eyes on her reinforced that to an alarming degree. "I have a healthy appetite for women and for their pleasure. I love to give a woman pleasure, to watch her melt . . . You really should go, you know."

He hadn't moved. During that extraordinary speech, he hadn't moved a muscle that she'd seen, but it was as if she could see herself through his eyes, in disorder, her long hair down her back, her gown sliding off her, clutched to her full breasts.

It was as if she could feel his hunger like the heat of a fire. She stepped back, but her foot tangled with her drooping skirt, and she stumbled.

He caught her in one arm. His other hand took possession of a breast, still covered by her loosened corset — but not well. He was looking at it almost as if a battle roared in him.

Then he removed his hand and turned her, somehow restoring her gown to her clutch. He steered her toward his open door and through it. "Good night, sweet nymph," he said, and closed the door on her.

She staggered into her room thinking of *Hamlet: "Nymph, in thy orisons be all my sins remembered."*

Sins. She should indeed be praying, for both of them. Instead, as she let her dress fall and then wriggled out of her corset, she acknowledged a shard of regret that he wasn't a more sinful man and hadn't tried to seduce her.

She noticed the earrings and banknotes, but couldn't even be bothered to pick them up. *Tried to seduce her?* He'd only have had to sweep her to his bed and keep on doing what he'd been doing.

She clambered into the bed in her shift and pulled the covers up over herself, still trembling. She had to be grateful for his willpower, but all the same, all the same, a bit of her wept for an opportunity lost, an opportunity that was unlikely to ever come her way again.

Cressida woke to strangeness. She remembered the events of the previous evening and where she was, but that in itself was the strangeness.

The Duke of St. Raven, playing at being the highwayman *Le Corbeau,* had snatched her from Lord Crofton and carried her off to his scandalous house, Nun's Chase. She could never have even dreamed such a scenario.

Now he was intent on saving her from ruin, and she'd given her word to stay here at least until they had breakfasted. She would keep her word, but she must complete her journey to Stokeley Manor. Everything depended on that.

Would her plan to outwit Crofton still work? It should, but if it failed, she would go through with the worst — she would become Lord Crofton's mistress for a week. But then she stiffened with dismay. Her plan depended upon a small vial of liquid in her reticule, and her bag had been left in the carriage!

She pulled the covers over her head as if that might save her. Could she get more of the emetic? If she convinced the duke to let her go on to Stokeley, he might find more of it for her.

She pushed back the covers and sat, sweeping her hair off her face. Her life had become disaster after disaster, but she would not fail. She *had* to win.

A slit of light through the heavy curtains said it was day, and it was time for her to face it. She wriggled out of the bed and squinted around the edge of the curtains to find a pleasant garden edged by woodland. From the angle of light she guessed it was about nine or ten o'clock. She heard whistling, then a stocky man in shirt, breeches, gaiters, and boots appeared, strolling down a path with a hoe on his shoulder.

She turned back into the room, disturbed in some way by that ordinary sight. Servants. Her host had advised that she not be seen by the servants, and she agreed. It hadn't seemed so terrible to go to Stokeley Manor and be seen there, especially as Lord Crofton had promised that she could wear a mask. To be seen here, however, in this ordinary house by ordinary servants, struck her as shocking.

She would stay in her room. But then she remembered that St. Raven had promised to bring breakfast himself.

She glanced in the mirror and yelped. Her rumpled calf-length shift was no cover at all, and with her hair all over the place, she looked like a blowsy slut! She hunted through her hair, pulling out stray pins, then tried to use her fingers to comb it into some sort of order. Hopeless. She checked the drawers in the dressing table, but there was no brush or comb.

Somewhere in the house a clock started to chime. She froze, counting. Two. Not two o'clock, surely, so half past something.

Oh, what did it matter? She needed to be *dressed!*

The key. She dashed over and turned the key in the lock. Now, at least, he couldn't walk in on her before she was decent.

Walk in on . . .

The incident last night crashed back on her, so she sagged against the door. The sight of his body, the look in his eyes, the way he'd kissed her . . .

The way she'd reacted!

She sucked in a breath and blew it out again. It was as if she'd wandered into another world. Not long ago she'd woken with no greater problem than what gown to wear for morning visits, and whether to attend a fashionable ball that was bound to be a boring crush. Back in that world *shocking* meant that a man had pressed too close in a dance or tried to inveigle her apart for a mild kiss.

She pushed away from the door, concentrating on clothing. She'd left her silk dress in a puddle on the floor, and when she picked it up it was as creased and crumpled as she feared. She shook it out and spread it on the bed, but she knew that nothing short of an iron would restore it.

And it was the only dress she had here. That, her shift, her turban, and her corset were her sole possessions. When had she lost her shawl? It had been Norwich silk and very expensive, but that wasn't her main concern right now — it would have been another decent layer. Her stockings and garters had been sliced, and heaven knew what had happened to her shoes.

She sat beside her poor sad dress, feeling poor and sad herself, frightened in a way she hadn't been before. She'd never thought that clothes could be so important to courage, but she longed to be decently covered, even in fustian.

A servant's clothes?

But this was a house of men.

One thing was sure, at this moment she was a prisoner here. Even if she decided to break her parole, she couldn't set off to rejoin Crofton in her bare feet and shift.

She stiffened her spine and stood up. She'd do what she could, and the first thing was to make herself as decent as possible before the duke intruded.

As a start, she drew back the curtains, letting bright summer light lift the gloom. Then she set to getting dressed. She picked up her corset from the floor. Beneath, she found her earrings and Crofton's money. Money would be useful. She'd tuck it back down behind her corset in a moment.

But then she realized that she could no more tie the laces than she'd been able to untie them. She tossed it on the bed, refusing to cry. She doubtless couldn't fasten the back of her dress, either, but if she put it on, it would be something.

The robe! The robe he'd brought for her. Where was it?

Struck by his thoughtfulness, she searched and found that it had slid off the far side of the bed in the night. She put it on, the heavy silk cold against her skin for a moment, that smell of sandalwood rising to torment her. She tried to gather it around her, but the sleeves were far too long.

With a slight laugh, she set to work. First she rolled up the sleeves until they cleared her hands. Then she fastened the buttons down the front. A foot or more of the fabric trailed on the ground, and when she looked in the mirror she saw a child playing in grown-up clothes. She was, however, covered. Decent.

Decent!

She'd lived twenty-one years in Matlock, a solid member of respectable Matlock society, decent from top to toe. Would she ever be decent again?

She pushed that aside. No point moping over what couldn't be changed, and anyway, if her plan worked, she and her parents would soon be back in Matlock and stolid decency. She must focus on her purpose and not let weak emotions get in her way. She sat on a chair by the empty fireplace and tried to plan a strategy to deal with the Duke of St. Raven.

He was never going to believe that she was a whore, which meant he'd refuse to take her to Stokeley Manor. Her choices, therefore, were to escape — which needed simpler clothing, good shoes, and a map — or to tell him the truth and gain his help.

She grimaced. Perhaps some of the truth. If she could escape this without him knowing her real name, she would.

Would he help her in her plan? She wouldn't normally think that a duke would be any use at thievery, but this was no ordinary duke. Could she spin a tale that — ?

A knock on the door.

She shot to her feet, clutching the robe around her.

He turned the knob. Knocked again. "Miss?"

A woman's voice!

Grabbing handfuls of silk to hold it up, Cressida hurried to the door to unlock it and peer out. She saw the blessed sight of a respectable middle-aged woman bearing a large steaming ewer.

"Good morning, miss," the woman said with an apple-cheeked smile. "I've your water here. His Grace sent for me to look after you."

Though Cressida felt that her world had taken another strange turn, it was a wonderful one. She opened the door. "Come in, please."

The woman did, bustling over to the washstand to pour water into the bowl there. She had extra towels that she hung over the rail, and from a pocket she produced a new bar of soap. "Nice flowery stuff, miss. You don't want His Grace's."

Cressida wasn't so sure of that, but it was doubtless for the best. She was touched almost to tears by this kindness. He'd thought of her predicament and sent for a maid.

She walked to the washstand, unbuttoning the robe. "The duke said he kept no female servants."

"That's right, miss, and if he wants any for the nonce he'll only have us older ones. Which is as well," she said, but added with a wink, "even if it does assume that we're dead from the neck down once we're forty."

Cressida laughed, not knowing what to say to that.

The woman came over to help with the buttons. "I'm Annie Barkway, miss. I live in the village, and I've one son who's a footman here and another working on the grounds. It's a grand thing to have His Grace here, miss. He's a good master even with his wild ways."

The woman stripped off the robe and began to lather a cloth. A delightful perfume of flowers and lemon rose to freshen the air.

Cressida woke from her daze and took cloth and soap from her. "Thank you." As she began to wash, she wondered what sort of story the duke had told to account for her being here in such a state.

Mrs. Barkway went to tidy the bed. Cressida turned to watch as she washed, and saw the woman grimace at the state of her gown.

"Lovely silk this is, miss. I'm not sure I'd dare try to iron it."

"It doesn't matter, though I'll have to put it on. The duke said he'd bring my breakfast. . . ." She realized there was no need now. Mrs. Barkway could do it. And just as well, she told herself.

"No hurry, miss. He's ridden out." Mrs. Barkway finished smoothing the coverlet. "He ordered breakfast ready at ten, and said he'd eat it up here with you, miss, so we'd best get you decent."

Cressida turned away to rinse her cloth, and hide her betraying blush of excitement. "Did he explain how I came to be here?"

"Such a shocking tale!" Mrs. Barkway exclaimed, flipping open a towel and holding it out for Cressida. "I didn't think men tried to kidnap heiresses anymore. Lucky for you that His Grace came upon you after you'd fled."

Perhaps Cressida's silence looked like fear, for the woman added, "All will be right now, miss. Don't you worry."

Cressida smiled her thanks, thinking that his ingenious story was no more outlandish than the truth. He did seem to be a man who thought of everything.

A good partner in crime, perhaps?

"And don't you worry about gossip, miss. His Grace pays well for closed mouths, and he knows I'll not say anything to embarrass you."

Cressida dried herself on the soft cloth. "Thank you, Mrs. Barkway. You're very kind."

The woman blushed. "Go on with you. Sit

down now, and I'll see what I can do with your hair, though I'm no ladies' maid."

The wonderful woman produced a comb from her pocket, and Cressida sat at the dressing table. There were knots in her hair, of course, but the woman was as gentle as she could be.

"No curl," Cressida apologized. She picked up her turban with the false curls dangling around the front.

The woman chuckled. "Very clever, miss, but they do look strange now, don't they? Like a scared cat hiding in a bag." She stroked a hand down Cressida's hair. "Your hair is lovely, miss. Like dark brown silk, it is, and thick right down to your waist. How do you want to wear it?"

Cressida realized how much she disliked her caps and turbans, with their false curls. It had seemed necessary because of her father's desire that she be fashionable, but there was no need for such folly now. In Matlock, she had worn her hair in a simple plait coiled on the back of her head. She tossed aside the turban and asked Mrs. Barkway to do something similar. As the woman worked away, Cressida let her tangled mind drift.

Matlock. Last year she'd welcomed the prospect of playing in fashionable society. Matlock had seemed so dull. Now it was the sanctuary she struggled to regain.

She had to admit to a pang about London, however. Hadn't Dr. Johnson said something about he who tired of London being tired of life?

It was the heart of the world. Men of power lived there, making decisions that would affect the fates of millions around the globe. It was the center of the arts and sciences, cradle of great discoveries. She had met fascinating people everywhere — explorers, poets, orators, scientists, sinners. And the theaters! They had a theater in Matlock, but it wasn't like Drury Lane or the Royal Opera House.

That stirred a memory — the Duke of St. Raven at Drury Lane Theater.

It had been months ago. She'd been there with her parents and the Harbisons at the opening of the play *A Daring Lady*. The theater had hummed with excitement, but then the hum had intensified. A stir had directed every eye to one of the finest boxes, to a glittering lady there accompanied by a dark and handsome gentleman.

"The Duke of St. Raven!" Lady Harbison had exclaimed in a whisper — one of the truly remarkable social skills. "He's here at last."

This had seemed a nonsensical statement, so Cressida had been pleased when her mother asked for more information. Since the whole theater was staring and whispering, it had to be important. In moments she had the meat of it. The duke had inherited from his uncle the year before and then disappeared. Now, without fanfare, he had stepped onto the stage that awaited him — an eligible duke, a prince of the ton.

However, according to Lady Harbison, his partner was killing many hopes. Lady Anne Peckworth was daughter of the Duke of Arran — a most suitable match — and by the looks of it, the match was already made.

He'd kissed Lady Anne's hand as if sealing the speculation, and Cressida remembered her own wistful desire. Not that the Duke of St. Raven would kiss her hand like that, but that some man would. Would kiss her hand with such elegant ease, gazing into her eyes in a way that spoke of deep devotion. She had suitors — being a nabob's heiress — but none had shown her reverence like that.

Presumably by now the duke had kissed Lady Anne as he'd kissed her last night, and more.

Lucky lady . . .

"Now, let's get you into your clothing, miss, even if it is all a bit the worse for wear. I'm sure you'll feel better then."

Cressida pulled out of the past. If any foolish notions stirred in her head about St. Raven, she must remember that he was the sort of man to attempt seduction of one lady while wooing another. So much for reverent hand-kisses.

She focused and saw that her hair was smoothly arranged. She thanked the woman and rose to dress.

Mrs. Barkway had a firm hand with the corset laces so that Cressida had to suck in an extra breath, but in a way it was comforting — a return of restraint and good order. Her evening dress looked out of place in the morning but it, too, brought respectability, even when crumpled. She picked up her pearl necklace and put it on again, then added her earrings.

"Where are your shoes and stockings, miss?"

Cressida turned from the mirror, knowing she was blushing. "I think they were lost in my adventure."

"Well, I never! And mine won't fit. If you don't

mind, miss, I'll go and see what I can find for you."

"I don't mind at all. You've been very kind."

"Go on with you. Anyone would in the same situation." She poured the dirty water into the slop bucket, hefted it, and left.

Chapter Four

Cressida checked her appearance again, longing for a sensible day dress, and especially for everyday stockings and sturdy shoes. Now she was dressed, her bare feet felt even more peculiar. Positively wanton.

She should have asked Mrs. Barkway to find a fichu of some kind to fill in the low neckline. Ah well, it wasn't as if she intended to go out in public.

She wandered to the window to contemplate the very ordinary world, wishing she belonged in it. Perhaps she should escape while she had the chance. Poor people sometimes went barefoot. It might not be so bad. She'd given her word, but she'd warned St. Raven that she might not keep it if she saw a chance of escape. . . .

The door opened, and she whirled, but it was only Mrs. Barkway again with — heaven be praised! — her shoes in her hand.

Cressida hurried over. "Oh, where did you find them?"

"Mr. Lyne had them, miss. But no sign of your stockings, I'm afraid. I can get you some from the village, but they'll be simple stuff."

Cressida was slipping her feet into the green silk slippers. "Anything would be wonderful. I had a shawl, as well, but I think that must have been lost far from here. Is there any chance of a fichu?"

"You poor dear. I'll see what I can do, miss. Now, His Grace isn't back yet. Would you like something to eat or drink while you wait? I don't see why you should starve at his pleasure."

Cressida chuckled at this, wanting to hug the woman. "I'd love something. Coffee, chocolate, tea. Whatever is most convenient. And perhaps a bit of bread."

"I'll fetch it, then I'll be off to the village. No woman wants to be without her stockings and a good, firm pair of garters."

Cressida agreed, feeling that nothing could be too terrible in a world that included Mrs. Barkway. Soon she was sipping rich chocolate and enjoying a fresh sweet roll spread thick with butter. The duke lived well in his simple surroundings, but that was hardly surprising. For all his casual ways and this simple house, he was next best thing to royalty.

Who played at highwayman.

She shook her head over that, but she'd learned that the ton often indulged in strange behavior. There were lords who played at coachman, so why not a duke who played at highwayman? Except that it was illegal and dangerous.

Was he mad, after all? It *had* been a full moon last night!

A knock on the door.

Cressida jumped to her feet as the duke walked in. He *looked* normal in riding dress of dark jacket, buckskin breeches, and top boots. No, not normal. The breeches seemed smeared with dirt, and his lip was swollen.

"Great Juno! Have you been *fighting?*"

"What would give you that idea?" But he smiled — then pulled out a handkerchief already spotted with blood and dabbed at his lip. "You look much restored, nymph."

Lunatic.

Duke.

Cressida was at a loss.

"I breakfasted. No one seemed to know where you were or when you would return."

He glanced at her plate. "That is not breakfast. I'll be back in a moment, and then we can talk."

She stared at the door. He was eccentric at the least, and now she had to deal with him. She sat down again and nibbled the last of her buttered roll. If she could persuade him to help, he could be a gift from heaven. She could be home soon, untouched but victorious — if she could harness a duke to her will.

He returned with a large tray and put a platter of ham and eggs in the middle of the table, then added a plate of bread along with butter and marmalade, then a bowl of plums. Last came a coffeepot, cup, and jug of cream. Clearly men, big men who rode out early to involve themselves in fights, needed huge meals.

He put the tray aside and sat opposite her. "You look shocked. Because I need sustenance?"

"Because you're a duke and carry your own tray."

"Don't be ridiculous." He helped himself to

three eggs and a lot of ham. "Please, take some of this if you want it."

Cressida repressed a shudder, but she did pour herself more chocolate.

"While I eat, tell me your story. It seems to be my day for knight-errantry."

"You've found another damsel in distress?"

His lips twitched. "After a fashion."

Mad. Truly mad. "This house must be becoming rather crowded."

"Oh, I stashed her in one of my other residences. Now, your story, Miss Whoever-you-are." He tucked into his meal.

Cressida dithered, but she needed help, so she formed a version of the truth. "Lord Crofton has stolen something from my family, Your Grace, and it is in Stokeley Manor. I need to get in there to recover it."

He swallowed, contemplating her. "If he's stolen it, go to the authorities."

"He's a peer. I don't think I'd be attended to."

"Worth trying, wouldn't you say, before prostituting yourself with him?"

It stung, but he was right. "Very well. He won it at cards."

"Cheated?"

That hadn't occurred to her before. Reluctantly, she shook her head. "I don't think so."

"Then it's his, fair and square."

"No, it isn't!"

He poured himself coffee and added cream. "Why don't you tell me the truth? We'll get there anyway eventually."

Cressida shot to her feet. "You have no right to

demand anything from me, sir! I am free to leave here anytime I wish."

"I'm afraid not." He cut another piece of ham.

"You can't keep me prisoner."

He just raised his brows and put the ham into his mouth.

Cressida eyed the heavy silver chocolate pot, but hitting him with it would not achieve her purpose. She forced herself to stay calm. *Only one thing matters,* she reminded herself. *Only one thing.* She squeezed her clasped hands once, tightly, then relaxed, and sat down again.

"My name is Cressida Mandeville, Your Grace. My father is Sir Arthur Mandeville." She watched for some sign of recognition, but didn't see any. Hardly surprising. Even in the London season the Mandevilles had moved in a different orbit from the Duke of St. Raven.

"He is recently home after twenty-three years in India."

"A nabob." He used the common term, which also implied wealth.

"Yes."

"You lived in India with him?"

"I was born there, but my mother was troubled by the climate, so we both returned home before I was a year old."

"Did your father return from time to time?"

"No."

His brows twitched again. "An interesting reunion."

That, thought Cressida, was a notable understatement, though her mother seemed to have accepted it well.

The duke continued to eat, but she had his complete and perceptive attention. She felt comforted to be telling the truth to someone at last.

"Having wealth and a new knighthood, my father wished to enter society. He bought a small estate, Stokeley Manor, and rented a London house so we could embark upon a life of pleasure and dissipation."

"My dear Miss Mandeville, I'm sure you know nothing of dissipation."

She met his teasing eyes. "After last night, Your Grace?"

His smile reached his lips. "A taste, perhaps."

That puffiness at one side didn't make those lips any less distracting. In fact, it gave his smile a wicked quirk. . . .

"Continue with your tale, Miss Mandeville. Or can I guess? Your father turned to gaming and lost Stokeley Manor to Crofton."

She stared at him. "You know about it?"

"Such stories travel, though I hadn't noted the names. How much did your father lose?"

She looked down for a moment and found her fingers clasped. She released them and met his eyes again. "I think he misses the excitement of life in India. Perhaps gaming provided that thrill, but he seems not to have been as good at it."

"He lost everything?"

A lump in her throat almost silenced her. "As best we can tell, other than my mother's and my personal possessions."

He'd cleaned his plate and now leaned back in his chair, sipping coffee. "Surely your father knows the state of his affairs."

"My father was struck down by shock. He does not speak and seems not to hear. My mother manages to feed him a little, but he is wasting away."

He inclined his head. "My commiserations. But I have to point out that, sad though it is, Crofton owns Stokeley and everything in it."

This was the crux that she did not want to share, but she saw no choice. "The truth is, Your Grace —"

"St. Raven, please."

She ignored him. "The truth is that my father kept a cache of jewels. It was a habit he'd acquired in India, when it was apparently wise to always have portable wealth in case a man had to flee. He told me about it. Showed me where it was hidden. I know that in strict legality those jewels go with Stokeley, but I cannot feel they truly belong to Lord Crofton. He has no idea of their existence, and I'm sure my father did not intend them as part of the wager. If he'd been able, he no doubt would have retrieved them before Crofton took possession of the house."

The duke put his cup on the table and refilled it. "Fascinating. I can see the temptation to try to get them back, but are they really worth sacrificing yourself for?"

"They are what will make life bearable. My father may never be restored, and even if he is, will he be able to make another fortune, or any money at all? My mother longs only to return to Matlock. We still have our house there, for it was always in my mother's name. We cannot support even a modest life there, however, without some money, and at present we have only what our possessions will raise."

She touched the pearls around her neck. A simple string of small beads. "We fought my father's inclination to give us extravagant adornment."

"You see, dissipation and extravagance are so much wiser. But, I have to ask, might your father not have sold his jewels to support his taste for gaming?"

He was like a vise, squeezing, squeezing for the truth. But it was invigorating.

"I don't think so. I checked my father's accounts. Everything is recorded there, including his losses. . . ."

She had to take a moment to compose herself. How anyone could throw away a fortune on cards she could not understand. "There is no record of the sale of the jewels, and no sudden increase in cash."

"What does your mother say?"

Cressida sighed. "My father's return was a great shock to her. She became fond of him all over again, but that didn't lead her to any interest in his business affairs. Now she can think of nothing but his recovery."

"So you face this alone. No longer. You have a knight-errant."

She eyed him warily. "I must retrieve those jewels, Your Grace."

"Of course."

"Whatever it takes."

"We'll see about that."

"You have no right to dictate to me!"

He raised a hand in elegant protest. "Fight that battle when we come to it. For now, we are comrades in arms against the foul fiend. However, if your father regarded these jewels as his emergency resource, why would they be in the country rather than to hand in London?"

Another excellent question. Despite his eccentricity, the duke's mind was sharp.

"I have a hypothesis. My father has many Indian artifacts — most, unfortunately, left at Stokeley. Among them is a series of ivory statuettes cunningly made to hold things. His jewels were in one of them. I think he took the wrong one to London."

"Careless. They must all be quite similar."

"Yes." She prayed he didn't ask for details.

He sipped coffee. "You have no guarantee that he hasn't gambled away the jewels directly, or pawned them, or moved them."

She had to relax her hands again. "No, but I'm not being blindly hopeful. I think that the statue he showed me was not quite the same as the one in London. I'm sure that someone of his acquaintance would have noticed him staking jewels. There was nothing furtive about his gaming, Your Grace. As for a pawnshop, I'm sure he would have recorded the money in his accounts. It is his way. He recorded everything."

"But is such a man likely to have been confused as to which statue was which?"

"He is a little shortsighted. And he did take one, just one. Why, unless he thought it was the one containing his treasure?"

He nodded. "Well argued."

"What's more, my father did not lose his wits when he lost to Crofton. He returned home at breakfast time and seemed normal except for being tired. My mother berated him for his unhealthy hours."

She swallowed at that memory, and at her mother's guilt over it. Though in truth he'd deserved worse.

"My mother went to apologize, and found him sitting in his study in the strange state that still chains him. I was there moments later, summoned by her cries for help. The statue lay on the floor, open and empty."

"So, his jewels were his family's salvation. Discovering that he had the wrong receptacle was the final straw." He looked at her. "Did it not occur to you to simply break into your old home? There are doubtless servants there who would help you."

She shook her head. "The house had stood empty before my father bought it, with just an old couple taking care of it. They were happy to be pensioned off. At least my father did it with an annuity, so they are safe."

"You have a very kind heart, Miss Mandeville."

"That is not kindness, Your Grace, but justice. One man's follies should not destroy others."

She saw a twitch that might be a grimace. Well, if the shoe fit, let him wear it.

"We lived there for only a few weeks in December, but my father had modern locks installed, and grilles on the lower windows. He came home with a great fear of sneak thieves. They are apparently common in India."

"They're common enough in England. No helpful servants?"

"None I could trust, and Crofton might have replaced them in the past weeks."

He nodded. "Right. So where in Stokeley Manor will we find the statues?"

The *we* speeded her heart with hope and nerves.

"If they haven't been moved, they're in my father's study on the ground floor at the back of the house."

"Alas for all those grilles and locks."

"Indeed."

He studied her, frowning. "What bargain did you strike with Crofton? A statue for your virtue would make him suspicious."

"And would rate myself very low." Cressida found she couldn't meet those eyes, and she studied the play of light on the chased silver chocolate pot. "I was to receive all my father's Indian artifacts. There are some valuable pieces, even without the hidden jewels."

"Do you have any idea what you would have been asked to do for such a price?"

She made herself look up, though she knew she was blushing. "I know the essential facts, Your Grace, and would have done it if necessary."

"If you were able."

She kept her eyes steady. "I believe my innocence was part of my appeal."

"You're a remarkable woman, Miss Mandeville, but a terrifyingly naive one."

"Nonsense. I was prepared for it to be appalling, but what choice did I have? Was I to huddle in my virtue and delicate feelings and end up in the workhouse? See my mother there, too?"

"It's what most people do, and the sacrifice was somewhat drastic."

After a moment, she confessed. "I hoped not to have to go through with it."

"Ah! You planned to get in by agreeing to give yourself to Crofton, then grab the jewels, and escape before he did his worst. Clever — but a trifle optimistic, I fear."

He was treating her like a child. "I had a plan."

"I don't doubt it."

His condescending amusement put her teeth on edge. "I had in my reticule a liquid that promotes vomiting. I planned to complain of carriage sickness, then sip a little shortly before we arrived, claiming that it was a restorative. I doubt any man would be eager to bed a woman who was throwing up her dinner."

He laughed. "Bravo! And you would need only a little time to seize the jewels and make your escape." He lifted her chocolate pot and poured the last of it into her cup. Then he raised his cup. "A toast to enterprising, courageous women."

She raised her cup and chinked it against his, unable to resist mirroring his smile. She'd had to pursue her terrifying plan in secrecy, and it was warming to have someone's approval.

As she licked chocolate from her lips she said, "I hope you see now, Your Grace, that you did me no service by stealing me from Lord Crofton."

"Alas, no." He put down his cup. "I commend your plan and your courage, Miss Mandeville, but you don't know Crofton's world. He might have found some novelty in using a sick woman, and he would certainly have locked you up until you recovered."

She stared at him, stomach churning at what might have been.

"Your other point of ignorance is that you were not going to Stokeley Manor to be there with Lord Crofton alone. He is holding a house party."

"A *house party?* He promised I would not be ruined in the eyes of the world!"

"Perhaps a truth. It's to be a masquerade. However, it is also to be an orgy. You know what that means?"

"A bacchanalia?" she said hesitantly. "Immoderate drinking and sexual license?"

"More or less. People who attend such events tend to be jaded. They demand novelty. I fear you were to be Crofton's centerpiece of novelty. Well-bred virgins are quite hard to come by, especially ones who go willingly to their fate."

Her shocked mind raced ahead of him. "In *public?*" She sucked in thin air, struggling not to faint.

"At least in front of privileged guests. Good Lord. My apologies!" He dashed around the table. "I should never have put it before you so bluntly."

Everything went gray; then a firm hand thrust her head down between her knees. "Keep breathing. It's all right. None of this is going to happen to you. My word on it."

That hand rubbed her neck. That and his

words helped. She pushed upward, and he let her straighten. Dark spots flickered for a moment, then cleared.

She looked into his concerned eyes and swallowed. "I find I must sincerely thank you for rescuing me, Your Grace."

She thought perhaps he blushed a little. "I certainly couldn't leave you with him. And we must go about our adventure carefully."

Cressida reached for her chocolate pot, but found it empty.

"Wait a moment." He left the room. He returned in moments with a decanter and glasses. "Brandy. Drink up."

She'd never drunk neat brandy, but sip by sip, she drained the glass. By the end she felt steadier, but also more frightened. She'd thought herself so clever and in control! But now . . . Was there no hope for her and her family? Then she remembered what he'd said.

"*Our* adventure?"

His eyes were bright with enthusiasm. "You can't deny me a part in this, Miss Mandeville. And I'm sorry, but I cannot let you go to an orgy without an experienced guide."

Chapter Five

Cressida put down the glass. "The term 'experienced guide' does not precisely reassure me, Your Grace."

She remembered thinking that he lived in another orbit, and it was true. A higher orbit of elegance and confidence. A much lower one of morals. The description "middle class" was singularly appropriate for her family, as well. Not the heights of pristine virtue, but not the degrading depths, either.

"I enjoy a gathering where men and women — all enthusiastic, of course — enjoy sensual pleasures more freely than is common."

He showed no trace of shame.

"I suppose you have an invitation." She regretted the tartness in her voice, but really!

"If you can't control that vinegar face, Miss Mandeville, I can't take you anywhere naughty."

"I have no desire to go —" She halted because she had. Or at least, had to go.

His eyes twinkled. "You could think of it as educational."

"There are some things best not learned."

"Wemworthy. Definitely."

That stung. "I am *not* . . . Oh, you are an exasperating man!"

"I try. Come, come, Miss Mandeville, you have the name of a romantic explorer." He leaned forward, bright eyes challenging her. "Is there not a tiny part of you that wants to see this through to the end, that wants to witness a licentious party? Did you not, perhaps, enjoy your bold venture with Crofton, delighting in the prospect of outwitting him?"

She stared. It was as if he could see into a secret part of her soul. Though terrified, though hating to let Crofton touch and command her, she had sung with excitement, with *life*, as never before.

"Yes," she admitted.

He smiled. "Would it not be a shame to return home, to return to Matlock, without seeing this through?"

"Perhaps . . ."

Tris was aware of being wicked, but it was harmless. He truly was an expert guide and could ensure Miss Mandeville's safety, and he wanted to see this world through her astonished eyes.

Time to put a twist on it.

"There is no need, of course," he said carelessly. "I am willing to go to Stokeley and retrieve the statue for you. It should present little problem."

She bit her lip — uncertainty, temptation, struggle, all as clear as if she'd spoken them.

He pushed a little more. "You can stay here in comfort and security."

Her neat white teeth released her lower lip. Her tongue poked out to lick. Such full, soft lips, especially when moistened. . . . He reminded himself that the amusement here did not include the lady in his bed. Virtuous ladies from Matlock were forbidden territory.

"It might be cowardly to leave this all to you," she said.

"Cowardice is sometimes the epitome of wisdom."

Let her talk herself into it.

"There are also practical considerations. I know the house, and you do not. I know which statue among others is the right one, and how to make it reveal its secrets."

"You could tell me that."

"It is not something easily described, and time might be short." She licked those lips again. "It is even possible that Lord Crofton will have moved them."

"Why?"

Pretty pink flushed her round cheeks. "They are . . . the sort of thing well suited to a bacchanalia."

Desire stirred. She made him think of swirls of cream on plump, sweet strawberries. "Then yes, he will have them on display. If you feel you can do it, your presence would be helpful. I can guarantee your safety."

Honesty compelled him to add, "I cannot guarantee that you won't see things that embarrass you. In fact, I can guarantee that you will."

He saw a flash of excitement before she frowned.

Ah, it would be criminal to deny her this treat. "So, do you want to come? Tonight?"

Cressida looked into his bright, challenging

eyes. Oh yes, she wanted to go. "Staying here would be like Wellington sitting in Brussels sipping tea while Waterloo raged."

He rose. "Delightful woman! Very well, we must make plans for battle, and the first is to disguise you. I can be recognized, but it's essential on all levels that you are not." He tugged on the bell pull. "How well does Crofton know you?"

"Not well."

"Then how did this extraordinary bargain come about?"

"He asked for permission to court me, but I had my father turn him away. I didn't like him, and he was clearly one of the ones after my large dowry." She looked up at him. "I worry that this is all revenge."

"Possible, but you could have done nothing else. And I assume he didn't force your father to the card tables."

She sighed. "No, and after the disaster, he offered me this chance to recoup. In exchange for my virtue, my family could keep all the Indian artifacts. He tried to express distress, to present it as a kindness, the louse. I almost had him thrown out, but saw a chance to get the jewels."

"It makes me wonder just how straight the play was, but the important matter now is your disguise."

He rose and went to open the door. "Harry?"

A young footman stepped into view. Cressida saw a strong resemblance to Mrs. Barkway. "Your Grace?"

"Find Mr. Lyne for me."

When the footman left, the duke turned and

looked her over. "You already look different. . . . What happened to the curls?"

She blushed. "They are false."

"Lord above. But their absense changes your appearance. With a mask . . . Or a veil. Yes, that's it! I have a sultan's costume somewhere. If you go as a houri, with a veil over the lower part of your face and a mask over the upper part, it will do. Is your hair as long as it looks? You can wear it down. . . ."

With a knock, a new man walked in. Another tall, fashionable man, though lighter haired than St. Raven and square faced.

Cressida raised her brows. "What became of the plan to keep me out of sight, Your Grace?"

"Cary's already seen you. Garters," he added, clearly to put her to the blush. "Stockings." Before she could respond, he said, "Miss Mandeville, may I present Mr. Caradoc Lyne. Cary, Miss Mandeville."

"You're looking more the thing, Miss Mandeville. I hope you haven't been too frightened."

"No more than is reasonable, sir."

He pulled an apologetic face. "We couldn't leave you in the hands of that loose fish, Miss Mandeville. Truly." He turned to the duke. "What's to do now?"

St. Raven efficiently laid out the situation. His friend argued about the wisdom of taking a lady to such a scandalous affair, but was overborne. Cressida reflected that the Duke of St. Raven was accustomed to having his own way.

"So, our pressing need is a costume," he said.

"Something vaguely Arabian with a face veil."

"There are some things . . . er . . . left behind, I think."

He returned in moments and spread a pair of purple silk trousers on the bed, adding a glittering, multicolored short-sleeved jacket.

Cressida stared. "I can't wear trousers!"

"This will be an *orgy,* Miss Mandeville." The duke's eyes were laughing at her again.

She went over and picked up the jacket. If she was lucky it would just reach to her waist. "My corset will show beneath this!"

Mr. Lyne cleared his throat. "I think you're supposed to do without. We could try for something else —"

"Nonsense." The duke cut him off. "The outfit's perfect, especially with my sultan's costume." Cressida tried to object, but he carried on. "We need a face veil and head veil, both fairly opaque." He studied her. "Mask, face paint . . ."

The door shut behind Mr. Lyne, who clearly followed orders. Cressida did not. "I am not wearing those clothes, Your Grace."

"Why not try everything on first? You can back out at any time."

"I don't want to back out. I simply want something more ladylike! Can't I go as . . . as a nun?"

He laughed. "Trust me, sweetheart, if you want to blend in tonight, the less ladylike you look, the better. The less likely that anyone will recognize you, you see."

She did, but she still rebelled. "Why would anyone even imagine that I'd be at such an event?"

"Most of the women there will be professionals, yes, but some ladies enjoy wild adventures. An unmarried lady would be a rarity, but not entirely unknown. The key, of course, is never to raise the thought."

He paused for a response, but Cressida didn't have one. Now that she'd seen the costume, she wasn't sure she could go through with this, but at the same time it was a challenge. She'd not known she'd react so strongly to a challenge.

"It is your choice."

Did he know that was as seductive as Lucifer's whisperings?

"I have a number of things to arrange," he said, "so you have time to think it over. It would be wisest for you to stay in this room. Can I send some books for your entertainment?"

Still frowning at the outrageous garments, she agreed, and he left. Cressida picked up the trousers, symbol of her extraordinary situation.

Trousers! Many people still thought ladies' underdrawers indecent because they resembled male clothing. Impossible to imagine wearing trousers and nothing else, and these silky things would feel like nothing.

They were opaque, at least. She'd seen drawings of Eastern women in similar trousers that were more like veils. These were quite pretty, too, braided with gold at the gathered ankles and up the sides, and tying at the waist with a golden cord. She held them against herself and thought they would probably fit. They'd be too long, but the gathered ankles would help there.

She put them down and picked up the jacket

made of purple and red brocade embroidered with gold thread. It was short sleeved, low necked, and buttoned up the front. She told herself that it would cover her as well as the upper part of an evening dress, but without underwear, that was scant comfort.

No shift? No corset? How could she go out in public like that?

She wanted to put the outfit on now, to see the worst, but was hindered by the usual problem. She couldn't get into and out of her fashionable clothes alone.

It had been different in Matlock. She and her mother had shared a ladies' maid, but most of their gowns had been made for practicality and comfort, and they'd been able to dress and undress themselves.

Matlock. She dropped the scandalous jacket back on the bed.

Their lives there had been so smooth and comfortable. She'd lived all her life in the handsome house provided by the money her father sent. She and her mother enjoyed good friends and solid positions in Matlock society. Not at the upper level, but the height of respectability, despite her father's strange absence. Her parents had been married there, after all, so no one could hint that the absentee husband had never existed. Her mother's many good works had kept them busy, and Matlock was a minor spa town, so there were concerts, plays, parties, and assemblies in the summer.

Soon, if this plan worked, they could return there. Even if her father remained unwell, she and her mother would be in familiar surroundings and among friends. If her plan failed, however, they could never return.

If only her father had stayed in India.

If only he hadn't taken to gambling.

If only she had noticed and done something!

That was the knife that turned in her. She'd been distracted by London. Society events had soon bored her, but London had fascinated. She'd begun to think that she might like to marry a man of that world. Not an idle aristocrat, but an active, involved man. A member of Parliament, perhaps, even a member of the government. That would be wonderful.

Or a merchant. She wasn't drawn by profit, but by the wonder of supplying masts to one country, wool to another, and spices to a third. Her friend Lavinia was engaged to marry a sea captain, and she looked forward to traveling to far ports. That was too much for Cressida, but she would like to be involved in the workings of the world.

All that was over now, unless she retrieved the jewels. It had been obvious during her season that she wouldn't achieve a fashionable marriage on her face alone, even with false curls.

She glared at them, still stupidly attached to the turban.

Fashionable circles were so stupid! Cruel, petty, and vicious, too. When her father had his wealth, many lords and ladies had visited, but since his loss and illness, they'd evaporated. Of course, it was summer now, when London largely emptied, but still, it showed their lack of heart.

Someone knocked, "It's Harry, miss." Cressida

opened the door and he carried in a pile of books and some cloth. He put the books down and, blushing, offered white cotton stockings, plain garters, and a piece of thin cloth. "Me mam sent these, miss. She hopes they'll do."

Cressida took them as if they were jewels. "Indeed they will. Do thank her for me."

He piled the remains of breakfast on the huge tray. "You just ring if you want anything, miss."

When he'd left, Cressida took off her slippers and put on the solid, comforting stockings, tying them firmly with the garters. Then she sat before the mirror and arranged the triangle of fine cotton around her shoulders and tucked the ends down the front of her gown. She pushed the edges under the neckline all around and at last was decent.

Decency was a strange thing. She'd not minded wearing this dress to a ball, but what was decent for night was not decent for day. She considered the bed. Trousers were not decent for anything.

St. Raven had offered to retrieve the jewels alone. With every passing moment, it became more sensible.

She hadn't been making feeble objections, however. Some of the ivory statuettes were similar. They all showed people . . . having sexual congress in strange positions. Five showed standing couples, and one of those was the one with the jewels.

She truly hadn't noted some precise detail that she could pass on, but she believed she could spot the right one when she saw it. And she did know the house.

know the house.

She pulled a face. Truth was, she wanted to go. She'd keyed herself up to be the heroine of this adventure, and she didn't want to back out now.

Think of it as a masquerade party, Cressida. She had attended a quite proper one in London, where some of the ladies and gentlemen had been outrageously dressed. There had been one woman dressed in similar Eastern garb.

She picked up the trousers and stood in front of the mirror, holding them against her. "Are you Cressida Mandeville, or Cressida Mouse?"

She was, she decided, Cressida Mandeville.

Having made up her mind, she sat in a chair by the window and went through the books. Had St. Raven chosen them? They were a careful assortment — poetry, history, a three-volume novel, and, she noted with a smile, an account of travel in Arabia.

A hint that she study for her part? She settled to it. She'd always loved accounts of travel to exotic lands. She'd sometimes thought that she was like her father and would thrive under foreign skies, but she had a strong streak of her mother's conservatism. Small adventures such as the move to London were enough adventure for her.

Time passed until another knock brought Harry, beaming as he carried in her valise.

"Oh!" To Cressida it was almost as wonderful as having the jewels presented to her. "Harry, thank you!"

"No thanks to me, miss. Mr. Lyne found it by the road and sent it back."

As soon as he'd left, Cressida opened it to find

her silk shawl on top and — miracles! — her reticule beneath it. Crofton must have tossed it out with her bag. She might no longer need the emetic, but it felt like a weapon in her hands.

She fingered through her gowns and underwear, delighted that Crofton no longer had them in his soiling possession. But then she stilled. He would have been furious. Might he try some revenge? Might he ruin her by telling the world she was seized by Le Corbeau?

No, he couldn't do that. He would have to explain her being with him. That would ruin her just as surely, but it would ruin him, too. Even the careless ton would shrink from such blackmail of a lady. If he turned his anger anywhere, it would be against the highwayman.

But, she thought, closing the valise, if she went through with the plan, she would meet Crofton again tonight. She must make very sure she could not be recognized. The outrageous garments along with mask and veil should do that.

She made herself settle again to the book, and enjoyed her vicarious journey to Arabia, broken only by Harry bearing a tray with some bread, fruit, cheese, and tea.

She heard the distant clock sound four before her host returned with pale, filmy fabric in his hands. "I hope you haven't been too bored, Miss Mandeville, but if you have, the adventure now begins."

Chapter Six

She leaped to her feet, mouth dry, heart speeding at St. Raven's words.

Or perhaps simply at his presence.

"I haven't been bored, Your Grace. I've been to Araby."

He dropped the material onto the table. "I thought it suitable. And it is fascinating."

"You've read it?"

"Why else would I have it?"

"Do you do business with the East?"

His brows rose. "Trade, Miss Mandeville?"

"There is nothing wrong with trade, Your Grace."

"Certainly not, but it does not fall within the province of a duke."

"Why not?"

"The stability and prosperity of England lie in the land, Miss Mandeville. They always have and always will. It is my honor to serve that."

There was no unpleasantness in his voice, and yet she felt put in her middle-class place.

"See what Cary found," he said, picking up the filmy material he had brought, and separating the silk into two pieces. He held the small one in front of his face. "Just thick enough to obscure your features."

She couldn't help but chuckle at the sight of his lashes fluttering over the veil, but her confidence in everything was shaken. "I'm not sure I can go in public in those clothes."

He dropped the veil on the table. "Time to try them on and see. You will have armor." He loosened the drawstring on a bag and spilled out a glittering pile. "Cheap stuff from a theater troupe, but it will serve. Do you want Annie Barkway to help you? I think her honest soul would be sorely tried to dress you in these clothes."

Cressida swallowed, but she gathered her courage and turned her back. "If you would loosen my clothing, Your Grace."

"If I am to be so forward, you really must call me St. Raven, you know."

He was impossible. "St. Raven," she said, and he started on her buttons.

Last night, even when she was fogged by shock and exhaustion, it had disturbed her to have him doing this. Now, every touch of his fingers sent something coiling through her, and she couldn't help thinking of him and her in other circumstances.

Married.

As wild and absurd as an orgy, but today she had been more at ease, more casual with this man than she'd been with any man in her life, never mind a young, strikingly attractive one. In their discussions, in their plans, she'd come to feel that she knew him. That they might even be friends.

It was an illusion. That clash of incomprehension over trade showed that. How could he be interested in foreign lands yet have no desire to explore business opportunities? How could he not want to be part of the fascinating advances in science and technology and, yes, the profits they were going to bring?

They were foreigners who did not even speak the same language, but that didn't make the illusion powerless. She was both exasperated by him and drawn to him, and he'd kissed her last night in a way she'd never imagined being kissed. What's more, if she was to believe what he'd said, he'd desired her.

He'd desired her. *Her,* Cressida Mandeville, the most ordinary of ordinary women . . .

Her clothes fell loose again. She clutched them again. She took a steadying breath and turned. "Thank you, St. Raven. I can manage now."

She saw that look in his eyes again.

Quieter, but still hot. It stirred something tentative but real and deep within herself. . . .

Cressida! He's a rake. He holds orgies here. He is doubtless aroused by any woman in loose clothing.

He smiled as if he could imagine her thoughts, and then he was gone.

She blew out a breath and let her gown fall. She wriggled her corset over her head and then, reluctantly, took off her shift. Now she was covered only by her drawers and stockings. She pulled on the silky trousers and tied the cord at the waist. They did fit, though they were a little snug around her hips. When she looked in the mirror, however, she gulped.

Snug! Her round hips and full bottom might as

well be naked. And she *was* naked on top. She grabbed the jacket and put it on. The silk lining slid cool against her skin but rubbed her hardened nipples. She hastily buttoned it.

Then she looked in the mirror again.

She was covered. As she'd thought, she was better covered on top than she had been in her dress, for the jacket's neckline was a little higher. She couldn't ignore, however, the fact that her breasts were unconfined beneath it. When she shrugged, they moved! And the long line of gold buttons down the front was the only thing between her and exposure. She stretched back, and they gaped.

Well, she'd simply not stretch back.

The worst thing was that the jacket only just reached her waist. At any movement a bit of skin showed there, skin that had never, ever been exposed to public gaze before.

Slowly, still watching herself, she raised her hands and pulled pins out of her coil of hair. A band of pale midriff showed, including the top of her navel.

Impossible.

And yet, moment by moment, she began to think that these garments might suit her better than conventional fashion. Her plait tumbled down her back. She drew it forward and loosened it, then shook her hair free, down to her waist.

Her hair went with the costume, with the stranger in the mirror. It was as if she were looking at someone else, an exotic foreigner from Araby.

She was plump, but she had a trim waist. The

high-waisted gowns of fashion did not flatter her, but the outrageous trousers and jacket did, making her full breasts and hips look right in some way. Indecent, but right. In balance.

She picked up the face veil and tied it just below her eyes. Perhaps it was true that no one would know her if she were dressed like this.

She broke connection with the exotic stranger in the mirror and went to plunder the jewelry. Bracelets. A half dozen narrow ones on each wrist. Two gaudy armbands on her upper arms. A necklace of red glass and false pearls that didn't look at all Eastern.

Reluctantly, she decided a "diamond" tiara wouldn't do. She'd always wanted to wear a diamond tiara. Even so, when she studied the whole in the mirror, she laughed with delight. She was someone else entirely, flamboyant as she'd never been.

She picked up the long blue veil and draped it over her hair, then had to use the tiara to hold it in place. She was laughing at the effect when someone knocked on the door.

She froze. It had to be St. Raven, and he was going to see her like this.

"Come in."

Her nervousness fled at the sight of him, another being from this fantasy world. His loose trousers were very like hers but in a deep red, and his jacket was black, sleeveless, and braided in gold. He wore it over a shirt with billowing sleeves, however, and she was a little regretful that he was so well covered.

"And why don't I get a shirt, Your Grace?"

He grinned, his eyes sweeping over her in a way both outrageous and flattering. She saw her own feelings about her appearance mirrored there. "Because," he said, "that would definitely spoil the fun."

She blushed, but couldn't help being delighted at his reaction.

"I'm not armed, either," she complained, noting the curved knife in a jeweled scabbard stuck through his black silk sash.

"Of course not. You're a lady of my harem."

She looked him in the eye. "Oh, no. I, my lord sultan, am your principal wife."

His grin turned wicked. "Including wifely duties?"

More blushes, but she didn't flinch. "Only with a ring and proper vows."

She couldn't believe she'd said that, but he didn't draw back in horror. Did that mean they were friends? Could they be friends for this little while?

She considered the rest of his costume, which had obviously been well thought-out and expensive. It included a black turban and a glittering "ruby" in his ear. Or at least, she assumed it was fake.

"Why do I feel that earring is real?"

"Because you have a good eye. Ducal privilege." He looked her over. "Most excellent, my dear Roxelana, though the tiara will not do."

"Something has to hold the veil on, O great Suleiman."

He held out a narrow black mask. "Try this. Your pale eyes are too noticeable, and if we tie this over the veil, it will hold it in place."

He came to do it, tossing the tiara aside. His hands on her head made her shiver, and peering through the mask moved reality one step further away. "Ah, yes. Look."

He turned her to face the mirror and truly, she would not have recognized herself. The gaudy creature looked brazen, wild, and ripely sensuous.

He put down something in his hand, stepped in front of her, and took her chin. "Your brows need to be darker." She felt something stroke there. Then it pressed on her cheek. "A beauty spot."

He picked up something and offered it. "For the lips. Even under the veil it will have effect."

Cressida took off the veil and drew the deep red cream over her lips. It was grotesque, but that didn't matter in this game. When she put the veil on again, those scarlet lips lurked indecently.

She looked up to see him using the black stick to draw a curling mustache above his lips.

"Why not use the false one?"

"We don't want anything to remind Crofton of Le Corbeau. There."

He stood beside her, and the mirror showed a matched pair — bold and patently false. Creatures who would exist for only a brief time, but that time could be magical fun.

But then he said, "The drawers will have to go."

She stepped away from him. "Impossible!"

"I can see them. No woman who attends an event in that costume would wear drawers."

She looked at his trousers. They were looser than hers, and she couldn't tell if he was wearing anything underneath them.

"No, I'm not."

That made her blush, but this was a challenge now. "Go away."

When alone, she stripped off the trousers, then, with a breath, took off her drawers and stockings. As fast as possible, she pulled the trousers back on and tied the drawstring. At least they were a little looser.

She turned to the mirror. She couldn't see any great difference, but she *knew*. The silk slithered against her bare skin and brushed between her legs in an outrageous place. No wonder women had been reluctant to wear drawers for so long!

She turned this way and that, gathering resolve. Then, back straight, chin up, she opened the door.

He was waiting, and he came back in, very obviously *not* smiling. "Much better, and you'll get used to it. But keep by me at all times tonight, or I cannot guarantee your safety looking like that."

Her heart did an excited, terrified dance. Was she really so dangerously attractive? "What about safety from you, sir?"

"Perhaps I should give you my dagger."

Something in his eyes warned her that this might not entirely be a game. "Am I in danger from you?"

For once he seemed serious. "No, but if you have any mercy in you, Miss Mandeville, don't play with fire."

Ah. That should be warning, but it felt more like temptation. . . .

"Right," he said briskly. "Can you go through with it?"

Cressida pulled back from a brink and turned to look in the mirror again. This felt very like the moment when she'd had to decide whether she could accept Lord Crofton's bargain. The situation, the necessity, had not changed, and the dangers were much less.

She met his eyes in the reflection. "I can."

"Bravo. We'll stay in costume for dinner, then set off. It will take about two hours to reach Stokeley."

Dinner was a pleasant, informal meal in her room, with Cary Lyne to preserve sanity. They talked of common topics — of the cool spring and poor harvest, the royal marriages, the state of Europe. Which led to talk of travel. The two men had traveled together last year.

They drew her out to talk of Matlock and of her experiences in London, but Cressida had little to offer in comparison to them, and she was not accustomed to the casual company of men. She preferred to be the listener.

Then St. Raven provided her with a cloak, and they slipped down the stairs and out to a waiting coach. She was surprised when Mr. Lyne joined them. Did St. Raven feel in need of a chaperon? Oh, she did hope so. Delicious to be a temptation just for once.

Talk started with carriages and moved on to travel again.

St. Raven was the sort of traveler who liked to

get to know the people of a country. He complained that once he'd become duke it was harder to stay in small inns and talk to the local people, even if he traveled as Tris Tregallows.

"English travelers are everywhere these days," he complained, swaying easily with the speeding coach. "I've met them in tiny inns in Charente and on snowy passes in the Alps. They then gossiped of me to their local acquaintances, and the next thing, I had a pressing invitation to stay at a schloss or château with a ball being held in my honor."

"All too true," said Mr. Lyne with an irreverent laugh.

"I took to using another name, but I still met people who recognized me. And then, of course, I felt ridiculous."

Cressida wasn't inclined to be sorry for him. "I wouldn't mind staying at a schloss or château."

"Then you should come traveling with me one day."

Longing burned in her like a brand, but she laughed. "Not," she said again, "without vows and a ring."

She heard Mr. Lyne laugh.

"You tempt me," St. Raven responded, but she could see the tease.

"You must know the Peak District well, Miss Mandeville," Mr. Lyne said, and talk moved smoothly on.

She learned that St. Raven was a patron of the arts. He dismissed it as an indulgence, and when she protested that, he claimed it a duty. She thought his energetic, restless mind reveled in the company of painters, poets, musicians, and actors.

She'd already let slip a desire to travel with him. She kept to herself the pull of "dutiful" indulgence in the arts. To have her own quartet, however. To support artists and poets whose work she admired. To see young artists blossom because of her care!

Ah, there was a prospect to enchant.

Then the coach slowed.

She looked out of the window and recognized the small village that lay a half mile from Stokeley Manor. Nearly two hours had passed with her scarcely noticing them.

She longed to command that they drive past the gates, that they carry on into the night in this pleasant companionship. But that voyage was at an end, and she was here to get the statue, or at least the jewels.

And then they would forever part.

Lyne pulled out a silver watch and flicked it open. "Almost two hours to the dot. Well guessed, Tris."

"Accurate estimation," St. Raven corrected, looking out of the window at the moonlit scenery. Was he regretful, too?

Soon the road carried them through fields, and then through trees — the trees around Stokeley. She'd always felt they gave the house a secretive, concealed atmosphere. She'd never much cared for Stokeley and wouldn't regret its loss except for the money it represented and the jewels in the statue.

The road followed the low wall around the estate, and she knew a break in the trees would soon reveal the house.

"It's on fire!" she exclaimed.

St. Raven leaned across her to look out, but then he relaxed. "Theatrical effect. Thin cloth streaked like flames and hung in some of the windows."

He settled back into his place. "Now we know Crofton's theme for the night, however. Welcome to hell, Miss Mandeville."

Chapter Seven

Their coach stopped, and for a moment it seemed a direct response to his words. Then Cressida realized that there was a queue of carriages. "Such a line waiting at the gates of hell," she remarked.

"But, of course. Doesn't Satan have the monopoly on all the most amusing occupations? Is there an inn in that village we just passed?"

She bit back an argument. "The Lamb."

"Then let's get out here." He gave the command to let them down. "We'll summon the coach when we're ready, Cary."

"Right you are."

St. Raven opened the door before the groom reached it and climbed down. Then he turned to grasp Cressida at the waist, to swing her through air to earth. . . .

She shivered. "The breeze is quite cool, isn't it?"

It wasn't the summer night, however, but his touch and her inadequate clothing that unsteadied her. She'd never been outdoors in such flimsy covering, not even on the hottest summer day.

Or perhaps it was the shouts, chatter, and even screams from the waiting carriages. Screams of laughter, she hoped.

St. Raven wrapped an arm around her and drew her past the raucous carriages toward the gates. Her pulse fluttered with nerves for a dozen different reasons, but by his sandalwood side, she felt that nothing could harm her, nothing could go wrong. Tonight, he was Great Suleiman and she was Roxelana. They would play their parts in this wild company, find the statuette, take out the gems, and leave.

Tomorrow she would be home again, her mission accomplished. But she would carry extraordinary memories with her, perhaps to record in a secret journal — memories of a scandalous evening in the company of this delightfully scandalous man.

And he *was* scandalous. As they strolled past the line of carriages, he was recognized. Women hung out of windows to issue blatant invitations, and were dragged back by complaining men.

"What charming friends you have, sir," she remarked after one raucous woman nearly fell out of the window.

"Don't nag, or I'll send you back among the houris."

One was supposed to act the part at a masquerade, so Cressida held her tongue. Keeping to her role would help avoid a revealing slip, and they'd decided she would put on a foreign accent to disguise her voice.

She used it now, trying for something guttural and German. "At least there would be no drunkenness in a harem, Great Suleiman."

"But all kinds of interesting drugs, I gather."

"St. Raven, by Hades!"

A fat red-faced man poked his head out of his carriage window. "Swap partners, St. Raven, there's a good fellow! Give you a monkey."

He was dressed as Henry VIII, and looked the part too well.

"Not this early in the game, Pugh."

St. Raven drew Cressida on. They could see the open door of Stokeley Manor now, and it was beginning to look like a haven despite the hellfire effect.

Henry VIII was yelling offers after them. *"A thousand, St. Raven. Come on, man! Stap me vitals, look at the tasty rump on the wench!"*

Cressida froze, but a strong arm forced her on. Heat rushed over every inch of her overexposed skin, and she wanted to go back and pull the stupid man's flat hat down over his stupid ears!

"There'll be more of that sort of thing. Ignore it."

"Ignore — ?"

"Yes." It was a command, and she realized they were close to the throng of people spilling out of carriages and into the house. "It is, after all, very flattering, nymph."

"I have absolutely no desire to be flattered about my posterior!"

In the red-tinged light from the house, his eyes laughed flames at her. "Then make sure to always face the enemy."

He swept her forward, and she didn't resist. This was her enterprise, it was important, and she had insisted on attending. Her reasons had been valid, but she had also been spurred by curiosity. She'd expected — anticipated — shock and scandal, and now she had it.

The scene near the open door was a good start. The paneled entrance hall must be full of red lamps to give such an infernal impression. Carriages disgorged fanciful creatures who rushed into the flames.

Thank heavens this had never been a true home to her and her family. To see it desecrated like this would be agony.

At the open door they tangled with a devil with a curly tail, a man in a toga, a nun, and a woman whose red costume she could not decipher. They greeted St. Raven as intimates and eyed her curiously.

The men were doubtless gentlemen by status if not by nature, and the women were not ladies in any sense of the word. Cressida remembered saying that she'd rather be a nun, but this nun's black habit was open at the front from the waist down, and she certainly wasn't wearing drawers.

The other woman's tight red dress was slit in at least four places, showing plump bare legs as she walked. Her large breasts were covered only by a wisp of veiling.

Cressida tore her eyes away, then froze at the sight of Lord Crofton welcoming his guests. He, too, was dressed as a devil, but he wore no mask. He leered at the daring lady, then snatched the veiling from her breasts. The woman shrieked.

Crofton swung her around so she was in his arms, back to him, and put his hands under her breasts, thrusting them up. The tips were painted as scarlet as Cressida's lips.

"Now, here's a fine welcome," Crofton called.

"Come in, come in, and kiss hell's tits!"

Cressida's breath stopped. She couldn't ignore such a cruel assault.

St. Raven's arm tightened. "It's Miranda Coop," he murmured in her ear. "Very much a professional."

She surrendered but watched, appalled, as St. Raven cradled the woman's right breast and kissed the upper swell. "Adorable as always, Miranda," he murmured.

The whore purred.

Those behind were pushing forward, the men eager to pay Crofton's fee for admission. Then a woman in a clinging black gown and tiara of stars took up the invitation. Mistress Coop slapped her so hard her tiara flew off, and in moments they were at one another's throats.

Crofton and some other men lunged to control them.

"Rather them than me. Trust Violet Vane to cause a riot." St. Raven steered them away from the screaming mêlée. Cressida twisted to look back, but he forced her onward.

The entrance hall wasn't large, and the yells and shrieks made Cressida want to clap her hands over her ears. Sounds of the fight had other guests pouring out of nearby rooms, assailing her with more din and stink, and crushing her between St. Raven and a bony man in a Harlequin costume.

Someone squeezed her bottom!

She jabbed back with her elbow as hard as she could, delighted to feel it connect. St. Raven laughed and switched so he was between her and the worst of the crush. They popped into a haven of space at the base of the wide, dogleg stairs.

St. Raven blew out a breath. "All right?"

"Of course."

And she was. Out of the press, she wanted to laugh at it all. It was as fascinating as a menagerie.

She ran up three steps to get a better view of the scene. The women were in the grasp of a couple of men each, but were still screaming at each other and trying to get back to the fight. The woman in black was bare-breasted now, too, and her pointy nipples were as red. Did all whores do that?

The crowd was cheering and urging them on.

Cressida looked down at the duke. "I suppose this sort of havoc happens at every orgy, since you aren't interested?"

He grabbed her at the waist again and swung her down. "I'd be pleased to ogle the show, but I, at least, remember our purpose. Which way to the study?"

Cressida swallowed a temptation to squabble for the fun of it, and tugged him through an alcove to the right of the stairs. This opened into the back corridor. It was deserted at the moment, though a couple of wall lamps provided light. The noises faded, and this area looked so like the house she'd lived in last year that she swallowed around a lump in her throat.

"It must feel strange." He was disconcertingly alert to her feelings.

"Yes, but this wasn't my home. We spent only last December here. Most of the furnishings came with the house."

She had herself in command again and led the way to the study. She listened but heard no sign that anyone was inside, so she turned the knob and went in.

She paused. It was so unchanged, she could imagine her father sitting at the large central desk keeping his meticulous records. They'd known each other for only a year, and these days she was furious that he'd thrown them into this disaster, but he was an interesting man. His talk of travel and trade and limitless possibilities had filled an empty place in her mind and heart.

A hand on her back pushed her farther into the room; then St. Raven closed the door. "Where are they?"

Cressida looked around. "Not here. They're not here!"

"Hush. Remember, I didn't think a man like Crofton would ignore such things."

"But what if he's sold them? Or given them away?"

"If they're as intriguing as you say, they'll be on display. Anything else you want while we're here?"

She stared at him, remembering that he never had explained the highway robbery. "Larceny in the blood, I see."

"One famous ancestor was a pirate. So? We're short of pockets, but if there's anything you want, I'm sure we can manage."

She thought about it, but her father had taken his important papers to London with him. The house, including this room, was scattered with his mementos of India, and she begrudged them to Crofton, but not enough to try to collect them now.

St. Raven had picked up something from the desk. A dagger, but with a design of flames around the edges and tip. "What's this?"

"A wisdom sword. I don't remember the Indian name for it. It represents cutting through knots of confusion and deceit."

"We need one of those."

Tris considered the flaming sword wryly, wondering what the devil he'd been thinking, to bring a lady to this event, particularly dressed as she was. Pugh wouldn't be the only one trying to buy her, nor Helmsley the only one to grope her. And she'd been witness to Miranda Coop and Violet Vane at their worst. The sooner they had the jewels and were out of here, the better.

He put the sword down. "You've had a taste now. Perhaps you'd prefer to wait."

"You can't leave me here!"

"There's a key in the lock."

"And master keys. And, anyway, you don't know the right statue."

Damnation, she was right, but her lush curves and veiled scarlet lips made him want to lock her in a dungeon. "Describe it to me."

She shook her head. "I can't. There are quite a few that are similar. I need to see them." She cocked her head. "Anyway, this is a rare opportunity to explore a foreign land. I'd be disappointed if the most I saw was a squabble."

"Here, however, be dragons."

"Made of ribbon and papier-mâché."

She was a child. "No. Here be dragons with real teeth and fiery breath. Don't let the tinsel distract you."

He'd given her a mask with narrow slits to mute the effect of her large eyes, but even so, he could sense them widening. Good. She had to understand the dangers.

"Be careful, and stay with me at all times. Yes?"

"Yes. Which is why you can't leave me here."

"Why do women always want the last word?"

"Because we're right?"

He opened the door. No screaming, so the fight must be over.

"Come on," he said. "We'll try the drawing room or dining room first."

"This way." She took his hand and pulled him to the right. The touch startled him.

And her, judging by the way she paused and stared at him.

He smiled and curled his hand around hers. "Lead on."

He'd touched many women's bare hands, which was not something every gentleman could say, but he couldn't remember when he'd last linked hands with a woman like this, in a friendly, almost childlike manner.

Cressida drew the duke toward the dining room, distracted by the effect of ungloved hands, by the way he'd wrapped his around hers. When had she ever linked hands with a man like this before?

At the end of the passage she turned to look at him again. He raised their joined hands and kissed hers. A strange unsteadiness swept over her.

This is a masquerade, Cressida. This is all play-acting. And if there is something more here, if there is a man you like, don't forget that he's a rake. He kissed that woman's breast with as little concern as he just kissed your hand!

She pulled free of him and led the way around the corner and into the small back parlor.

And stopped.

This wasn't unchanged. The dull and rather dark paneled room now blazed with red lights — or rather, lamps with red glass chimneys. In this lurid glow, naked women posed on tables, obscenely.

Not entirely naked. They wore veiling, but every detail of their bodies was clear. With their slim hips and tiny breasts, they looked like children.

Men pawed at them, touching them in unthinkable places, and the girls only laughed. They had protectors — dwarves and hunchbacks dressed in black with horns on their heads. Imps from hell, she supposed. They didn't protect them from much.

She turned to St. Raven and murmured, "Are they so young?"

"No, whores who can look young."

"But why?"

He pulled her on. "Some men have strange tastes. Remember our purpose. I can't see any statuettes here."

The statuettes! The lurid light made it hard to be sure, but they certainly weren't on display. She let him lead her away, despite a lingering feeling that she should do something about those posing girls.

The dining room was a relief. It looked almost normal. The lighting was simply from candles, and refreshments were laid out in a conventional manner.

In fact, it looked much the same as when she and her parents had dined here, sometimes with guests. Giggles threatened at the thought of the neighboring Ponsonbys, or the vicar and his wife at this feast.

She looked around the guests. Tight and revealing seemed popular. The fight must be over, because the woman in black was here — Violet something? — her dress clinging to every curve and torn open to expose her small, pointy breasts.

She was . . . flirting? — which did not seem to be the right word — with a pirate in thigh-boots, breeches, and a shirt open to his waist. Those breeches might as well have been painted on. A large bulge was unignorable, and Cressida knew what it was. She'd seen classical statues.

The woman in red was here, too, though on the other side of the room, breasts still exposed and marked by scratches. It didn't seem to bother her. She was laughing as Henry VIII — Pugh? — fed her some sort of long pastry.

Cressida placed him. He attended some society events. Lord Pugh, fat, florid, and loud, but she'd never have guessed him debauched. She thought he was married.

She'd foolishly assumed these entertainments

were for bachelors, but clearly not. St. Raven was a bachelor, but she didn't suppose he'd change when he married Lady Anne, which made a mockery of that lovely moment in the theater.

And he recognized harlots by name.

She looked again at Pugh, and the harlot called Miranda, and couldn't help but notice that as the woman slowly ate the pastry, her hand played around that strange article of fashion called a codpiece.

She'd always thought it peculiarly indecent. Even kings, such as Henry VIII, had worn it. She wondered what ladies had done in such times. They could hardly have pretended not to notice.

Then Cressida's mind made a connection between the long scarlet protuberance at the front of Lord Pugh's puff breeches and the long pastry he was feeding to the woman. . . .

After a moment she tore her gaze away — and found St. Raven watching her, darkly inscrutable. He picked up something from the table and offered it to her. Something long and cylindrical.

"No, thank you." She hoped the words sounded like icicles.

"It's only a half cucumber filled with —" He scooped some of the pink stuff up with his finger and tasted it, sucked it. "— potted shrimp."

"Perhaps I don't care for shrimp."

"But you are supposed to care for . . . shrimp, Roxelana."

She cast him a look she hoped *felt* like icicles. He was reminding her of her part — mistress of the harem, but also the sort of woman who would attend an orgy like this. A slight flick of her eyes made her aware that some people nearby were paying attention.

"Do you fear poison, my love?" St. Raven asked. Eyes on her, he turned the cucumber and bit off the end.

More outrageous images flooded into Cressida's mind.

"Ouch," she said.

He exploded with laughter, covering his mouth and almost choking. Grinning with victory, Cressida rescued the remains of the delicacy before he dropped it.

They had the whole room's amused attention now. She must play her part, but truth to tell, she was enjoying this. She was very partial to potted shrimp, so she raised her veil, and slowly licked the pink filling out of the scooped-out cucumber.

Applause, but her attention was all on him.

His eyes sparkled, but his look said, *Your move.* It seemed cruel to bite, so she put the end in her mouth and sucked the last of the shrimp off.

Applause and even cheers burst out all around.

Not knowing what she had done, Cressida stared at him for guidance. He stared back. Had sparkle turned to fire? Something tightened her throat, so she had to work hard to swallow.

She pulled the cucumber out and turned away, turned to the table, pretending to study the selection of food, only too aware of the hubbub around her. Men were demanding to know who she was, and was she available. Henry VIII was bidding again.

Then a big body pressed against her from behind. Hands appeared on the table on either side, caging her. Hot breath stirred at her nape. She tensed to fight, but then she knew him. Perhaps it was sandalwood, but perhaps it was a more secret sense than that.

"Hungry?" he almost growled.

Quivering, she looked down, and her eyes were caught by his right hand, the one with his large gold signet ring, bold declaration of identity, here among the masquerade.

It was a hand, that was all. It melted her sinews and tightened her muscles, shortened her already unsteady breath. Long fingered, elegant, but nakedly strong and masculine. For the first time she noticed some scrapes on his knuckles and could imagine it as a fist.

She breathed in cool sanity. Last night the Duke of St. Raven had held up a coach, then engaged in a brawl. Now he was at an orgy and known to all. This was his world, and it most certainly was not hers.

She dragged her eyes away from that seductive hand and pushed back to gain more room, turning to meet his eyes. "I was merely taking a moment to look around the room. The statues aren't here."

Chapter Eight

Tris realized with shock that he'd forgotten the damned statues entirely. That little play with the cucumber had him hard and aching. He'd been pressing against her delicious bottom, mind turning to a different quest entirely.

Cressida Mandeville, he reminded himself.

Not Roxelana, either wife or whore, but Cressida Mandeville, virtuous merchant's daughter from Matlock, a walking marriage trap if he fooled around with her.

"Come on, then." He turned them toward the door.

She stopped halfway, and he looked to see what had caught her attention.

Roger Tiverton, in his usual guise of pirate, had a jam tart in his hand. He was holding it in front of his mouth, his long tongue dipping into it, swirling, scooping up the red filling, which he then drew into his mouth and swallowed.

Three women were watching appreciatively.

Plus Cressida Mandeville.

If Tris had been with Miranda Coop, he might have thrown her down among the suggestive delicacies and shown her what it was really all about. But Miranda wouldn't need to be shown, and Miss Mandeville, devil take it, needed to be protected from all this lewdness.

He gripped her chin and turned her head to him. Her eyes were wide, startled, but not at all confused. And to think that he'd always liked a clever woman.

"We are not here for these amusements, Roxelana." But those eyes asked questions he longed to answer. It could be done without taking her virginity. Without ruining her. Without trapping him . . .

"Unless I can interest you in other games," he said. When she didn't pull away, he added, "If you wish to explore further, I am completely at your service."

"I'm not a whore," she said, but softly.

"I'm not offering you money."

He saw her draw a deep breath. "Then let us agree that I am not a wanton fool."

Ah, Cressida, you want this, you know you do.

"It isn't only whores who enjoy unsanctioned pleasures." He drew her closer, let her feel his arousal. "I would enjoy pleasuring you, and I guarantee that you would enjoy it, too. Aren't you curious?"

He thought for a precious moment that she was going to agree, but then she broke the spell and looked away. "That curiosity will be satisfied at a more sanctioned moment."

For one brittle second he resisted sanity, but then he let her go. "For better or worse," he said, steering her out of the room.

Cressida let him lead her out of the dining room, feeling as if she were leaving an opportunity she might regret for the rest of her life. She was not, however, a whore, and to surrender to a rake would be folly of the most extreme kind.

She would lose her maidenhead.

She might get with child.

And there was no possibility of marriage. Even with her father's fortune intact, it would have been an unequal match. Without it, it was unthinkable.

She didn't even want it. Oh, she acknowledged the wicked duke's appeal, and the appeal an event like this stirred in the sanest mind and body. But she could not live with a husband addicted to this sort of game, a man who would laugh at fidelity. She could never share a husband with the likes of Miranda Coop.

The hall was still a riot of noise, a tempest of smells, and the revelers continued to pour in. Many were already drunk, and all of them grabbed drink from the trays carried by twisted servants in black imp costumes.

This was more a theatrical than reality, she told herself. As silly to be upset by this as it would be to scream against Othello smothering poor Desdemona. Could the house hold any more actors without bursting, though? Her senses throbbed with the din and stink.

Crofton, in his horns and scarlet robes, still welcomed people to his sensual hell, but now she found him more suited to farce than drama. Lucifer could not have horns and tail. To trap sinners, the devil must be beautiful and seductive.

Like the beautiful, seductive Duke of St. Raven.

How many of these raucous characters were

people she'd met at events in London? Most of the women must be whores. The strident laughter, the shocking costumes, and something in the way they moved marked them. No wonder St. Raven hadn't believed her claim.

Perhaps it was the whores who contributed the coarse perfume that hung so heavily in the air, though the smell of dirty bodies could be from anyone. She'd come across it in the best of society. Crofton was one who was careless in those matters.

Crushed against St. Raven by the crowd, she caught that scent of sandalwood. It was a saving antidote as they worked their way toward the drawing room.

He continued to be recognized, and he kissed three bold women who thrust themselves against him. Nothing to do with her, she reminded herself.

While he chatted to people, his hold became tighter and his hand squeezed — her hip, her bottom. She understood why, but it was another sign of what he was. Then, when he was again fending off questions about her identity, he turned her head and kissed her through her veil, his hand, low on her back, pressing her hard against his side.

Tired of being a puppet, she put her left hand on his silken hip and kissed him back.

His lips stilled on hers.

"Don't worry, luv," a woman said. "St. Raven don't need rubbing up."

Cressida froze. She'd missed.

The hard shape under her hand wasn't his hip.

Oh, Lord — it moved, and only a thin layer of silk lay between her hand and it! She knew she mustn't snatch her hand away, but wished something, anything, would whisk her back to her real life. She felt, heard, his soft laughter as he broke the kiss.

She opened her eyes to stare into his, silently begging for help. She could tell he was having as difficult a time as she was, but it was because he was fighting laughter.

His hot hand covered hers. Thank heavens. He was going to move it. Instead he pressed. The hard shape moved again. Perhaps it grew.

Her heart thundered, and a good part of it was fury. The swine was exploiting this. She couldn't rebel, but she could glare, and she did.

"So impatient," he murmured, but somehow loud enough for others to hear and laugh. Then he gathered her hand in his and stroked it up his body to his lips, to kiss the palm. "Later, my houri. . . ."

"No need to wait, St. Raven!"

Cressida felt her eyes stretch wide as panic swamped anger.

Crofton!

St. Raven held her attention, kissing her fingertips one by one, giving her time to gather herself, then turned them both to face their host.

"I'm sure we'd all be most grateful for a display of your prowess, Duke."

The disgusting man was leering, but that wasn't what made her feel sick. His attention was fixed on her. Would he *recognize* her?

If her identity was exposed here, she would die.

Literally and eternally. The respectable Cressida Mandeville, dead in a lewd costume after a lewd display at a lewd orgy. Matlock would be talking about it for the next fifty years.

"I never give public displays, Crofton. And as I'm sure you know, pleasure is enhanced by the torture of exquisite anticipation."

Something in St. Raven's tone killed Crofton's bonhomie.

"Later, then." Leer turned to sneer. "Though I cannot guarantee a private room as the night grows wild. You might end up giving a public display anyway, Duke — if anticipation wins out. But you're not drinking. . . ."

He snapped his fingers, and a horned imp hurried over with a tray of beakers. Crofton took one and pressed it into Cressida's hand. "My devil's brew."

She accepted it, but didn't drink. It would be the height of folly to get drunk here. She watched St. Raven take a beaker and toast their host, but she noticed that he took the merest sip.

Crofton looked at her. She raised her veil and sipped, somewhat let down to taste only spiced cider. Surely if it were dangerously heavy with spirits, she would taste that.

Crofton smiled. "I'm sure you'll agree, Duke, that anticipation is enhanced by stimulation, and here we have it in plenty. Display in the back parlor, some clever birch work in the master bedroom. You could order your houri a pretty stinging."

He smiled at her, showing the long teeth that had always appalled her. She worked hard at not speaking, and not glaring in return. She obviously failed.

"I see you haven't broken her spirit yet. I would be happy to do it for you. . . . No? Let me see, what else would amuse? Catamites in the back bedroom — appropriate, wouldn't you say?" He let out a peculiar high-pitched titter. "But I know that's not your vice, St. Raven. Certainly not with your own slave girl at your side." Crofton's eyes slid back to her. "I feel I might know you, my dear."

Cressida turned every faculty to looking stupid and not at all like Cressida Mandeville.

"Impossible." St. Raven's tone was absolute. "She is my personal discovery."

"Ah, fresh from the country. Not for sale, I assume? I had planned something similar. . . ."

Something stopped his words, and without looking, Cressida knew it was St. Raven. She could feel it — an emanation that raised every hair on her skin.

Crofton's disgusting smile turned a bit sickly.

. . . *planned something similar.*

Her! If not for St. Raven, she would be at this debauch as Crofton's whore. By his side, dressed in something appalling, fondled at his whim. Perhaps presented bare-breasted at the door.

To stave off a faint, she gulped her drink. An imp took her empty beaker and replaced it with another before she could say she didn't want it. The drink was sickly and left a sour taste in her mouth.

Crofton was groveling now. "No offense, Duke. No offense. I only seek to please all my guests.

There will be a competition in a little while which might amuse you. In the drawing room. Something a little different."

"I'm not competitive in these matters, Crofton. I have no need to be."

Crofton flushed. Oh, yes — he was furious, but he didn't dare lash out, and Cressida didn't think it was rank alone.

"I meant you might find *watching* amusing, Duke. Excuse me."

Crofton scuttled off to greet a new guest, leaving Cressida trembling with the aftereffect of the confrontation, aware of tension lingering in the man beside her.

"Why do I think the drawing room is our target?" St. Raven's voice was calm and light. Perhaps too much so.

Cressida swallowed and matched it. "The competition?"

"If I had a set of erotic statues, that's what I might do with them. I'm surprised Crofton showed such imagination, but let's go and see."

He took her beaker and gave it and his own to a drunken couple nearby. They thanked him and drained them with surprising enthusiasm. Cressida worried about that. Perhaps there was more spirit in the drink than she'd thought. She checked herself, but could feel no sign of inebriation. She had occasionally drunk more wine than she'd intended and felt the effects of it.

Enough of this. She was here for an important purpose and must keep her mind fixed to it. Then, with heaven's assistance, she would soon be home and could arrange her family's return to the safe sobriety of Matlock.

Tris put Crofton out of mind. His disgust at the man was a distraction, though coming here might encourage his pretensions, damn it. Cressida Mandeville had a great deal to answer for, including some physical discomfort which was unlikely to be eased as he would wish.

Temptation still burned in him, temptation to seduce her. He was her guide here, however. He'd promised she would be safe.

But, desire whispered, he could satisfy a great deal of her curiosity without putting her at risk. She might even be safer for it, less likely to plunge into danger, more careful about whom she eventually chose as husband.

Surely no woman could be so frankly curious without chafing at the boundaries of propriety. The memory of her hand on him, of her startled, *curious* eyes —

Perdition! He had to settle for the novelty of guiding a tourist through this dangerous territory and returning her to her own country untouched. Didn't he always say that he liked a challenge? Well, he had one now.

An event like this was designed to stimulate the erotic senses and break down barriers, though he found Crofton's style crude. That drink, for example. Thank heavens Cressida hadn't drunk much of it. He'd been distracted for a moment. She could have drained a whole cup.

He certainly didn't need it. Cressida herself was an aphrodisiac. He found her costume more enticing than Miranda's vulgar exposure, and her ladylike movements more stimulating than the whore's undulations.

Miranda was nearby, laughing with a man in a fool's costume. It struck him that she was of similar height and build to Cressida, and yet the effect was so very different. Vulgar curves on one, luscious curves on the other.

He indulged in a sweeping assessment of his houri's charms.

Her breasts were too big for fashion, but he loved it, and Pugh had been right about her rump, damn him. That bottom, firm, high, and round, made his mouth water and his hand itch to stroke and squeeze. . . .

Devil take it! The sooner they found the statue and could leave, the better. He wrapped an arm around her dainty waist and forced a way through to the drawing room.

Chapter Nine

Tris paused in the doorway to assess the drawing room, but also to regain his sanity. Get the statue and get out.

He could see them now — a line of ivory statuettes on the oak mantelpiece on the far side of the room. They were interset with candles so the fireplace resembled an altar, but the crowd could hardly be seen as worshipers. Some were pressing close to study the statues, others milled around drinking and laughing. A few were attempting the poses.

In front of him, Cressida went on tiptoe. "There they are."

She sounded relieved. She couldn't be any more relieved than he was.

Another brush of her delightful bottom against his body and he might snap. He wished he could move away from her, but the crowd pressed them together, and anyway, they needed to be able to talk secretly.

"Do you know which one?" he murmured, close to her ear, tormented by a scent he was coming to know too well.

Her scent.

She turned her head slightly, bringing her lips close. "One of the vertical ones. I can't distinguish which from here."

Tris focused on their target.

"One of five, then. The other four are more or less horizontal. How will you know which is which?"

St. Raven's voice was soft in Cressida's ear. She felt his warm breath against her lobe. The aroma of sandalwood was all around her, along with something more, something deeper, something pounding like a pulse in the air.

Perhaps that was why she felt so strange — hot, dizzy, and peculiarly sensitive all over her skin, but especially in secret places. She longed to rub herself against something.

Against him.

He was saying something, about feet on the ground. . . .

". . . There's a limited range of possibilities."

Possibilities. She'd thought all the poses of the statuettes impractical, but now, crazily, her body ached to turn to him and attempt them.

"Well?"

Cressida swallowed and inhaled. "I'll recognize it. But we need to be closer. To them, I mean . . . ," she added desperately.

"Very well."

The center of the drawing room was even more crowded than the hall, which was probably why he steered a path around the edges. She supposed he had to tuck her close to his side as they threaded between chattering, laughing groups, but she wondered how long she could stand it and stay sane.

She inhaled his sandalwood with every breath

so it wove into her brain and spiraled there. Despite the noise all around, she could hear his heartbeats, feel his pulse pounding along with hers. Her shocking silk costume stroked her skin with every movement.

His mask looked at hers, and his eyes seemed larger, darker. Was he as frustrated as she by how little of the eyes the masks revealed? His lips parted, and she could see his chest rise and fall with deep breaths.

Sounds seemed magnified, but at the same time distant. That drink must have been full of brandy or some other spirit, but she forced herself to behave normally.

What on earth was *normally* in a situation like this?

She'd always assumed that she would enjoy the marriage bed in some cuddly sort of way. She'd never imagined this wild, wanton fire within her ready to flare at the first scandalous opportunity.

Tris had to keep torment close by his side. He could cope with her curves against him, beneath his hand. He was an experienced man. He could control himself, protect her.

Could he prevent her seeing what was going on in the middle of the room? At least everyone had all their clothes on — for now.

Since most members of English society lacked the flexibility of Indian gods and goddesses, the results were humorous rather than erotic. Still, they were more than a lady should see.

He felt her twitch and looked closer to hand. Damnation. One couple was up against the wall, the woman's thin white legs around the man's waist, the man's bottom pumping. He blocked her view and pulled her on despite a pulse that pounded through him in time with the man's thrusts.

"It's not polite to stare."

"Here?" she snapped. "I thought it was part of the fun."

She'd spoken too sharply, so he countered it by swinging her hard into his arms, hard against him. "I warned you that you'd be embarrassed. And confess, you stopped to watch."

"I was startled." She shifted her body against him in a way that was pure torture. "I thought the statues fanciful. Do people often do things like that?"

Now she wanted to *talk* about rutting while she moved against him? If she weren't such an innocent, he'd think she was set on killing him.

"Against a wall?" He tried to pretend they were talking about the weather. "I doubt many could do it standing without support. Anyway, there's a lot to be said for comfort. It's what I prefer. . . ."

Don't think about what you prefer!

Then a man pushed past, and the damnable woman pressed against him again, wriggling. Oh, for an armored codpiece.

"There are times," he heard himself say, "when less comfort has its own delights. . . ."

Just a kiss. That wouldn't hurt. . . .

The damn veil was in the way.

"Comfort," she echoed, her breath fluttering the veil.

Was that longing he heard? Hunger? Need that

equaled his? There was a bit of wall free over there.

He pulled back. Hades, that was the worst trap to fall into, to begin to think that a decent woman hungered for the same things an indecent man did. He broke the connection and headed straight toward the fireplace.

Get the statue and get out of here.

He bullied a path through to the display. A couple of men turned to protest, but then they either recognized him or someone said his name. He detested using his rank like this, but he had to get this done.

"Tell me which one you prefer, Roxelana," he said, to give her an opening.

When she didn't reply, he turned to see her frowning. Hell, if she couldn't pick the right one, what were they going to do?

So, think, Tris. Drag your mind away from your damn prick, and come up with a strategy.

He could try to buy them all from Crofton.

That would be dangerous. Crofton might simply charge an outrageous amount, but he might refuse out of spite. Worse, he might suspect something. No matter how cunning the hiding place, would it resist a search?

"Well?" he prompted.

Did her eyes look worried behind that mask? "I need to get closer." After a moment she added, "I, too, am a little shortsighted, Your Grace."

Her slip into using his title showed how much she hated to admit that.

"Suleiman," he reminded her. Beneath the veil, her scarlet lips tightened with annoyance. He imagined them tightening around —

He blocked that thought. But he couldn't help feeling tender that his Miss Mandeville so disliked having to acknowledge any weakness or error.

"And I don't suppose you have your spectacles with you," he teased.

Her red lips parted as if she was breathing deeply, with annoyance no doubt. "That would be a spectacle indeed — a houri in eyeglasses. I only need them for fine print and fine needlework, and I did not expect to do either on this venture. . . ."

He saw the sudden change in her expression as she remembered what she might have been doing here, and he slid his encircling hand up to the side of her breast to distract her.

Ah, she had the sweetest, softest breasts, Miss Cressida Mandeville, and he'd bet his soul she didn't have a notion of the pleasure they could give her. Not to mention him.

A pity she's not a whore.

Gads! He was stroking her breast. He stopped. Judging by her dazed look, she wasn't going to be the control here, so it was for him to do.

Then he realized that people nearby were watching them. When in doubt, be bold. He shifted to take Cressida's hand high in the old-fashioned style, and led her in a review of the line of statues, commenting loudly enough to be overheard.

"Which position do you favor, Roxelana? I have to confess that I don't care for the one with the gentleman upside down and cross-legged."

"I'd like to see anyone try," she muttered.

Tris glanced at their audience. "The lady doubts it's possible. One does wonder what happens during the . . . climactic distraction. I look forward to watching the experiment."

People chuckled.

"Watching, St. Raven?" said a man unimaginatively dressed in his grandfather's wide-skirted court suit. Lord Seabright, an amiable idiot. "Bet you could do it, even if your luscious houri is a bit heavy for it."

Tris felt Cressida stiffen, and choked back a laugh. "Bountiful with delicious curves," he said quickly. "So," he added to his Lady Bountiful, "which do you favor? Perhaps if you please me well enough, I will buy it for you."

He thought for a moment that she'd rebel, perhaps grab one of the statues and whack Seabright over his dense skull with it.

A scenario with possibilities . . .

Before he could suggest it, she turned her back on the man. "Such a hard choice," she said in her foreign accent, studying the line of statuettes.

If she couldn't recognize the right one, they'd have to wait. Eventually the debauch would render most people oblivious.

He could have groaned. Linger here for hours? Even now, with Cressida simply standing still, he was aware of every delectable curve. He could imagine the taste of her skin on his tongue, feel her nipple full in his mouth. . . .

He dragged his eyes away from her body, and his mind from the pit, and focused on the vertical statues. What distinguished them for her? Did she remember whether the woman had her right or left leg up over the man's hip? Surely she'd know if it was the one with both her legs raised. The fourth was a complicated stance with both partners on one leg with the other hooked up around their partner's hip.

Three showed the woman with one leg raised. In two it was the right leg, in the other, the left. Was that the one?

He looked at the two with the right leg up, wondering what the differences might be. Ah, in one the man was holding her around the waist with both arms. In the other he had one hand on her breast.

So, had the one in London been mistaken for one with the left leg up, or for one with the man's hand on a breast?

She reached out and touched the one with the woman's right leg curled around her mate's hips, his hand on her breast. "This one, my lord Suleiman. This is the one that pleases me."

Casually, he picked it up. "Then let us find our host and ask his price."

It was worth a try, but there was an immediate outcry that his ducal status didn't seem to quell. He was about to proceed anyway when Crofton pushed through the crowd.

"My dear duke, I cannot permit even you to claim a statue just yet!" He was showing the pleased spite Tris had feared. "You, like everyone, will have to win it. Each statue will go to the couple best able to reproduce the act."

Tris ran through some choice curses in his mind. It might just be possible to persuade

Cressida to enact the pose in public, but not to complete it. And even if she were willing to try, he would never allow it.

"I see you have chosen one of the easier ones," Crofton added slyly.

He kept his voice level and bored. "My Roxelana chose it, my lord Satan. She doubtless recognizes the position most likely to give her pleasure."

"Then she will enjoy performing it, but I must insist that you replace the prize until then."

Tris could see no way to resist. To start a fight over it would draw attention, and the thing might pop open if dropped. Damnably frustrating. All they needed was a few minutes with it in a shady corner.

"When will the contest be held?" he asked.

"At midnight, of course. Please, do enjoy my many little treats until then." Crofton moved on to watch and applaud the performance of those attempting the poses.

For the first time Tris wondered how much the jewels were worth, and whether the Mandevilles would accept money. Probably not, and if the value was substantial, it wouldn't be an easy option for him. He was rich, but not so rich as a duke should be, and he was cash-poor.

His uncle had always resented not having a son. When he'd given up hope, he had diverted all his unentailed wealth into lavish portions for his six plain daughters, and ceased to take interest in managing his estates. If not for reliable staff, the dukedom could be in a disastrous state.

As it was, things were bad enough. The end of

the war had brought hard times, and most of the estate income was needed to repair neglect and provide employment. Yet a certain show was part of the role.

And besides, it was a matter of justice. In any real sense, these jewels belonged to the Mandevilles, and they should be returned to them. There had to be a way.

People began to object to them blocking the view, so he moved to the left of the fireplace. From there he could watch for an opportunity to slip the statue out of the line. If the ones on either side were nudged closer, it might go unnoticed.

He pulled Cressida into his arms, her too-curious eyes facing his chest. She looked up at him almost desperately.

He nuzzled her neck so he could speak into her ear. "Don't worry. We'll get it. How did you know it?"

"The hat," she murmured back. "The woman has a longer, more pointed hat."

He glanced at the statue, wishing that she wouldn't keep moving against him. She was a damned twitchy woman. "The hat," he repeated, not knowing whether to laugh or groan.

"And a different style of belt."

He did laugh then, softly against her sweet-smelling neck. He recognized the soap he'd sent to her room. It was his favorite on a woman, but now, strangely, he decided to find a new one for future guests. This perfume would always remind him of her.

She turned in his arms, and short of force he

didn't see how to stop her. A laughing Harlequin was attempting the cross-legged shoulderstand with the help of two friends. Tris hoped they didn't try to get a woman on top of him. He feared Hopewell might break his neck, and he rather liked the man.

Hopewell folded his legs down, ankles crossed, and someone lifted one of the smaller whores to sit backward on top. The girl locked her legs with Hopewell's and they achieved a sort of balance, but she was squealing that it was no fun without a prick inside her. Tris wanted to put his hands over Cressida's doubtless wide eyes.

The whore sounded about thirteen. He blocked that. He couldn't take on more damsels in distress, and that damsel seemed delighted with her situation — except for the prick, of course.

Cressida turned back to look at him. "Not just the pose?"

"Not just the pose. Don't worry. We're not doing it."

"We have to!" But he could hear the gulp in it.

He rubbed his knuckles up and down her spine. "No, we don't. Trust me."

Trust. When he wanted to slide his hand under her jacket and feel the satin of her back, slip his hand down inside her trousers to feel her scrumptious bottom.

Raise her right leg . . .

Cressida felt she was going mad. They had to plan how to steal the statue, but she couldn't think straight. The itch was worse. Twice now she'd had to stop her hand going between her legs to rub there!

It had to be the alcohol in that drink, though she'd never felt like this before. If they could get away, she could wash. That might help. Or she could take laudanum and sleep it off.

Now, however, pressed against St. Raven, the raucous sounds of the room a dim backdrop, she burned, longing to rub herself against him, to spread her legs and rub against him *there*. Her hands were frustrated by his shirt and jacket, and her mouth watered for him. She wanted to lick his skin. . . .

She shivered and realized why she might be feeling like this. It was him. This was all his doing, the wicked, skillful rake!

He'd been squeezing and fondling her all evening, and now he was running his knuckles up and down her spine, sending shivers and shards of excitement throughout her body.

Every scrap of silk she was wearing stroked her skin as she moved, as she shifted so her eager nipples rubbed through silk on silk. The seam between her legs whispered against an exquisitely sensitive place. Her breasts felt swollen, and the tips demanded more than a touch.

She pressed against him.

He was so hot, as hot as she was. . . .

His hand kept on making casual, knowing havoc on her back.

Then his hand arrived back at the bottom of her jacket and slid up under it, hot and subtle against her bare skin. She made a sound into his chest as his splayed hand commanded her back, crushing her chest against his as if he knew exactly how she felt.

Oh, what a devil he was to be able to do this to her.

She should stop him. Stop all this. She knew he would stop if she insisted. She trusted him. She trusted him. . . .

Her frantic breaths caught. If she could trust him, could she let him keep on doing what he was doing? Doing what she wanted so desperately?

"Move your veil for me," he murmured, and she obeyed, pulling it down beneath her chin.

Oh, yes. Kisses. Her mouth thirsted for kisses.

She was dimly aware that they were in public, but it didn't matter.

Still pleasuring her back, he took her lips, and this time she opened them, eager for a kiss like the one last night, but more. A kiss as wicked as the statues, as entwined, as involved. A kiss that seared through her, engulfed her.

She raised her right leg, sliding it up his thigh, silk on silk. He was too tall. She went on tiptoe to try to stretch her knee to his hip.

This was what she wanted. *This.* To be openmouthed to him, above and below, that aching, stinging place loving the pressure, wanting more.

He put a hand under her knee to help her hold the pose. She hadn't thought their kiss could be deeper, but he made it so. The ache grew almost to pain. She pressed harder for relief. He moved his other hand to the small of her back and held her there.

It wasn't enough. She moaned. . . .

He pulled his head back. *"Hell."*

After a moment, he eased her leg down. She felt him suck in an enormous breath. "My apologies. That went entirely too far."

Or not far enough. She ached, she shook, in a horrid, stomach-churning way. She could almost burst into tears.

"Or not far enough," he agreed, making her realize that she'd said it out loud.

He was rubbing her back again, but in a soothing way. "I'd do something about it, nymph, but not here. And we don't dare risk leaving, for here's Crofton again."

He helped her replace her veil, then turned her in his arms so she could see the room. He kept his arms around her, however, kept her pressed to him. Even shattered, even shaking, Cressida felt wonderfully protected.

Crofton. She pinned her mind on the red devil, author of all her disasters. He had moved to the center of the room and was demanding attention.

"My friends, you have found my new treasures! Are they not intriguing? And direct from India. Product, along with this rather boring house, of a lucky evening at cards with an upstart merchant who thought he could mingle with his betters."

Laughter and jeers. Cressida stiffened, but she felt St. Raven's arms tighten. It could be control, but it was also sympathy and comfort.

A new ache beat inside her. Crofton's words were a jagged reminder that she came from a different world. Once they left this event, she had no place in the intimate world of the Duke of St. Raven.

And I don't want one, she told herself, fearing it was a lie.

"Some of you have been attempting the poses," Crofton said. "I have arranged a demonstration."

He clapped his hands, and a dark-skinned couple entered the room dressed in a fashion similar to the statues. They bowed to the company and began to take up the poses, starting with the simplest, but bringing to them a grace that Cressida admired, even in her disordered state.

Then they moved into the one where they both had one leg on the ground, the other around the partner's hips. Her intimate place began to throb again, but she could appreciate their graceful ease. All around, people applauded.

"Ah," said Crofton, grinning, "but could they hold it when rutting? Could you? We will find out, eventually."

Cressida didn't think anyone could. Surely she and St. Raven would have tumbled to the floor if not supported by the wall.

But no, St. Raven hadn't been affected as she had been. He had been stirring her lust. He had been seducing her, and so easily, too. His horror came when he remembered that she wasn't a whore, but a lady he might have to marry after having his wicked way.

She blinked away tears as she watched the couple break their interlocked pose. Then the man went into the shoulder stand, legs crossed, as if it were the most simple and comfortable position in the world. "Two must lift and support my *sakhi*, my lord."

Two guests leaped forward to lift the woman onto his thighs, facing backward. She steadied herself with a hand on each assistant's shoulder, but as she and the man locked legs, she looked astonishingly comfortable. After a suitable pause for appreciation, she let the men lift her off.

Cressida watched as the two went through the horizontal poses, able to imagine all too vividly the way their bodies should connect. In the last pose, in which the woman was on her back with her legs over her head in a position that looked painful, the man moved his hips up and down, causing cheers and applause from the avid crowd.

Cressida remembered the couple up against the wall earlier and knew exactly what the man was simulating. Then she realized that she'd tightened her own muscles, moved her own hips. . . .

Oh, heavens, she had to get out of here!

Crofton leered around. "Mahinal and Sohni are available for training sessions with generous guests. Or you may wish to practice with your chosen partner. I gather a similarity of height is useful. Alas, St. Raven" — he suddenly focused on them — "your little houri is too short."

"You're suggesting that you have a woman here of my height?"

Everyone laughed, and Crofton looked as if he'd like to spit hell's flames. He turned away. "Drink, feast, and make merry! Explore. At midnight a gong will announce the beginning of the competition. Lord Lucifer — myself — will be the judge, and each victor will receive as prize the statue they have best imitated."

Many guests swirled away to explore. Cressida ferociously focused her wits on one thing. She watched for a chance to slip the statue from its companions. Alas, enough people remained to study the statues to make the task impossible.

She had to do something.

Could she plunge the room into darkness? She couldn't see a way. Fire? She could set Stokeley Manor on fire. . . .

No, no, she couldn't do that. She despised Crofton and his sort, but they didn't deserve to perish in flames.

Chapter Ten

She turned in St. Raven's arms to face him, refusing to let herself be distracted by her wanton body, even though the brush of silk against silk, of silk against skin, made her feel she was on fire. "What are we going to do?"

He looked thoughtful, too, and not the slightest bit affected by silk and skin. "It's a pity we don't have the one your father took. We could manage a straight switch with a momentary distraction."

"I should have thought of that."

"You expected to have a moment to extract the jewels."

"True." He shifted against the wall, sending that feverish sensation over her skin, tormenting her nose with warm sandalwood — and that something else. Deeper, mysterious . . .

She pulled her mind back from that abyss. "What do we do now?"

Lewd answers swelled in her mind, and she watched his face, irrationally longing to see the same needs there.

"Get out of here." He put an arm around her and led her away from her treasure and out of the room.

There was no heavy crowd in the hall, and the

front door was shut. A deep chime made her jump, every sense jangling. The staid hall clock — which must be quaking in horror at the display before it — was chiming eleven.

An hour to pass before the contest. Doing what? She no more wanted to be part of another lewd display than she wanted to plunge herself into a fire. And how were they going to get the statue? She knew she couldn't take part in a public display to try to win it, but she wouldn't let herself leave here without it. To have come so far and then turn back. Never!

For the moment, she went where St. Raven took her, which was toward the back of the house. If he was looking for privacy, he didn't find it. People were everywhere, in couples and groups. In corridors and rooms, all engaged in debauchery.

Cressida was astonished at the number of people kissing, fondling, and even copulating in the corridors. She was even more astonished at the way her body twitched and yearned at every heaving, gasping glimpse.

She focused ferociously on St. Raven so as not to see anything, though that stirred all kinds of other undesirable thoughts. A woman cried out. A man grunted.

An ache shot right up her legs and into a place that burned.

Had that muttered curse come from St. Raven?

His arm tightened, and he hurried her down the corridor. They bumped into the group.

Group?

Such a tangle of bodies. One of those childish whores was on her knees kissing. . . . Surely not! St. Raven forced her past at speed. Perhaps he was carrying her. Her legs felt as if they might fail, might stagger her. Or send her to the floor. Where he might . . .

He was a rake.

He would, wouldn't he?

That place inside her throbbed, like an extra pulse, beating fast like her heart.

He paused in a quiet corner. "Can you think of anywhere in this house that might still be private? Cellars? Attics?"

He sounded desperate.

Excitement skittered down her disordered nerves, and up her heated body. He'd said he didn't give public demonstrations, and now he was desperate for privacy.

"Not the kitchens. Servants." she explained. "Attics — storage and maid's bedrooms." She couldn't even make sentences anymore. "We could try them."

"And hope others don't have the same idea."

"Or go outside."

"Good idea. What's the quickest way out?"

She led the way this time, as eager as he for privacy and what would come next, even though it would be a leap into hell.

When they stepped outside he gasped, "Thank God."

A country-fresh breeze ran over Cressida's hot, damp skin, clearing away some of the insanity. Wickedness still throbbed in her, tingled in her, seethed in her newly informed mind, but now she could fight it.

Maybe.

Remember! she commanded herself, looking up at the pure white moon. *You don't want to give your virtue to a rake at an orgy!*

"Lead the way," he said. "You must know what's here, and even with a full moon, the light's chancy."

"What are we looking for?"

"A place where we can wait until midnight without tripping over people."

Midnight. The competition. "But you said we wouldn't compete."

"Of course not, but it will present opportunities. We'll get the jewels if not before the contest then afterward. The winners will be a rare couple here if they're sober enough to notice."

So simple, and it could work. And in the meantime, they had an hour. . . .

"So, where?" he prompted.

"The stables? No. The grooms will be there. The brewery? . . ."

"Not if we can help it. They stink."

"Storage sheds . . . They might be locked. Laundry . . ." She ran through her memory of the house.

"The bakehouse!" she exclaimed. "Even if they used it earlier, I doubt anyone is baking bread now. There's nothing unpleasant about the smell of baking."

"Nothing at all. Lead on, Roxelana."

He put his hand in hers, clearly expecting her to lead him, so she did so, relishing that slight, warm touch as a starving beggar might lick up crumbs. Heart pounding, mouth dry, she led him around the flaming, rowdy house.

Some of the guests had also ventured outside. The shadows and the shrubbery seemed alive with giggling, grunting misbehavior. Her naughty imagination tempted her to drag the Duke of St. Raven into the bushes. She made herself think of mud, twigs, and ants.

There were nettles near the stables. *Think of nettles, Cressida.* They would soon replace one itch with another.

The stables were almost as bad as the house as far as noise went. Coaches stood all around, shafts sagging to the ground; the nearby fields were packed with horses; and all the coachmen and grooms seemed to be in the stable block getting drunk in the company of a number of shrieking women.

"I see why you sent your coach to the village. But won't your men feel deprived?"

"Not as deprived as they would if I summoned them and found them drunk. The bakehouse is next to the kitchen?"

At his sharp tone, she speeded past the kitchen window, then stopped at the plain wooden door to the bakehouse. Gingerly, she opened it.

Blessed quiet welcomed her, along with the warm smell of past baked bread. It swirled around her, antidote to the wicked madness that reigned everywhere else this night. This was too wholesome a place for sin. She released his hand and moved away, farther into the safety of the dark room.

"I thought your father had this place secured

like the Tower?" he said, closing the door, sealing them in darkness cut only by moonlight through three high windows.

"There's no door from here into the house." She inched away from temptation.

"But still, things to steal."

He moved. Away from her, toward the far side of the room. Relief collided with bitter disappointment. She prayed not to show either.

"There's nothing of much value here. Bowls, bins of flour, rolling pins . . ."

"There are people desperate enough to steal anything."

"True." She turned her mind to that. "Perhaps my father is more afraid of murder in the night than of thievery. He doesn't seem greatly concerned about possessions."

"Obviously."

It carried a sharp edge of condemnation, but she couldn't argue about that now. She wasn't sure there was an argument to make. She rubbed her arms, fighting a need to be rubbed elsewhere.

"From stories my father told, he won and lost a number of fortunes, though at trade, not cards. In India, he says, there is always more for a man of wit and courage."

"And in England, even when wagering everything, he had the jewels to fall back on."

She could just make out the silver-edged shape of him beneath the high windows. He was wandering the far side of the room, perhaps exploring by touch. Cressida watched him, using what she knew of the room from before. The large table for kneading, shaping, rolling. The sideboard holding rolling pins, bowls, and the smaller tins.

"Adventurous," he remarked, "but not willing to risk everything. It makes me wonder why he made that mistake."

"He is shortsighted like me."

"Or wanted to lose everything."

Cressida stared across darkness at shadow. "That's absurd!"

"Is it? My observation is that people often get what they truly want, however undesirable it might seem on the surface. There are people who find calm so intolerable that they destroy it whenever it happens to them. Perhaps your father felt trapped by his tame English life and tried to escape in the only way he knew."

"By making a new adventure a necessity?" She spoke in disbelief, but was chilled by a sense of truth. "But what of *us?* What of my mother?"

"Perhaps that's why his mind is frozen. Perhaps he forgot . . . Ah, no. He went mad upon finding the jewels gone, did he not? They were for you and your mother. It must have been like teasing a tiger for fun, only to find that it has eaten his loved ones."

Cressida put her hands to her face, finding mask and veil. She stripped them off, dropped them, felt the head veil slither after them. She wished she could deny St. Raven's analysis, but it rang true — oh so true. She had not known her father long, but she'd sensed a growing restlessness in him.

He must have wanted England, wanted to reunite with his wife and child, wanted to taste the highest levels of society as Sir Arthur, rich nabob. But perhaps within a year the novelty had palled.

Had he been conscious of what he was doing, and why?

"All those stories," she said. "Fortunes won and lost. Gambling with his life. Do you think he knows what he does? That he seeks out risk?"

"Who's to say? But I've known men like that, and they never admitted knowing. They complained of their misfortune, but kept doing what caused it." He moved something with a heavy grating sound. "What is this huge wooden box?"

She welcomed the distraction he offered.

"The trough for kneading the dough. I came here now and then to watch. The making of bread fascinated me because I'd not seen it before. In Matlock we bought bread from a shop down the street."

How provincial that seemed. She was sure the Duke of St. Raven had never bought a loaf of bread from a shop.

"I used to love the bakehouse at Lea Park," he said, as if to confirm her thought. "I didn't study the processes, but it was always warm, always with this lingering smell of baked bread, and generally provided a treat for hungry boys."

"Is Lea Park your home?"

"What's home?"

She pinned her restless mind to that strange question. "Home is where your family is."

"Your father was in India, but that wasn't home for you."

"Home is where a person grows up, then."

"Until they move."

She stirred. Conversation wasn't working. His voice alone brushed over her skin, deepening her breath.

Or perhaps her hands twitched to touch him. She swayed with the need to press her face against his chest, to inhale the sandalwood she was sure she could smell now, even over the ghosts of past baking. . . .

She moved back and came up against the warm, smooth plastered arch of the big bake oven. Letting that soothe her, she concentrated on what he'd said, on what she did not understand. "So Lea Park is your home? Where you grew up?"

She saw him settle, too, probably with his hips against the sideboard, where it ran beneath the windows.

"No. I grew up in Somerset, in a house called Cornhallows. A small manor house not much different from this place. It didn't have a bakehouse, because it sat almost in the village and there was a baker there."

"So you did buy bread from the shop."

He didn't immediately reply, and she sensed puzzlement.

"It sounds like a pleasant home," she said quickly.

"It was until my parents died."

The sudden taste of sorrow seemed to pass from his words to her heart, swamping irrelevant itches. "How?"

"Drowned crossing the Severn."

"Both together?" She couldn't imagine that.

"I tried to stay on at Cornhallows, but of

course, no one pays any attention to a twelve-year-old. It was only leased, so others live there now."

Cressida breathed in, feeling the air rough against her mouth and throat at the thought of that poor child. Twelve years old. No wonder he'd asked what home was.

"But wasn't your father the duke?"

"The duke was my uncle, but I was his heir even then, and likely to inherit."

"So you went to live with him? At Lea Park?"

But that seemed wrong. She didn't know much about the Duke of St. Raven, but Lea Park didn't sound right.

She was attacked by a sudden sequence of memories. The duke seen at a distance, at theater, ball, rout, and soirée. Smiling, laughing, life burning in him like a torch so that he seemed the center of every event. He had been the center of every event — as the stag is the center of a hunt.

"Lea Park is the seat of the Duke of Arran. He was a friend of my father's and agreed to foster me. I was educated with his heir and thus learned the ducal trade."

Sympathetic talk seemed to be working as an antidote to lust, but now Cressida was trapped in a new insanity. Now she desperately needed to *know* this man, to understand him.

To ease him.

Ah, new folly, but she couldn't resist, here in the fragrant dark. "Why didn't you go to live with the old Duke of St. Raven?"

She heard a wry chuckle. "I wasn't the most popular person at St. Raven's Mount. My father and the duke had been at odds almost from birth. The duke — he was never referred to as anything else in our household — was ten years older, and had apparently been haughty all along. My father had always refused to bow down to his brother. He was a lighthearted iconoclast."

"A republican?" she asked, surprised.

"Not ardently, but any enemy of his brother was his friend. A twelve-year-old doesn't understand such things, but he left a sort of diary recording his approval of the revolution in France. He would doubtless have cheered beside the guillotine when it sliced off the duke's head."

"Oh, surely not!"

"We'll never know. But you don't want to listen to my sordid family history."

Yes, she did. She wanted to know everything about him.

"Most of England would gobble up your intimate family history, my lord Duke."

She was rewarded by a laugh that sounded genuine.

"Very well, then. My father and the duke hated each other, and much of it coalesced on the succession. The duke regarded keeping his mad brother out of his shoes as a holy duty. I confess to some sympathy, given my father's flaunting of his revolutionary views.

"Each daughter must have been an infuriating disappointment, and he didn't spare his wife that. She was not the sort to be beaten down by his disapproval, so instead she turned hard and bitter. Which I give thanks for, as it was the reason I was not sent to live at Mount St. Raven.

She vowed never to live beneath a roof with me."

"How foolish. If she had been kind, you could have become like a son to her."

He laughed again. "Dear Cressida . . ."

The disbelief shriveled her.

"Do you see her as the motherly sort? Even the Duchess of Arran saw her children for only an hour a day until they came to an age to be interesting. I gather my aunt did even less. Her daughters were raised in a separate house from birth until they had their courses. Then they moved into Mount St. Raven and were presented to her daily for examination of their progress in ladylike accomplishments. Not, I assume, life as it is lived in Matlock."

"There's no need to sneer. It is not, I assume, life as it was lived at Cornhallows, either."

"*Touché.* But my father was a mad republican."

"Your father sounds more sane than his brother."

"Possible. I have reports that my uncle frothed at the mouth when told of my birth. I suspect my father would have liked to have dangled a string of six boys in front of the duke — he could probably have driven him into the grave that way — but he married late, and had more sense than to marry a young miss. My mother was thirty-five when he married her, an independent, intelligent woman."

Cressida recognized a deep fondness there. Beneath adult cynicism and bitterness, did that shocking childhood loss still bleed?

"She could have no more children?"

"Apparently not. She suffered two miscarriages

after me. My father probably made sure she didn't conceive again, for she was more precious to him even than points in his rivalry with his brother. And he had, after all, achieved his aim. His line would continue the duchy, not his brother's. My father's early death must have been some solace to the duke and duchess, but not much."

She wished they were closer in all ways and that she could offer sympathy in a touch. "Can it really have been as hateful as that?"

"Oh, yes. I encountered them once in London. I was eighteen, and I remember the shocking awareness of hatred. The duke merely looked through me, but the duchess . . . I believe she would have put a dagger through my heart if she could have avoided hanging for it."

It was so far beyond Cressida's ability to imagine that she could only shake her head. "But you had a good home at Lea Park?"

"Thanks be to the Peckworths. They're a kindly family."

Peckworths. Cressida's memory made connections. "Lady Anne Peckworth! Daughter of the Duke of Arran."

"You know her?"

Cressida almost laughed, though she supposed she might have found herself involved in charity work with a duke's daughter. It was one way for outsiders to push their way into the circles of the great.

"I saw you with her at Drury Lane. It was the first night of *A Daring Lady*."

And you kissed her hand in a way that could

break my heart now if I were so foolish as to care.

Cressida concentrated on that image of him and Lady Anne, looking into one another's eyes, connected, intimate. If she had the slightest temptation to idiotic dreams, it should remind her that he was already committed.

She tried to pity poor Lady Anne, bound to this feckless rake. She failed. Perhaps even crumbs were worthwhile. . . .

"An amusing play, don't you think?"

His words dragged her out of her thoughts.

"Amusing? Shockingly so. My mother didn't approve, but my father laughed uproarishly."

"And you?"

Remembering that night, she was amazed that she'd paid so much attention to the stage when she could have been looking at him. "I think I missed some of the witty references."

She saw him move. Saw and heard him begin to cross the dark room toward her, though his Eastern slippers made no sound.

"Are you feeling more enlightened now?"

The air was suddenly thin. "A little."

She remembered a joke in the play about proud cocks that made altogether too much sense now. Her wickedness began to stir again, and he was almost here.

Their purpose.

Their quest.

Think of that, Cressida!

"What are we going to do?" she blurted.

There was a ticking clock in the room so the bakers could tell how long their loaves were in the oven, but in the dim light she couldn't make out the time. Most of the hour must still need to be passed, and he was too close. Only a few feet away.

She turned, trying to avoid him without seeming to, and her hand touched the iron door to the oven. She flinched, expecting a burn, but then realized that it was only warm. She pushed down the handle and opened it between them. Hot aromatic air rolled out.

"They must have baked those tarts and rolls and such earlier in the day." Succulent tarts. Long rolls . . .

Don't think about those things!

He moved around the door, came closer.

She needed a new barrier. "What of Lady Anne?"

"What of her?"

"Rumor says you will marry."

He was only inches away. "Rumor, as usual, is wrong. She's my foster sister, and she's in love with someone else."

Her insane heart leaped.

Then he asked, "Jealous?"

"No!" Cressida retreated, but she was trapped, her back against the other side of the oven.

"We are comrades in arms tonight, Cressida. Nothing more, but nothing less. And I like you in my arms."

He took the extra step, trapping her between his heat and hardness and the oven's, resting his arms on either side of her, leaning in to kiss her in the dense darkness his body created.

This was wrong. Worse, it was foolish. All that talk about his family, about his childhood pains, could have been a rake's trick, designed to weaken her. It suggested an intimacy that did not exist.

And yet, he had just warned her of the truth. Nothing more, nothing less. They had this night, and only this night. She thought that her lips were silently speaking this uncertainty against his. Whatever they were doing, it was enough to stir the turmoil inside her to fever pitch again.

"What are you doing?"

"Pleasuring you," he murmured. "Trust me. Surrender to pleasure."

"I shouldn't. We shouldn't. What are we *doing?* . . ."

"Exploring. Explore with me, nymph, and we will all the pleasures prove. . . ."

"Marlowe. A very naughty poem."

He moved back a little, but his hands still caged her. "Don't run from this, Cressida. You have the name and the heart of an explorer. Explore me, Cressida Mandeville." He brushed her mouth with his, more torment than kiss. "Come on, sweetheart. Explore. I promise you a safe return to harbor."

He slid his hands down her arms to capture her hands, to draw them to his sides and put them there. "Pull my shirt loose."

It was as well she was leaning back against the oven or she might have slid to the floor. Hands over hers, he pulled his satin shirt loose of his trousers inch by inch and then — oh, Lord! — he pressed her hands to his hot skin.

He held them there for a moment, then played his hands back up her arms and across her shoulders to feather-stroke her neck.

She couldn't help but stretch, but lean her head back against the curving oven. Couldn't help but flex her fingers against his skin, so soft and smooth over bone and muscle.

His knowing fingers explored her neck and traveled up into the edge of her loose hair, where his gentle play was like magic sparkles.

She pulled him closer. When his lips touched hers again, she pressed. Then, hesitantly, she put out her tongue to lick.

Chapter Eleven

Tris smiled and deepened the kiss. Cressida Mandeville had been driving him mad for hours, and now she was willing to play. Besides, he'd left her dissatisfied earlier. How very ungallant.

But then she pulled back. "I'm afraid."

Her retreat gave access to the buttons down the front of her jacket. As his fingers crept there, he asked, "Of what, love?"

"Of this."

He undid the first button. "Do you want to stop?"

"No . . ."

He smiled at the breathy hesitation and undid another button.

She reached up and grasped his hand. "We can't! What if I . . . conceive?"

"You won't. I promise." Despite her attempt to control him, he had another button loose.

She grasped the edges to keep her jacket closed. "Any rake would say that. Let me go!"

He stilled, but did not retreat. "You trust me, Cressida."

"No, I don't!"

"Then why are you here? Why are you so sure I won't toss you to Crofton? Or obtain your jewels only to steal them?"

"You're rich. They would mean nothing to you."

He could feel her agitated breathing. To give her time, he surrendered the top of her jacket and slid his hand down and under the bottom edge. There he used his nails to tease the skin of her side. When she inhaled and shifted her hips against him, he knew it would only take patience. He could be very patient in pursuit of what he wanted.

"I don't know how much the jewels are worth, but I could do with more money."

"A duke?"

"Would you believe me if I explained?" He lowered his head and nuzzled her neck.

"Yes."

"Because you trust me," he stated, then licked around her ear, heard her catch her breath.

Waited.

"I suppose I do."

He loved the grumpy reluctance of it when every movement of her body showed how much she wanted what he was doing, and more.

"So, trust me in this, sweetheart. Come explore with me. There are many things we can do without risking a child. Trust me. . . ."

He eased aside her clutching hands, found one sweet, full breast, and tickled her nipple with his thumb.

A gasp escaped her, and she went up on her toes. He couldn't stop a soft laugh of triumph. "See?"

"Yes . . ."

He slid his hands up to her shoulders, pushing the jacket away —

She put both hands to his chest and shoved.

He stepped back, shocked, his eyes adjusted enough to see how she had her jacket clutched shut again, how she was looking at him, eyes wide.

Frightened.

Frightened.

Dear God.

He raised his hands. "It's all right. It's all right. I won't force you." His heart pounded as if his life depended on her response.

She looked down and fumbled at the gilt buttons. He wanted to help but kept his distance. "Talk to me, love. I thought you were enjoying that."

Her hands stilled. "I was," she whispered.

Despite everything, he melted at her gallant honesty.

She made short work of the remaining three buttons and then looked at him. "But it would be wrong. You have to know it would be wrong."

"I told you I wouldn't get you with child."

"That's nothing to do with it! At least it is . . ." She stared at him. "I'm not sure we speak the same language."

The chill he felt was quite steadying. She was right. Miss Mandeville of Matlock was absolutely right. Insane to imagine more than this quixotic quest.

"We have indeed been speaking in foreign tongues. I thought I heard you say that you trusted me."

"I do, I do! But it's *wrong*. Perhaps not in your world, in this world. But in mine. In mine, people — decent people — don't do things like this."

"You'd be surprised."

He should be finding this laughable. Why was his heart pounding? Why did the gulf between them cause such pain?

"I think we have understanding now," he said, with all the cool he could summon. "You are denying your body's very natural desires, Miss Mandeville, because Matlock propriety has triumphed."

"As it should!"

"Nonsense. Propriety is a straitjacket, but if you feel comfortable *locked* up in it, so be it."

He meant the words to be cool, but hot anger flickered along the edge of his words like the flames along the blade of a dagger. Wisdom sword. God, he needed wisdom here. He needed to show her that this didn't matter.

He looked away, looked at the clock. "It's fifteen minutes to midnight. Time to retrieve your other treasure."

He looked around and saw the pale puddle of her discarded veils. Why had she shed them if not to invite him? He gathered them up and offered them to her.

Cressida snatched them. She wanted, she needed, to be angry at him — for sneering at her, for trying to make virtue seem like folly. She needed to gather her wits, but her dissatisfied body tangled her, suggesting that impossible things were still possible. . . .

She was right. She knew it. She had to believe it.

But he was angry, and something more than angry. She wanted to go to him, surrender to him, as much for him as for herself.

It had to be another rake's trick. It wasn't her fault if she didn't belong in his world, wasn't willing to play his lewd games!

She had to put on the things in her trembling hands. She wasn't sure she could. She must. She couldn't, mustn't, ask his help.

As if he sensed something, he took another step away, freeing her to move into the center of the room without going near him. She walked to the big table and dropped the things in her hand there.

What order? Head veil. No, face veil first. Or mask? No, that held the head veil on. With shaking hands, she tried to tie the strings of the face veil at the back of her head.

"Let me help." It sounded strangely like a plea.

Perhaps that was why she said, "Very well."

His slippers were silent again, but she felt his approach. She was prepared and did not shiver when his hands touched hers as he took the strings, when his fingers stirred her hair, brushed it as he tied the knot.

The shiver was there, however, deep inside.

Painfully, she was aware of his care, aware that he stood not an inch nearer than he had to, when once he would have pressed close. When once he would have teased. Would have kissed her neck . . .

Ah, Cressida Mandeville of Matlock, you are a

fool. But which part of this is the folly?

With her back to him, she picked up the blue veil, shook it, and draped it over her head, then let him tie the mask to hold it in place. She was Roxelana again, queen of the harem, wife to Suleiman. . . .

He stepped away from her. She felt the space where once he had been. Now that she had been clear, he would not intrude again. It *had* been a case of different languages.

She turned to him. "I'm sorry."

"It is I who should be sorry for upsetting you."

"You didn't upset me —" But she stopped that, for it was a lie, though perhaps they weren't talking about the same upset.

She longed, against reason, for some scrap of the closeness they'd had before. She reached for an explanation. "I was not myself. I'm sure it seemed to you that I —" She bit her lip. "I think it was the spirits in that drink."

"Crofton's brew? But you hardly took a sip."

She was glad the dimness concealed her red face. Intoxicated. She had been intoxicated! "I drank a cupful. One of the servants replaced my beaker with another."

"Good Lord." But then he laughed, even if it did sound a bit wild. "Poor Cressida! That, my dear, was a potent aphrodisiac. It's what caused all that rutting in the corridors. Even at the wildest parties, people usually seek a bit more comfort than that."

"Aphro—"

"*Aphrodisiakos,*" he said, and it had to be Greek. "From Aphrodite, Goddess of Love, or to be more precise, of sexual pleasure. Cressida, forgive me. I did not know —"

"It was my fault. How could you?"

Aphrodisiac. That burning lust came only from a drink? She remembered that time in the drawing room and the raw desperation she'd felt then. If he'd not stopped, would she have had the strength to?

"Thank you," she said again.

"There is nothing here to thank me for," he said flatly. "I should never have brought you, but having done so, I should have guarded you better. And I never should have even attempted what I did. I should have known it was not truly what a woman like you would want."

A woman like you.

A lady of Matlock.

Locked in Matlock.

And this lady of Matlock *did* want, and she wasn't sure it was all aphrodisiac anymore. Temptation flickered. She stamped on it.

"It is almost midnight," she said in the most prosaic voice she could muster.

"Yes. We should go. As soon as someone wins that statue, we can get the jewels and this will all be over."

Over.

"How strange that after all this, it will be so simple in the end."

He laughed. "I'll believe that after the event."

"It will work, Your Grace."

"St. Raven."

Folly, but she surrendered. "St. Raven."

"Tris." It whispered on the air toward her like

an invitation to sin.

She tightened her lips and would not give in. Did she seem foolish to be afraid of a name?

"It might slip out in public," she offered as excuse. But that was foolish, too. "Not that I think we're likely to meet in public."

"I do attend the occasional ball and rout."

She could have pointed out that during weeks of the London season and a surfeit of balls and routs, Miss Cressida Mandeville had not once been introduced to the Duke of St. Raven. Instead, she said, "But I will be returning to Matlock."

"I assume even Matlock is not barred to outsiders."

"You have need of the restorative waters?"

"After this, almost certainly."

It was a joke, and it broke her heart. If only they could be friends. "It's time to go, St. Raven," she reminded him, "if we're to know who wins my statue."

"Yes." Still he didn't move. Then he said, "Let me be your agent in this, Cressida. Let me deal with it while you stay here."

Until relief unsteadied her, she hadn't realized how desperately she didn't want to return to the disgusting house.

"You should be safe. Everyone not mightily engaged elsewhere will be watching the contest."

"But what if there's a chance to grab the statue for only a moment?"

"Tell me how to open it." He glanced at the ticking clock. "Quickly."

She gathered her wits. "It's not easy, but the

statues are carved on all surfaces except the base. On the man's back, you have to slip something thin — a strong fingernail or a fine blade — at the base of his belt, right at the middle. At the same time, you pull down at his heels. When you get it right, you'll feel a slight movement, but only slight. Then you slide the back of his legs to the left. That opens the door to the cavity."

"It sounds as if it won't open by mistake. How long a fingernail?"

She remembered fingernails against her skin and managed not to shiver. "Longer than yours, I think. Your blade?"

"Is probably too thick. What of the blade in the study?"

"Yes, one of the points will work. I used that when my father showed me."

"Let's hope it's not already been filched. Is there anything else I need to know?"

"Not as long as you can detect the right one."

"The hat and the belt. I remember."

There seemed to be a smile in that, but it was still as if he was delaying. She stepped forward and pushed him. "Go!"

The touch shocked her. He seemed to be staring at her. . . .

He grasped her shoulders and kissed her — short, hard, and hot. And then he was gone.

Cressida hugged herself. Without him, the gloomy room no longer seemed warm and comforting, and what had happened here had spoiled something sweet. Even good. How could anything about this place be good?

It must be the potion still disordering her

mind, making her want what she would never normally want. She focused on the matter in hand. She had to trust him with the business in the house, but in the meantime she had to be safe here.

What if someone came — another couple looking for a private spot? She was tempted to go out, to hurry after her experienced guide, but she never wanted to step inside Stokeley Manor again.

Instead, she opened a drawer in the sideboard and felt around until she found a large wooden rolling pin. Thus armed, she sat where she could see the clock and prepared to wait.

Chapter Twelve

Tris was astonished by his reluctance to return to the house. It was not the sort of event he enjoyed, but returning to it felt like jumping into a sewer. The noise had lessened, but it was probably stupor rather than calm.

A smell made him halt. Vomit. He detoured around it.

This disgusting affair was typical of Crofton. Excess as a substitute for excellence. But could he really say all his own parties had ended up more decorously?

Yes, but sometimes not by much. He didn't serve the sort of brew Crofton had been ladling out, however. That had been a concoction designed to drive people to extremes as quickly as possible — a sure sign of a host uncertain of his success.

Tris wished Crofton to the devil he was impersonating, and regretted bringing Cressida here. He could have persuaded her to stay behind at Nun's Chase, but it had seemed an amusing novelty at the time. He'd never given a thought to protecting her innocence of mind. He'd never thought that important. In fact, if asked, he'd have said that innocence was generally ignorance and dangerous.

It would seem he had overlooked questions of purity.

No, he thought, pausing by the door back into the house, that wasn't the right word, either. It sounded so damn preachy.

Loveliness, perhaps. The loveliness of a flower at its peak, or a fresh summer morning, or a piece of fine, white linen. Something that should be treasured, not soiled.

He laughed at himself. Nature of itself faded the flower and wore out the morning, and linen was designed to be dirtied and then washed. It was all part of a natural order — but it shouldn't be hastened by an event like this.

An event like this should never exist.

That was a strange thought, since it was probably his own successful events at Nun's Chase that had put the idea into Crofton's head. He shook away his wandering thoughts and went into the house.

Stink assailed him, and he almost tripped over the legs of a snoring gladiator. The gladiator was on top of an equally oblivious, half-naked, billowy fat woman. Tris heaved the man off her a bit to make sure she didn't suffocate. He couldn't see anything to cover her with. She was clearly a whore, so he didn't suppose she'd care.

He made his way past other guests to the study. Unfortunately they weren't all unconscious and, damnation, but some of the whores looked too young. It was enough to turn a man off rutting for life.

He opened the door to the study with relief — to find Jolly Roger copulating with the whore who'd wanted a prick earlier. She sprawled on the desk, knees up, looking either bored or exhausted. Neither seemed to notice when he retrieved the wisdom sword. It was an act of charity, since the blade looked likely to poke the girl's buttocks at any moment.

"Come on," she whined. "Get on with it or give over!"

Tris glanced and rolled his eyes. Jolly Roger wasn't in a state to get on with it, and why he thought pounding would help Tris couldn't imagine. None of his business, however. He was backing away when the girl kicked Tiverton away. "Get off me, you wilted pansy!"

"Shut your mouth!"

Tris acted on instinct. He caught Tiverton's raised arm, swung it behind the pirate, and dragged him back. The girl scrambled to her feet. She did look young, but an ominous sore blossomed by her mouth. Tiverton wouldn't have touched her when in his senses.

Tiverton wouldn't hit a woman when in his senses.

Damn Crofton.

"Let her go," Tris said as soothingly as he could.

"I'll bloody murder her!" Tiverton howled, breaking Tris's hold. "I'm no bloody pansy!"

He turned on Tris, swinging, but staggering with drink. No hope of talking sense to him. Tris knocked him out, then winced, rubbing knuckles still sore from his earlier fight.

Had that only been this morning? Highway robbery, forcing himself on a woman, drunken brawls. A fine career for the Duke of St. Raven . . .

A gong jerked him from his thoughts. Then he heard the clock chiming. Midnight.

Tiverton was snoring, and the whore had slid away. Tris tucked the wisdom sword into his belt and headed for the drawing room. Perhaps he would take the sword when he left. He needed wisdom, and Crofton was beyond hope.

If he hadn't known where the event was taking place, the noise would have drawn him. Screeching, laughing, howling — Crofton's guests sounded like wild animals in a pit.

And not, after all, in the drawing room. The event had moved into the hall so that people could use the dogleg stairs and the landing above as a gallery. More candles had been brought to cut the fiery red gloom, and Tris wondered if Stokeley Manor would become a true inferno before this night was through.

Maybe it would need fire to cleanse it. The floor was sticky beneath his feet with spilled drink and other things.

Crofton the red devil was presiding from the lower stairs, eyes glittering as he egged his guests on. At least the drinking seemed to have stopped, which explained why so many were still conscious. Probably more a case of the supply running out than of Crofton having any sense of judgment or good management.

The statuettes were there, however, on a small table at the base of the stairs.

Tris blocked the cacophony and ignored the cavorting already going on in the central space, concentrating on that table. This might be a lot easier than he'd hoped.

The statues were no longer in a neat line. He might be able to slip one off there long enough to empty it with no one the wiser. He began to move that way, easing through the drunken crowd, exchanging a word here and there when he had to, but making as little contact as possible.

Then a body pressed against him. He looked down into the heavily kohled eyes of Violet Vane, Queen of the Night, as usual stinking of sickening *poudre de violettes.*

She walked her fingers up his chest. "Where's your little bit of Turkish delight, St. Raven? Need something stronger now?"

He caught her hand. "She wore me out. For now."

She chuckled. "Not you. I've heard stories about you, my lord duke. You need a real woman. One who's up to your strength . . ."

The sickly perfume was in danger of turning his stomach. And why the hell was he acting the gentleman with a woman like this?

"Not tonight," he said, turning her and pushing her into the arms of a Roman senator. He ignored her screamed insults and moved on toward the table, but now, dammit, all eyes were on him.

"Ah, St. Raven," said Crofton. "Come to participate after all?"

"Merely to observe," Tris replied, leaning against the stairs, armed crossed, within reaching distance of the table, praying all attention would return to the three couples attempting a horizontal pose.

Cheers indicated that someone had at least connected. Tris glanced around. Attention seemed to be off him. Crofton was avidly watching the competition. Time to make his move.

He studied the statues on the table. Right leg raised. Hat and belt . . .

It wasn't there!

Heart racing, he looked again.

It wasn't there.

He counted.

Eight.

Hell and perdition. Had the contest started early? If so, by what foul luck had that statue gone first, and who had won it?

Ignoring a sudden burst of applause, he looked around the hall and stairs, seeking a person holding the trophy.

He didn't see it.

But his eye caught a man in a fool's costume leaning against the wall near the front door. Dan Gilchrist. A decent enough man and a friend. He wondered why he was here, but thanked heavens for it. Suppressing something close to panic, Tris worked his way around to him.

"A wild affair," he said when he arrived.

Dan grimaced. "Too wild by half." He was an amiable, plump young man who was also a clever and hardworking official in the Home Office. Tonight he'd chosen a fool's costume, but he seemed sober, and if anything, bored.

"Why are you still here, then?" Tris asked, not wanting to go straight to the matter in hand.

"Came with Tiverton and some others. I don't suppose they'll want to leave until this is over."

Tris thought of Tiverton — unconscious in the study still? — and almost offered Dan a ride away from here. Then he remembered that he'd have Cressida with him. The fewer people who had a long look at her, the better.

Oh, Lord — Cressida. How was he going to tell her he'd let the statue get away? It was because he'd been late, and that was because he'd lost control and tried to seduce her, because he'd misread her, because he'd not watched her closely enough, so she'd drunk that damn potion.

He'd never felt such a failure in his life.

He wasn't a complete failure yet. He could still execute their plan. "Has the contest been going on for long?"

"Started at the witching hour." Gilchrist smiled and jingled his belled stick. "I admit, I'm looking forward to seeing someone try that headstand one."

Tris looked across at the table again, but even from here he could count. There were still eight.

"Seems to me one of the statues is missing. I could have sworn there were nine."

"Miranda Coop talked Crofton out of one. Or did something for it." Gilchrist jangled his bells again.

Tris struggled not to show any reaction. "One does wonder what. He seemed set on his contest."

"It was one of the more ordinary ones. I'm sure La Coop could come up with something interesting enough to change any man's mind."

"So am I." Tris indulged in some mental curses. Miranda wouldn't be as easy as some to deal with, but he could do it.

If worst came to worst, he could come up with something interesting enough to persuade her. She'd been trying to get her claws into him for months. The idea of pandering to any woman turned his stomach, but this was his mess to correct.

"Where is she now? I'd like to find out what she came up with."

"Then you'll have to pursue her to London. She left."

Tris looked at the ridiculous contestants as blankly as possible. "Wise woman. I think I'll do the same."

He moved away before Gilchrist thought to ask for a ride, and headed back to the bakehouse. He'd predicted that nothing about this would be simple, and it seemed he'd been damnably right. What mad freak of fate had made La Coop take a fancy to that statue? And what was he going to tell Cressida?

A plan. He had to present her with a new plan. He paused by the stables to come up with one — and thank God, he did. It should work, too, and if it pushed him to doing things he'd rather not, that was suitable penance for a string of stupidities.

He turned to the stables and pushed open a door, finding himself in a tack room strewn with drunk or sleeping servants. However, one young lad was rolling dice on the floor and looking more-or-less sober. He jumped to his feet. "Yes, sir?"

A smart one. He'd figured out that some guests might want their rigs and would be generous to anyone able to help them.

"Ride down to the village and tell the Duke of St. Raven's men to bring the coach to the end of the drive. And tell my man to give you a crown."

The boy's eyes widened. "Yes, Your Grace!" Then he was off into the stables to find a horse.

Pleasant to still impress someone. Tris headed for the bakehouse. He hesitated outside the door, trying to come up with happier news, but of course there was nothing to tell her but the truth.

"It's me," he said as he opened the door. That proved to be wise, since his houri had a large rolling pin in her hands and looked ready to use it.

"You have it already!" she exclaimed in delight.

"No. It had already gone." He closed the door behind himself and took the rolling pin from her hands, though she seemed more likely to drop it than hit him with it. "I'm sorry. It seems Miranda Coop struck a private bargain with Crofton before the contest began. We couldn't have prevented it if we'd been there."

It was true, but it sounded like an excuse.

"Then we have to get it off her. Where is she?"

He broke the news. "On her way back to London."

He felt her dismay, even if he couldn't see it. "Le Corbeau?" she suggested faintly.

"I would if I could, but she's ahead of us. By the time I made it to Nun's Chase and into the costume, she'd be home. But all is not lost. We know where it is. Unless La Coop knows the secret, the jewels are in no danger. We can get it back."

"Are you sure?"

Such a piteous plea. She'd come so far, done so much, gallant Miss Mandeville of Matlock, but now her voice trembled.

"I'm sure." By Hades, he'd make it sure. "At least now we can leave here. I've ordered the carriage to meet us at the gates. Come on."

She seemed stunned, so he put his arm around her to lead her out into the night, only realizing a moment too late that she might reject his touch. She didn't, but perhaps only because of her shock and disappointment.

Why the devil couldn't he wave a magic wand and make everything right for her? What use being a duke if he couldn't straighten out the lives of his . . . friends?

In fact he could and would. If they didn't get the jewels, he'd find a way to give her money, a way that she and her parents could accept. He thought of somebody he knew who'd won a lottery. Was it possible to fix them?

"I'm sorry for bringing you here," he said.

Every step away from the house seemed a blessing.

"No, I thank you. It might have worked, and it has certainly been an education."

"There are many lessons best unlearned."

Unwise words. It was doubtless thought of lessons yet unlearned that made her pull away from his side. He let her go, but felt absurdly relieved when she took his crooked arm.

Like a lady and gentleman strolling, they

moved onto the short drive that led toward the open gates. Clouds veiled the full moon, but it still gave light enough for walking. As the sounds faded and the world became more peaceful, this could almost be an ordinary occasion.

Except for their clothing. The silk of his shirt seemed inadequate protection from her bare arm. . . .

"I'm not sure that's true."

He had to scramble for the subject. Ah yes. Learning.

"Knowledge is always useful," she carried on, "even if only in telling us what to avoid."

Men like him, if she had any sense.

"And what to change," she added. "I've been thinking —"

He suppressed a groan.

"— I don't believe those whores were older women acting the part of girls."

He could say nothing but, "Perhaps not."

"And they weren't only doing those poses. In the corridor . . ."

"Yes. But no one was forcing them to it."

"Except poverty."

"Perhaps." Thank heavens they'd gone nowhere near the catamites. "Cressida, there's nothing to be done. The world's a brutal place, and people survive as best they can. Which is why I'm trying so hard to restore your fortunes."

"I am not in such danger!" The way she went silent showed she remembered that she had been. And perhaps that he had saved at least one lamb from the butcher.

"I still have the wisdom sword," he said. "Do you want it?"

"Not particularly."

He'd meant it only as distraction, but she'd clearly taken it as a rebuke. As well. The two of them were acid and milk and could only create a curdled brew.

"Then perhaps I can pay your father the value of it. I would like to keep it, but I don't care to be a thief." And it would be a small amount in their coffers.

"Take it as a gift, Your Grace. A reward for noble service."

Your Grace.

It stung, but he bit back a protest. They were almost at the road, the road back to reality, where milk and acid could flow in safely separate channels.

He didn't care about right and wrong, Cressida acknowledged.

As well, all in all, that they were drifting apart. The move from in his arms to arm-in-arm had felt like a tearing separation, and now every scrap of space between their bodies was chill and aching, but it was right.

She still longed for wicked things, but every step away from Stokeley Manor took them toward her own decent world, and she wanted that even more. She had visited, she had experienced, and now she wanted to be Miss Mandeville of Matlock once more, even if it meant never seeing the Duke of St. Raven again.

She turned her mind to Miranda Coop, who

had her statue. He'd said they would get it back.

They?

Was the connection perhaps not quite over yet? A flutter of excitement betrayed all reason and common sense.

"How will we get the statue?" she asked as they passed through the gates and stopped by the empty, silent road. "I don't think I can pay a morning visit to Miss Coop."

"Hardly, but I can. It might be as simple as that."

Not *they* after all. She looked down the silvery road, wishing the coach speed. She couldn't endure much more of this.

Then she realized that it wouldn't be over when the coach arrived. They had a two-hour drive. Thank heavens Mr. Lyne would be in the coach. But should she, could she, return to St. Raven's house?

A true shiver shook her, one of weariness and cold. "Can you return me to London?"

"In those clothes?"

She rubbed her bare arms. "I suppose not."

"Your luggage is at Nun's Chase, Cressida, and there's no point in collecting it and then taking you home in the small hours of the morning. You'll be able to get a good night's sleep, dress properly, then return to London in decent form."

He was right, of course, but to her desperate, dismal mind, Nun's Chase felt almost as intolerable as Stokeley Manor.

"Trust me."

When she looked, he was watching the road, face cool in the pale light of the moon, but it mattered to him. She knew it. He was careless in many ways, but he had been careful with her.

"Of course," she said softly. "I do trust you."

She saw tension leave him and was tearfully glad she could give him that, at least. She was also glad the tears didn't fall, for he turned to her and held out his arms.

"You look cold. Won't you share my heat?"

For his sake as much as her own, she went into his arms and snuggled to his side. It was warmer. It was better as well in other, more dangerous ways.

"I never asked what story you told in order to leave with Crofton, or how you intended to return. I hope we can still use that plan."

She rested her cheek against his silk jacket. "I'm visiting a married friend who lives near Lincoln. I was taken to Cecilia's house by a friend who happened to be traveling there from London."

"But in fact you traveled with Crofton. Did no one question this?"

"My mother is too distracted by my father's state to notice or question much, and we've let most of the servants go. And Cecilia really does exist."

"Does your friend know of this pretense?"

She looked up. "Of course not. She would hardly condone something like this."

Cressida immediately wished that unsaid. It was true, but it was a sweeping denunciation of his tastes and lifestyle.

But then, in her saner moments, she did condemn his tastes and lifestyle.

The jangle of iron and thump of hoofbeats brought relief. The coach was coming, and she wanted this over, the event, the intimacy, everything. She pulled free of him again. From here they would have a chaperon, and in Nun's Chase she'd lock her door and go straight to bed.

The coach drew to a halt, and Mr. Lyne stepped down to hand her in. Cressida entered the coach and sat. St. Raven spoke to his friend, then ducked to take the place beside her. The door closed with a firm click.

Her stomach dropped. "Is he not traveling with us?"

"He's staying to check that the story about La Coop was true."

Chapter Thirteen

The coach jerked into movement, and for a moment Cressida actually thought of throwing herself out of it. Alone with him? Alone in this confined space for two hours? After all that had happened? At least there were two candles in here. It was more light than they'd had for most of the evening, and light surely brought sanity.

He stretched out his long legs, long legs covered by satin that draped down to mold to his thighs. Thighs she could reach across a very little distance to stroke . . .

The speeding coach swung around a bend, and she clutched at the strap.

"My informant was probably honest and correct," he said, "but I realized that I should have checked. He might have been wrong on any number of details. Cary will find out and follow on."

"He's not costumed."

"By this time, I doubt anyone will care."

Swaying with the movement, Cressida became aware all over again of their clothing. During the evening she'd grown accustomed to her costume, but now she felt as if she were in her underwear. As if they were both in their underwear.

In the underwear neither of them, apparently, was wearing.

Satin over thighs. Satin over a mound that must be . . .

Cressida!

It was like Adam and Eve suddenly becoming aware of their nakedness. What apple had she bitten into, back there in hell? . . .

He opened a flap in the wall of the coach and took out a silver flask and two small silver cups. "Brandy. Would you like some?"

She suppressed a shudder. "No, thank you, Your Grace." She used the formal address as protection. That potion must still be fermenting in her blood! With yet more spirits, what might she be weakened into doing?

He put it away untouched. "It would warm you. We should have brought blankets."

Blankets. Bed . . .

"I'm not cold, Your Grace." They seemed to have reached a more level piece of road, so she let go of the supportive strap. "What are we going to do, Your Grace, if Mistress Coop will not give you the statue?"

He turned sharply toward her. "If you call me 'Your Grace' again, I will not be responsible for my actions."

The leashed violence stopped her breath and shuddered her flesh. She stared at him, speechless.

"At least," he said tightly, "call me St. Raven. But it would be a kindness if you would call me Tris."

"Tris," she whispered, feeling as if she pacified

a wild animal. Yet she also saw that it mattered to him, that she had hurt him by addressing him so formally. Surely she could give in on such a little matter without disaster?

"Tris," she said clearly, and to remove a barrier she took off her veils and mask.

It was as if the air changed and she could breathe properly again. He even smiled a little, that slight, teasing smile that had become so dear to her.

"Tristan Hugh Tregallows at your service. You are not to worry about the jewels. They are now my affair, and I will not fail. My pride and honor are at stake."

Too late, she knew a twitch of her brow had expressed some doubt about his honor.

"Do I detect an edge? 'Tis not important what honor is, Cressida, only that once settled it is adhered to."

"A very aristocratic view. I assure you, honor is much more clearly defined in Matlock."

She winced inside, but what point in denying what she was? She was a provincial nobody from Matlock with beliefs about right and wrong that he disdained.

"You are referring to decency," he said, "which is another matter entirely."

"There is nothing wrong with decency."

"Except that it gets in the way of pleasure. Like underwear . . ."

She stared at him. "Don't."

A sudden bounce of the carriage threw her toward him. He caught her, held her, but then returned her to her side of the seat. She gripped the strap again, vowing to hold on to it all the way to Nun's Chase.

"Pray tell me what form of honor had you out holding up honest travelers on the King's Highway?"

"Ah yes." He stretched his long legs at an angle to find the most space. Cressida inched her slippered feet over so they wouldn't touch.

"It's a maudlin tale, but probably better than you assume. I think I told you that I was Le Corbeau only for the night."

"Yes."

"When I returned to England in the spring I found there was a notorious highwayman who appeared to be creating a link to me. The name Le Corbeau is generally translated as 'the Crow,' but in French it can also mean 'the Raven.' In addition, he has only worked the roads in a radius around my house at Nun's Chase. Even the look he assumed had a point, though not one most people would recognize. At Mount St. Raven, we have a portrait of my great-great-many-greats grandfather who was a Cavalier painted in exactly that costume."

"My goodness. How could he have known that?"

"One of the interesting questions I wish to ask him. I've been investigating the matter for most of the summer and eventually discovered his base — a broken-down cottage within half a mile of Nun's Chase, damn his impertinent eyes."

He looked at her. "Are we friends, or should I apologize for that?"

She knew what she should say, but she could

surely be a little weak here. It was only for a few more hours. "Friends," she said. "I can imagine your outrage. So, did you trap him there? Were you responsible for his capture?"

"No, he slipped up and was seized. But I had already discovered something in his possessions that put a different slant on the situation."

"Well? Don't tantalize!"

He grinned. "But it's a tale worthy of a play, and I fancy myself as a raconteur. And we do have hours to pass."

She inhaled. Was he as aware of the tormenting time ahead of them as she was? Was the rocking of the coach as bothersome to him, the thought of being thrown against one another again as tempting?

"In a chest in the cottage I found a number of letters and objects. I did not immediately read the letters, of course, but the objects showed that there was a connection to my family. One in particular being the missing family betrothal ring."

"Shouldn't that have belonged to your aunt?"

"Yes, but apparently she refused to wear it. It is a heavy piece over two hundred years old, containing a large star sapphire. Quite magnificent, but old-fashioned, even barbaric."

"And the highwayman had it. Stolen? No," she answered herself. "Who would be wearing it on the road? Did your uncle not miss it?"

"He must have done. He was almost miserly in his attention to his possessions. They were inventoried every year, and a special inventory was done on my aunt's death. Before 1790, the ring is listed as being in the locked treasure room at the Mount. After that it is listed as being in the duke's possession — which of course meant that no one need actually see it."

"So in 1790 he gave it to someone?" she asked, enthralled by the mystery. "And now this highwayman has it. Who is he?"

"Jean-Marie Bourreau, it would seem. Given the ring, I felt I had to read the letters. They were in French, but I am fluent in French. They revealed that my uncle kept a mistress in Paris — no surprise in that — and had a son there, Jean-Marie, in 1791. I can imagine how infuriating that must have been. A son at last, and yet no chance of him inheriting the dukedom."

The coach jolted again. She wasn't thrown about, but one of the candles died. St. Raven — Tris — unhooked the scissors, trimmed the wick, then relit it from the other. Her maudlin mind couldn't help noting and appreciating the elegant deftness of his long-fingered hands.

She had never known that she was such a susceptible woman.

He settled back. "It must have seemed another malign twist of fate. His wife was fertile and produced six healthy children, but every one of them was a girl. And then — to paraphrase him — the damned woman lived on until he was too feeble to try again."

"He sounds like a disgusting man."

"Just a duke," he said dryly.

Instinctively, she reached out to touch his hand. By the time she realized it was unwise, it was too late.

He turned his hand and took hers. She couldn't snatch it back, and she didn't want to. She was offering comfort, but she was also drawing strength from him, from his strong hand. Then he winced.

She relaxed her hold. "Am I hurting you?"

"Not as long as you don't squeeze."

She raised his hand a little. "Have you been fighting? Again?"

"I'm not in the habit of it. At least, except for sparring practice."

"Who did you fight at Stokeley? Crofton?"

"Alas, no. It was Jolly Roger. And don't ask for details."

She was tempted, but she had learned something over the night. It could make her weep, however, how he constantly slid into rough, unsuitable behavior.

"As long as you weren't fighting over a woman . . ." Then she winced at saying anything so intolerably coquettish.

That smile curled his lips and flickered in his eyes. "Jealous?"

"No!"

His brow rose.

"All right, a little. You were my partner for the night."

"And still am —" He raised her hand and kissed it. "— Roxelana."

She licked her lips, realizing that she'd let go of the fortifying strap. How had she ever thought desire dead, danger past? At a touch, at a look, she longed to lean to him, to touch, to taste, to kiss. The pounding hooves felt like the pounding of her blood.

She pulled her hand free. "So you found the ring and the letters," she prompted.

His brow quirked again, but he responded. "There was only one dated after the birth, and in it he denied any responsibility for the child. It would appear that some money was sent along with it, but it was clearly a parting gift. The rest of the letters in the chest were rough drafts of the desperate ones Jeanine Bourreau wrote to him, begging for assistance, citing his promises. She seems to have thought he would take her to England and set her up in style there. He may have received them and ignored them, or he may not have received them at all. Soon after Jean-Marie's birth, the revolution ripped the country into chaos."

"Do you know what became of her?"

"No, but we have to assume that she survived by selling her body. She would know no other means of supporting herself and her sons."

"So Jean-Marie is here and seeking, what? Money? Revenge?"

"I don't know. He's never contacted me except through his taunting behavior. I intend to find out, but first I have to get him out of jail. I don't want my family's sordid dealings in every broadsheet and on every tongue. That meant that Le Corbeau had to ride again."

"And you held up Crofton. . . . Oh dear. I don't suppose he reported it to the magistrates."

"Nor do I. I tried again. That was why I had to leave you tied up so long. I apologize for it."

It seemed so long ago, that time lying bound and blindfolded, not knowing her fate.

"I did manage to intercept an irascible old lawyer hurrying to a deathbed — as he made very clear — and relieve him of his gold watch and a few guineas. I hope that does the trick, because I'm not trying again."

"Yet you offered to do so for me."

Did he look a little uncomfortable, the sophisticated duke? "Unfinished business."

Cressida smiled at him, a smile of true fondness. There was much about the Duke of St. Raven that she had to deplore, but at heart he was a generous man who took his responsibilities seriously. Even, it would seem, responsibility for a bastard, foreign cousin.

"What are you going to do about him?" she asked, head resting in her corner of the coach, rocked by the motion to a state almost of peace.

"He should be out of jail soon, and I know where Jean-Marie Bourreau lives and what he does in his ordinary life. He has to return to that to allay suspicions, so he will be easily caged and forced to reveal his true purpose."

"That sounds positively tyrannical."

"Am I not a duke?"

"But in this civilized age?"

"This age is not so civilized as you assume, Miss Mandeville of Matlock. I'd have thought you'd just seen evidence of that."

"Don't sneer at me."

"Did I? I do beg your pardon. But the world isn't tame, Cressida. It comes beaked and clawed. Step carefully. As for tyranny, I do have the power and influence to make life very unpleasant for a Frenchman if I wish.

"Le Corbeau must cease," he said, as if his word were law. "The sort of scandal that would arise from his capture cannot be permitted. However, my uncle appears to have treated him and his mother abominably. If he wants some sort of restitution, I'll do my best to provide it."

"What if he wishes to continue as the highwayman?"

"It can only have been whimsy."

"A family trait?"

His eyes flashed to hers. "Don't sneer at *me,* Miss Mandeville. I can be serious and even dignified on occasion."

She flinched at his anger, but then realized it was something closer to hurt. She was throwing darts at him as if he wore armor, and perhaps he didn't. . . .

"Being a duke is not a round of pleasure, you know. I've spent most of this summer on business, not on Bourreau's affairs. Or on orgies, for that matter. I spent the past six years officially under my uncle's tutelage, but we disliked each other so thoroughly that once I came of age we avoided each other. I have much to learn. It didn't help that, in a fit of funk, I fled abroad as soon as I inherited."

"Why funk?" she asked, her resistance melting at this more vulnerable side of him.

"The duke died of a heart attack very suddenly. He wasn't well, but there'd been no sign he would die soon. I wasn't . . . prepared. I think in a way I'd been pretending that it would never happen."

"You didn't want to be duke?"

Flickering candlelight could play tricks, but he seemed honestly surprised by her question. "Where's the appeal, except to the sort of person who loves to see others grovel? The responsibilities are huge, and not just in terms of property."

"Wealth? Luxury? The ability to do as you will?"

"I am not finding that I can do as I will."

The tone, the look, told her he spoke of her. Of them.

"As for wealth and luxury," he carried on, "it's possible to have those without high rank. Wealthy Tris Tregallows would have an easier life, believe me. What use are twelve houses in six countries, vast acres, hundreds of servants, and thousands of tenants? All dependent on me."

"Twelve houses?" she repeated. "Six countries?"

"England, Scotland, Wales, Ireland, France — I may have repossession of it — and Portugal. A quinta, and I know nothing about producing port."

"You could do a great deal of good."

"With what time?"

With the time you waste on debauchery. But she said, "You could support a great many charities."

"Which is still work."

She couldn't resist a tease. "I see. It's the hard work that bothers you."

"Damnation, woman, it is not!" It was all right. He was laughing as much as he was angry. "A duke is a duke, Cressida. People don't just want my money, they want my patronage. They want my presence at events. My presence generates money as if I were a two-headed pig."

She couldn't stop a spurt of laughter, but she could imagine his trials, and she ached for him.

"People pay attention to my most casual words. They seek to please, especially the young ladies. There are some who would rip off their clothes and lie on the floor at my feet if they thought it would win them a coronet. And the men imitate me. Look at Crofton!"

"I see," she said, and she did. Crofton had imitated St. Raven's popular bacchanalia and created that disgusting debauch, and he felt it was his fault.

And he'd sworn at her without even noticing. She saw it as a strange accolade. For this little while, they were friends.

He sighed. "If I took to wearing a fool's cap, half the men in London would be sporting one the next day."

"I'd think that would be a strong temptation."

He looked at her, startled, and then laughed. "You're a minx at heart, aren't you, Cressida Mandeville? Did I really just swear at you?"

"Yes, but I don't mind. My father claims that fussing about language in front of ladies is to pretend that we are a weaker species. My mother insists that it is a matter of respect, but my father's opinion makes more sense to me. What harm will the word *damnation* do me? It is even in the Bible."

"Context, Cressida, context. And I swore *at* you, which is outrageous."

"I was goading you. You are allowed some retaliation."

His eyes were fixed on her. "You're a remarkable woman. Why were you goading me?"

She cocked her head, then gave him the truth. "I thought you wanted to talk about these things."

"You were right. I don't know why."

She knew the answer she preferred, but it would never pass her lips. The coach swayed her against him for a brushing moment. She noticed, but it no longer bothered her.

They were at peace.

Chapter Fourteen

Cressida smiled at him. "Tell me more about the terrible burdens of being a duke. It will be great comfort to me when I'm stuck in a dull round of poverty and plain living."

"You will never be stuck in a dull round of poverty and plain living."

She saw where he was going. "I will not allow you to fund my family, Your Grace."

"Tris."

"Tris, I think, is less controllable."

The words escaped without thought, and she saw him become intent. "Ah, now that is interesting."

Perhaps not so at peace as she'd thought. "Interesting or not, I will never accept money from you. You have been more than kind as it is."

"I have been amusing myself, and you know it. The money would let me sleep at night."

"The Mandevilles are not among your thousands of dependents."

"But Cressida Mandeville is among my limited number of friends. Is she not?"

"That's not fair!"

"Dukes don't have to play fair."

She met his teasing eyes. "It isn't possible, Tris. There's no acceptable connection point between us, and you know it. I could only be your friend if I was also your mistress."

Did the flickering reaction in his eyes match the one in her heart? Astonishingly tempting, especially if her family were to end up in poverty. All chance of a good marriage would be gone, and by her "sacrifice," she would earn the money to help her parents. . . .

His lashes lowered, but he still watched her. "I'm the last of the Tregallows, and I must marry. Quite soon. I should have done it years ago, but the more my uncle commanded, the more I resisted. And there are not, in the end, that many young women suited to the rank."

"Lady Anne?" she said, but then remembered. "No, you said she is in love with someone else. So, who?" She was proud of her calm and level tone.

"I've not yet stuck a pin in the short list."

"Oh, you mustn't do that!"

He shrugged. "Lady Anne's mother is fond of saying that anyone can fall in love with a suitable person if they set their mind to it. I have a strong will."

Cressida felt like a distant witness to a tragedy, but she'd already said too much, and what did she know about life in high places? He wasn't free to pick as he wished any more than a king or royal duke was.

Except when it came to mistresses.

She looked up to find him watching her.

"I will doubtless set up a mistress," he said. "One woman for duty, one for pleasure."

It might be an invitation, but phrased like

that, it was unthinkable.

"I hope you don't. I hope you marry for love. Now," she added lightly, "list some more of your ducal burdens."

A wry smile flickered. "Let's see. . . . Duty obliges me to attend the House of Lords and even — horror of horrors! — to pay attention. I've had to inform myself on subjects a lesser mortal is allowed to ignore — export of coal, import of cochineal. Do you know what cochineal is?"

"A red dye used in making pink icing."

"Do you know it's made from crushed insects?"

She stared at him. "No! Ugh! You wretched man. I'll never be able to eat a pink cake again!"

"Nor I. You see — a burden of my rank. What other exciting subjects have I had to read about? Port, of course. I enjoy the drink, but the production is dry stuff. Transport between the Island of Newfoundland and a place called Labrador — a problem with ice, I gather. The peace establishment of the army — important, but stunningly tedious. I was pleased, I must say, to have a part in abolishing punishment in the pillory for most cases, and in a bill for easing the situation of bankrupts."

"I suspect most of the peers do not pay such close attention."

He shrugged. "And perhaps in time I'll grow too bored or cynical to bother. At the moment, I find I can't slide away — though I'll confess to abandoning the cochineal debate in favor of more enlivening amusements. There are too many important matters. The situation in Ireland, agricultural distress, and a restless population. See? If I weren't a duke, I could ignore all this and enjoy my orgies."

She laughed, wanting to hug him. "I don't think so. You are cursed with a sense of responsibility, you poor man — especially when you lack the sort of pride that would delight in the groveling rewards." She cocked her head. "But dare I say that it will get better? In time we do become accustomed to almost anything. Do you have a secretary to help you with all this?"

"I inherited my uncle's. Leatherhulme's a dried-up old stick, and thinks he knows everything. He does, in fact, but he also thinks everything must go on as it has since the king was a lad."

He sighed. "I probably should overhaul the whole administration. It's antiquated and rooted in the idea that the duchy exists for the duke's satisfaction. But all the people there are doing their jobs as best they know how. Am I to throw them out?"

Such a thoughtful man. The right wife could turn his restless energy to good works. . . .

He raised a hand and rubbed the back of his neck, dislodging his turban. He pulled it off and tossed it and his mask on the opposite seat. "I can't believe I'm boring you with all this."

You could never bore me, she thought, wanting to smooth his tousled hair. "Perhaps you don't have enough people to talk to like this."

"Enough? Any. No, that's not true. I have friends, but should I bore them with cochineal when they live in blessed unconcern?"

She would be a good listener for him. She could be a good helpmeet in so many ways. She already took an interest in political matters and would enjoy delving deeper. She was seriously involved in charitable works. She'd always been a good organizer. She was enough of her father's daughter to love the thought of helping to run a duchy in a modern, efficient manner.

But she knew that what he'd said about the pressures of rank was true. Her dreamy image of their life together was of them in their slippers by a comfortable hearth in a house like Nun's Chase, talking over the day's events. It was not of occasional meetings in an echoing mansion amid hundreds of servants and thousands of dependents, and a whole world fascinated by their smallest doings.

Perhaps he'd raised those things in order to make that clear to her, though she did hope not. It would mean that he'd detected deeper feelings in her than she even wanted to admit to herself.

A duke did not marry a provincial nobody, and for good reason.

She shuddered at the thought of having her every word hung upon, her every folly imitated — of having people groveling for the favor of her company. It was the reality, however. It was the reality in Matlock with the local lions such as Lady Mumford and Lady Agnes Ferrault. In London she'd seen it in all its blatant glory. The terms *toadeater* and *lickspittle* were not gross exaggerations.

He broke the silence. "So, what of you,

Cressida Mandeville? When you have your jewels, what will you do with your life?"

She made sure to smile. "Return to Matlock with my parents and help take care of my father."

"Hire a nurse."

"We probably will, but Matlock is my home. I have a full life there."

"You were in London looking for a husband."

"I was in London because my father hoped that I would find an impressive husband. I had nothing against the idea, but" — she shrugged — "it didn't happen."

"All London is blind?"

She gave him a look. "I'm no beauty. After all, you never noticed me."

"We met?" He might even have blushed.

"No, but I was in the same room with you a time or two. You were not drawn irresistibly to my startling beauty and charms."

She meant it as a joke and was relieved when he laughed. "I was probably so busy avoiding the fashionable pursuers that I wouldn't have noticed you if you'd had a glowing halo around your head. But I'm sorry."

He took her hand and kissed it.

After a frozen moment, she pulled free. "Don't, Tris."

"Don't what?"

"Don't flirt with me."

He didn't look away. "I will never hurt you, Cressida. My honor on it."

How can you promise me that, you fool? I can feel the pain coming as surely as if I faced the surgeon's knife.

"I have enjoyed your company as much as anyone's I remember. Don't ask me to be cold."

It took courage, but she went straight to the heart of the problem. "As long as we admit, now, that there can never be anything but friendship between us."

When he hesitated, her foolish heart trembled, but then he asked, "What constitutes friendship?"

"You should know that."

"I'm wondering if it will preclude this." He drew her into his arms.

Cressida could have resisted. She knew that, knew that he was giving her all the chance in the world to stop him. This would soon end, however. The surgeon's knife would bite. She couldn't resist just a little of what her heart and body longed for.

Still as a statue in the full moon's light the highwayman watched the road, controlling his mount without effort and without bit. His clothing was dark as the shadows, his face concealed behind a mask and a delicate beard and mustache of the style of Charles I. He would be invisible if not for the splash of a sweeping white plume on his broad Cavalier hat.

Jean-Marie Bourreau prayed for a rich carriage — the richer, the better. He was pleased to be free from jail, but his pride stung. Who had impersonated him? Who had dared to take his creation, Le Corbeau, and use it for his own advantage?

Jean-Marie and his men had returned cautiously to the cottage. They had found the ramshackle place untouched, except that he thought perhaps the bedding in the concealed room had been changed. His impersonator had slept in his bed? He would have his eyes, his innards, his genitals! He'd found his chests as he'd left them, however, including his costume.

Perhaps the impostor had made his own version, as the Drury Lane theater had when they'd included him in that play, *A Daring Lady*. He had become something of a hero to the foolish English. During his days in jail fashionable women had flocked to visit Le Corbeau. Some had bribed his jailers to let them spend time with him, intimate time.

It had not been so unpleasant. Now he was free, he must take back his identity. He was Le Corbeau. He!

Ah. Wheels approached. He saw his target. A light traveling chaise with two horses and only one man on the box. Excellent. Poorly guarded but promising wealth. He surged out onto the road. "Stand and deliver!"

The coachman drew the horses to a plunging halt. "Bloody hell, I thought you were in jail!"

"A mistake, as you see, *monsieur*. Do not make ze trouble."

He looked inside the coach and smiled. The traveler was a beautiful woman, alone. That and her painted face suggested that she was not the epitome of virtue, but then, neither was he. A courtesan rather than a whore, he suspected, to be traveling in such a carriage.

"*Madame,* I require a toll for the use of zis road."

"You're the king, then, are you, since this is the King's Highway?" His ear was not good with English accents, but he thought she spoke quite well.

"Perhaps. After all, your king, he is mad."

"And yours," she pointed out, "is dead."

"Alas, no, *madame*. Ours is now very, very fat."

She smiled, and then she laughed, a glorious full laugh, showing excellent teeth. The new king of France had spent his exile stuffing himself and was known as Louis le Gros.

"Then you are certainly not he." She frankly appraised him. "What sort of toll did you have in mind, *Monsieur Le Corbeau?*"

Jean-Marie almost growled, and he was in danger of becoming uncomfortable in the saddle. "Alas, *madame,* a hasty one. Zis crow must fly or he might dance in the air."

"And yet I am worthy of a great deal more than haste."

He knew what she was suggesting. Would it put his head in a noose? Life, he believed, was risk, but a long life demanded some common sense.

"Perhaps, *madame,* one day we could explore zese t'ings with a great lack of haste."

"Indeed, sir, perhaps we could. . . ."

"For now, alas, I must ask you to leave ze coach so I can assess ze toll of your . . . er . . . wealth."

Her expression chilled, and she thrust open the door to step down. His brows rose at the full sight of her. Her well-rounded body was revealed by a formfitting dress with many slits in the skirt.

Plump thighs, round calves, slender ankles, trim waist. His mouth watered. The bodice of the gown was cut below her magnificent breasts, which were covered only by veiling.

He sighed again, making sure she heard it. "Your wealth, I see, is in your natural assets, *madame*. No jewels?"

"I am returning from a wild entertainment not worthy of jewels."

He ran his eyes up and down her again, which was no hardship, but showed her words true. Little could be concealed beneath that gown. He often took a kiss from ladies in lieu of trinkets, but a kiss from a whore hardly seemed payment. He glanced inside the coach. On the seat lay a pale statuette. He looked back at her and saw a sudden tension. Ah, so . . .

"I will take zat."

"It's a paltry thing."

"I will be ze judge."

She glared, then reached in, picked the thing up, and held it up for him to see. "It's a trinket. An Indian statue awarded to me as a prize."

It was about eight inches high, intricately carved, and almost certainly of ivory.

"I'm sure you deserved the prize, *madame,* but I have my pride, and it would be worth something if sold. Surrender it to me."

Her eyes flashed anger, heightening his interest. Why did this thing mean so much to her, and how could he use that for greater profit?

"I thought you only took half a person's assets, Crow."

"We can hardly cut it in two." He moved the

horse forward and plucked it from her hands. "Perhaps, *madame,* I will let you buy it back."

She was not as good as she should be at hiding her emotions. She was furious, then calculating, then hopeful.

"For zat," Jean-Marie pointed out, "I will need your name."

"Miranda Coop." She spoke with the arrogance of a duchess. "You will find that my address is well known. Return that within the week, sir, or I will see you hang!"

She climbed back into her carriage.

Jean-Marie held the door so she could not close it. "I wonder where zis so lively party is taking place. . . ."

Her eyes met his with a spark of understanding amusement. "Stokeley Manor, over an hour from here. And yes, most of the revelers are now quite drunk."

It would seem that the lady bore no goodwill toward the people there. He inclined his head, shut the door, and gave the coachman freedom to go. As it rattled off, Alain and Yves came up beside him.

"You're not thinking of taking up that invitation, are you?" asked Yves. "She'll wrap you up and present you to the hangman."

"Will she?" Jean-Marie smiled at the statue, which was most interesting. "Do you think this pose is possible?"

"I think it's possible we'll be caught if we linger here. And if you're not going to sell that, we're risking death for nothing."

Jean-Marie laughed. "You have a mercenary

heart, but now I have an enterprise in mind that might satisfy it. Come! The Crow flies north."

Cressida played her mouth against Tris's, astonished by how long a couple could simply kiss. Though *simply* was perhaps not the precise word. She was on his lap now, and every bouncing movement of the coach shifted silk against silk and shape against shape.

His hand was under the back of her jacket again, moving rough-hot against her skin, creating the most delicious feelings. She wished she knew how to do the same to him, but she was too uncertain to ask or try.

She had her arms around him, however, and the freedom of his mouth. How strange that was. Such an intimate place, a mouth, and yet their joining had lasted so long that his had become a part of hers, dissolving all barriers between them.

The coach jolted her against him again, and she felt him tense. He was hard. Hot prickling desire ran over her, but she broke the kiss. "We must stop."

"Must we?" Heavy lids shielded dark, smiling eyes, and his lips looked more sensuous than ever. More tempting. More delicious . . .

She hated to try to put words to this mystery. "I can't let you ruin me, Tris. It would be disastrous. For both of us —"

He captured a length of her hair and wound it around his finger. "I'd marry you if you conceived."

If that wasn't temptation, what was? To have him always, and a child of his!

Wielding the surgeon's knife herself, she said, "I'm sorry. I . . . like you, Tris, but I could never be a duchess. Perhaps we can be friends, at a distance. Perhaps we could write. . . ."

"Write," he echoed.

"Or not." She grasped her hair and tugged it free of his distracting play. "We are like travelers who meet in a strange land and become companions there simply because they are so far from home. Once back in their own land, they have no connection."

"We just discovered a very powerful connection."

"Kissing isn't everything."

His lips twitched. "True."

"In terms of connection."

"Very true."

"Stop it! We have nothing else in common."

"Don't we?"

She knew they did, and feared he was about to list examples.

"It doesn't matter. I'm too conventional for you, too proper. You'd soon lose patience with me. You are attracted to this," she added, gesturing at her outrageous costume, "and I am not."

"I'd be happy with you without it."

She pushed off his lap entirely, back to her own side of the seat. "See! Only you would say such a thing!"

His brows rose.

"You and your sort." She put hands to her hot cheeks. "Why am I going on like this? You aren't serious about marriage. You're trying to seduce me. And you promised you wouldn't!"

He leaned back in his corner. "No, I didn't. I promised that you could trust me. That is still true. You weren't reluctant to kiss me, Cressida, so don't pretend you were."

He seemed relaxed, amused, and seductive as Satan. "As for seduction, I still think it would be a good idea."

"It would be disastrous!"

"Don't be so hasty. You, my intrepid explorer, do not know what is around the next bend."

"I sincerely hope it's Nun's Chase."

"Where there are two convenient beds and many hours left of this adventurous night. Your voyage is not over until you are back in your parents' home, Cressida. Don't you think it would be a shame to miss the most exciting . . . scenery?"

Her skin shivered, and her muscles tensed. "That's Satan talking."

He laughed. "You think me possessed by the devil?"

"I think you *are* the devil."

He was. He knew just how to play her. His mind was as skillful as his knowing hands and mouth.

That was why he wasn't trying to touch her now, why he was leaning back in his corner, as far away from her as possible. He knew it made him more desirable, not less.

As if to prove it, he spoke. "I want to make love to you, Cressida, and I can do it without risking a child, without even breaching your virginity. I want it for my own selfish satisfaction and delight, but also for you. As you say, this voyage will soon be over. As your guide, it wounds me to let you leave my land without experiencing the best, especially when I have taken you to the seedy and downright disgusting stews. I offer you intense pleasure, Cressida, at very little risk."

Her body clenched on itself in direct, hungry reaction to his words. She prayed he couldn't tell.

Very little, she made herself note. *Not no risk.*

It emphasized that he was being scrupulously honest, however, which was seductive in itself. She valued honesty, and if she were honest now, she'd admit that the past twenty-four hours, the time in his company, had been the most honest she could remember. Here in this outrageous situation, in this skimpy costume, she felt real for the first time in her life.

Was this what her father had felt in India? Was this why he'd not been able to return home, even to be with his wife and child?

But Arthur Mandeville had found a place in India. There was no place for his daughter in this wild land except with strumpets and their customers.

"I wish you would speak your obviously troubled thoughts," he said.

"Then you would try to fight them."

"Of course. I can see no rational objection other than fear of ruin."

She laughed. "You think that nothing?"

He shrugged. "If your presence at Stokeley comes out, you are ruined. Nothing you do now will change that, and of course, if that happens, I will marry you."

"And I will refuse!"

"I will not be distracted by a hypothesis. You have no rational choice, Cressida, but to return with me to Nun's Chase for what remains of the night. What we do there, no one will ever know."

"*I* will."

"A platitude unworthy of you."

That stung. "You make virtue sound vulgar!"

"Perhaps it is."

"You *are* a devil."

"Not until I die. And no," he said, forestalling her, "do not try to save my immortal soul. I don't feel it is in danger, but I am what I am, and I am the expert here. What you risk tonight — the only thing you risk — is that once you enjoy your body to the full, you might hunger for that pleasure too much. It might lead you into rashness."

"You are very sure of your skills," she snapped.

"Yes. But don't forget, I know you a little by now. You are not cold or hard to please. Our lovemaking will be a continuation of what we have enjoyed together thus far, and that, you must admit, has been very promising indeed. What do you want, Cressida? What do you *want?*"

"We cannot always do what we want! Or at least, we lesser mortals cannot."

He shook his head. "Once there were sumptuary laws, which regulated what people could wear according to their rank. Under those laws, it would be wicked for you to wear those purple trousers. Laws, and even sins, change, Cressida. There is no immutability about them. The only thing that matters in the present is to not get caught."

She rolled her eyes. "There are the Ten Commandments."

"Which forbid only adultery."

"Oh, you are outrageous!"

He smiled, an eloquent statement of wickedness. "That, I do not dispute. What I offer is honest, however, and I thought we had already established that you trust me. Haven't I proved worthy of your trust?"

Cressida pressed her hands to her temples, into her loose hair. "The devil is bound to be enticing, and even convincing."

"You disappoint me, Miss Mandeville. This is very conventional thinking."

She seized on it. "I'm a very conventional woman."

His brows rose, and his lips twitched.

"I am! This is an aberrant voyage. My home, my true place, is Dormer Close, Matlock. Can't you see?" she asked, suddenly seeing the truth herself. "If I give in to you, I may never be at home there again."

As her father had failed to find a home back in England.

Had she already gone too far?

"But is Matlock such a good choice?"

It echoed her sudden doubts and fears.

"It is my home, and I need it. I need family, friends, habitual activities, routine comforts. I need to be someone I know and am comfortable with. I am not a wild spirit like you, Tris. I'm not."

She begged that he'd understand, that he'd believe.

He studied her, then sighed. "As you wish. But it would be as well, I think, if we do not touch or talk until we arrive. My willpower, dear Cressida, is not as strong as yours."

Chapter Fifteen

By the time they arrived at Nun's Chase, Cressida was heavy with weariness, but most of it was of the spirit. She wasn't sure she would be able to sleep. She knew her decision was right, sane, and even logical, yet it churned in her like a mistake.

It wasn't only lust. It was something else. Instinct? She'd never felt she was a person who relied on instinct. Yet here, instinct said she had taken a wrong path despite all the evidence of her more rational side.

When the coach drew up before the house, she hastily restored her disguise of veils and mask. St. Raven got down on his own side even though it was away from the front door. Cressida wondered if she were supposed to scramble over there, but then the groom opened the door on her side and offered her a hand out.

The man was impassive, but for the first time in an age she felt all the peculiarity of her costume. Trousers! Nakedness beneath thin silk! The memory of Henry VIII bellowing comments about her posterior made her think longingly of her forgotten cloak.

She didn't know the time, but it must be gone two, that dead hour of the night when everything feels bleak, even when there's no cause. And she, heaven help her, had plenty of cause. No wonder St. Raven thought her ripe for seduction. In the cold light of reality, she saw that she'd behaved improperly all night.

He walked with her toward the door but without offering his arm. The hour and the chill air had her almost aching with cold, and she thought wistfully of his warm body against hers, but he was following the path she had insisted upon.

The door opened before they arrived, and Harry stood aside to let them enter. What did they look like to him? What on earth did he think?

Was she ruined anyway? If so . . .

St. Raven turned to her. "Do you require anything before you retire, Miss Wemworthy?"

She felt she should drop a curtsy, though it would look ridiculous in these clothes. "No, thank you, Your Grace."

There should be something significant to say at the end of their adventure, but all she could manage was, "Good night, Your Grace, and thank you for your efforts."

She turned and walked up the stairs, praying that the men weren't watching her behind. Once in her room, she turned the key in the lock, then sat on the bed and sank her face in her hands.

Tris watched for a moment, but then Harry said, "Some papers arrived by courier, sir. They are in your study."

The last thing he needed now was paperwork,

but then he sighed. If Leatherhulme had sent them urgently, they were urgent, and perhaps fusty paperwork would chill lust.

A glance showed that they weren't as urgent as all that. A signature needed for an investment. Documents on sale of property in Lancashire. They were probably more Leatherhulme's way of reproaching him about his continued absence from London.

What he needed was a secretary who could travel with him, and not be easily shocked. Cary would do except that he had no interest in such dull work, and money enough not to need employment.

He tossed the papers aside, but then picked them up again, glanced over them, and signed them. He put them in their leather pouch and sealed it shut with wax and his ring. Poor Leatherhulme would throw a fit if he thought papers were left open to casual eyes.

Tris leaned back in the chair, rubbing his hands over his face. Thoughts, questions, doubts, regrets tumbled at him from all sides, and all to do with recent events, but he couldn't think straight yet.

He'd return Cressida to her precious propriety and get her damned statue. He'd pay Leatherhulme a visit and catch up on all the paperwork. And then — ?

He'd like to flee the country, but the best he could permit himself was a repairing lease in Cornwall.

Or no. He'd made a promise to himself that once he was duke, he'd marry and procreate.

That was now a year overdue, and he'd met all the fashionable contenders.

He might as well get it over with and choose a bloody wife.

Cressida would like to cry, but she might make noise. Tris might hear. He'd come to her then, and it would all be to do again. She couldn't bear to hurt him anymore.

She straightened, frowning.

Hurt? The Duke of St. Raven?

That was extreme. And vain. Her rejection of him was a minor inconvenience, not a wound. He'd probably already forgotten it.

And yet, she sensed something, some kind of pain. He was, she thought, largely what he appeared to be — a healthy, privileged young man who enjoyed life. Beneath, however, lurked a nugget of unhappiness.

Perhaps it came from the death of his parents.

How old had he been? Twelve. His parents had clearly loved each other, and he must have loved them. She tried to imagine it. Everything lost, everything changed, in one stroke of fate.

She remembered him asking, "What is a home?" Foolishly, she longed to give him one, a cozy simple home like her home in Matlock.

He had many houses, but no home. Cornhallows, his home from birth, had passed into other hands. Officially his home was Mount St. Raven in Cornwall, where he'd clearly spent little time. Nun's Chase? She had the impression it was mainly used for his wicked entertainments.

He must have a house in London as well as all

the other ones listed among his burdens.

Poor Tris Tregallows.

Poor orphaned child . . .

She stood, pushing that away. If she indulged in such thoughts, it would sap her willpower. She dragged off her veils and mask, remnants of a wild night. Tomorrow morning she would return to reality, and soon this would all be like a dream.

She slipped off the bed and went to the washstand. A glance in the mirror showed Roxelana's face — her darkened brows, a hint of the paint on her lips. Had it faded with time, or been worn off in those endless, endless kisses? . . .

She washed her face, scrubbing until she looked like Cressida Mandeville again. How peculiar to find that that conventional lady still lived beneath.

She opened her valise to look at the small selection of clothes she'd packed for her ordeal with Crofton. He'd insisted that she wear an evening dress for the journey, and bring another for her stay, but she'd also packed two day dresses and changes of underwear.

She could laugh at herself now. She'd had no idea of what she'd face.

She pulled out her nightdress, which was quite pretty, but had no place in Crofton's milieu. It was her summer one, of light, fine lawn with short sleeves and a scoop neck trimmed with green ribbon.

Almost reluctantly now the moment had come, she stripped off her two wicked garments and put it on. Strange that one garment was more decent than two. No, the point was that she would not be going out in public in her nightdress. She was going to bed.

Her hair. She had her bristle brush now.

She sat at her dressing table and brushed it out. She normally plaited it, but more because that was "proper" than from necessity. Straight and heavy, it didn't tangle.

Tris was right about that. So much of propriety was nonsense. That a lady should always be gloved when she went out, and wear a hat or bonnet. That if she had need to refer to a man's pantaloons or breeches she call them "unmentionables." That she never walk down St. James's Street, where the men's clubs were.

In a moment of defiance, she decided to leave her hair loose, and turned toward the bed.

And stood there.

After a while she accepted that she wasn't going to get into that bed. Strange how clear things had become, as if a mist had lifted.

Tris was right. She could not leave here, end this voyage of adventure without exploring what he offered. Her fatal curiosity pushed her, but the main impetus, the force that overwhelmed her will entirely, was the compelling sense that it mattered to him.

She didn't understand his precise needs, but she knew they went beyond lust. Perhaps, above all, he needed her trust. He had, she decided, won the right to that.

So she turned her back on propriety and left the room, still sensible enough to peer out to be sure no one was around. She went to his door.

Walk in on him again, or knock?

She knocked.

No response.

Then, faintly, she detected his voice from downstairs, probably giving orders for tomorrow, for their journey to London. That was that, then. She should go back to her room and go to bed. . . .

Then the voices became louder. She heard, "If Mr. Lyne returns soon, pass that on. . . ." Then soft footsteps. He was coming up the stairs!

Cressida had a momentary decision point. She had just enough time to rush back to her own room — or to enter his.

She opened his door and went in, closing the door with exquisite care in perfect silence. Once she was committed, doubts struck.

What if the mood had passed for him?

What if he'd thought better of the risks?

What if he was the rake she'd first thought and she ended up with child?

She was tempted to hide behind the curtains, but she made herself stand her ground. She was shaking, though, with her hands clasped tight in front of her, when he opened the door.

He stopped. Then slowly, without moving his eyes from hers, he closed the door and leaned against it. His eyes, his breathing, told her that one fear was groundless. The mood had not passed. But still, he did not come to her.

"I see no buttons to undo," he said at last, his voice deep, almost hoarse.

Her fingers were pleating the thin cotton. "No."

"Are you here only to torment me?"

"I don't know." She swallowed. "You're the expert guide."

He looked down, laughing a little. "At this moment, I don't feel like it." He looked up again. "Why, Cressida?"

Her feeling of confidence weakened. "Has it all changed? Do you want me to go?"

He came forward then, took her hands. "God, no. No. Never. I'd given up. If you'd planned to turn me on my head and shake all coherence out of me, you couldn't have managed this any better. Are you aware, woman, how much more devastating that pristine nightdress is than your harem costume?"

She could feel heat prickling all over her, and relief bubbling up. "No, truly. I didn't plan to come. I intended to go to bed. To my own bed . . ."

"But changed your mind." He still only held her hands, but her mind swooped down to that touch and for the moment found it enough. "Can you tell me why, Cressida? I hate to question such a precious gift, but I couldn't live with myself if I do anything tonight to harm you."

She looked at him with tenderness and laughed. "Only you, St. Raven, would balk now! Aren't you afraid that if I probe my motives, I'll flee?"

"If you flee, you flee. First rule. Call me Tris. If you can't do that, we have no business moving an inch closer."

It should have been easy, but she hesitated.

"Tris is such a simple person."

"No, he's not."

"I mean, ordinary. A man, not a duke."

"True."

"Tris is the duke, though."

"True enough. But not tonight. Tonight it would be Tris and Cressida. Hot, sweaty, and naked. Tonight you will be more intimate with another person than you have been since the day you slid messily from your mother's womb. That's what we're talking about here, Cressida. Do you want it?"

She stared at him. "Oh, you wretched man. You know me so well! How can I resist after that? Yes, I want it — Tris."

He pulled her into his arms. "Don't you realize that those words would have sent most virginal ladies screaming?"

"They're afraid of the mess?"

"Or of the hot, sweaty, and naked."

She felt hot, sweaty, and naked already. "Perhaps it's because I've been through the orgy."

"Perhaps it is. . . ."

His hands began to move on her back. Through the fine linen, his touch almost felt as if nothing lay in the way.

"I hope to please you, too," she whispered.

"You will."

"I mean, to do things that please you. I want . . . I don't know what I want, but something for you."

He lowered his head to brush her lips with his. "Be quiet. We've done our duty. We've thought and we've talked and we've tried to be sensible.

Now we can simply feel. . . ."

He reached behind himself for her hands and brought them forward, rubbed them slowly over his brocade jacket, then settled them on the buttons down the front. "If you want to do something for me, love, undo them."

Undress him?

Oh, yes.

Cressida began to release the buttons one by one, aware all the time of his heat, his spice, and his deepening breaths. When they were all free, she pushed the garment open, then off his shoulders, uncovering his white silk shirt.

She glanced to see if he had further instructions, but he was relaxed, almost passive, letting her do as she wished.

"You know me too well," she whispered, tugging the shirt out of his loose trousers. When the shirt was loose, she slid her hands beneath it, onto his hot, firm flanks, slightly dizzy just from that.

"You can take over now."

"Carry on. I'll catch you if you fall."

He did know her well. No, he knew women well. Or knew this mystery well. That, by the laws of propriety, should deter her but for the life of her she couldn't imagine why. An experienced guide seemed an excellent idea when slip-sliding down into this torrid jungle.

She should probably undo his cuffs and take the shirt off, but she wanted to discover him first by touch. Eyes closed, she let her fingers wander, let her palms stroke and feel.

Other senses would not be denied. Her sense

of smell still reveled in him, and her hearing caught his rough breathing along with the slither of silk.

Or perhaps it was just that she could feel his breaths beneath elegant bone, supple muscle, and silken skin. The change from hard ribs to firm abdomen seemed a marvel, and the soft indent of his navel made her smile.

She pushed the silk up and touched her lips there, inhaling his scent. Then she reached with her tongue to taste. . . .

Distraction. His hands light on her shoulders, then sliding into her hair, stroking the back of her head, raising her hair. She straightened, arching her neck, moving her hands behind him, to skim there, to run her fingers up the bedazzling hollow of his spine.

She'd never seen his back.

She fluttered her eyes open and stared up at him, having trouble focusing for a moment. His eyes spoke of desire even to her, who scarcely knew the language.

He kissed her forehead.

She swayed, but then she turned all her attention to his right cuff. She undid the three buttons there, then did the same on his left. Then she tried to take the shirt off, but it was awkward because of his height.

"You'll have to do it."

He dropped to one knee.

Chapter Sixteen

So. She walked behind and eased it over his head as carefully as if he'd been a child.

Then she had his back. A work of art, all hers. Slowly, she stroked across wide shoulders and back to his nape, drinking it in with every sense she possessed and a few she was just now discovering.

Her head buzzed as if that potion still maddened her, but this intoxication was him, and him alone. Her eyes didn't focus quite as they should, and her heartbeat, her pulse, beat an urgent rhythm.

Shaken, she clutched his shoulders. "I'm falling. . . ."

He rose slowly, letting her hands fall away, and turned to her, kissed her. "My name?"

"Tris. Tristan Tregallows."

"I was that all my life until last year. Sometimes I'm afraid he's lost, poor Tris Tregallows. Find him for me, Cressida."

He kissed her, gently at first, as if they'd never kissed before, then carried her deeper into dark and dangerous places. She swirled down with him, not realizing her legs had given way until he lifted her and carried her to the bed, to place her there.

He stood back and untied his sash to drop it, slithering, upon her. "You can tie me up with it later if you like."

Her dreamy wits stilled on that. "What?"

"Only if you want to." Eyes on hers, he loosened the tie holding up his trousers and let them drop. A shiver rippled through her, part nerves, but part knowing hunger.

His expression seemed wary, as if he thought she might retreat. She could see why, but all she felt was an aching hunger. A lustful man was so beautiful it was astonishing artists could resist portraying it.

"I'm feeling somewhat impatient, guide."

Watchfulness gave way to sparkling, wicked delight. "Anticipation, wench. The key to everything."

He pulled her up to her knees, then pushed her nightgown off her shoulders. He stripped her slowly, eyes on the skin he revealed, pausing when the white cloth was beneath her breasts. She looked down to watch his hands holding the cloth there, to see as well as feel his lips trace across the upper swell of each.

She thought of Crofton, and Miranda Coop, and what a debasement that had been of this.

"Most men adore the mystery of a woman's breasts, Cressida. Such sweet softness. Such pliant firmness. Wise nature has arranged that a man's touch here gives a woman pleasure, but men being men, we'd play with them anyway for our own delight."

His lips moved down to her left nipple to brush, finding a new, exquisite sensitivity in her.

Then his tongue teased. She waited breathlessly for more, but he turned his attention to the other one, then left it equally unsatisfied.

She stifled complaint. She would be satisfied. She knew that. He was mapping the path that they would take, preparing her.

Her nightdress was down to her hips now. His mouth followed, down a line to her navel, where his tongue played. Then he straightened to lift her free.

Free of cloth.

Free of thought.

Free of anything but anticipation.

He whirled with her in his arms, dizzying her so that she wrapped her legs around his waist.

Still turning, he kissed her, swirling every sense down to the place where she was open to his heat.

Walls could shatter, fire could rage. Nothing mattered except this.

He broke the kiss, eyes dark and dazed as she felt, and lowered her onto the bed, gently freeing himself of her hold. One knee on the bed, he stroked up the insides of her spread legs, ending with his hands between her thighs, his touch so close, so close. . . .

Then he was beside her, an arm cradling her, his hand where she ached for it to be.

She remembered the orgy, the tormenting itch, the need to press, but this was nothing like that. As strong, perhaps, but nothing like.

His mouth on her breasts again.

"Tris? . . ."

"Yes?" he murmured.

"What do I do?"

"I'm the guide, remember? Come where I take you." His hand still circled between her thighs. "In this new land, there is a treasured custom. We throw ourselves off high cliffs into mist. Those with the courage to fall free find it worth their while. Let go, Cressida. Let go."

He brushed his lips back to her breast and sucked. She felt pushed, pushed to an edge, but she clung, afraid. Afraid to fall, afraid of the mist, as if she would dissolve there, die there.

His mouth, his hand, would not let her retreat. They were forcing her on, arching her to breaking point.

She could break, or she could fly.

Trust.

She let go and fell, screaming in her mind as she spiraled down, down, down through the mists and into a deep, dark peace.

With him. Pressed to him, kissing him, holding him one knee up over his hip. Claiming him. Needing him . . .

"We can't, can we?"

His breathing seemed ragged. "We won't." He kissed her hair, stroked her, but his hands shook.

"Tris . . ."

"Hush." He moved off the bed, pulling her with him, tugged back the covers, and settled her onto the sheets. He covered her. "I won't be a moment."

Then he walked out of the room, magnificent enough, her dazed mind registered, for a marble statue.

A warrior.

No, an athlete.

Cressida pulled the covers higher, suddenly cold and bereft.

It was only night air on sweat.

"More intimate with another person since the day you slid messily from your mother's womb."

Oh, yes. But it hadn't been complete. And now he wasn't here. She must have done something wrong. Had he left her for the night? Would she not get another chance?

It seemed an age, but she didn't think it was long before he returned, a wicked smile on his face and a red glass vial in his hand. He didn't look angry or disappointed. He also didn't look . . . rampant. He had been when he'd left. Like a rod.

She looked a question at him, and he shook his head.

"Always curious. I couldn't trust myself so I . . . got rid of it."

"Got rid of it?"

"Dammit, Cressida, do you have to question everything!"

He was blushing. The Duke of St. Raven was actually blushing.

A part of her wanted to laugh with delight at that, but she focused on the vial in his hand. "What's that?"

"Oil. For massage."

Cressida's skin tingled with anticipation.

But then he said, "I am hoping that you are willing to rub it into my skin."

Oh.

Oh, yes!

He'd given her such pleasure. Now she could pleasure him. She smiled, knowing she probably looked too tender, showed emotions she mustn't have, but she couldn't help it. She slipped off the bed and took the vial from him. "Lie, my sultan."

He pulled the covers all the way down but then paused, looking at her.

"When a man desires a woman, his penis enlarges and becomes hard. So he can enter her. It's pleasure, but also close to pain. Being like that can make control difficult. The ideal relief is a woman's body, but a hand can serve." His lips twitched. "Sometimes it's called an encounter with Mrs. Palm and her five lovely daughters."

Cressida bit her lip, but then let the laughter escape. "Thank you. For telling me."

His smile might be a little wry, but it was tender all the same. "We're past protecting your purity, so you might as well be informed."

She'd remembered something from the orgy. "Or a mouth?" she asked.

He winced. "Or a mouth."

She stared at him. "That cucumber!"

"Quite. Now can we progress?" He lay down on the sheets, head pillowed in his arms.

She held back her laughter this time, but ideas were stirring. She didn't know if she'd be brave enough to put them into action, but they intrigued her.

For the moment, she had oil and what she wanted more than anything was to give him a gift that was at least a little as wonderful as the one he had given her.

She took the glass stopper out of the vial and

sniffed. A subtle smell, neither flowery nor the familiar sandalwood.

"What is it?" she asked, pouring a little into the palm of one hand.

"Various eastern spices."

"With interesting effects?"

He just smiled.

She put the vial aside, rubbed her hands together, then raised them to her nose. It didn't instantly drive her mad with lust, but it wove sweetly into her mind.

She climbed on the bed and began circling her oiled hands on his back. Her intent was to give him pleasure, but soon the glide over seductive curves and hollows had her drifting into delight herself.

She closed her eyes and lived in feel alone, pressing a little harder to test the firm resilience of his muscles, to feel his bones. Then lighter, skimming.

Too light?

She looked at him. Eyes closed, mouth relaxed, he looked as blissful as she'd wanted him to be. Then he said, "Write your name on my back."

"How?"

"With your nail. Lightly."

She began in the small of his back and wrote upward — *Cressida*. Up his spine she wrote *Elizabeth,* then on the skin closest to her she wrote *Mandeville*.

Beneath her hands he moved, like a cat stretching.

"It feels so wonderful?" she asked.

"I'll show you later."

Her skin hummed with anticipation and her mouth dried, but surely there was more she could do here for him. She reached for the vial and reoiled her hands. "Do you have any other suggestions, Suleiman?"

"It's simply Tris and Cressida, naked and honest."

She rubbed her hands — the warm, elusive scent encircling her — recognizing hovering tears, then pushing them away. "What more can I do to please you, Tris?"

"There are parts of my available skin as yet un-oiled."

His long, strong legs.

She shifted to his ankles and rubbed oil there, then circled up his legs, up onto his thighs, aware of approaching his buttocks. His rump, as Henry VIII would doubtless say. Round, firm. Teeth in her bottom lip, she slid her hands there, up over the high curve.

He tensed beneath her touch, and she froze. "If it hurts when you desire —"

He chuckled. "I can bear it."

Temptation stirred again. This massage had aroused her as much as it had him. She ached to give him the true release, to experience that completion herself.

It would plunge them into disaster, however. They were sharing wild magic here, but they had to be careful. Neither of them wanted this night to bind them.

Not really.

Not really . . .

There were delights that were safe, and this

was one. She kneaded his firm flesh, tears aching behind her eyes.

Safe! They skimmed a knife blade of disaster, and she knew it — and the biggest danger was her weak will. How unfair of fate to bring her to this place, to this man, but make marriage impossible.

A spasm in her leg jerked her back to the mundane. Her body was complaining at her position. She straddled his thighs. Ah, much better. From here she could skim, press, or knead as she wished, and even rise up to put her weight behind it.

She did that to work at his shoulders, pressing harder and harder. He didn't complain and he wouldn't break, so she worked out some of her frustration there before sitting back on her thighs to circle his buttocks and the hollow of his lower back.

So, she would never visit this land again. Even if she married, it would not be like this. Decent people didn't do things like this.

So, she would experience everything she could tonight. She leaned down and pressed her lips into his lower back, tasting oil, and Tris, and magic.

Lazily, loosely, he began to turn beneath her. She sat up and saw that he was firm again.

She looked away, but then she looked back to study the long veined column, the darker cap divided by the cleft where his seed must come from. Finding the courage to do as she wished, she touched, with just her fingertips.

"It's so very hard. How?"

He laughed. "If you're asking about physiology, I'm not your guide." His hand covered hers, wrapping her fingers around him. "If we're talking other things, then it's you, Cressida. You."

Sweet misty sentiment. She found she had no taste for it.

"That would imply you've never hardened before we met."

"Men are men. We're animals. Here, now, this is you."

"Or massage."

"I've been massaged by professionals, love, and not reacted like this."

Love. Their eyes met, then shifted. He probably addressed all women in his bed as *love*. Men addressed women as "dear lady" without holding them dear, and vowed themselves to be "humble servants" without being either.

She shifted to what truth they had. Here, now, he desired her. The proof was in her hand — in custody of her palm and fingers. She moved, sliding up and then down, glancing to see any reaction.

His lips parted again. That was what she wanted, but oh, it was dangerous to look. He was such a handsome man, but now, aroused, lids lowered, hair tousled, he could break her heart.

Here be dragons, indeed. Dragons, serpents, and cockadrills, according to that ancient explorer, Sir John Mandeville.

Here be perils she had not considered when setting out on this journey. She had been prepared to sacrifice her virtue if she had to, but she'd never thought to lose her heart.

Not because of a man's good looks, or his charm, nor because of his wealth and rank. Not even because of his skill and mastery over sexual matters.

But because she liked him, ached for his sorrows, and loved his free response to her touch.

His lids fluttered open, and she saw the beginnings of alertness, of concern. She smiled and moved her hand again.

What to do? She knew he would tell her if she did anything she shouldn't.

It seemed natural to use both hands, to stroke up with one, then the other. It became a soothing, slow rhythm; then she let one hand continue up and over the top, gingerly. It looked sensitive.

As sensitive as she was between her thighs, where she wanted to rub herself against him?

She heard him gasp, felt his sudden movement.

"Clever Cressida," he murmured. "But are you willing to deal with a little mess?"

She knew what he meant. A drop of fluid already glistened on the tip. "Yes."

"Drape the sash over the top."

She heated with embarrassment, but it wasn't uncomfortable and it didn't make her want to retreat. It was a hot, prickling excitement at this new mystery.

Heart thundering, she picked up the black silk sash. But then instead of dropping it over him, she trailed it over him, watching his reaction.

He laughed shakily. "Intrepid voyager. But the hands are what I want."

A straight request. Loving that, she dropped

the silk over him, then underneath it she stroked him as before, trying to sense every reaction. And this time she watched his face.

After a moment, his eyes shut and he almost frowned. She hesitated, but she remembered his directness. He'd tell her if she were hurting him.

His hips began moving in time with her hands. His expression became almost pained, but now she recognized the same desperation she'd felt.

Before the fall.

She found herself speeding her action, racing along with her pulse and his breathing, pushing him.

Did everyone need pushing?

Then he stiffened, and a gasping groan broke from him as she felt his seed pump free. She used one hand on the silk to catch it, to hold him as his body tensed again and again.

Then it was over.

She was breathing deeply, too, recognizing where he was and how it felt. Loving having done that for him, but greedy for more for herself. Aching for the thing they couldn't do.

His lids rose and he smiled. "Thank you."

"It was truly my pleasure. But . . ."

He sat up, taking the sash from her and dropping it to the floor. "But?"

She'd almost said what she was thinking, that her life would seem empty after tonight. She scrambled for a substitute. "But are we finished now?"

He broke into laughter. "Oh, no. As long as we can both stay awake, we will not finish. My turn to rub oil all over you. All over . . ."

Chapter Seventeen

Cressida awoke wondering what time she'd fallen asleep, and what time it was now. She couldn't seem to care. The curtains were drawn and the room dim. Not too dim to see him, to see Tris, to see her lover, asleep on his front, head facing her.

She longed to stroke the dark hair off his forehead, to touch him while he slept. In the night it had become the most natural thing in existence to touch him. Any way and everywhere.

And to be touched.

She smiled in memory of his oiled hands all over her body, of him tracing lazy patterns on her ecstatic back. Then she'd insisted on massaging him again, on the front that time. She'd helped him to his release again. He'd kissed and stroked her into oblivion at least two more times.

She sighed at the delicious memory, but under it all lurked sadness. Sadness that the wild journey was incomplete, yet was over. That she could never return.

She was destined for Matlock, he for a grand marriage.

She had to accept that he would be as good a lover to the high-born lady he married as he had been to her. His kindness and honor would demand it. Doubtless his duchess would learn to pleasure him in turn, to rub him with exotic oils. Poor Cressida Mandeville would be the one barred from the land of delights.

She shook that off. A poor gratitude to show any sadness, and they still had work to do. They still had to retrieve the statue, or at least the jewels, from Miranda Coop.

He opened his eyes. "Good morning. Or is it afternoon? I wouldn't be surprised." He rolled onto his back and stretched. The covers fell down to his waist, stirring all kinds of unwise thoughts.

"You have no clock in here."

"I dislike the ticking. And I have plenty of servants to make sure I rise at the right time."

She couldn't help but play her fingers on his abdomen. "Servants not much in evidence."

"Servants I told not to disturb us until we rang." He met her eyes. "I wasn't expecting this, love. Just that we might both need extra sleep."

Her hand stilled. "Will they know? About me?"

"They'll know I spent the night in this bed with you."

The oil. The smells. Hot, sweaty, messy . . .

Unease crept over her, and for the first time she felt wrong, perhaps soiled. How many women had he massaged on this bed? How many would follow her? An endless parade.

She turned her dismay into starch for her spine. She'd known what he was. He'd never hidden it. He felt no shame. It was why she could never marry him even if it were possible.

"But will anyone know it's me — Cressida Mandeville?"

He gathered her hand and kissed it. "I don't see how. No one except Cary knows your name. Harry and his mother are the only ones who've had a straight look at you undisguised. I trust their discretion, and in any case, they'll likely never set eyes on you again."

So honest. So direct. So brutally blunt.

"You're safe as long as you can return home without raising questions. You'll be returning earlier than planned."

She took back her hand. "I'll tell my mother there was sickness in the house and I was in the way. But how am I to return? Hardly in your coach."

"My coach has no markings. It will do."

He sat up, looking toward the future with no apparent ghosts from the night to trouble him, the insensitive brute.

She blocked that. She was glad. The last thing she wanted for him was a broken heart to match hers.

"What of the statuette?"

"Leave that to me. Miranda will welcome a visit from me. With any luck, I'll have the chance to empty the statue with her none the wiser."

A clean cut, then. Once she climbed into the coach it would be over. Unless . . . "How will you return the jewels to me?"

He frowned at her. "Are you worrying that I'll do something to ruin you? I hoped for more trust than that."

And she'd thought he could read her mind.

"Of course I trust you. I'm just worrying over details. I'm a worrier like that."

He cradled her head and drew them together for a kiss. "Soon you and your family will be secure. You'll have your life back as it was before. I promise."

Cressida wanted to hit him with a large object.

Instead, she said, "Thank you," and climbed off the bed with a smile on her face. She grabbed her nightdress and pulled it on. "I'll need help to dress."

"My privilege."

She tried to frame an objection, but when she looked at him she saw she'd have to fight him over it. She didn't want to fight. He'd never lied to her. This had always been a journey of just one night.

"I'll come as soon as I'm dressed." He left the bed and pulled on his crumpled silk trousers. Lust stirred all over again as she watched him walk to the door, open it, and look out. "All clear."

The night wasn't over yet. . . .

He opened the door wider.

She pushed aside folly and walked forward. Perhaps she should say something significant at this moment, but instead she scurried through the doorway and into the safety of her own room.

How cold it seemed, how empty. The bed was smooth. Though she knew it was pointless in this house, she pulled the covers back and tousled them, and pushed an indentation into the pillow.

The washstand held only the cold water from last night. At least no one had come here and found the bed empty, but it was almost as bad. No one had come because they'd known, or at least suspected, what was going on!

She pressed her hands to her cheeks and smelled the ghost of that oil. Quickly she washed, lathering off all trace of it, but then she was plagued by the flower scent. A scent, she reminded herself, doubtless carried by dozens — hundreds! — of women in this house before.

She rinsed it off her hands, but then found she had to wash all over. She must stink of the oil, the sweat.

Of him.

She turned the key in the lock and then stripped. Why did she feel naked now, when she hadn't in the night?

Because she was racing back to propriety as in a boat on a raging river. It would eventually pour her into the pool of Dormer Close, Matlock — small, calm . . .

Stagnant crept into her mind, but she blocked this, too.

Using cloth, cold water, and soap, she cleaned every inch of her skin, trying not to let her mind remember the way he'd touched her there, and there, and there. . . .

At last it was done and she could put on her simple shift, her stockings, and her drawers. His silk robe still lay on the chest, but she couldn't bear to put it on. She'd put on her dress so he'd only have to button it — but she needed the corset underneath.

She picked it up from the chair where she'd placed it so long ago, loosened the laces some more, then wriggled into it. She settled it around herself, sturdy and secure, but if she didn't hold it up at the front, it fell down, looking ridiculous.

What was all this but ridiculous?

With the boned garment hanging, she sat at the dressing table to brush out her hair. Every long stroke reminded her of how he'd played with it, combed his fingers through it, raised it and let it fall, then brushed it off her oiled and sweaty skin.

She remembered him winding his hand in it to bind her, to hold her for deep, powerful kisses. . . .

The brush fell from her fingers, and she closed her eyes.

It wasn't fair!

A knock!

She sucked in breaths, checking in the mirror to be sure she wasn't crying. Clutching her corset up, she went smiling to open the door.

He came in fully dressed and shut it behind him, his eyes flicking over her. "I'm sure there's no alternative, but that clothing isn't designed to encourage sanity, you know."

Her mind could leap ahead of that. This bed could be well used, too, and there was no great hurry. Her mother didn't expect her back for days. . . .

But she wouldn't survive it. This had to stop or she'd run mad, as Lady Caroline Lamb had for love of the poet Byron. For the first time she had some sympathy for the disturbed lady. She could imagine sending St. Raven embarrassing letters, and haunting his doorstep dressed as a page.

She turned her back on him. "Then we had best get me dressed."

The first tug on the laces was like the first step back toward propriety. She settled the front and held it in place. "Do it up firmly."

"I think I know how to lace up a lady."

Was he deliberately reminding her of what he was? Oh, she wanted this over before she burst into tears.

"What time is it?" she asked in as ordinary a tone as she could manage.

"Nearly noon."

The cups around her breasts were snug now. She could relax her hold. "We should have pursued Mistress Coop last night."

"Nonsense. The last thing we want is to stir her curiosity. A visit in the middle of the night would be sure to do that. Even one first thing in the morning would be as bad. Cyprians, like the ton during the season, do not know what morning is."

Cressida heard an edge in his voice. Too late, she realized that her words could imply that last night had been a waste of time.

Better so.

He continued to tighten the laces with a sharp tug between each set of holes, working his way down her back, sealing her in propriety again. She adjusted her spine, straightening her shoulders, becoming completely the lady again, tug by tug.

At the waist he gave an extra pull, and she felt him tying the knot. If she cut herself out of the corset tonight she could preserve that knot. . . .

Oh, folly!

"Thank you." She stepped away and drew one

of the simple day dresses out of her valise. She shook it out, lifted it over her head, and tugged it down. She checked in the mirror that the pleated bodice was straight to the high neckline — and saw him behind her, watching her.

Caught an expression, of what?

Regret?

Her heart contracted painfully. She was Cressida Mandeville again, the woman who'd been invisible to him during the London season. Of course he regretted becoming entangled with her. He was probably worrying that she might try to use this association to intrude, even to try to force him into marriage.

She wished she could address that and set his mind at ease, but only time would prove it. She smiled at him in the mirror. "Just buttons this time."

She swept her hair up and to the front to clear the way. Now the mirror showed no sign of distress. No sign of anything. Perhaps she'd been mistaken about that expression, or perhaps he was politely hiding it. Politeness would do. Good manners could carry people through almost anything — even through his hands brushing her back as he did up the buttons.

He fixed the last button, tightening the small ruffed collar that circled her neck. It had never felt so tight before. His fingers seemed to brush her nape one unnecessary time, but she kept all reaction to herself.

"What of your hair?" he asked.

"I'll plait it." She moved away from him to sit before the mirror, and picked up the brush.

He took it from her hand. “I’m sure it’s easier for someone else to do it.”

Being a weak woman, she didn’t fight him.

She had strength enough not to watch in the mirror as he brushed her hair back and began to weave it. Who would have thought how maddening it could be to have a man’s hands in her hair?

She’d always loved having her hair brushed and arranged. It had always made her feel like a stroked cat. But not like this. Not when it was him.

She realized too late that he’d plaited it to lie down her back, not up on her head. She couldn’t bear having it done over again. She picked up the pins, pulled the plait up and coiled it on the back of her head, fixing it there.

“That doesn’t look quite right,” he said.

She rose and turned. “It will be fine under my bonnet. You can go now. I can manage the rest.”

He didn’t take the hint, and she didn’t have the nerve or heart to command him. She didn’t want him to see her putting on her false curls, but it was better so. He could see her at her foolish worst.

Her maid usually moved her false curls from headdress to headdress, but she had more than one set. In addition to the turban, she’d brought along a lacy day cap with curls. She put it on and adjusted it in the mirror. The glossy ringlets on either side of her face altered her appearance remarkably. They even made her cheeks seem rounder.

“That is absurd.”

"This is the fashion, which means you're probably correct."

As she lifted her bonnet from its box, he said, "If you want side curls, have your hair cut."

"I don't want my hair cut."

"Then have the courage of your convictions!"

She pulled out the high, silk-covered bonnet and turned on him. "It is my conviction, sir, that I'd better wear these curls as long as I'm in London, or someone might recognize St. Raven's houri!"

He winced, then rubbed a hand over his face. "You're right. I'm sorry. As long as you know you don't need those curls to be beautiful."

Her heart slipped into weakness. She pulled it back. "I have never thought that. I only began to use them because it is the fashion, and my father so wanted me to be fashionable. . . ."

Tears threatened then, when she'd been able to control them over other matters. She turned to the mirror and put the white silk bonnet on. It was quite a foot high with a deep brim caught down by pale blue ribbons to match the pale blue trimming on her dress. She tied the ribbons in a big bow beneath one ear as fashion dictated.

She returned to the valise to add the short and completely ornamental blue spencer jacket that completed this outfit, and to stuff her nightdress into it. At the last minute, she remembered her shoes and pulled the bag from the bottom.

She sat to put them on, but he went on one knee before her. "Allow me."

Short of fighting him over it, she had no choice but to let him slip the kid half-boots on her feet and tie the blue ribbons against her anklebones.

Feet. Another extraordinary sensitivity they'd explored in the night.

"What a pity that I'll never be able to tell my grandchildren that I once had the Duke of St. Raven on his knees before me."

He looked up, smiling. "Tell them. By then, I doubt anyone will be shocked. I wouldn't tell them the rest of it, though."

She realized then that she'd never be able to tell anyone the rest of it.

Still on one knee, he took her hands. "Regrets?"

A million, but they didn't outweigh the treasures. "No. You?"

He stood and pulled her to her feet. "When a lady gives a man the gift of a night like that, the word *regret* is an impossibility." He raised her hands and kissed each. "I consider the past days a wondrous gift, Cressida. Needless to say, you can call on me for any service, at any time."

Parts of her leapt at that erotic promise, but she knew he meant it in a mundane sense.

"Gloves," she said, seizing an escape.

She turned and dug in her valise again, taking longer than she needed to find the lacy summer gloves. She pulled them on as she turned back, able to look down until she was sure she could smile. "And in the unlikely event that I can be of service to you, my lord duke, I will always be available."

"Then I think I will visit you once a year to hear you call me Tris Tregallows."

She prayed he was too wise for that. "Then,

Tris Tregallows, restore me to my home, please."

He offered his arm, and like a proper lady, she placed her gloved hand upon it.

"You've forgotten something."

She turned back. "Oh, my valise."

He put her hand back on his arm. "Breakfast. It's not the end yet."

Her stomach abruptly rebelled. She couldn't sit and have breakfast with him.

"No?"

"I'm not hungry."

After a moment, he said, "I'll have something packed for you to take with you. But in that case, I have to go and call the carriage to be ready."

He considered her a moment as if he would say more, but then he turned and left the room.

Cressida stood looking at the mahogany door as if it might provide a revelation, then turned sharply away. She walked to the window to look out at the charming garden. If only Nun's Chase were the home of an ordinary man and they could live here forever. How perfect that would be.

But the man who owned this was no ordinary man. He lived clothed in his rank, but so unconsciously that he hardly knew it. He'd talked of having to work at being a duke, but she didn't think he'd had to work very hard. His father had been a duke's son, after all, and he'd spent many years as part of the Duke of Arran's household.

Truth to tell, she thought with a tender smile, the Duke of St. Raven had as much idea about ordinary life as the Regent, and it spoke in everything he did. He could walk into a shop incognito and receive instant, groveling attention.

Nun's Chase was a playground as artificial as Marie Antoinette's farm, Le Petit Trianon. As artificial as Crofton's hell. And here, she must remember, St. Raven held orgies. Events more orderly and subtle than Crofton's affair, she was sure, but at heart the same.

She'd fallen in love with Tris Tregallows, but he admitted that to be his past. His present and future was the Duke of St. Raven — great lord, great philanderer.

She turned her mind to the practicalities of her future, and started with a resolution to think of him only by his title.

How much money did the jewels represent? They weren't large, but quality mattered. Surely there had to be enough for a decent, comfortable life.

Then . . .

Then?

Then it would be up to her mother, and her father if he was able, to decide where to live, and in what state. She assumed it would be the house in Dormer Close, and that she would return there with them. She was needed, but on top of that, where else did she want to be?

In London, likely to see St. Raven at any unpredictable time?

She shuddered.

At any fashionable spot?

Ditto.

No, Matlock was safe.

As long as he didn't pursue her there.

Might he try to persuade her to become his

mistress? . . .

She licked her lips, praying he not do that. Because she wasn't sure she could resist. Perhaps she should hide. Under an assumed name . . .

She turned away from the window, shaking her head. No point in that unless she was willing to go, like Sir John Mandeville, to the ends of the earth. If the Duke of St. Raven wanted to find her, he would. She smiled wryly at the painful stab of hope that caused in her.

Her costume still lay neatly folded on a chair. Unable to resist, she took the long blue veil that had covered her hair and stuffed it into the bottom of her valise.

Last night hadn't been wise, but she wouldn't have missed it for all the jewels in India.

It was the footman, Harry, who came to tell her that the coach was ready. Cressida followed him, thinking St. Raven must be planning to say farewell in the hall. Probably better so. Less temptation than in a bedroom.

However, when she went downstairs, the hall was empty, and the door stood open to show a plain coach waiting, four horses in the shafts. She walked out, head high, fighting tears. Had that been farewell, so thoughtlessly incomplete? Had their time together meant so little to him?

She raised her chin and crossed the gravel to where a groom held the carriage door open, eager now to get away. She put her hand in that of the groom's as she mounted the steps, then froze and looked at him.

The Duke of St. Raven wore a plain jacket,

breeches, and a battered low crown hat.

He winked. "I found I need to see you safe to the end of your journey. I just heard that Le Corbeau was out last night."

"What? Isn't he in jail?"

"My adventure had its result. The magistrates let him go. The ungrateful bird took immediate flight. He's never operated in the day, but when I feel there's some connection to me, I daren't risk anything. Don't worry. I don't think anyone will recognize me."

"True enough. I only knew you by your touch."

Foolish that, but he smiled, kissed her hand, and pushed her gently into the coach. Cressida settled, the door closed, and they were off, rolling smoothly down the excellently maintained drive.

Rolling like an inexorable river home.

That had been farewell, and there was peace in it. She took comfort from knowing he was on the box, even though they would not speak again. She also noted a basket on the floor, doubtless containing the food he had promised.

Her appetite stirred. She opened it to find buns crusted with pink sugar crystals, fruit, a corked jug, and a cup and saucer. The earthenware jug contained café au lait, still almost hot. She half filled the cup so as not to spill, then picked up a bun and took a big bite.

She was certainly no fine lady. After all she'd been through, a fine lady would sicken at the thought of food. She, however, found it comforting, even though her mind was stuck on the charming, devastating, beloved, and perplexing

Tristan Tregallows, Duke of St. Raven.

She didn't understand men at all. How could he bear sharing nights like last night with a succession of women? How could he put each one out of his mind and move on to the next?

She didn't understand this man. Was he saint or sinner? They'd met when he'd been acting the highwayman — but it had been for a good cause of sorts.

He'd carried her off by force — but again, for a very good cause. When he'd leaped to her aid, he hadn't known her from Eve. They'd become friends, but he would have done it for any woman in that situation.

Yet he admitted to hosting orgies at his house and showed no shame at being an expert guide to a disgusting bacchanalia. And he had been with many women.

She looked at her half-eaten bun. Was she just another naive woman seduced out of her wits by a charming rake? After all, he'd involved himself in her quest out of idle mischief.

Growing up in a house without men — they had not even had male servants — she had never had much to do with them, certainly not in informal circumstances.

Informal! She took another bite out of the bun. A classic understatement.

She knew her inexperience made her ripe for folly, but it did feel as if they were friends. Every time an imperious blast on the horn alerted an upcoming tollgate to be ready for an important traveler, she could imagine how much he would be enjoying playing the groom.

Yet wasn't that another black mark against him? A man of his age, a man of high rank, should be more sober and responsible.

But then she remembered him talking of taking up his duties as duke. He had spent much of the summer touring his estates, and applied himself to learning about Newfoundland and cochineal.

She looked at the pink sugar crusting the last of her bun, shrugged, and popped it into her mouth. She was definitely not a lady of fine sensibilities.

A light drizzle started as they approached London, and she wondered if St. Raven was regretting his quixotic journey, especially when drizzle developed into a steady rain. It would serve her purposes, though. There would be no one on the street to see her arrive, and every excuse for hurrying into the house.

By the time the coach halted before her door, the rain was a downpour, sheeting past the windows and frothing in the puddles on the ground. Oh, poor Tris.

She waited as the boot was opened and he carried her valise to the door, slogging through puddles. At least he was wearing boots and had a cape with him, but his hat poured water around the brim.

Regrettably, Cressida had to fight the giggles.

Sally opened the door a crack, then wider to take the valise. Then she turned to get something — her father's big, black umbrella. Tris opened it and came to open the carriage door. He held out a hand while shielding the place where she would step down. Their eyes met for a moment under the concealment of the umbrella.

"Thank you," she said, meaning everything.

"Thank me later when you have the jewels. I'll dry and change and then go to Miranda's. If I need to send a message, I'll send Cary."

That was all they had time for. They hurried to the door, where Sally waited, preventing further words. But before he left he bowed slightly. "Bon voyage."

Cressida went into the house, then turned to watch as the Duke of St. Raven climbed back onto the box, and the coachman set the horses into motion to carry him out of this world and back to his own.

Good journey, she thought back at him, meaning, as she knew he had meant, the rest of their lives.

Bon voyage, my love.

Chapter Eighteen

Sally closed the door and popped the umbrella back in the elephant-foot container. "Nasty weather, miss. What a shame you had to travel in it."

"Dismal. Is my mother with my father?"

"Yes, miss."

Since they had only the one maid now, Cressida carried her own valise and hatbox up to her room, trying not to imagine the handle still warm from St. Raven's hand. In her room, she paused to take off her gloves, bonnet, and curl-trimmed cap, then went to visit her parents.

She found her father asleep and her mother knitting. Louisa Mandeville had always claimed that knitting was soothing. Since her husband's attack, she must have knitted enough shawls and mufflers for half the poor in London.

She looked up, gray eyes weary, but they brightened. "Cressida, dear! I didn't expect you back for days. Did I?" she trailed off uncertainly.

Her poor mother had always been so quick, so certain, but this whole debacle had shaken her.

"I was supposed to be away for the week. Chicken pox," she explained, kissing her mother's cheek. "Fortunately a neighbor was returning to

London and offered to convey me home. How is Father?"

"Much the same. The doctors say there's nothing wrong with him, but if there's nothing wrong with him yet, there soon will be from lying in bed so long."

She looked at the still figure in the bed, and Cressida looked, too, seeking any sign of change.

Mouth slack, her father snorted with each breath. In sleep he looked fairly normal. It was between sleep he was so strange, staring at nothing and acting as if deaf and dumb. Her mother was right about the effect of this state. His thick head of grizzled hair remained the same, but his sun-browned skin wasn't wearing well, and she knew it was a struggle to get any kind of food into him.

Her mother sighed. "I have told him and told him that I forgive him for losing all the money. I don't know what else I can do."

Cressida was sure it was the loss of the jewels that had shocked him into this state. Would their return be the key to recovery? When would she hear? Tris would hardly be at his London house yet, never mind tidied up and at Miranda Coop's.

Her mother's shoulders straightened, and she rose to lead the way out of the room and close the door. "There are times when I could slap your father," she said, sounding more like her old self. "To throw away a fortune on the folly of gaming! . . ." Hand over mouth, she stopped and inhaled.

She lowered her hand. "I have been thinking

while you were away, Cressida. It is time to make plans. Our lease on this house will soon expire, and there's no money to renew it. I have sold most of my jewelry to pay the doctor's bills and to buy food and pay Sally. We can live cheaper in Matlock, but we need money to get there. I'm not even sure if your father can travel. . . . Oh, Cressy, what are we to *do?*"

Cursing her father, Cressida squeezed her mother's hand. She didn't want to raise hopes. "An inventory," she suggested. "We need little of this fashionable stuff, so we can sell it."

And, she thought, that would explain her discovery of a cache of jewels.

"I doubt we can raise much. Most things here came with the house. When I think of all those Indian things your father scattered around Stokeley Manor. And the house!" She put her hand to her head. "I can't bear to think of it."

Cressida took her into her arms. "Then don't, Mama. Leave this to me."

To her embarrassment, tears leaked from her mother's eyes. "What would I do without you, darling? But this is so unfair. You should be enjoying parties, finding a husband."

"Not in London in August, Mama. And truly, though this has been an adventure, I will be happy to be back in Matlock."

"If we can even afford to run the house there."

Oh, dear. Her mother must have been going round and round all this for days. "We'll manage," Cressida said with as much confidence as she could find.

Her mother pulled free, smiling sadly. "You

have such a practical, enterprising nature, darling. You have it from your father, of course. Or did. I mean, he used to be so very practical. . . ." She shook her head. "I must return to him. By all means, inventory the house — once you are recovered from your journey."

Cressida watched her mother return to her vigil, then wandered back to her own room, fending off assorted thoughts about the nature of love and loving responsibility. She'd always assumed that a happy marriage required complete approval.

Did her mother love her father, even in the face of his appalling behavior, or was the bond simply duty? Louisa Mandeville had shown no sign of missing her husband over twenty-two years, but she had accepted him back with apparent pleasure. In the past year, they had seemed a happy couple.

Her mother was angry with her father now, she saw how foolish he had been, and yet she still seemed devoted. Cressida sighed. It was too complex a situation for her troubled mind.

She unpacked her valise, finding at the bottom Roxelana's blue head veil. She didn't regret bringing it, but as she wrapped it idly around her hand, she recognized a disturbing link. It was like a ribbon stretched from here to there when a clean break would be much better.

It was over. Or would be once Tris . . . Once the Duke of St. Raven retrieved the jewels from Miranda Coop. Would he be able to open the statue quickly if he had the chance?

Oh! If she'd thought, she could have brought

him into the house to practice on the one here. . . .

No. The Duke of St. Raven could never come here. The servants would speculate. Nor could a rain-drenched groom be taken to her father's study. But she could have given the statuette to him. Why couldn't she have thought of that in time?

Her recent life seemed to be a dreary parade of if-onlys and what-ifs, and not a one of them was a pennyworth of good. The past could not be changed.

The future, however, could.

She could send the statue to him. She hissed with frustration. The same problems applied. How could she explain sending something to the Duke of St. Raven, and through pouring rain? Nothing, nothing, could connect them.

She suddenly realized how true that was.

No one from Stokeley Manor was going to wonder if St. Raven's houri had been that dull Miss Mandeville, the nabob's daughter. Even the fact that Stokeley had been her father's house, and those statues her father's possessions would not stir the notion.

If the idea were forced to anyone's attention, however, it was a different matter. Her protection from ruin was the complete impossibility of it, the total lack of contact between them.

She acknowledged the fierce pain of that prospect, but it made no real difference. Their worlds did not connect.

She turned her mind to the practical. By now he might be dressed and on his way to Miranda

Coop. She looked out and saw that the rain had lightened. It had been a summer storm. He need not get wet. Perhaps an hour?

She'd go mad waiting, so she started the task she'd set for herself — the inventory of their salable possessions. She began in the dining room. The silver epergne with tigers gave her hope. That was theirs, as was the china. Perhaps there was enough here for survival, at least, even without the jewels. . . .

Tris drove up to Miranda Coop's house with reluctance, even resentment. Damn Cressida Mandeville for making this necessary. Damn the woman for the whole affair, for forcing him into Crofton's company, for putting herself in danger, for laughing gray eyes and luscious curves and insane curiosity, and courage, and spirit, and will. . . .

Ah, hell.

The rain had forced him to travel here in the coach, so a real groom came to open the door. He stepped down and glared at the green lacquered door. Then he smoothed his expression and went to knock. He'd sent a note to ask if Miranda would receive him, never doubting the answer. Her reply had come back swiftly and predictably, but at least on elegant cream paper, not perfumed.

This house was better than he'd expected, as well. On the fringes of fashion, but in a new terrace, quiet and well maintained. Miranda was one of the top courtesans in London, but it would appear she knew how to be discreet.

She was a lover in great demand who refused

to be set up by any one man as a mistress yet charged exorbitant rates for her favors. He wondered what Crofton had paid to get her to attend his affair. He also wondered why she had served Crofton for a statuette that would probably not bring fifty guineas at auction.

Too many unknowns and improbabilities for comfort.

The door was opened by a stone-faced middle-aged maid, and in moments he was with La Coop. He gave her the courtesy of a bow.

"A delight to encounter you again last night, Miranda."

She inclined her head. "Please, Your Grace, be seated."

She settled gracefully onto a sofa, leaving the choice of seating to him.

He chose a chair facing her while doing rapid assessments. Miranda Coop had a number of guises. At riotous events she could be wild, but at the opera or other such public functions, she could appear a lady, if a painted lady. At home it would seem she chose to be an epitome of propriety.

Her olive green dress was the height of fashion and showed off her lush charms, but it could have been worn by Princess Charlotte. She was painted, but with discretion. Her only flaw was a hint of a Cockney accent.

"A surprise to see you at Crofton's, St. Raven. I thought you and he were at odds. *I* was well paid. . . ."

He smiled at the subtle question. "My little houri insisted."

"Ah. Then I hope she paid you well? Forgive me, but she seemed a little . . . unskilled."

"*Innocent,* I believe, is the word."

Her eyes twinkled. "How novel for you. No longer, I assume."

The truth of that hit him, and he kept his smile in place with an effort. "No longer," he agreed, revolted to be speaking of Cressida with this woman. But he must. For Cressida.

"Therein lies this visit, Miranda. My Turkish delight took a great fancy to one of those statuettes at Crofton's. When I went to buy it from him, it appeared you had already . . . won it."

"Paid for it," she corrected. "And paid quite dearly."

That said something about Crofton, coming from a whore. It made Tris worry even more about why she'd wanted it. She couldn't possibly know.

"I see. I, of course, am willing to pay you what you think the item is worth — within reason. You know, none better, how men are in their first flush of ardor. My houri wishes this little gift. I must do my best to obtain it."

She cocked her head. "I have no great need of money, Your Grace."

"Then you're a damn unusual whore."

He was deliberately rude but saw no flinch.

"Yes, I am. I am no man's property because my appetite is too great for any one man. And," she added, her eyes traveling over him, "I like variety."

Even as parts of Tris's body reacted to a message in her knowing eyes, he knew that he didn't want to bed this woman. No, that wasn't strong enough. He was revolted at the thought of bedding this woman. Which surprised him.

He drew on every scrap of control he possessed not to show it. "Which does make you a whore," he pointed out.

"Then what does it make you, Your Grace?"

He was on his feet by reflex. "You are impertinent."

She looked up at him, eyes laughing but hot. She wanted him. He felt it, and his skin crawled.

"You do not charge," she said. "That is true. But you are, at the least, promiscuous."

Damnation. The woman's impudence had pushed this to an edge. If he didn't react the right way, she'd know there was something important about that statue.

"You cannot possibly be suggesting that I turn whore with a whore. Sell my body to you for a piece of carved ivory?"

Her expression became watchful. "You requested this meeting, Your Grace."

"To humor a bint's whim." He turned and walked away. "No more. Good day."

"Your Grace!"

He paused at the door and turned back, blanking out any sign of hope. She was standing, not looking at all nervous, but watchful.

"I appear to have made a mistake, Your Grace. I assumed I knew what you wanted. Men do," she added wryly. "Want. Almost invariably. Any question of barter was mere amusement."

His heart was beating as if before a crucial roll

of the dice. "Then may we discuss monetary payment?"

She considered him. "I really do not need money, Your Grace. You find me here in London in August, when the *haute volée* have flown elsewhere, simply to rest. The Crofton affair" — she shrugged — "it was a diversion. I do enjoy raw crudity now and then, and I wondered just how far he would go."

"Unless you will take money, madam, and a reasonable sum of money, you are wasting my time."

"Even if the price is merely that you escort me to Sir James Finsbury's house party next weekend at Richmond?"

"You lack an escort?" he asked, assessing this new move. He had to confess that though he wanted nothing to do with Miranda Coop in bed, she was an interesting opponent.

Finsbury was a friend, and he had an invitation to the party. On the surface, it would be mildly respectable, but the company would be a combination of racy couples and men with their whores.

"Of course not, Your Grace." She cocked her head. "I think perhaps you do not understand the essentials of my trade. All, *all,* is reputation. In matters physical" — she dismissed that with an idle hand — "my reputation is well established. In other ways, it requires constant attention.

"You, my lord duke, are the prize of the world. Every virtuous maiden desires to wed you. Every wicked woman lusts to be the object of your admiration. If I arrive at Sir James's house on your arm, my cachet rises many rungs up the ladder."

"I thought you were already at the top."

"How kind. But in these things there is no top, is there? And there are always so many climbing hard below."

"I'm sure you know how to stamp on fingers."

She laughed, seeming genuinely amused. "Most unwise, wouldn't you say? Even Miranda Coop will one day outlive her charms. I intend to have plenty of money for my retirement, Your Grace, but friends will be useful, too. So, does my proposition offend you? I assume you plan to attend, and I'm sure I need not say that my body is not included in this bargain. For that, Your Grace, you must pay, and pay high. It would never do for it to get out that I had to pay for a man."

He laughed at the sheer impudence of the woman. "Why did you get that statue from Crofton?"

She regarded him, then smiled. "Because you tried to buy it, which showed that your little houri was taken with it. I *do* know the ways of men in their first ardor, and I hoped for this visit. There, that's the plain truth."

And it probably was. He silently cursed the action that had led to this, but it wasn't too bad. He hated having his hand forced, but to escort Miranda to Finsbury's would be bearable. The danger here was that she suspect some importance in the statue. How would he react if his story were true?

"I intended to take Roxelana to Finsbury's."

She simply waited. If she gambled, she was doubtless excellent at it.

"Very well. It will teach the girl not to be so demanding, and by the weekend I might welcome a break from her. However, I promise nothing but that we arrive together. I may leave shortly after if I wish."

"I don't think that would do my reputation any good at all, Your Grace."

He made himself smile. "Your audacity is amusing, Miranda, but don't test my tolerance. Very well. I will stay at least one night."

How should he behave? How? By demanding more.

He let his eyes assess her charms. "It might be worth your while to make your skills available to me gratis. I might become besotted. That should crown you queen."

Her lids lowered, though she was still looking at him. Despite himself, his body reacted just to that.

"A consideration." She ran her tongue along the inner edge of her upper lip, smiling. "We shall see, shan't we, Your Grace."

She was playing him like a fish, damn her. He matched her smile. "Apparently we will. Now, the statue?"

Her eyes widened — with shock? "I will give it to you at the weekend, Your Grace."

"You dare to doubt my word?"

If there'd been shock, it had been shielded so quickly he couldn't be sure. Now she looked hard, and her age. "I'm a whore, Your Grace. Men do not seem to consider their word binding to me."

Tris remembered Cressida's astonishment and pleasure at being asked for her word and having it believed. It touched him when he needed to be untouchable. What now? He could push for the statue, but he shouldn't seem to care so much.

He shrugged. "As you wish. It will do the girl no harm to wait. Five o'clock on Friday?"

She dropped a graceful curtsy. "You are all kindness, Your Grace."

Tris bowed and left, and didn't allow himself to suck in the deep breath he needed until he was back in the coach. Damn the woman's bloody impudence!

Should he have told her to go to hell? Had he convinced her that this was a whim rather than a necessity? Mistakes, mistakes. He'd made a whole string of mistakes. Was this another one?

What's more, his pride rebelled at being used like this.

Bought!

Almost as bad as being a whore.

Perhaps, he thought, stretching his legs, it was time for a little larceny.

Miranda Coop let out a breath. Now, why had she done that?

Because she wanted the glory of having the Duke of St. Raven on her arm in front of her rivals. American Indians apparently displayed the scalps of defeated enemies on a spear to prove their prowess. She wanted St. Raven's escort on her spear. That alone would be enough, but given the chance, perhaps she could have him at her feet, as well. Or rather, in her bed.

"One of these days," she said to the empty room, "your impulses will get you into trouble, Miranda." And that day could be soon if she didn't get that bloody statue back!

She could find Crofton and get one of the others. But he'd probably given them away as prizes as he'd planned. So she'd have to find out who'd won them, and who'd won the ones that looked the same.

It could take forever, and she couldn't be sure St. Raven and his Turkish bint wouldn't spot the difference. She blew out a breath and paced the room.

There was only one sure way. She had to find Le Corbeau and get that statue from him. Getting it shouldn't be difficult if she could only find the man. Half London was trying to catch him.

Then she paused. She knew someone who could be of use. Peter Spike of St. Albans. Ostensibly he was a prosperous merchant, but he also dealt in stolen property on the side.

She sat down to write him a letter, then sent Mary with it to the post office. For what she'd promised, Peter would find Le Corbeau for her. She laughed dryly. For what she'd promised, he'd find the devil himself.

Chapter Nineteen

"Ho, Tris!"

Tris winced. The rain had stopped, so he'd abandoned the coach to walk home. Now he was paid for such eccentricity by an encounter with Lord Uffham, heir to the Duke of Arran.

Uffham was a handsome, robust, but increasingly tiresome fellow. Tris suppressed another wince at the sight of a virulent green waistcoat and so many fobs that his foster brother jangled as he strode over. It reminded him distressingly of Gilchrist's bells.

Tris had enjoyed some good times with Uffham in his youth, but their differing tastes and natures became more obvious every day. In addition, Uffham seemed put out that Tris was now a duke, whereas he must wait until his healthy father died.

Tris thought Uffham should count his blessings and enjoy his freedom. What's more, he admired the Duke of Arran and didn't think Uffham ready to administer such great responsibilities. He was finding his own duties a strain, and he knew he was more ahead of the game than poor old Uffham would ever be.

"Didn't know you was in town," Uffham said. "Been in a fight?"

Tris had forgotten his bruises. "A minor disagreement."

"On your way to White's?"

"On my way home." There was no way to avoid it. "Care to come along? I dashed up to town today and scarcely broke my fast. I intend to eat."

"I'm game." Uffham fell into step, swinging a gold-topped cane. "Emergency?"

"Paperwork. What brings you here in the summer?"

"Invitation to a saucy do at Crofton's. Misread it. Thought it was at his London house. Fellow should make things like that clearer."

Tris didn't remember the invitation being particularly obscure. "It was not a well-run affair."

"No? When are you going to have another prancing party at Nun's Chase?"

Tris was astonished by an impulse to say, *Never.* "Not for a while." They turned into Upper Jasper Street. "Summer, after all."

"Summer's just the time for a house party. Everyone's drifting about with nothing to do."

"Speak for yourself. Or be grateful you don't have a dukedom to run yet." He planted the seed deliberately.

Uffham shrugged and followed Tris into the dark-paneled hall of the St. Raven town house. "Bit gloomy, this. Should have it painted."

Tris handed his hat and gloves to a studiously impassive footman. "Interior decoration? You'll be falling into the parson's mousetrap next."

That was enough to turn Uffham's eyes wide with panic. "Don't even say that! The ball-bitches are even worse this year. I think you've set 'em off. That and Arden marrying that damn governess. Now any of 'em thinks they have a chance!"

"Arden married a governess?" Tris absorbed that as he gave instructions for simple but substantial food. The Marquess of Arden was heir to the Duke of Belcraven, and if he'd married a woman of low birth without disaster . . .

Tris led the way up to the small drawing room he'd made his own.

"Talk of the town a year or so ago," Uffham said. "Suppose it was about the time you inherited and went abroad. Just hatched a son, so I suppose that's something to be said for peasant stock."

"Peasant?" Tris queried as they entered the room, which was furnished with comfortable chairs and plenty of books. Arden was an arrogant bastard, as high in the instep as they came.

Uffham had grace enough to blush. "Not exactly. Daughter of a sea captain or such, but no money. Employed at a ladies' seminary in Cheltenham! Not much to look at, either. Turned his back on the Swinamer filly for that."

"That, at least, shows some sense."

At Uffham's blank look, Tris decided to try to plant another seed. Phoebe Swinamer was exquisitely beautiful if one cared for china dolls. And as heartless as one. Uffham's marriage to her would cut up the peace of the whole Peckworth family.

"Miss Swinamer is an ice queen in pursuit of a coronet, preferably a ducal one. Any man who marries her will feel her claws all his life. She's coquetted around me, but I know that if I were plain Mr. Tregallows she wouldn't spare me a smile. Nor would she notice you if you were plain George Peckworth."

Uffham pouted, looking like a child who'd been forbidden a sugared treat, but perhaps that meant the words had sunk home. Tris decided to add to it.

"Men like us," he said, settling into his favorite chair, "need to choose a wife with care. It's demanding work being a duchess, so she needs to be raised to it, and be robust and intelligent."

"Like a good hunter."

Tris managed not to roll his eyes. "Quite. On the other hand, high rank tempts some people to arrogance and cruelty. We owe it to our family and our dependents to choose a duchess with a kind heart. And of course, with Devonshire as an example, one who can be depended upon not to game away our fortune."

Uffham dropped into the opposite chair, legs sprawled out. "You're turning into a prosy bore, Tris. I suppose there's always a tasty mistress for the other."

"Exactly." If that was the way to get Uffham to take a comfortable wife into the Peckworth household, so be it.

"It's what m' father did in his younger days. M' mother didn't kick up a fuss. That's what you mean about a duchess being raised to it, I suppose."

"My uncle had three that I know of. One for Cornwall, one for London, and one for France before the Revolution."

Uffham laughed. "As bad as a sailor, with a whore in every port! Not a bad idea, though."

Tris suddenly regretted this whole conversation. Would this be any better for the Peckworths than Phoebe Swinamer as duchess?

Yes, sadly, it would. Infidelity would be preferable to a cold, heartless woman ruling over them.

He had no intention of marrying a cold, heartless woman, but he'd always assumed he'd marry one who was suitable rather than delightful, and keep mistresses for pleasure. It was part of the way he'd been trained to be duke.

The Duke of Arran had started the process, and his uncle had coldly continued it. He'd been taught to drink without passing out, game without getting fleeced, and rut without getting the pox or too many bothersome bastards — and to do so without embarrassing decent women.

And, of course, to always remember that a duke ranked only a couple of steps below God, and everyone had damn well better remember it.

He hoped his uncle was rolling in his ornate vault.

The footman arrived with a tray laden with beer, bread, cheese, pickles, and pies. Tris thanked him.

Uffham grabbed a wedge of pork pie and a tankard of ale and half of each disappeared with a slurp. "Wish I had a place of my own. Could get food like this, then, instead of the fiddly stuff m' mother's chef turns out."

"Order what you want."

"It's all right for you. . . ."

Tris took a bite of crusty bread and ripe cheese and let Uffham ramble through his complaints. That was Uffham's line these days — that he was hard-done-to.

"So why are you here?" Uffham asked, swabbing his mouth with a napkin, then belching.

"Some routine business. My secretary is here."

"Can't be much to do in summer."

"The work never stops, I assure you. Where will you be off to next?"

"Thought I'd pop down to Lea Park. Haven't seen the parents in a while. Then nip down to Brighton. Caroline and Anne are there, you know."

Tris drank more beer to hide his expression. Uffham's sister Lady Anne was not, in fact, in Brighton. With Tris's aid, Anne was on her way to Gretna Green with an upstart her family would not think suitable.

She could end up cut off from her family for life. At the moment of decision, with love shining between the two of them, it had seemed a worthwhile risk. But if that was the case, why had he not fought to win Cressida?

"Why don't you come?" Uffham asked.

Tris had to pick up the thread of the conversation. "I don't care for Brighton."

"You could come to Lea Park."

"My business will keep me here a few days. Perhaps later."

Anne was prepared for loss and scandal, and thought it all worthwhile. Could he and Cressida be the same?

But no. Unlike Anne and Race, he and his

duchess would never live far from the world's attention.

"I'll be back in town on the weekend," Uffham said. "Do at Finsbury's down in Richmond. You'll have an invitation."

"I haven't checked. I may be gone by then."

Uffham refilled his tankard. "Dining with Berresford tonight, then we're off to Violet Vane's. They say she's some new tender morsels. Care to come?"

Tris almost shuddered. *Poudre de Violettes* and giggling girls. He'd always avoided the woman's place, but now he wondered about her business. She specialized in young-looking whores, but just how young were they?

Lord above, London was awash with abandoned, feral children willing to do anything for a penny. If they didn't thieve or whore, they'd starve. Trying to change that would be like trying to make the Thames flow upstream.

Tris rose, hoping Uffham would take the hint. "I was at Crofton's until the early hours. Tonight I need to sleep."

"Were you, by gad! What was it like?"

His earlier comment had clearly passed Uffham by. He worried about the dukedom of Arran, indeed he did. However, he obliged with a lascivious description that had Uffham drooling.

Of course, he didn't mention Cressida. How was she? Had her return been accepted without question? Damn. She would be waiting for news, and he here was nattering with Uffham!

"Naughty statues, eh?" chortled Uffham. "Wonder who won 'em. Wouldn't mind a peep."

"I'm sure if you ask around, you can find out. Pugh was there, and Tiverton. Hopewell, Gilchrist, Bayne . . ." Tris moved toward the door. "Now I must go to my taskmaster. Leatherhulme insists that I actually read documents before signing them."

"Good God! Sack him."

"The thought has crossed my mind." Tris steered his foster brother down the stairs, and out of the house, his mind already turning to Cressida's cause.

He'd told Uffham he was exhausted, but at the thought of her, arousal stirred. Arousal focused only on her, on her soft, sweet curves, her long silky hair, her wide gray eyes, her full, luscious lips, her clever hands, her frank enthusiasm.

They'd only started their exploration. . . .

He realized he was standing before the door, and the footman was surreptitiously eyeing him.

Cressida. Waiting for news!

"Find Mr. Lyne, and send him to my study."

Damn the fact that he couldn't go to her himself. He went upstairs, realizing with every step how completely impossible he had made any further connection.

Crofton was stupid in some ways, but not that stupid. Miss Mandeville had been snatched by Le Corbeau. Crofton wouldn't cause talk over it because that would expose his disgusting blackmail of her. He probably assumed she'd been ravished, however.

If talk started about the Duke of St. Raven and the same Miss Mandeville, he'd have to speculate. He'd probably assume — wrongly — that

Tris was Le Corbeau. He'd also realize that she'd been the houri. The disguise had been good, but not good enough.

It would all be a damned mess, and not even one to be solved by marriage. Bad enough to thrust a woman like her onto the cruel, exposed pinnacle of society. Impossible with scandal like that attached.

He was staring into nowhere when Cary came in. "Trouble?"

Tris laughed. "An eel-bed of it. I'm just realizing how deep a toil we're in here, with Miss Mandeville the one most at risk."

"Gossip's started?"

"No, but . . ."

Tris outlined his thoughts. Perhaps he'd hoped to have the problems argued away, but he saw Cary accept everything as seriously as he did.

"She'd never have a chance at a decent life," Cary said. "It wasn't . . ."

"Wise. Dammit, I know. And I could have gone after her damn statue by myself." Tris raked a hand through his hair. "What's done is done. Now we have to take care of her. I can't be seen near her, but you should be safe enough. I won't risk a note."

He recounted his visit to La Coop's house.

Cary grinned. "That's a fine, bold sort of woman for you."

"If you want her, have her."

"No, thank you. We're not going to let her get away with it, are we?"

Tris matched his smile. "Of course not. I hope you're skilled in housebreaking."

"No, but I'm ready to learn. Could lead to more trouble, though."

"Dammit, I know. I'm thinking it's time to settle down. Perhaps I'm getting old."

"Bite your tongue. You're a year younger than I am! Perhaps we've just run through our wild oats. It's been a deep sack of them, but every sack must empty in the end."

"So what do we do now? Starve in the wilderness?" But Tris shook his head at his own question. "I'll be going on about bitter bread soon, and eating locusts. Which is almost as bad as cochineal."

"What?"

Tris laughed. "Go to Miss Mandeville. Assure her that she'll have her jewels within the week. My word on it."

Cary gave an ironic salute and left.

Tris knew he should go to Leatherhulme, but after his friend left, he lingered. Never to see her again. That's what it came down to. He'd expected that, hadn't he? So why did it seem so bleak a sentence now?

"What a pity that I'll never be able to tell my grandchildren that I once had the Duke of St. Raven on his knees before me."

Grandchildren. That meant marriage to some other man. Some other man stroking her to pleasure, being driven to ecstasy by her. He put a hand in his pocket and pulled out the scrap of white veiling stained with red from her lips. When he brought it to his face, a soft perfume rose from it.

He clenched his fist on it and broke free of

thoughts that could drive him mad. But, God, were they doomed to travel the rest of their lives in different lands?

Not doomed. Not her, at least. She would soon be back in the world she found comfortable, and surely she had sense enough to marry the right sort of man. She would live a comfortable life, wife to a prosperous professional man, or perhaps to a gentleman with a small, cozy estate. She would be a bustling, energetic wife and mother, a blessing to any community. . . .

As for himself . . . He stuffed the silk back in his pocket. As the Duchess of Arran said, it only took resolution to form an attachment with the right person.

Cressida duly noted each book in her father's library. He was not a great reader, and most of his books were to do with business. Directories of cities, merchants, banks, stocks, ports, ships . . .

She knew such things would have little value, but this mechanical recording blessedly numbed her mind.

Travel books. Some about India, but mostly of other places. China, Japan, Mongolia, Russia . . . Did her father still dream of travel to yet stranger lands?

No copy of the travels of Sir John Mandeville here, but he'd sent her one on her tenth birthday. There had always been letters and occasional gifts, and of course the money they lived on. But he'd been as real to her as the Faerie Queen.

Why had he come home to spoil everything?

Then she came to the same book on Arabia

that St. Raven had lent her, and couldn't help taking it down to flutter through the pages.

Where was he now? Had he returned from Miranda Coop's yet? When would she hear? The sensible parts of her mind were anxious for that, but the deeper parts could hardly care, because she knew he would not, could not, bring the news.

What point to a handful of jewels, if not — ?

Oh, folly! She snapped the book shut and shoved it back on the shelf. But the next one was a directory of London. St. Raven's address would be in there. It seemed positively unnatural that she not know his address. . . .

Almost against her will, she took down the plain-bound book. Did it list houses by proprietor? No, by address and by trade. She laughed. They would hardly list him under "Peers of the Realm" would they? She checked, but of course not. Between "Pastry Cooks" and "Pepper and Spice Merchants"?

But when she riffled through, she realized that it started with a section on the homes of the great.

The first page entry, of course, was the king. His Royal Majesty King George. The listings continued through the royal family and the members of the cabinet. She flipped along, but didn't have to go far to find it.

His Grace, the Duke of St. Raven, 5 Upper Jasper Street.

Even that was enough to set her heart speeding.

Another book. A map book, with sheets that

unfolded to show various parts of London in fine detail. She spread it on the desk and consulted the index.

Upper Jasper Street. There it was, close to St. James's, each house delineated by an outline with the number neatly penned inside.

The meticulous mapmaker had even drawn the garden behind the house, implying a central flower bed, though whether he could have known that, she didn't know. The house had an extension at the back that was only half the width of the main part. A scullery below, but what above? A small bedroom? A box room?

As she concentrated on these details, it almost seemed that if she found a magnifying glass, she would be able to see the actual house. With a strong enough glass, perhaps she could look in windows, perhaps even see him. . . .

She pulled back and quickly, clumsily, refolded the map and put the book back on the shelf. There was nothing there for her but inked lines.

Chapter Twenty

Tris went downstairs and toward the back of the house, where the offices lay. In the outer room three clerks rose from their desks to bow. "Your Grace."

Tris smiled and turned to his senior clerk. "Good afternoon, Bigelow. All's well with my dominion, I assume."

The man, who was a merry sort when he let down his guard, winked. "I believe so, Your Grace."

Tris nodded and went into the inner sanctum, where Mr. Nigel Leatherhulme ruled. Leatherhulme, pale, scrawny, and with thick spectacles, must be seventy if he was a day, but his mind was as sharp as Tris's own, and his knowledge and experience far deeper. The man had terrified Tris when they'd first met. By now Tris could hold his own, but that was about it.

"Your Grace."

Leatherhulme began to rise, but Tris waved him back to his seat. The brain was holding up, but the body wasn't, which was why the man now lived here. His wife had been dead twenty years or more, and his children were practically pensioners themselves. Tris had thought it ridiculous that Leatherhulme was traveling a mile every day to this office when there were empty rooms available.

Leatherhulme had not completely approved, but eventually he had accepted the offer — but only after Tris had agreed to deduct a version of room and board from his wages.

In making the offer, Tris had not thought how difficult it would be to replace the man when he lived here, but he was going to have to in order to bring about change. Another rash mistake.

He pulled up a chair to the side of the desk and passed over the pouch of documents. "Here I am. Tell me where else to sign."

Leatherhulme's thin lips tightened almost to a hole. "Either you will read the documents, Your Grace, or I will summon Bigelow to read them to you."

Tris was aware of playing a game — like a dog fighting over a bone. "If I sit and look at them, how will you know if I am reading them?"

"You are sensible enough, Your Grace, not to waste your time like that. In fact," Leatherhulme said, looking over the top of his spectacles, "I am beginning to suspect that if I tried to prevent you from reading what you sign, I might have a fight on my hands."

Tris leaned back in his chair. "You see, you made assumptions."

"Your uncle had no high opinion of you, sir."

"You think better of me now?"

"I would think more highly of you, Your Grace, if you had not arrived here playing the groom."

"Gossiping, Leatherhulme?"

The man stiffened as much as his curved spine

would allow. "Sometimes one cannot help hearing things, sir, especially when all the domestics are gossiping."

"Honor of a Tregallows, I was engaged in a good deed."

The old man sighed. "You are very like your father, sir."

It was the first time Leatherhulme had mentioned his father, and Tris was tempted to ask for more. It was too sensitive to rush into, however.

"Another black mark against me?" he said lightly. "Very well, push over the first document."

Tris started on accounts from various estates, signing or initialing them once he understood them, asking questions when he didn't. For the first time he felt a sort of partnership here, and he began to think it a shame that Leatherhulme would have to go.

He would, though.

The man sat ready with the ducal seal and sealing wax to apply it to the appropriate documents, always precisely centered in the wax. The sharp smell of hot wax mixed with the dust of old documents and a faint, aged lavender smell from the wrinkled man. There was something unfortunately tomblike about this room.

Tris moved on to a request for improvements at an estate in Northumberland, reviewing the costs against income, present and anticipated, keeping in mind the overall income of the dukedom in these hard times.

"Can this be sold?"

"That is part of your family's original holdings, Your Grace."

He was in hot water now. "Yet far from any other property. I see no sense in clinging to the past when the money could be put to use elsewhere."

"There are always economies, Your Grace."

"Dammit, Leatherhulme, how much tighter do you want the belt? I'm not cutting staff when it's so hard to find positions these days. And I'm not," he added, "selling any of my horses. I deserve some pleasures."

"Undoubtedly, sir." Leatherhulme took the document. "I will let it be known that the property might be available. But it would be unwise to sell beneath its value."

"Of course." The old man hadn't mentioned Nun's Chase and women, which were an expense, but not enough to break a duchy, unlike his uncle's avid collecting of Italian paintings. Which, alas, would now fetch a fraction of what he'd paid.

He took the next document, thinking that a rich wife would undoubtedly be a blessing.

He thought of Phoebe Swinamer, who brought a handsome dowry as well as her cold beauty, and shuddered. A Mary Begbie had been trolled through the season by Lady Trent — plain, dull, but heiress to a wealthy West Indies merchant. He'd vaguely considered her, with the idea of a mistress to make life bearable.

He wondered why he hadn't noticed Cressida Mandeville, daughter of an East Indies nabob. Her father had probably not been as rich as Begbie, and perhaps they had been too refined — or too ignorant — to hire a needy or greedy aristocrat to dangle her before the highest-bred noses. He did find it astonishing that he had been in the same room with Cressida a number of times and not been aware of it.

Leatherhulme cleared his throat, and Tris realized he'd been staring at the same page too long. He put it down. "Why am I suing a convent? It seems sacrilegious."

"A convent can also be a landowner, sir. You are suing them because their estate has encroached upon your land in Berresby Studely. They cite boundaries that go back before the Reformation, but it is a Catholic convent removed here because of the turmoil in France, so they do not even have history on their side."

"Lying nuns?"

"It would be a mistake to assume virtue merely because of religious vows."

"Would it, indeed?" Tris asked with a grin. "Bring on the nuns, then."

"Your Grace . . ."

But was that a hint of a twinkle in the faded eyes?

"Are you sure I can't tempt you to Nun's Chase, Leatherhulme? I could arrange delights especially for you. A mature mother superior . . ."

"Your Grace!"

The exchange gave Tris courage. He put down the documents.

"Leatherhulme, I need to talk to you about your position." He thought he saw a flash of alarm and raised his hand. "On my honor, you have your place here as long as you want it, and your home here, too. With my gratitude. But I think it is time to hire an assistant for you."

"I require no assistant, Your Grace, other than suitable clerks."

"Then I must be selfish. I require that you have an assistant, and for two reasons. One, I need someone able to travel around the estates, to travel posthaste to deal with an emergency. I do not like leaving matters so completely in the hands of inadequately supervised local employees. Two, when you do decide to rest, I want someone ready to take on your burden, someone who already knows my affairs."

For a fleeting moment, Leatherhulme's expression was like Uffham's pout, but then he glared at Tris. "You are a surprise to me, Your Grace."

"You were hoping for an idle nodcock?"

"Not idle, no . . ." Leatherhulme took off his glasses and rubbed the marks on either side of his nose. "Your uncle gave me complete control, and I confess I have become accustomed. What you say, however, is judicious and wise. If I have clung to the reins, it is — forgive me — because I have not held a high opinion of the morals and judgment of your predecessors."

"Good God. You served under my grandfather, too?"

"And your great-grandfather, though he died shortly after I joined his service — as assistant to his aging secretary."

Tris laughed. "At least they had the wisdom to hire and keep good servants."

Leatherhulme nodded in acknowledgment of the compliment. "I assume you wish to hire my assistant yourself?"

"Yes, but I'll give you a veto. It will not serve if you take each other in dislike."

"Very well, sir."

Sixty years in the family's service. Gad!

Tris glanced again over the explanation of the case of the Duke of St. Raven versus the Sisters of Divine Purity. In the end, he authorized it, feeling that a lightning bolt should shoot down to fry him.

He pushed the final paper back across the desk and accepted the heavy summary account book for his perusal at leisure. He'd never had a tutor as exacting as Leatherhulme. Which gave him a mischievous thought.

"I wonder if you have any advice about brides, Leatherhulme."

"I sincerely hope you mean that in the singular, Your Grace."

Tris smiled. "Certainly at a time. And if I marry, I hope never to wish my wife dead."

"In my opinion, sir, there is no *if*. You are the last of a long and noble line."

"Of whom you have not held too high an opinion."

The thin lips tightened in what might even have been a suppressed smile. "I have hopes for the future, sir. As for advice, I recommend that you choose a sensible woman who will be a good companion and helpmeet. To a young man that doubtless sounds dull, but the fires of love often burn down, and the fires of — your pardon, sir — lust always do."

"I promise not to marry out of lust. One of the benefits of my rakish lifestyle is that I have no need to."

He didn't know what reaction he'd expected, but it wasn't a sober nod. "An excellent point. I have observed some straitlaced young gentlemen who fell into that trap."

Tris couldn't believe he was having this conversation, but he leaned back in his chair. "Do you have any suggestions?"

"I do not study the social registers, sir."

"But should I go for birth, wealth, or helpmeet?"

"All three."

" 'Struth! Plums like that don't hang on every tree."

"But they hang on plum trees in season, sir. Have you been looking in the right orchards?"

Tris laughed and stood. "Damn you, man, you're right. Perhaps I should go to Brighton and peer more closely at the fruit. But I have business here first."

"Business?" Leatherhulme queried in obvious alarm.

"Nothing in your sphere. More like Nun's Chase business."

"I see." Leatherhulme replaced his spectacles, becoming the withered dry stick Tris was accustomed to. "That will be all, Your Grace?"

Despite the query, it sounded like dismissal.

"It will." But Tris added, "Thank you."

He left feeling strangely lightened, even though he was sure that Leatherhulme's advice would be against a penniless bride of ordinary birth and training.

The old man had no need to worry. It could never be.

Was Cary back yet?

An inquiry turned up no evidence of it. Tris tossed the account book on a chair and paced his room.

London, even in August, was ripe with amusements designed to wipe foolish attachments from a young man's mind, but he ran through them and found nothing that appealed.

He picked up the book and sat to go through it. As for the evening, he found himself looking forward to a plain dinner and an early night.

It wasn't that he was becoming a dull dog, he assured himself. It was simply that he'd need a clear head if he was going to get that statuette from Miranda Coop without obeying the woman like a dog on a leash.

A growling stomach alerted Cressida to the fact that it was a long time since her picnic breakfast, and a body must eat. She went to the kitchen to beg kindness from the cook, who cheerfully cut a slice from a pie and arranged some fruit on a plate.

"If you'll pardon the suggestion, miss, why don't you sit down here with Sally, Sam, and me and have some tea? We're about to, and it must be lonely for you upstairs."

Cressida accepted, though she worried that the servants wanted to question her about their futures. They chattered among themselves, however, about their families and other servants. Cressida sat there, drinking tea out of a plain cup, relaxing in this very ordinary world. Even in Matlock, she'd not taken tea in the kitchen.

Then they started on a scandal. According to the Onslows' maid — met just this morning when filling jugs from the milkmaid's pails — Miss Onslow was growing plump. Not surprising that there was to be a hasty marriage to a Lieutenant Brassingham, who wasn't what the family had hoped for when they'd brought the young lady to town. And what's more, according to Miss Onslow's maid, he was not likely to be the responsible party. . . .

Poor Miss Onslow. Cressida sipped her tea, finding it all too easy to imagine her scandalous story trickling all over London over pails of milk and baskets of bread.

That Miss Mandeville. Rumor says she was at a gentlemen's party in a wicked costume. And according to her kitchen maid, she wasn't at home that night. Visiting a friend . . . Or so she said . . .

How could she have been so foolish? But, of course, originally she had seen no choice. And as Tris had said, by last night it made no difference what they did. Except to her guilty conscience.

Someone rapped the knocker, and Cressida started, imagining scandal on the doorstep.

Sally leaped up. "Who can that be?" She hurried out, but was soon back. "It's for you, Miss Mandeville. A Mr. Lyne."

St. Raven's messenger! At least something was turning out right.

"It is to do with my father's affairs. I had better see him."

She hurried to the reception room and immediately read his expression. "You don't have the jewels."

"I'm afraid not. But don't panic!"

Cressida shut the door and sat down. "I'm not panicking. Yet. What happened?"

He sat down nearby. "St. Raven went to the house as planned, but the woman would not immediately give up the statuette."

"Why? What can she possibly want with it?"

He pulled a face. "St. Raven's company in public. He's agreed to it, Miss Mandeville, never fear, but it's not till the weekend."

Agreed to what? She pushed that aside. "Won't she think it strange that he agreed just for a statue? Its value is not very great."

"His concern exactly, but he thinks he played it all right. His story is that his little houri wanted it — that's you, if you'll excuse the notion. He cut up stiff at the idea that he demean himself to please a whore — if you'll excuse the term." He was beginning to blush. "He let himself be persuaded to give only his escort, and only for one day."

Could she believe that? Here was a whole new layer of society beneath the balls and promenades. No wonder gentlemen were often in short supply at the more respectable events!

"Saturday. I wish we didn't have to wait so long."

"Please don't worry, Miss Mandeville. St. Raven bade me to assure you that you'll have your jewels within the week, no matter what."

No matter what he had to do for them? Yet what right did she have to disapprove of his behavior if he was acting in her cause?

She rose and gave him her hand. "Thank you,

and please convey my thanks to the duke. This is no affair of yours or his, and I do appreciate your help."

He squeezed her hand for a moment. "He will do whatever he can to ensure your happiness, Miss Mandeville."

Cressida watched him leave, contemplating that. Happiness at the moment seemed out of reach. She was a practical person, however, and knew that such feelings would pass. In the meantime, she had the numbing inventory to soothe her.

Except that it no longer soothed.

As she plodded along with the task, impatience began to nettle her. Her statue was so close. Was it impossible to get into the house and . . . repossess it? It wouldn't exactly be stealing, especially if she took only the jewels.

Even as her mind spun out the adventure, she knew it was fantasy. She didn't even know where Miranda Coop lived.

She had the *Directory of London*.

Just as it lacked a section for "Peers of the Realm," it lacked a section for "Prostitutes," but Cressida was not in a mood to give up. The book did list each street, and the names of the householders.

Where would a woman like Miranda Coop live? Not in one of the most select areas, surely, but not completely outside them. A fashionable whore would want to be close to her clientele.

Not in the City. That was for merchants and businessmen.

This wasn't a rational occupation, but it obsessed her — or perhaps just distracted her anxious mind. It felt as if she were doing *something*.

She unfolded the street map and began a check of every street on the fringes of Mayfair against the directory. Her eyes began to tire, but by now she couldn't stop until she'd checked each street in London.

And then she found it.

Number 16, Tavistock Terrace, Miranda Coop. Not, in fact, that far from this house. She felt as if she had achieved a miracle, but she had no idea what to do with the information. She couldn't visit such a woman. It would be improper and could stir dangerous speculation.

It wouldn't hurt, however, to walk past the house tomorrow. It was, after all, a respectable street, and it would be something to do other than waiting, waiting, waiting.

Chapter Twenty-one

The next morning, Cressida dressed in one of her Matlock gowns. Though of good quality, it was made of a quiet print of blue on gray that would never attract attention, and it was, of course, high necked and long sleeved. She added her deepest-brimmed bonnet with the curls beneath. When she looked in the mirror, she was sure that even if she came face-to-face with Miranda Coop, the woman would never imagine she was St. Raven's houri.

In the night, the memory of him cradling the Coop woman's full breast and kissing it had come back to her again and again like torture.

"That is what he is," she reminded her reflection, and turned to leave. "Be grateful to be saved from the misery such a man would cause you."

She visited her parents and told her mother that she was going to the lending library.

"Take Sally, dear."

"She's needed here, Mama, and I'm not going far."

Her mother sighed. "Very well, dear."

Tavistock Terrace turned out to be exactly what Cressida had expected — a line of new houses, stucco shining white, large windows gleaming. Railings at the front guarded steps leading down to the basement doors used by servants. These houses would be owned or leased by those on the fringe of the highest circles, or by merchants and other professionals who aspired to wriggle their way in.

Like her father.

She put that aside and amused herself with wondering whether the worthy inhabitants of Tavistock Terrace knew the profession of the woman who lived at number 16. She doubted that the mother and daughter emerging chattering from number 5 did, or the sober man striding out of number 8 to enter a waiting hackney. She walked down the street purposefully, though not too fast, but in the end it did no good. What had she expected?

Miranda Coop's house was just like the others. A passing glimpse through the front bow window showed an ordinary drawing room with no sign of the figurine. Cressida turned left at the end of the street and walked on, thinking.

She could return and go down the steps at the front to the servants' area and . . . what? Pretend to be looking for work? She should have dressed even more plainly for that. Pretend to be lost? Pretend to be looking for an old servant?

Possibly, but it was still a risk. An unnecessary risk, because it would gain nothing. The figurine wouldn't be in the basement, and the servants were hardly likely to give her the freedom of the house.

However, she couldn't simply go home. When she saw a sign saying TAVISTOCK MEWS, she realized that the narrow road must circle behind the houses. She turned into it. A little more strange to be back here, but not a crime.

The lane was bordered on either side by high stone walls concealing back gardens. Above the wall to her left, she could glimpse the roofs of Tavistock Terrace broken by the small gable windows of servants' rooms. On her right lay houses that looked much the same.

The walls were broken by wooden gates. Tempting to try one, but they would be bolted on the other side.

She arrived at the mews area and paused. The yard was surrounded by buildings with large wooden doors, all closed. Some would contain coaches, some horses. Poor city horses, to spend all their time here with scarcely anything green around them.

This might be more of a livery stable with horses and coaches for hire. After all, only the very rich kept their own horses and carriage in London. Her father certainly didn't, even before the calamity.

Another fascinating aspect of London that she hadn't explored — the whole business of how people moved around, of how the thousands of horses were provided and cared for.

A door opened and an elderly, bowlegged groom came out leading a saddled gray. He touched his hat. "Can I help you, ma'am?"

"I am curious about how horses are managed in the city."

His eyes narrowed. "Not one of them reformers, are you?"

His reaction told her that there was something

that should be reformed. "Merely one who likes to understand how things work."

His look said that she was loose a great many screws, but he touched his tricorn again — "Got to get Hannibal to Mr. Greeves, ma'am," — climbed nimbly into the saddle, and rode off, the horse's hooves clattering.

But now another man appeared, a younger, bigger one with huge forearms exposed by his rolled-up sleeves. Cressida's nostrils flared, aware of his maleness as she would never have been before. He wasn't a particularly handsome man, she wasn't attracted to him, but by heaven she was aware of him!

"What can I do for you, miss?" he asked with an edge of impertinence.

Though he hadn't made a threatening move, Cressida wanted to step back. She stiffened her spine. "I'm curious about how a mews like this works."

"Those who 'as a need to know, know, miss."

"Now where would the world be if everyone took that approach, sir? Curiosity spurs invention. It creates wealth and conquest!"

His eyes widened a bit at the word *wealth.* Cressida pressed her advantage. "After all, someone's curiosity doubtless led to the invention of —" She searched for something to do with horses. "— horseshoes!"

His heavy brows rose. "That were a long time ago, miss." But he seemed amused, and the sense of threat lessened.

"Very well, tell me something that has improved recently."

"Bits. And coach springs. And I did hear tell that the horse collar was a mighty change long ago. Horses can't pull with a yoke like oxen, you see."

"Fascinating," Cressida said, and it was. "My father told me that coaches now are much more comfortable than when he left for India in the last century."

"India, eh?" The young man's eyes lit. "Always fancied travel, I have."

"Then you should do it. You could find employment with a gentleman going out to India. My father could perhaps help you. . . ."

Cressida realized that her enthusiasm was carrying her into perilous waters. The logical step here was to give her father's name and direction. Oh, well — she could see no way to retreat, and the young man looked so bright-eyed, so excited, that she wanted him to have his chance to see the world.

"Sir Arthur Mandeville, Twenty-two Otley Street. My father is unwell at the moment, but if you leave your name, I will see if he can put you in contact with suitable gentlemen."

The man was rubbing his chin looking a bit dazed. "Well, I dunno, miss. It's a big step. . . ."

"Of course it is, and there's no need to take it if you don't wish to. India can be an unhealthy climate for Englishmen, though my father thrived on it."

"Sir Arthur Mandeville," the man repeated to commit it to memory. "Twenty-two Otley Street."

"And your name? Then I will know to admit you."

"Isaac Benson, miss. Do you want me to show you around here?"

Cressida hadn't been angling for this, but it was proof that virtue was not always its own reward. "Mr. Benson, I would like that very much."

Her natural curiosity delighted in the tour of the stables and coach-houses, where she also met a young lad who was busy cleaning out a stall. She was aware of indulging herself with no real purpose, however, unless she could find out more about Miranda Coop.

As she suspected, the place was more like a livery stable, with stabling for horses belonging to residents, but also with horses and three carriages available for hire. Isaac Benson always spoke of gentlemen.

"What of ladies? I don't see any sidesaddles."

"Don't get much call for them, Miss Mandeville. If we do, there's a big stable over in King Street that we can send to. We does have to do that sometime — get something from elsewhere for our people here."

"And ladies don't travel alone." Cressida wondered if Miranda Coop preserved an appearance of propriety. Surely she must.

"Well, it depends a bit. There's a very nice lady lives on Tavistock who's of an independent turn. She'll call for a carriage and go off on her own. A widow, you see. Mrs. Coop."

"Ah." But if La Coop took one of these carriages, wouldn't the driver talk about where he took her? Not to mention her costume! "I'd think she'd want to be very sure of the driver you provide."

"Has her own, miss. A manservant who does footman or driver as called for. Can't say as I liked it at first, but Mr. Jarvis knows the ribbons." He touched his forelock. "I'd better get back to my work, miss, but look around some more if you'd like."

Cressida indicated that she would like, but when he left the saddle room, she pulled a face. It had been a more interesting morning than expected, and learning was never useless, but she was no closer to recovering the figurine than before.

She walked through the feed room and into the stables, grateful the big horses were all inside high-walled boxes. At the end of the room, she paused in the open doorway to the yard. This spot gave a reasonable view of the back of Tavistock Terrace. The house numbers were painted on the back gates, but it still did no good. The statuette was not conveniently sitting on a windowsill in number 16. And if it were, what could she do?

Break in? She was not brave enough for that.

As she watched, the gate opened and a solid older man in riding clothes walked out. Cressida stepped back so as not to be seen.

"Morning, Mr. Jarvis," she heard Isaac Benson say.

"Morning, Isaac. Mrs. Coop would like the traveling chaise if it's available. If not, she'll need you to get her one from elsewhere."

"It's free, sir. When does she want it?"

"As soon as possible."

"One pair or two? I'll have to send for two."

"One'll do. Just a jaunt to a friend in St. Albans."

"Right then. Jimmy!" Benson called for the lad to help and went into the carriage house. Jarvis came toward the stable.

Cressida almost ran, but she couldn't get away before he came in, and she mustn't seem furtive.

He walked in and stopped, then touched his tall hat, looking, if anything, amused. She realized that he thought she was Benson's young lady. She stifled a clarification and dropped a curtsy. He winked and walked by to check on the horses.

Cressida racked her brain for something to ask to get information. "I have an aunt in St. Albans," she lied.

"Do you, pet? If you're angling for a ride out there, forget it. My mistress wouldn't consider it."

"I wasn't! I was just making conversation." Cressida heard herself sliding into speech like Sally's and wanted to giggle.

"Don't you have work to do?"

"Not today. My mistress is away."

"Lucky you." He turned to study the horses.

"Mr. Benson said you drive the coach for your mistress."

He went into a stall to inspect a big brown horse. "Mr. Benson shouldn't be gossiping."

Cressida prayed she wasn't getting the young man into trouble. "He only said it because he admired you, sir. You being able to do so many things."

"That's true enough. Held up by a highwayman the night before last. I had my pistol and could have picked him off, given a sign."

Cressida didn't have to feign excitement. "Not that Le Corbeau!"

"The very same." He looked at her. "You another totty-headed admirer of the rogue?"

"No, but he is exciting."

What sort of crazy twist was this? Miranda Coop had been held up by the real Le Corbeau on the way home from the orgy?

"I thought he was under arrest," she said.

"Got the wrong man, apparently." He came out of one box and went into another. "Didn't get much for his pains, though. My mistress only had a little statue she'd been given as a present."

Cressida thanked heaven that he was inspecting a horse's hooves and not looking at her. "He surely didn't take that."

"Said it would spoil his reputation not to take something."

Benson came in then and looked taken aback to find Cressida still there.

"Sorry, Mr. Jarvis. . . ."

"No matter. Your young lady's a lovely lass. I'll have this one and that." He indicated his choice of horses. "I was just telling her about us being stopped by the Crow."

Benson gave Cressida a puzzled look, but he didn't contradict Jarvis's assumption. "At least you're in no danger from him during daylight, Mr. Jarvis."

"True enough." Jarvis went out to the coach, leaving Benson to deal with the horses. Young Jimmy dashed in to help.

Benson looked a question at her.

"I'm sorry. He assumed I was a maidservant here to see you, and I couldn't resist playing along."

He shook his head. "You're a right one."

"No, really. I'm normally a pattern of propriety. I'll leave you to your work now. If you wish to travel, please do take up my offer."

"I appreciate your kindness, Miss Mandeville."

Cressida went to the doorway, but paused there. "Mrs. Coop truly was held up by Le Corbeau?"

"Unless Jarvis is telling a tall tale."

"And lost only a small statuette."

"Aye, but from something he said, she was right put out about it."

I am not at all surprised, Cressida thought as she crossed the mews and headed for the wider streets, head whirling.

La Coop was using the statuette she no longer possessed to force St. Raven to escort her to an orgy. The woman had to be desperate to get it back.

And she was going to St. Albans at this hour. A whore — who didn't know what morning was. Did Miranda Coop know where Le Corbeau's hidey-hole was?

Cressida stood in the street, breathing deeply, trying to decide what to do. So tempting to walk down Tavistock Terrace again, but that would do no good.

She had to follow Miranda Coop.

But she couldn't just disappear like that.

She had to get word to St. Raven. What was the quickest way? . . .

She wasn't looking at anything, but then her eyes focused. Was she dreaming, or was that the man himself walking along the other side of the street in his groom's costume?

It was! With Mr. Lyne alongside, similarly dressed, and they were turning to cross the street, heading for Tavistock Terrace. She stifled an urge to call out to them, but walked briskly to intercept. Tris turned and saw her just as she reached the corner.

Did she see the same breath-catching moment in him as in herself?

"Cressida — !"

"She doesn't have the statue."

"What?" He looked as if she'd hit him over the head with it.

"Miranda Coop doesn't have the statue," she repeated, glancing around to see if anyone was watching this strange encounter.

"Don't worry." Mr. Lyne sounded amused. "I'm on lookout. You just tell your tale."

"Yes," Tris said, "tell us what the devil you've been up to."

"Language, sir!"

"I'm a rough groom. The sort who wouldn't know any better. Spill it."

Cressida glared at him, but this was no time to argue. "Miranda Coop was held up on the way back from Crofton's, and Le Corbeau stole the statue. She's ordered a coach to take her to St. Albans, and it has to be to try to get it back."

"It doesn't *have* to be, but it's a thought. How did you find this out?"

"I was in the mews when her man came to arrange it."

"In the mews? . . ." He came to the alert. "Did anyone see you?"

"Of course. I was talking to them. That's how —"

"Then get away. As soon as that coach drives around to the street, they'll see you."

"Why would that matter?"

"More to the point," Mr. Lyne said, "they'll see you talking to two disreputable characters."

"Oh." She glanced around. "But what are we going to do?"

"You are going to do nothing." Tris turned her to face down the street. "You are going to go home and behave like a lady."

Cressida whirled back. "Only when you go home and behave like a duke!"

She heard his friend stifle a laugh. "Why don't we all get out of the line of fire? There's nothing to do here."

"Right." Tris took Cressida's arm to march her up the street away from Tavistock Terrace. Then they heard hooves.

Tris shifted to stand in front of Cressida. His friend stood beside him to make a solid barrier. Heart pounding, Cressida untied her bonnet, which might be visible, and took it off.

She hated not being able to see. She hated having nothing to see but his broad shoulders. His broad shoulders . . .

She knew what they looked like naked. Her body softly melted at the memory of what he looked like naked. She slid a hand under his jacket and up to the coarse shirt covering his beautiful back. . . .

"Stop that."

She bit back laughter. She did stop, but literally. She kept her hand there, drawing something magical from the warm contact as the clop of hooves and rattle of wheels moved away into Tavistock Terrace, to collect Miranda Coop.

As he turned to her, she snatched away her hand. "What are we going to do?"

He looked angry — or something. "You are going home, and I am going to find Le Corbeau."

"He's in St. Albans."

"Why should Miranda know where he is? She's doubtless going to someone who might know, but I already have a couple of ideas."

"On the other hand," said Lyne, "it would be as well to follow her in case it leads to anything. I could get a horse in time."

"Good idea."

Lyne strode away, and Cressida thought to question things. "What are you doing here?" But then she guessed. "You were going to try to break in and steal it!"

"True," he said.

"You're mad! I thought she promised it to you for your escort."

"I dislike having my hand forced. And what precisely were you up to poking around the mews?"

"I wasn't poking. I couldn't help but come to see the house. In case there was anything . . ."

He rolled his eyes. "You're Miss Mandeville of

Matlock, remember? She of impeccable behavior?"

"Yes, Your scruffy, ungrateful Grace."

He shook his head but laughed. "Very well. Your ill-advised adventure was fruitful, but please don't do anything like that again. I couldn't bear for you to come to harm."

Her lips threatened to wobble. "I was in no danger."

"How can you tell? Go home, love. Leave the rest to me."

Love.

It sapped all her fighting spirit, leaving only sadness. She began to say farewell, but then she rebelled. "I don't want to. Go home. I want to be part of this."

"How? And — forgive me — what use could you be?"

Hooves and rattling wheels alerted them.

"Hell!" He took the bonnet from her hand and dropped it down the nearby stairwell, then pulled her into his arms. She was pressed against the railings as if he were kissing her. Unfortunately, he wasn't.

"We might as well," she murmured.

"I need a scrap of sanity."

She kissed his set jaw. "But madness is so appealing."

"Only if you aspire to Bedlam."

"A heaven if there with you . . ."

He pushed away from her. "Cressida! The woman is supposed to be strong enough for both."

The coach had passed.

"How very unfair. And if true, we should be ruling the world, not men." She read his eyes. "You don't want to part any more than I do."

"Of course I don't, but even though I'm but a frail man, I'm trying to be strong enough for both."

She slid her hand up to his shoulder. "I know. We have to be sensible, and I will be, I promise, once we have the jewels. But until then, I want to be this wild creature a little longer."

She touched his cheek. It was rough. Because of this disguise, he hadn't shaved. "Take me with you to hunt the Crow, Tris. I can't bear to sit at home waiting!"

He trapped her hand. "How? How can you leave again and get away with it?"

He wasn't saying no.

It all suddenly seemed clear. "I'll tell my mother some of the truth. I'll say that I have a way to repair our fortunes, but it means my going away unchaperoned for a few days. And that she must trust me to do the right thing."

"She will permit this?"

"She's a realist now she has her wits back. She knows we face disaster."

"This could *lead* to disaster."

"Only if we . . . I don't think we should . . ." Words failed her.

He turned his head and kissed her palm. "You credit me with Herculean strength."

"Yes, I do. Will it be unbearable torture?"

He pushed away from her. "You damnable woman. You know I can't deny you when you look at me like that."

She blinked. "You can't?"

He pulled her back and gave her a quick kiss. "I can't."

He released her and went down the narrow stairs to retrieve her bonnet, then came back and put it on her head.

"Go home," he said, tying the ribbons. "If you can get away without disaster, meet me at the corner of Rathbury and Hay. It's not too far from your house, but it's a place unlikely to be under the eye of anyone of fashion. I'll be driving my curricle."

Cressida knew her smile was too bright, too wide. "Thank you!"

"Thank me when you're safely home in Matlock. Go on. We need to be ahead of Miranda."

He turned and walked away.

Chapter Twenty-two

Cressida watched for a moment for the sheer pleasure of it, then hurried in the other direction, excitement fizzing. Such wicked folly, this new adventure, and it would make the rest of her life seem even bleaker, but she couldn't pass it by.

In fact, she thought, as she turned into Otley Street, she was wicked at heart. If not for her parents — if she were alone in the world — she might become the Duke of St. Raven's acknowledged mistress and to hell with propriety and pain!

As she entered her house, however, the practicalities hit her. How was she going to do this? She hated to lie. She'd hated to lie before, but going with Crofton had been essential. This excursion would be for her own wicked pleasure.

She needed time to think, and she didn't have time.

But she needed to take the statuette. Tris would be able to practice opening it, and they might have a chance to do a switch. She was in the study picking it up when her mother walked in.

"Oh, I thought you were still out, dear. I thought it might help your father if I read to him.

What book would interest him?"

"A good idea, Mama." Feeling as if guilt were written all over her, Cressida took down the book about Arabia. "Try this."

Her mother took it, but sighed. "If he revives, it will only be to the burden of disaster."

Cressida licked her lips. "As to that, Mama . . . There might be a way."

"What?"

Cressida used her thumbnail to click the back of the figurine free and slide it open. "There's another figurine very like this one, Mama, but it contains jewels."

Her mother stared. "But . . . But all the rest are at Stokeley! Oh, how infuriating that that man should have even more!"

"Except that I have learned that he doesn't have them." How much to say? But then Cressida realized that she was treating her mother like a child.

"Lord Crofton gave the statue with the jewels to someone else, and then the highwayman, Le Corbeau, stole it. Someone I know is willing to take me to try to get it back. I need to do this, Mama."

Her mother was staring at her. "But how do you know all this?"

Cressida felt her face burn. "I can't tell you that."

"Were you at Cecilia's these past days?"

Cressida gulped. "No."

"Cressida!"

"Please don't think the worst of me, Mama. Father showed me those jewels at Stokeley

Manor, and I've been trying to get them back. We must if we're to have any kind of life. We can return to Matlock, return to our comfortable life there. . . ."

She felt that future winding around her, binding her, but she pushed that away.

"My goodness. What a lot of goings-on I've been blind to. And you think you can find these jewels?"

Cressida made it more certain than she felt. "Yes."

"Who is this friend? Is it . . . a man?"

A lie formed, but she resisted it. "Yes, but there will be no impropriety."

By putting it in the future, she could be truthful, though it was scarcely proper to be fondling a man's back on a public street, or kissing him.

"A *young* man?"

"Yes, Mama."

"Are you sure you can trust him, dear? Men can be carried beyond good manners so easily when a lady does not behave with complete propriety."

Cressida felt as if wild laughter might choke her. "I'll be strong enough for both, Mama. Please. Will you trust me to manage this?"

Her mother bit her lip, but then she stepped forward and took Cressida's hands. "You remind me so much of your father, darling. Confess, a little of this is sheer adventure, isn't it?"

"Yes."

"But will you be content to return to Matlock when it's over?"

Cressida sighed, staring at a wall of books. "I doubt I'll have other exciting possibilities."

Her mother touched her cheek. "I am a conventional woman, but I've suspected for a while that you are not. I set your father free. He would have returned to England with us, but I knew it wasn't his place to be. He loved me, but he loved adventure more. So I set him free. Now, I set you free, too. Go adventuring, Cressida, but always know you have a home to return to, tomorrow, or twenty years from now."

Cressida saw her mother through tears, understanding so much, but not really understanding at all. Now, however, she felt she had to tell more.

"It's the Duke of St. Raven, Mama. My friend. We met . . . by accident. It's amusement for him. A quest. But —"

"But you've fallen in love with him. Hardly surprising." Her mother sighed. "Poor Cressy. It seems you have the most dangerous parts of your parents. My tender heart and your father's bold spirit. The duke is very handsome."

"That's not why I love him."

"No, it wouldn't be. If he asks, will you become his mistress?"

The direct question made everything clear.

"No. It wouldn't be right for us for long, and the wounds would last a lifetime. And he has to marry, so it might be hardest for him. . . ." She breathed deeply. "If I'm going, I must go. Thank you!"

"Remember, I'll always be here, waiting for the wanderer's return. I believe I can deal with little wounds, at least. A touch of basilicum ointment, some soothing warm milk . . ."

Cressida gave her mother a fierce hug, then ran upstairs to gather a change of linen and her toiletries. How to carry them? Walking through the streets with a valise could look strange. She pulled out the hatbox for her tall bonnet and packed her things into that, adding the statue.

She didn't wear that bonnet, however, but kept the small one from Matlock days. Would she still be recognized? Talk would fly if anyone saw Miss Mandeville driving out of town with the Duke of St. Raven.

She really shouldn't go.

But she couldn't give up this opportunity.

She glanced at the clock, then grabbed Roxelana's thin blue veiling. She tied it around the brim of the bonnet and then pulled it down over her face. Ladies did sometimes wear veils when driving in an open carriage.

It turned everything a dim blue, however, making it hard to see. That reminded her. She pushed the veiling up, but grabbed her spectacles. She'd never worn them in public in London, so they'd be another disguise.

After one last hasty glance around, she picked up the hatbox, rushed downstairs, and left the house. She knew that one way or another, her life would never be the same.

Cressida forced herself to walk steadily to the rendezvous, praying that she not meet anyone she knew; praying especially that no one delayed her by wishing to speak.

She turned into Hay Street and saw him. At least, she saw his back and his splendid curricle. She faltered for a second, then hurried on. Her soft half-boots made no sound, so when she said, "I'm here," he started.

He must have jerked on the reins, for his horses sidled and he had to work to settle them. Then he held out a gloved hand and pulled her up into the seat.

She couldn't tell if he was surprised, pleased, or reluctant.

"Hatbox?" he queried.

"I thought I should bring a few things. Including the statuette. We might be able to exchange them."

"Ah, good thought. Ready?"

I don't know! Cressida tugged the veiling down over her face, relieved to be able to hide her expressions. "Ready," she said.

He flicked his long whip over the horses, and they set off.

As he turned into a wider street, she became desperate to say something. "I'm sure I should make some admiring comment in praise of your horses, but the best I can manage is that they seem good at this."

"So they are."

She thought she saw the hint of a smile, but through the veiling it was so hard to tell.

She could see when they came up behind a huge cart laden with bales of something. It was traveling at a walk and taking up most of the road. Occasional vehicles coming the other way pinned them there until she wanted to scream.

There wasn't that much urgency, she supposed, but she couldn't stand this dawdle.

Then he said, "Hold on."

Cressida realized a moment too late that he meant it literally, and had to make a mad grab for the rail beside her as the curricle surged forward to fly past the cart in a small gap in the traffic. Once they were past, the road ahead was clear, and they whirled by people and houses at terrifying speed.

"All right?"

Cressida unglued her stare from the buildings flashing by at her side. "Can we go a little slower?" She sounded strangled.

"Come now" — he steered around a hole in the road with alarming nonchalance — "is this my intrepid Roxelana?"

"No, this is your terrified Miss Mandeville of Matlock, who doesn't want to die just yet!"

"You won't. Trust me."

Trust. Trust. She forced her fingers to release the rail.

Then he added, "I haven't overturned in at least six years."

"You've overturned?" she squeaked, gripping again.

"When I was young and foolish and racing with Uffham."

"Uffham?" Talking was some distraction. She prayed it wasn't distracting him.

"Heir to the Duke of Arran. A kind of foster brother."

"Oh, yes." She remembered there being almost as much flurry among the society hopefuls about

Lord Uffham as about St. Raven. "Do you know anyone who isn't from a ducal family?"

"Don't be ridiculous. Feeling better?"

Cressida realized that she was, a little. She eased her painful grip on the iron rail, though she didn't let go entirely. "This is a foolhardy way to travel."

"This is the best way to travel as long as the weather is fine. It's also the fastest."

"That's what I mean."

"We need speed. We want to be ahead of La Coop. Now, why are you swathed like a veiled mourner?"

"So that if anyone who knows me sees me, they won't. Know me. With you." Her brains must be blowing away with the wind of their speed.

"Ah. Quick wits, as always. You can put it up for now, though. We're passing through nursery gardens with no vehicles in sight. I can't see anyone from the ton strolling here."

Cressida pushed the veiling up as best she could with one hand. She still was not ready to release her grip on the rail. Clear vision did help her nerves, and Tris's relaxed confidence helped even more.

He, after all, wasn't holding on to anything except the reins, and they wouldn't keep him from falling out. Instead he was riding the movement of the curricle with a foot braced on the board in front of him. Unfortunately, her foot wouldn't reach there.

She made herself release her grip on the rail and tried to sway with the carriage. The road was quite smooth, kept in good condition by the tolls. Even though they were whirling past pedestrians and people on donkeys and placid cobs, she was not tossed off the flimsy vehicle into the air.

She began to almost enjoy it.

But then he said, "Coach up ahead. Mail or stage coming this way."

Cressida yanked down the veiling, and in moments the coach passed by and was gone on its way to London in a swirl of dust. At least, it was them speeding by. The coach was doubtless trundling on its steady way.

"You're better off where you are than traveling on the outside of that," he said.

"I don't doubt it." She'd always thought that being an outside passenger would be uncomfortable and dangerous. Miss Mandeville of Matlock had never had to contemplate such a fate. If she didn't get the jewels, she might end up traveling that way.

Dread tangled with screwed-up tension, making her want to scream. Instead she fixed on their purpose. They were going to get the jewels, and that would solve most of her problems. She and her parents could live in decent dignity — and she would never travel in a curricle again.

That meant, she knew, that she wouldn't travel with Tris Tregallows again, but that was an old wound by now.

"What is our plan? Where are we going?"

"Hatfield, where a certain Jean-Marie Bourreau lived before he was arrested for being Le Corbeau."

"Oh, of course. How clever! But will he still be there?"

"Having been proved innocent, I hope he'll have stayed put. Anything else might look suspicious. He has lodging and employment there."

"Employment?"

"He does portraits in pastels, and is quite good at it."

This struck Cressida as very peculiar. "An artist? Are you sure he is Le Corbeau?"

"Artistic skill guaranteeing virtue?"

A tollgate blocked the road ahead, and he slowed to toss a coin to the waiting toll-keeper, whose son was already swinging open the wide gate. In moments Cressida was pressed back by speed again, and Tris's attention was all on the road.

"So he's in Hatfield." She concentrated on that, not on the speed. "And he has the statue. Didn't you say he has a cottage?"

"But he knows that cover is blown. I had the place checked before we left Nun's Chase. He's cleared out all his important possessions."

"So if he has the statue, it is probably with him in Hatfield."

"That's the hope. If he's found a new hiding place, I'll squeeze it out of him."

"And how are you to do that without revealing that it has some importance?"

He flashed her a glance. "I'll find a way. Do you truly think me hotheaded enough to forget the need for discretion?"

Had her thoughtless words hurt him? "No, of course not. You're coolheaded. I'm in a fret."

"Trust me, Cressida. This is the last stage. We'll soon have your jewels."

The last stage. She certainly couldn't accuse him of sugarcoating things.

"How are we to get it from him without him knowing its true value?" After a moment, she answered herself. "Perhaps I should handle that. It doesn't sound as if he'll be disposed to please you."

"I'm willing to beat it out of him if necessary — but the less fuss, the better."

They slowed to pass through a small place called Finchley.

When he didn't say any more, her lips twitched. "Do you have any less violent plan?"

She saw her humor echoed in him. "Robbery still appeals."

"Unless we get caught."

"I am a duke."

"Which doesn't make you immune to criminal arrest."

"But makes it unlikely. Unjust, I know, but there have to be some compensations. He's living at an inn called the Cockleshell. We could take rooms there and be enterprising."

One word registered. "Rooms?"

"Rooms." He slowed the team and glanced at her. "We can't pretend to be married, Cressida, even under a false name. There's too great a chance of being seen by someone who knows me. And anyway, that outfit and hat cry out a lack of funds. A fine husband I'd look to be dressed by the best and driving this rig but with my wife in servant's clothes."

"I thought they would be inconspicuous," she muttered, and did not tell him they were part of her everyday Matlock wardrobe. She could point out that they were made of durable cloth, and very well made, as well, but what was the point?

"Penny for your thoughts?"

Cressida snapped alert. "I'm constantly worrying about being thrown out of this ridiculous vehicle."

"I've slowed."

"We are still going too fast."

"Be bold. Be brave. You were far away, weren't you? Are you worrying about the night? You can trust me."

"That's what I feared." It slipped out before she thought.

"Devil take it, Cressida. You'll drive me mad. We can't. It's too dangerous. And it won't make it any easier."

It — the inevitable parting.

"We'll doubtless be too busy in the night anyway. Switching the statues," she added, in case it was unclear.

"Yes." But the horses broke step as if he'd given them some conflicting signal.

She found some satisfaction in that. The noble Duke of St. Raven wanted another night, perhaps as much as she did. What's more, she believed that he wanted more than her body. There was a bleak sort of comfort in that.

They drove for a while in silence, and the less-than-suicidal speed allowed her to think more clearly. She noticed that even at their moderate pace, they passed three coaches of the slower sort, lumbering north on this busy road. She was grateful for her veil.

"Perhaps," she said, "we should arrive separately."

"Why?"

"It would avoid any chance of a scandalous connection, and allow us more options. . . ." Before he could interrupt, she added, "At the next coaching stage, I could take a coach to Hatfield. They seem to pass by quite frequently."

"Impossible! You could end up traveling on the outside."

"If I don't succeed in this venture, I could end up traveling there for the rest of my life!"

He drew the horses to a halt and faced her. "We are not going to fail."

"Even you can't shape fate to your choosing."

"I should at least be able to shape this. We're dealing with a foreign petty criminal who doesn't realize what he has. There's no need for you to take risks."

"Yet nothing in this seems to go smoothly, remember?" When he didn't agree, she said, "You cannot dictate to me in this. My plan makes the most sense."

"Does it, indeed? Then what is this plan other than to travel in discomfort?"

"You call hurtling along in this thing *comfort?*"

She wouldn't have thought that his jaw could tense any further, but it managed to. "The plan, Cressida."

She swallowed another retort. "You will arrive and demand to speak to Bourreau. I will arrive separately and search his rooms when he's with you."

"Out of the question. As soon as you enter his rooms, you're a criminal."

"Surely my lord duke can extract me from jail."

"I may decide to leave you there if you 'my lord duke' me again!"

The desperate violence behind his words stilled her breath. She pushed up her veil so she could see him more clearly.

"I'm sorry, but you're bullying me. I did not grow up trained to the male bridle. Your word is not my law."

"So tempting to marry you, to hear you promise to obey me."

"A prime argument against matrimony!"

But they were dancing close to an impossible edge, and she saw that knowledge in his eyes, along with a great many other painful things.

"You can distract Bourreau," he said, "and I will search the rooms."

"And how am I supposed to do that, dressed like a servant?"

His brows twitched. "Did that offend you? For heaven's sake, Cressida, you can't deny —"

"These clothes are my everyday wear in Matlock, sir, and I like them."

"Then I wish you joy of them. But," he added, his expression softening, "you won't make yourself any less attractive to me that way."

"I didn't. I wouldn't . . . Wretched man, you will not distract me that way! I cannot guarantee to hold Bourreau away long enough. You can. I will search the rooms. I have come up with a story."

"What?" She heard a disbelieving sigh.

"I'm an abandoned lover come to beg him to take me back. That gives me an excellent reason to sneak into his rooms and one not likely to land me in jail."

He seemed angry at its reasonableness. "Not if you're caught red-handed."

"How would that be? I have the similar statue in my hatbox. I need the merest moment to switch them, and only a little more to remove the jewels from the one he has."

"Dammit, Cressida, I don't like it!"

"Clearly, since you're swearing at me again."

"You'll hear worse than that before this is over."

She bit back laughter and touched his tense gloved hand. "It is not so outrageous a plan as that, Tris, to travel by stage for a few miles and then sneak into a man's rooms."

His raised brows were sufficient commentary.

"Not outrageous for mere mortals, at least, my lord duke."

"Harpy."

"Winged and clawed."

"I'm running blood to prove it." He turned his hand to take hers. "Cressida, I need to keep you safe."

Ah, that could break her heart. "Truly, the risks are not great, and the advantages are. Especially one. Think. We will not be linked. Even if we meet someone who knows you, or who knows me, there will be no connection, so no scandal."

She put into words what had not yet been said. "After Stokeley, we can't afford any scandalous connection."

His thumb rubbed against her hand. "I'd marry you, Cressida, but it would only make matters worse."

She knew what he meant. "It would put me in the center of the world's eye, and somebody would put two and two together and realize that I was your houri at Stokeley. Crofton would make the connection between you and Le Corbeau —"

"That doesn't matter, and we can stare down scandal —"

"No! No, I don't want that, Tris. Truly I don't. Bad enough to be the center of the world's attention, but to be the center of the world's disgusted whispers all my life? No, no, no!"

She controlled herself. "We're running away with things anyway, aren't we? We both know I am not the stuff of which duchesses are made, so there's no future for us. This is a fleeting folly. We'll forget each other within days when this is over."

"You're doubtless right," he agreed in an indifferent drawl that was as artificial as her bobbing curls. "And given that, your plan does have merit. But Bourreau may have the statue hidden, along with any other loot he owns."

She slipped her hand away from his. "Then you must try to create time for me to search. Do we know if he has any servants?"

"I doubt he'd have any personal servants at the inn, though he has accomplices when he is Le Corbeau. It's too dangerous —"

"No, it's not. As long as his accomplices are not in the rooms. And if they are, I have my story."

"What happens when he declares that he's never seen you before?"

She raised her brows. "Well, he would, wouldn't he?"

"Cressida . . ."

"You have to let me do this, Tris. It's the only rational plan. For heaven's sake, I was willing to risk whoring to get the jewels. Risking jail seems a lesser evil to me."

His jaw worked. "We'll stop at Barnet and see if there's a suitable vehicle passing north soon. We can't delay too long. We don't want Miranda there ahead of us."

"You can go ahead to watch for that."

"And leave you unescorted?"

A laugh escaped her. "Were you going to drive this ridiculously expensive vehicle alongside the stage to keep me safe?"

He gripped her chin. "Funny, am I? I've enticed you from your home, Cressida Mandeville. Your safety is my responsibility. How am I supposed to wave you off on a common stage and put you out of my mind?"

She cradled his gloved hand. "Have you ever traveled on the stage, Tris?"

"Don't sneer at me for my pampered life."

"I'm not, but . . . among so many, rape and pillage becomes a little difficult, you know."

"Squeezing and fondling would not be."

"I'd throw a fit of the vapors, and the other passengers would have the villain ejected."

"Tell the truth. Have you ever traveled alone on the stage before?"

Cressida might have lied except that she knew she was blushing. "No, but I have traveled by stage with my mother. It will present no particular hazard, and it will only be for a few miles. It is the sensible thing to do, Tris."

"Sensible. Oh, by all means let us be sensible." He leaned forward and pressed his lips to hers. Their hat brims collided, and they moved apart, laughing.

"Our headwear has more sense than we do," he said.

Such tender longings washed over Cressida that she could not speak, and had to fight not to cry. He reached beneath the seat and produced a long, flat piece of metal.

"What's that?"

"The man who provided it called it a winkler. You push the thin bladed end under the hasp of a lock or hinge and lever it off."

"I can't use that."

"You're the one who wanted to do the thievery."

Cressida took the implement, which was about twelve inches long and surprisingly heavy. "Perhaps I won't be strong enough."

"The power of leverage. I tried it. It's quite effective as long as you can force the blade beneath what you want to move. How else are you going to deal with a locked drawer?"

He was expecting her to back down at this point. Cressida opened her hatbox and stuck the tool in there. "Right, then," she said, pulling down her veil.

"Right." He cracked his whip above the horses' heads. They were off again in a spurt of dust and anger. Cressida clutched the rail again, resolved not to lose courage now.

If he was angry with her, it was doubtless for the best.

Chapter Twenty-three

They slowed to take the hill up into Barnet, then pulled up by the Green Man. They had arranged the details, and Tris followed the plan. He leaped down and spoke to an ostler in an offhand manner of his passenger who required a ticket to Hatfield. Everything about him made it clear that said passenger was not worthy of his particular attention.

Cressida was helped down by an inn servant and went to purchase a ticket. A suitable coach was due to arrive in under fifteen minutes and should have space.

That disposed of Tris's strongest argument — the need for speed. When she turned with the ticket in her hand, she saw his lips tighten. However, he strolled into the inn for some refreshment. The ostler was walking his horses, obviously awed by their quality and by his. And obviously convinced that Cressida was a servant.

This, she decided, was a very useful exercise. If she ever deluded herself that she and the Duke of St. Raven could blend their lives, here was evidence that it could not be.

She took a seat on a bench beside a weary-looking couple also waiting for transport. She knew Tris was hovering to see her on her way, and that he would be in Hatfield, equally watchful, when she arrived.

From such a hazardous journey.

Soon this watchful protection would be over. It would all be as it had been before, with her going about her life in Matlock with no one fretting about her safety. And better so.

"Sad journey, love?" asked the countrywoman to her right.

Cressida said, "No," too brightly before she thought. "I'm just tired."

"Aye." With that universal endorsement, the woman lapsed into silence again.

"And you?" Cressida asked.

"Sad enough."

Cressida couldn't ignore the weight of grief she heard in those two words. "What's happened?"

She saw then that the man and woman were holding gloveless hands. Two rough, work-worn hands twined together probably unconsciously.

As her hand had twined with Tris's now and then. But they had been forced to pull apart, and these two were bound for life. They provided support for one another, even now, when life was hard.

"Not long ago we had a smallholding on Lord Sunderland's estate," the woman said, "and four fine sons to come after us. Those were happy days, happy days. But three of our lads were 'ticed away by the recruitment men and died, and then our eldest — he took a scythe in the leg last harvest, and it festered."

All four sons dead? "I'm so sorry."

The woman shrugged. "Now Lord Sunderland's steward says we can't do the work, and I suppose he's right. My man's heart isn't as good as it was. So we've had to leave our cottage."

Cressida knew that a farm laborer's home was tied to the land. "Where will you go?" Her instinct to help was stirring, but what could she do here and now?

"Don't you worry, miss. We're off to my sister near Birmingham." But then she added, "Though what's to become of us there, I don't know."

"I'm sorry for your trouble."

Cressida hated feeling so helpless. She knew how to tell the conniving storyteller from the truly tragic, and this woman's story was true. Three of their sons had served to fight Napoleon, and for reward, these folks had been thrown out of their home. It was unjust. Something should be done.

She didn't blame their landlord, who doubtless needed the place to house a new family of farmworkers, but she blamed the government, which had made no provision for its soldiers and their families. If she were in Matlock, she would know many resources to turn to, but now she was struggling to survive herself.

If only she had a magic wand. . . .

How much time did she have? She asked the woman to keep an eye on her hatbox and hurried into the inn. She peeped into a number of rooms, wondering where Tris was. Had he hired a private parlor for such a short stay?

Then she saw him in the lowly tap, drinking beer from a pottery flagon and chatting with a bunch of local men. They all looked, of course, dazzled as if a faery prince had landed among them.

She wasted a moment simply loving him, then snapped her wits together. How to get his attention without walking in and demanding it? She hovered, willing him to look her way.

He did. His brows twitched, but then he drained his flagon, took farewell of his fellows, and sauntered out into the corridor. "I thought I was hardly aware of your existence."

"There's a problem with the ticket," Cressida said in case anyone was listening, but she pulled a face at him.

All the time she listened for the coach. She knew it wouldn't wait for her.

"What?"

She looked around, but no one seemed to be nearby. "There's a couple outside with such a sad story. Three sons lost in the war, and the last dead of a wound at home. The husband is sick and the wife worn out. They've been thrown off their land. . . ."

He rolled his eyes. "There are a thousand such. What am I supposed to do?" Then he added, "Stop looking at me as if I can turn water into wine!"

"That would be little use," she said tartly, then wondered if it was blasphemy. "You could let them go to Nun's Chase until I think of something. Once I'm back in Matlock, I'll be able to arrange help. Light work or an almshouse. If not, they'll end in the workhouse, I'm sure of it. And they're holding hands, Tris! It would kill them to be parted, and you know they separate couples in the workhouse. . . .”

He put fingers on her quivering lips. “Lord above, Cressida. How are you to survive with such a tender heart?”

She blinked at him. “By making things better, of course.”

“Of course,” he said, rather faintly.

“I’m sure it’s easy from your elevated eminence to ignore all the little people, but down here, my lord duke, I cannot.”

“Stop my lord dukeing me!” He almost snarled it. “All right, I’ll take care of them. But that’s your coach.”

She heard the rumble, then the call.

“Thank you!”

She smiled and touched her fingers to his lips, then hurried out to grab her box and climb into the coach. She only had time to squeeze into her seat before it headed off again, new horses between the shafts.

Tris watched the coach go. Another excellent reason to cut free of Cressida Mandeville and the insanity she had brought to his life. She was a do-gooder. A reformer, probably. She’d sweep the roads of England for waifs and strays for her husband to support. . . .

Husband.

He accepted for the first time how much he wanted that, how much he wanted Cressida as his constant companion. She was an impossible duchess and generations of Tregallows would spin in their graves, but he no longer cared.

But it had been his own rash indulgence in taking her to Stokeley Manor that had made it impossible. It could make a damn Greek tragedy.

He shook his head and looked to see what she'd left for him to deal with.

The couple wore decent but shabby clothing. The man had probably been wiry and strong for most of his life, but now he was just thin and weak. The woman was more substantial, but there was a gray sagginess to her that spoke of bone-deep weariness and threatening disaster.

Grief, too, of course. He knew from losing his own parents how quickly a golden situation could shatter into a lifelong shadow.

Cressida was probably right about their fate. Wherever they were heading now with their two bundles of possessions, they would be in the workhouse soon — housed, fed, and clothed, but in the meanest way, and kept apart, one in the women's section, one in the men's. And there they would soon fade away.

Did they really want to go on living? But he'd promised.

He strolled over.

The woman looked up first, startled. She pulled her hand free and pushed to her feet. The man stirred to do the same.

Tris put out a hand. "Please, don't. I only wanted a word with you."

The woman stood anyway, but she put a hand on her husband's shoulder to hold him down. "He's not well, sir."

"So I can see. I gather you have lost your home."

The woman's eyes skittered around, perhaps seeking the informant, or help, or to see who was watching their shame. Damn, he didn't know how to do this. How could Cressida throw him into this situation and then abandon him? It was as bad as him putting her on a horse and walking away.

"I mean you no harm. My —" No, he couldn't say Cressida was a friend. "The lady you spoke with mentioned your situation to me."

Under the pressure of their blank stares, he soldiered on.

"She thinks she may know of a place for you, but she was in a hurry to catch her coach. She asked me to direct you to my home, where you could wait until she contacts you."

The man and the woman shared a long look; then both pairs of eyes returned to him. What the devil did they think could happen here to make things worse? They were hardly candidates for the white slave trade.

Then he realized that they needed a name. They were not going to trust him without a name.

"My name is St. Raven," he said, and left it at that. "My house is called Nun's Chase, and lies a few miles from Buntingford. I will give you a letter that will take care of you."

Those guarded, weary eyes just stared at him.

"You will have a room and food," he continued doggedly, praying there was a spare servant's room at Nun's Chase. How the devil should he know? He supposed he could offer them the cottage Bourreau had been using, but it was deserted precisely because it was falling down. Disturbing to think this couple might be grateful for it.

"Miss Mandeville will contact you shortly," he said bracingly.

The eyes connected again, for long silent seconds, and then the woman looked back at him and dropped a curtsy. "You're very kind, sir. We thank you. And the lady."

Tris almost blew out a breath. "Good, good." He pulled out some money, wondering what simple transport to Buntingford might cost. He'd give them guineas, but he suspected too much largess would have them fleeing.

He offered a crown, watching to see the reaction. She colored, but not with alarm. "We have money, sir."

"I would prefer to cover the cost of your journey to Nun's Chase. You may require your money later to continue on your way."

She took the money, pulled out a knitted purse, and popped it in. There was clearly not a great deal else in there. "You're very kind, sir." After a hesitation, she added, "I'm Rachel Minnow, and this is my husband, Matthew."

He cursed himself for not bothering with their names. He might even be blushing.

"Well, then," he said, hearing himself sound overly hearty, like the good-natured squire in a play, "I hope to see you at Nun's Chase when I return there, Mrs. Minnow, Mr. Minnow. Or not, if Miss Mandeville has already arranged something else." How to end this? "I'll . . . er . . . leave you to it, then."

He backed away a few steps before feeling he could turn his back on those fixed eyes, now brighter. There might even be tears on the man's cheeks. God! Perhaps there was good reason for dealing with tenants thirdhand.

He strode toward his curricle, but then realized he had arrangements to make for them. On the other hand, Cressida was rolling on her way to Hatfield, where she could get up to any sort of trouble. He was ready to wring her neck.

He hurried into the inn, commanded writing materials, then dashed off a quick letter to the landlord of the Black Bull at Buntingford requesting that the couple be transported to Nun's Chase in the gig.

Then he wrote another to Pike, his butler at Nun's Chase, ordering him to take care of the Minnows. He had to swallow laughter, imagining Pike swallowing the poor Minnows whole, as would happen in any stream. He didn't try to explain the visitation. He didn't have time, and he wasn't sure he had an explanation to offer.

He almost gave the letters to Mrs. Minnow, then realized the poor man must be feeling beaten down, so he gave them to him instead. The gnarled hands took them as if they were precious glass, and the man sat a little straighter to say, "We do thank you, sir."

"It's little enough," Tris replied, with perfect honesty.

He climbed into his rig and sped on his way, aware of the attention of his new dependents.

Once out of Barnet, he gave the horses their head. After the rest they were frisky, and soon the wind was blowing away uneasy thoughts about dependents, about the smothering mass of need and suffering in the world.

He had worries enough of his own, the chief one being that Cressida might make it to Hatfield ahead of him. He whipped past the lumbering coach about halfway, however. He glanced to the side, but could only see the two people in his side's window seats. She had to be there. She couldn't have managed to get into some new tangle in the past half hour.

Anyway, Miss Mandeville of Matlock didn't like him fussing about her safety or her reputation, damn her!

Arriving at Hatfield ahead of her felt like a triumph, though it was an ordinary enough little town. He found the Cockleshell, but it was not a staging inn. That was only two buildings away, so she couldn't get into trouble between there and here, could she? Damn. They hadn't taken that into account. He should have known her plan would create problems.

He had to settle in here, before he could deal with that. Once he admitted to his identity and an intention of staying, anything he requested was his, including information.

He inspected the rooms shown him by the groveling innkeeper. "I am here because my cousin has expressed a desire for a pastel portrait by a Frenchman who, I am told, lives here. Is he in?"

"Mr. Bourreau." The fat innkeeper bowed. "Yes, indeed, Your Grace! I believe he is in, but with a client."

"He executes his art here rather than in clients' homes?" Tris asked with surprise, adding a touch of ducal disdain for effect.

"Sometimes, Your Grace. It is as the client wishes, Your Grace."

Tris shrugged. He ordered food, but when the innkeeper backed his way toward the door with many bowings and Your-Gracings, he halted him.

"Where are the artist's rooms? Are they nearby?"

"Quite close, Your Grace."

Tris could read the doubtful note. Did the eminent guest want the artist nearby for his convenience? Or would he resent having the rooms of a lowly artist close to his?

"This is a small house, Your Grace. . . ."

Tris let silence turn the screw.

"Sixteen and seventeen, Your Grace. Quite the other end of this corridor, Your Grace, but close enough if necessary."

Tris couldn't help a slight smile at the poor man. That answer had been quite brilliantly diplomatic.

"Excellent." He waved the innkeeper on his way.

He hated being groveled to, but a ducal aura might be useful if things went awry. And the damnable thing was that people enjoyed it. They wallowed in the reflected glory. The innkeeper was doubtless bursting with importance and looking forward to telling everyone about a duke, no less, gracing his house.

Noblesse oblige. The words of another duke, the Duc de Lévis, but echoing the more ominous words of Euripides. "Those nobly born must nobly meet their fate."

He had been given no choice about his fate, but had always intended to bear the burden as well as he could. He had not expected public performance to be such a large part of it.

He wandered to the window of the parlor and found it looked out onto the street with a view of the staging inn. Excellent. He would be able to see Cressida's coach arrive. He pulled out his gold watch and flicked it open.

Where was it? Had something delayed it? They did sometimes overturn, causing much injury. Sometimes wild young men bribed the coachman to let them take the reins. . . .

He controlled what he knew was illogical panic. If he could not bear to let Cressida out of his sight for a half hour, what of the future? Perhaps he could install a servant in her Matlock house to report to him on her welfare. . . .

He shook his head.

He was running mad.

More to the point would be to check on his bastard cousin's rooms. Perhaps there would be some way to get the statue without putting Cressida at risk. Bourreau had two rooms, presumably a bedroom and a parlor. Surely he would practice his business in the parlor, and he might well have his loot stashed in the bedroom. Shame he didn't know which was which, but he had a fifty-fifty chance.

He opened the door into the corridor and looked out.

The long passageway was deserted with closed

doors on either side. His rooms took up the whole of this end, giving the largest spaces and the most windows. Bourreau's, according to the innkeeper, were at the other end. A door there opened.

Tris moved back. A maid emerged, carrying a loaded tray. His food. Damnable efficiency. He closed the door and retreated to the window. So, that door led to the serving stairs.

After a knock, the pretty, buxom maid came in, dimpling and blushing, to lay out the food on the table. Cold pie, cheese, bread, butter, and a carafe of claret.

He thanked her and gave her a coin. She curtsied, blushing a deeper pink. "If that'll be all, Your Grace?"

He hoped he misunderstood her invitation. "Yes, thank you."

She pouted, but left — with a twitch of her buxom behind.

Rump.

Lascivious thoughts of Cressida washed over him in an embarrassing manner. He poured and drank a glass of the wine, checked the street for the coach, and then opened the door again. All was quiet.

The thing to remember here was that he was not, at the moment, up to anything illegal. If he wanted to stroll the corridor looking at the numbers on the doors, there was no reason why he shouldn't.

With that in mind, he put action to the thought, even though he felt transparently guilty, especially as he crossed the landing at the top of the stairs that led down to the entrance hall of the inn. There were people down there, but none seemed to be looking up, thank goodness.

He realized something else they'd forgotten. How did Cressida find out which were Bourreau's rooms?

Damnation! He could intercept her. Should he prepare for that, or continue with his mission?

Damnation again.

He'd better prepare.

Chapter Twenty-four

He turned back toward his room, almost colliding with the innkeeper, who was leading some new guests upstairs — a prosperous middle-aged couple.

"Your Grace! Is something amiss, Your Grace?"

Tris could see his concern, but also his delight at being able to reveal his eminent guest so easily. The eyes of the couple had widened.

"Just taking a stroll," Tris said genially. "Always do before eating."

He nodded to the staring couple and sauntered back to his rooms. At this rate he'd soon be the "eccentric Duke of St. Raven." Once inside, he went straight to his window — and there was the coach, swaying and rumbling down the street.

So much for stealing the statue before she arrived. He could at least get the room numbers to her. He pulled his small tablet of paper out of his pocket, slid out the attached pencil and wrote the numbers *16* and *17*. He folded the piece of paper small and left his room to go downstairs.

He didn't encounter the innkeeper again, but he crossed the path of three inn servants who pressed out of his way in an awestruck manner. He strolled to the front door of the inn and outside, glancing down the street.

There she was, walking briskly toward him ahead of a stern, soberly dressed man accompanied by a servant bearing his luggage.

He noted with amused approval that she was wearing her spectacles. Another touch of disguise, and a distinct aura of dull respectability. She was carrying her hatbox, and that meant she'd look somewhat strange at an inn.

She saw him, but hardly hesitated in her approach to the door. He deliberately didn't move so she had to brush against him. She gave him the sort of look a decent woman would at that maneuver, augmented by those round spectacles. He couldn't help a smile, and quickly turned it into a lascivious leer as he pressed the piece of paper into her hand.

Her eyes widened and he thought she'd muff it, but then she swept on, head high.

His behavior let him watch her, watch for a glimpse of her luscious behind. No chance beneath that deplorably dull and full dress. He turned back to find the other passenger glaring at him with profound disapproval.

Knowing he was coloring, Tris turned and headed back into the building. Lord above, his reputation would be in the mud soon.

His *reputation?* When had he ever bothered about his reputation in matters such as this? It was his birthright to be wild.

He passed Cressida in the hall, waiting patiently for someone to pay attention to her needs. Dressed as she was, it might take some time, which was as they wished it.

In theory.

In reality, he wanted to grab one of the servants who groveled to him and command service for her.

Silently steaming, he returned to his room to set the plan in motion. The sooner this was over, the sooner she would be safe in her proper world. And he'd damn well find a way to teach her to demand more from it. She was clever, brave, and adventurous, but her training would trap her in Matlockian mediocrity for the rest of her life if something wasn't done about it.

He yanked the bellpull with more force than he intended, and winced at the vision of the Duke of St. Raven's clamoring for attention. In moments, the maid burst into the room, breathless.

"Is something the matter, Your Grace?"

A ducal tantrum seemed in order. "I'm tired of being kept waiting. Tell Bourreau that I must see him immediately."

The maid gaped. "I think he has a client with him, Your Grace."

Tris produced his quizzing glass and stared at her through it. "And that is supposed to take precedence over my wishes?"

The poor girl went pale. "No, Your Grace! Of course not, Your Grace!"

She whirled out, and Tris winced. He'd leave her a handsome douceur. Now, he supposed, he'd better decide what to say to his bastard cousin in this underplanned encounter.

A moment later, the door opened without a knock, and a man walked in, shutting it behind him.

"What need to terrify ze servants, Your Grace?"

He was in shirtsleeves and waistcoat, and the resemblance was clear. Not too clear, thank heavens, for Jean-Marie Bourreau had brown hair and a more rugged build, but he reminded Tris a little of the face he saw in the mirror every day, and rather more of his uncle. In fact, he had quite the look of their ancestor, whose portrait hung at St. Raven's Mount, complete with Cavalier hat.

"When did you visit St. Raven's Mount?" Tris asked.

"In ze spring when you were still away." Bourreau's English seemed good, but was heavily accented.

Tris switched to French. "I'm tempted to say something dramatic, such as 'So, sir, we meet at last.' "

"To which I reply, 'Foul fiend, you destroyed my family.' "

Tris came *en garde* for a moment, but saw the humor in the other man's eyes and laughed. How surprising. He liked — recognized, in fact — his bastard cousin. Was there something in the saying that blood is thicker than water?

He'd never felt close to his six female cousins, and his mother had been an only child. He had a bond with some of the Peckworths, but they were not blood.

He gestured to the wine. "Alas, I lacked the foresight to demand two glasses."

His cousin strolled over to the washstand and appropriated the tumbler there. He poured wine into it and into the glass, offering the glass to Tris. An impudent rascal, but then, so was he.

He toasted Bourreau. "Your health! So, I hope for an explanation of your recent career."

The Frenchman sipped. "Can it wait? I have a client waiting in my room."

Tris froze, wondering how he could have overlooked that obvious problem. The innkeeper had said as much, then the maid had been specific, and he'd ignored it both times! What had turned his mind into a block of wood?

He knew. A woman with big gray eyes. He stretched his sense of hearing, seeking sounds of alarm from the other end of the corridor.

"Can he wait a little?" he asked.

If Cressida tried the bedroom, she'd be all right. If not, surely she'd find some quick-witted way out of the situation. She had quick wits.

"A little." Bourreau seemed amused. "An explanation . . ." He regarded Tris from heavy-lidded eyes that must drive women wild. "Are you disposed to deliver me to the hangman?"

"God, no. I don't think you've done anything to hang for, but once in court, there'd be nothing to stop you from throwing my family's name in the dirt."

How long did this need to last? They should have arranged some sort of signal. Truth was, neither of them had been thinking clearly.

"Then," said Bourreau, "what will you pay me to keep your family's name out of the dirt?"

Tris yanked his wits back to the matter in hand. So much for cousinly friendship. "Why should I pay anything? You cannot do harm without revealing your identity as Le Corbeau."

"Perhaps." But the Frenchman had a worrying

smile in his eyes. "Tell me, Your Grace, why did you arrange for someone to pretend to be me?"

At least Bourreau didn't realize who it had been.

"How did you know it was my doing?"

"Who else? I knew you would not want me to hang, for the reasons you gave. I was preparing to send you an encouragement to engage yourself on my behalf when — poof! — I am proved innocent and released."

"Then you know why."

"There were surely easier ways for a duke to obtain the release of a prisoner?"

"Are matters still so arbitrary in France, even after revolution? A duke in England has many powers, but riding roughshod over the law is not one of them. It would have been exhausting work, but more to the point, it would have revealed an uncomfortable interest in you. Now, why don't you tell me exactly what you want — bearing in mind that you are in no position to demand anything."

"Am I not, Your Grace? . . ."

Tris felt a prickling down his spine. He had no doubt that Bourreau was an old hand at risky games. He also had no doubt that the man thought he had a winning hand.

Cressida paused outside the door of number 16.

Her lowly garb had worked to her advantage thus far. What with Mr. Althorpe, the self-important scholar, and the separate arrival of a demanding couple, no one had leaped to ask her business.

She had realized too late, however, that she and Tris had not planned when each should do what. How could they have been so muddle-headed? Heart beating too fast for comfort, she had counted to a hundred while also watching the landing at the top of the stairs.

At the count of eighty-four she saw a man in shirtsleeves walk briskly across that landing. No guarantee that it was Le Corbeau obeying Tris's summons, but he didn't look like a servant, and who else would be moving about so informally dressed?

The hall was empty for a moment, so Cressida took a breath and walked toward the stairs as if she had every right to do so. Her heart raced so fast she thought it should be audible, and her feet longed to dash up into the concealment of the corridor.

She climbed the stairs primed for a voice calling for her to stop. When she reached the top she turned in the direction the man had walked from, halting to regain her wits. She couldn't remember the last time she'd felt in her right wits. What was she doing here on this mad, criminal enterprise? She could end up in jail!

She took a series of steadying breaths, then straightened and set off down this side of the corridor, looking at the numbers on the doors. She reminded herself that she was an abandoned lover of Monsieur Bourreau, here to beg him to take her back.

Twenty, 19, 18. That must have been Bourreau. The plan was working. Sixteen and 17 were the two doors at the end on the left. There were two other doors opposite — 14 and 15 — which meant the door in between, the one facing the corridor, led to the service stairs.

For some reason, now that the time had arrived, she was terrified of actually turning the knob to one of the doors and going in. Well, not just for some reason. For an excellent reason. Once she did that, she was — in the eyes of the world — a thief.

They hanged thieves! Not often these days, at least not petty thieves of previously good character, but they whipped them, or transported them to Australia.

Clinging to the idea of her story, and to the fact that Tris was keeping Le Corbeau occupied, she turned the knob of room 16. If worst came to worst, surely the Duke of St. Raven could prevent her being hauled off to jail.

She opened the door, went in, and shut the door behind her.

She scanned the room — the bedroom — then froze, blind panic lancing through her.

A naked woman lay on the bed, staring back at her.

Idiotically, Cressida almost screamed the alarm. When the woman did nothing except raise her brows, her terrified brain noticed an easel and an excellent picture forming there, all pink curves and sinuous invitation.

Artist. Bourreau was an artist.

Model. Not quite the society portraits she'd expected.

The woman smiled. "Early for his next appointment, luv?"

Cressida managed to breathe, and leaped at the explanation. "Yes! I didn't know there'd be . . ." She glanced at the woman, then away. "I mean, do you want me to wait next door?"

She looked to her left and saw a door that must lead into 17, the parlor. She inched toward it, but then gathered her wits enough to look around this room for the statue.

It wasn't in sight, and now there was no way to search. If Tris could swear, so could she. She silently borrowed one of his.

Damnation.

"If you want," the woman said, "but I don't mind. I daren't move — he'd be that upset. But if you want to sit and talk, it'll pass the time."

The idea of chatting to this completely naked woman dumbfounded Cressida, but her main turmoil was how to deal with this barrier to her search. She decided to move around the room. Surely the woman wouldn't be surprised that an intruder wished to look elsewhere.

"Have you been his model long?" she asked for something to say, strolling toward the empty fireplace. There was a portmanteau near the bed. What possible excuse could she find to look into it?

"A couple of months. You?"

Cressida remembered she was supposed to be a model, too. So many different parts to remember. "This will be my first time."

"No wonder you look wound up. Don't you worry. There's nothing to it once you get around to it, and he's a proper gentleman. No funny business."

Cressida's wandering had brought her back to the easel. She paused, struck by the picture's quality. Highwayman or not, Jean-Marie Bourreau had a gift. The picture was accurate, and yet it made a fantastical confection of the woman's large breasts and swelling thighs, her neat waist and dainty feet.

Cressida knew by instinct that the picture would be arousing for many men.

For Tris?

"Aren't you cold?" she asked.

"A bit. Why don't you drape that blanket over me, luv? He does when he wants to work on things a bit without needing us. Like I say, a proper gentleman. He was called away, but he didn't expect to be gone this long."

Lord, time was ticking! What was she to do?

Cressida put down her hatbox, unfolded the woolen blanket on the end of the bed, and draped it over the woman. Should she try to tie her up in order to ransack the room?

"I'm Lizzie Dunstan. You?"

"Jane Wemworthy."

"No need to look at me like that."

Cressida only realized then that she'd put on a Wemworthy face. Oh, well, she'd build on that. She stuck her nose in the air and grabbed her hatbox. "I prefer to wait next door. Good day to you, Miss Dunstan."

"It's Mrs!" the woman shouted after her, alarmingly loudly.

Cressida shut the door and stood there, ears stretched for any sign of alarm or approach.

The inn was not a quiet place — she could

hear wheels and hooves in the street, and someone giving orders outside the window — but nothing sounded unusual. Lizzie Dunstan was fixed in her pose. Cressida could only pray that Tris could keep Le Corbeau in conversation for a while longer.

But as soon as Bourreau returned, the woman would tell him he'd had another visitor. If he missed the statue, he'd know who'd taken it.

Jane Wemworthy. Oh, poor Mrs. Wemworthy. It was to be hoped that she never visited Hatfield!

With any luck, he'd not know anything had gone. She was going to take the jewels, not the statue. At worst, she was going to switch the statues.

She put the hatbox on the table and looked around, failure chilling her. The statuette wasn't on view, and there was nowhere to hide it. It must be in the bedroom. Perhaps in that valise.

There was little in this room that belonged to a guest — just a jacket tossed over the back of the faded sofa and three books on a table beside the only armchair. A clock ticked on the mantel over the empty fireplace, bracketed by two figurines, but they were cheap pottery pieces.

The furnishings didn't offer hiding places — the sofa and chair were accompanied by a table with four chairs around it and an old-fashioned box bench against the wall.

Box bench.

She hurried over and tugged on the seat. It moved. It was heavy, but she heaved it up, and lo and behold — a chest!

By then she was so sure of failure that she just

stared at it, as if it might vanish into pixie dust. But it remained as it was, a simple leather-bound chest with brass corners and a brass hasp-and-plate lock secured by a padlock.

She gave a little whoop of victory and set to work, praying Tris could hold Bourreau long enough.

She pulled the winkler out of her hatbox. There was not a lot of room between the lock and the side of the bench, but if she could lift the brass plate on the top, the padlock would be useless.

She put the edge of the tool against the metal and pushed. It went under the edge a tiny way. She gritted her teeth and put all her weight behind the tool, her senses quivering to catch someone coming. Her heart was racing with nerves, but also with triumph. All she had to do now was force open the lock, get the jewels out of the statue, and everything would be well.

Not everything, but she wouldn't pay heed to that now.

At last the tool was a half inch under the metal. She paused to catch her breath and listen to the world beyond her pulse.

Nothing unusual.

Now to test the power of levers. Someone had said, "Give me a long enough lever, and I can move the Earth."

The tool had a curve to it. She leaned down and the plate lifted a bit. It was working!

She paused again to listen, then had a thought. She dug the statue out of the hatbox. If she was caught before she could extract the jewels, she might still be able to make the switch.

Of course, being caught forcing open the lock was going to be hard to explain, but she couldn't think like that now.

She pushed the statuette into one of her pockets, thinking that it was just as well, milord duke, that she was dressed in lowly wear rather than fashion, since fashionable skirts were too slim to allow use of pockets at all. There was certainly a bulge, but under the fullness, it might go unnoticed.

Then she saw the key on the inside of the room door. She dashed over and turned it. There. Now no one could burst in on her from the corridor. There was no key in the door to the bedroom. She shrugged. She'd done the best she could.

She turned back to her task, wishing her heart-beat would slow, that she didn't feel dizzy. Wishing didn't make it so, however, and at least her hands were steady when she leaned on the winkler again. The metal rose a bit more, and she saw the nails that held it in place.

It was going to work, and with any luck, when she'd finished she could push it back into place so it wouldn't be immediately obvious. . . .

Then she heard noises.

Shouting.

A bang, as if something heavy had fallen.

She froze, as if being still might save her. But then she breathed again. The noises were loud rather than close. Somewhere people were shouting. She even heard a hunting halloo. Some rowdy rascals in or around the Cockleshell, but that was excellent. They would keep the inn servants tied up.

She turned back to the job and put all her weight to levering. And the metal sprang free!

Cressida suppressed another whoop, put aside the tool, and raised the lid. If the statue wasn't in here after this, she was going to have a fit of the vapors. . . .

She stared.

The chest contained a jumble of jewelry and other precious items, many of them Indian. She thought she recognized some as very like pieces her father had owned — including, her bewildered mind noticed, a lot of erotic ivory statuettes.

Were there hundreds of these statues in England? Did Le Corbeau collect them as part of his dealings in risqué art? She had a nightmarish vision of searching through piles and piles of them, trying to spot the right one. . . .

She shook herself. Le Corbeau had stolen one from La Coop — she knew that — so it was here. She pushed her spectacles up her nose and began to disentangle the statues from chains, necklaces, and weapons, looking feverishly for the right style of hat.

"I could call your bluff," Tris said to his cousin. "I doubt you have the money to drag this through the English courts, and I'd win in the end."

The Frenchman still wore his gambler's smile. "Perhaps. But you can avoid all with just a little generosity. And your family does owe me something."

"You're my uncle's bastard. That doesn't carry any claim at all."

"The duke treated my mother heartlessly."

"He treated everyone heartlessly —"

Riotous sounds cut off what Tris was saying. Loud voices down below. A bang that shook the old building, as if a heavy piece of furniture had been overturned. A cry that sounded like a hunting halloo.

Tris shared a look with Bourreau, and in accord, they went to open the door. The disturbance could have nothing to do with his affairs, but Cressida . . . He had to keep her safe.

Was it Miranda? He couldn't imagine her causing a riot — at least, not of this sort. It sounded more like a drunken mob down there. Was there a by-election going on?

But then he heard boots rumbling up the stairs.

He and Bourreau were halfway down the corridor when the drunks spilled out at the top of the stairs, crying, "Halloo!" and "Tallyho!" and banging on all the doors.

"Corbeau!" someone bellowed. "We have you now!"

Crofton!

Tris turned to Bourreau, but his cousin was already hurtling down the corridor straight for the mob. With a curse, Tris took after him. Cressida was in Le Corbeau's rooms!

Some of the rioters burst into the farthest room, and a woman shrieked. With a roar, Tris battered his way into the room. Bourreau was hauling a man off the bed.

Off a woman.

Three animals were on her. Tris hurled one across the room to crash into the wall before he realized that the woman was big, naked, and not Cressida.

The man he'd hurled had been Pugh, still in his Henry VIII clothes. Bourreau had knocked out a tiger and was rolling on the floor with a Harlequin and a man in crumpled ordinary wear.

The wild-eyed woman was wrapping a blanket back around herself and seemed safe. Tris whirled, searching the room.

Cressida?

He heard a crashing, splintering noise from the adjoining room and leaped over the fight on the floor —

Then froze in the doorway.

There she was, pale, wide-eyed behind spectacles, and clutching the statue, facing Crofton and a bunch of wild, drunken men who had just battered down the door. She glanced at Tris once, their eyes held for a heartbeat, then she looked back at Crofton and his drunken pack.

Every muscle tensed to dash to her side but Tris knew instantly that her best protection might be the duke not the man.

She was caught, and too soon. A quick glance showed no sign of another statue. They'd failed, but now to get her safely away from here.

To do that, he had to act as if she were a complete stranger.

He brought his quizzing glass into play. "What," he drawled, "is the cause of this disturbance?"

Crofton swung around, eyes narrowed. "St. Raven?" Then he turned back to eye Cressida. "Well, well, well . . ."

Chapter Twenty-five

Tris maintained a bored demeanor, turning his quizzing glass on Cressida. "And who, may I ask, are you, ma'am?"

Her eyes were still huge, but she had some of her color back. Perhaps it was faith in him. He hoped it was justified.

She dropped a curtsy. "My name is Cressida Mandeville, Your Grace."

"You know him, I see," sneered Crofton.

Her surprise was beautifully done. "All London knows the Duke of St. Raven by sight, Lord Crofton."

"Then what are you doing in a man's locked room, eh?"

"I was unaware that door was locked, sir. I entered by the other one."

The innkeeper arrived then, pushing into the room, puce and sweating, some menservants behind him. "I've sent for the magistrates! I'll have the law on you all." Then he saw Tris. "Your Grace! Oh, Your Grace, I'm that sorry you've been disturbed —"

Tris raised a hand and took control. He strolled into the room, closer to Cressida, eyeing both her and the statue through his quizzing glass. "Your statue, ma'am? How very . . . peculiar."

He saw her lips twitch and prayed she could hold to her act. "It belongs to my father, Your Grace."

"I won everything off your father," Crofton snapped, "including his dirty statues. I call you thief, Miss Mandeville, and doxy to Le Corbeau, and I'll repeat that when the magistrates arrive. I'll see you whipped at the cart's tail."

Tris turned, ready to step between Crofton and Cressida if necessary. He prayed the man would make the move. He'd never wanted anything in life as much as he wanted to smash Crofton's face to a bloody pulp. For the moment, he managed not to even let his hands form fists.

"You won nine statues, sir," Cressida said with icy disdain. "There were ten, which can be proved. You did not win the possessions in our London house."

Crofton's snarl was pure frustration. How he must hate Cressida for escaping.

"Then what about Le Corbeau? Explain what you're doing in his rooms, if you can."

Before Cressida could try, Tris intervened. "More to the point, Crofton, what are you doing here?"

"Hunting crow. Perhaps you'd left my party, duke, before Le Corbeau invaded to filch my property."

"Certainly I had. It was a tedious affair. But why here? Monsieur Bourreau was cleared of suspicion."

"Easy enough for one of his colleagues to take to the road in his distinctive getup. Fooled the magistrates, but it doesn't fool me."

Jean-Marie burst into the room then, bruised, disordered, but visibly simmering with rage. He had his model in a protective arm, swathed in her blanket. He sat the woman on the wooden settle and turned on Crofton.

"You accuse me!" he snapped, eyes blazing.

Ah, the French temperament. Very useful.

"Moi! Un artiste! Un homme innocent!" Eloquent hands emphasized every point. "You accuse me — *me!* I was proved innocent. What does an honest man have to do in zis wretched country to be left in peace? You have invaded my room! Damaged my property! Assaulted my respectable model —"

"Respectable?" chortled the tiger, staggering in and heading straight for the blanket-wrapped woman. Jean-Marie whirled and kicked the man in the balls. The tiger shrieked and rolled into a knot of agony.

Tris couldn't help it; he laughed. "Bravo!"

Not sure where the next throw would take them all, he turned to Crofton. "My cousin, Jean-Marie Bourreau," he introduced, "whom I was visiting on family matters."

"Cousin?" Crofton exploded.

"Cousin. My uncle's son on the wrong side of the blanket. I suggest you leave, Crofton, and take your detritus with you. Kindly pay the innkeeper for damages as you go."

Crofton's eyes shifted around. "Not until I know what Miss Mandeville is doing here with that statue. We have only her word that there was one at her father's London house. I think the whole set was at Stokeley Manor, which means that is one of the ones the Crow stole. And that," he said, confident enough to meet Tris's eyes, "proves that your 'cousin' is the Crow, and that Miss Mandeville is in league with him."

Tris could almost hear the gears of Crofton's mind turning. "Would I be completely mistaken, St. Raven, to think that particular statue is the one that your bit of Turkish delight expressed such an interest in?"

Tris worked at not showing any effect, and inspected the statue again through his quizzing glass. "It is perhaps similar enough to serve. Is it for sale, Miss Mandeville?"

She curtsied. He hoped her pink cheeks could be seen as natural in this outrageous situation. "Certainly, Your Grace. I came to offer it to Monsieur Bourreau, as he was recommended to me as a collector of such items. As you know, Lord Crofton," she added with false sweetness, "my family has need to sell everything that is not essential to survival."

She was a queen among women.

This damnable scene, however, was hammering nails into their coffin. All these men, despite drink, would remember this encounter and talk about it. Her being here was unfortunate but not ruinous. It was, however, a springing point to hell if anyone decided that Cressida resembled St. Raven's houri.

Tris glanced at Crofton. He looked baffled, and no wonder. He had a string of events that seemed to suggest an unholy alliance. On the other hand, who was going to believe an illegal connection between a French highwayman, a virtuous provincial lady, and a duke? Especially when the virtuous lady was the image of propriety in her dull clothing, tidy bonnet, and spectacles.

Jean-Marie strolled toward Cressida and took the statue, turning it in his hands. "An excellent example of erotic temple art from Kashmir, Miss Mandeville, zough not, I am desolate to say, of great rarity."

Tris wondered if he had a clue what he was talking about.

"I could offer you no more than t'irty pounds for it. What a shame it is not a pair."

"It was a set of ten, monsieur. We do have some other Indian artifacts, though, alas, most passed into Lord Crofton's hands."

"I am only interested in — your pardon, mademoiselle — ze erotic art." He returned the statue to her. "Let me know if you wish to sell."

"Allow me to offer first, Miss Mandeville," Tris said. "As Lord Crofton mentioned, I have someone in mind who would like that piece."

Most of Tris's attention was on Crofton, however. The man was thwarted and thus dangerous, and a hint of humor in Jean-Marie was not helping.

Crofton glared at Jean-Marie. "I still say you're the Crow, Froggy, and that you raided my house last night. I'll search this hole before I leave, and no one's going to stop me."

Good, thought Tris. *I still might have a chance to batter him to bits.* "You forget, Crofton, Monsieur Bourreau is my uncle's son — and thus under my protection."

"Protection," Crofton snarled, his face reddening. "Let's talk about protection! That woman" — he jabbed a finger at Cressida — "who looks so prim and proper, was your companion at Stokeley Manor, dressed to suit her nature. And she's a known cohort of Le Corbeau —"

"I most certainly am *not!*" Cressida cried.

Tris raised a hand again and turned his quizzing glass on her, looking her up and down. He dropped all the acid disbelief he could into his words. "Crofton, I think you are mad."

Crofton turned to his followers. "You saw St. Raven's houri!" he yelled. "That's her. That's *her!* And the little bint had the nerve to act so prim and proper with me. No wonder she let herself be snatched by Le Corbeau. It was a setup!"

"You're raving," Tris said.

He was, too, flecks spitting from his mouth.

"St. Raven's houri?" It was Pugh, staggering in, clutching his head. "Where? Want a go at her."

Tris didn't let himself serve Pugh as Jean-Marie had served the tiger. Instead, he indicated Cressida. "Lord Crofton thinks that this Miss Mandeville was with me at his party."

Pugh stared, then shook his head. "Man's mad. Suspected it for a while. That houri was a tasty morsel."

Tris saw spots of color bloom deeper on Cressida's red cheeks and wished he could reassure her that she was the tastiest morsel imaginable.

He turned to Crofton. "Since Miss Mandeville seems to lack male protection and you have linked her name to mine, it is for me to defend her honor. Do we need to take this any further?"

Sir Manley Bayne was sober enough to grab Crofton's arm. "Must be mistaken, Croffy. I remember that bit of Turkish delight. Really, Croffy, no resemblance. Look at all those bobbling curls, and the glasses, and the tight little mouth. Remember that bit with the cucumber? . . . No, really."

Crofton turned to look at Tris, and Tris saw pure hatred. A duke was untouchable by this, but Cressida . . .

Cressida, with her longing for peaceful, conventional Matlockian propriety. Tris knew how small towns worked. They were worse than London. A touch of scandal was like leprosy. A person was never clean again.

And such gossip couldn't be stopped, not even with a pistol ball. Especially gossip as juicy as this, involving both a duke and a romantic highwayman. Killing Crofton, dammit, wouldn't help. Her only safety was if there was never any believable connection between Miss Mandeville and the wicked Duke of St. Raven.

He gave her a slight bow. "Miss Mandeville, I deeply regret that due to a coincidence your name has been linked with mine in a distasteful connection. I doubt that the slander will be repeated, but if you should experience any repercussions, please inform me, and I will take care of it. As for that statue, I am still in the mood to purchase it."

Her eyes met his, and he saw she had made the same grim, logical journey as he. But perhaps she had been too sensible to ever be teased by hope.

"Monsieur Bourreau valued it at thirty pounds, Your Grace."

"Then allow me to make it fifty to compensate for this encounter. You will take my note for payment at my London house?"

"Of course, Your Grace."

He pulled out his tablet and scribbled the promise, then gave it to her, taking the statue in return. He had no idea if it was the one with the jewels or not, but it would be safer in his hands.

If she didn't have the jewels, that was still to do.

He couldn't stop a touch of hope. This adventure would not then be over.

He turned a frigid stare on Crofton and the invaders. "I cannot imagine why you are still cluttering this room."

They began — even Crofton — to back out the door. He followed to make sure the innkeeper was paid for the damage. At that belated point, the local magistrate turned up with reinforcements.

Tris left Crofton to deal with him, though he knew it would all be smoothed over with a little talk and some money. A viscount was almost as immune to the law as a duke.

But Crofton swung back. "There's a noose in this somewhere, St. Raven, and damme but I'll find it."

Tris's patience broke so completely, he was surprised no one heard it snap. "Even bring yourself to my attention again, Crofton, and I will crush you like the insect you are."

It sounded like his uncle, but for once Tris

didn't mind. He enjoyed the way Crofton blanched, and the way his friends hurried him away, though not so much as he'd have enjoyed his fists crunching bones.

As the corridor emptied, he took a moment to cool down. They'd won this round, but that still left the war. Crofton would not openly repeat his accusations, but the other men would describe this encounter. Cressida couldn't escape gossip about that. He was sure Crofton would find other ways to drip his acid, ways that could never be traced directly back to him.

His first move had better be a preemptive strike. Hasten back to London and start another story circulating. One about Crofton's base behavior and idiocy here, and about poor Miss Mandeville, insulted when she'd been trying to scrape up some money to save her family from the poorhouse.

He returned to Jean-Marie's rooms to find his cousin and Cressida alone in the parlor, talking. Tris hoped she wasn't being too confiding. Jean-Marie might seem an ally, but he was a scoundrel and a blackmailer and didn't need any new weapons.

"Your model?" he asked.

"Is dressing and will soon be gone. I t'ought perhaps we needed time and privacy."

"Undoubtedly, but there's no excuse for Miss Mandeville to linger, and I must take her home."

Cressida stared at him. "You can't. How would that look?"

"As if I am a gentleman," he snapped. "What else is the Duke of St. Raven to do with a stray lady he befriends at an inn?"

"Put her on a coach?"

"No."

Into silence, Jean-Marie said, "A houri at an orgy?"

Tris turned on him. "No."

His cousin hastily raised an apologetic hand. "Quite! Impossible, of course."

"Miss Mandeville and I have only just met."

Jean-Marie rolled his eyes, but shrugged.

Tris was aware that he was letting his icy rage spill, but he seemed unable to stop it. Then he remembered other aspects. "You invaded Crofton's orgy and stole from him?"

"But, why not?" Jean-Marie switched into French. "I hear about this so wild party, and I think that such things go on for days, and that those few who linger will not be in a state to oppose me and my friends. And they are not. Not many valuable trinkets on the guests, alas, but so many interesting items! Some statues such as the one you have just bought from Miss Mandeville. Do you care to explain that?"

Tris saw a trap and thought quickly, but Cressida spoke first, in adequate French.

"It is simple enough, sir. As you will have gathered, my father lost nearly everything to Crofton at cards. Then I learned that you had stolen one of the statues from someone leaving the party. I took the idea of stealing it from you. A tiny part of the whole, but something. These things represent my father's memories of India."

"But how," Jean-Marie asked gently, "did you know that I was Le Corbeau? I am assumed innocent."

Tris stepped in. "I knew better, and in a fit of folly, I brought her. There's no need to dance around this. All we need is to make sure there's no scandal." He met his cousin's irreverent eyes. "If I agree to your terms, Le Corbeau will cease to fly, and you will return to France and stay there. Yes?"

"Terms?" Cressida asked, looking between them.

"My cousin has created a situation where it would be . . . convenient for me to share some of my good fortune with him."

"I can't allow that!"

"This is nothing to do with you. Truly, Cressida. This all predates your adventures."

"True," said Jean-Marie. "I decided that as the old duke's only son, I was owed something by fundamental right and justice. Perhaps even the dukedom itself."

"What?" Cressida gaped at them.

Tris took her arm. "As you said, we mustn't linger. I'll explain it all to you another time."

"Another time?" she echoed faintly.

"At least this outrageous encounter gives me an excuse to visit you. I will need to assure myself of your recovery from the overwhelming shock and distress."

"You think me too calm?" she snapped. "I could faint if it would please you."

Jean-Marie laughed. "A woman of spirit! You should seize her, cousin."

Tris looked at him.

"Ah. A shame . . ."

Cressida's mouth threatened to quiver, and she

pulled it in — then remembered Crofton's disgusting associate sneering at her "tight little mouth." She snatched off her forgotten spectacles and put them in her pocket, but that didn't change her unflattering clothes, her plain face, or her tight little mouth.

Bourreau lifted the lid of the bench and pulled out the winkler. "A most resolute bit of thievery," he remarked, opening the chest. He looked at her. "I am fortunate that you only had time to take one before you were interrupted."

He suspected something, and her strength was close to exhausted. She didn't know how to counter this.

Tris moved forward and looked into the chest. "A set! I wish to purchase all of this. Any payment goes to Miss Mandeville, of course."

"But this is the reward of my labor, cousin."

Cressida saw the power of the look that Tris sent to the Frenchman. "Fundamental right and justice?"

Bourreau shrugged and smiled at her. "I give you a present of the set, Miss Mandeville, and the rest of the Indian treasures I took from Stokeley Manor. Your father's property, his sentimental souvenirs. It is right and just that it return to him."

Cressida worried that there were hidden traps here, but she could see nothing to do but to say, "You're very kind. Thank you."

Tris and his cousin were looking at each other, the family resemblance clear more in manner than in looks. "You will have it all delivered to Miss Mandeville's house?"

"On my honor as a Frenchman."

Tris nodded. "Then you could call on me, too, to arrange the final details."

The Frenchman nodded, with a strange, almost regretful expression.

Cressida still worried that in some way Tris was buying her safety, but she had no energy now to pursue it. She let him guide her out of the room.

Once in the corridor, however, she halted. "Tris . . . St. Raven. Truly, I would rather return to London by coach. It would be safer, and I can't . . ." *Can't bear the long farewell,* she thought, but could not say.

He closed his eyes briefly. "Very well. As you argued before, you'll be safe enough."

He escorted her to the staging inn and purchased a ticket for her, giving an excellent impression of a duke doing his duty by a lowly dependent. As he gave it to her, however, he asked softly, "The jewels?"

Undeniable pride swelled in her. "Are in my pocket. I had just extracted them when Crofton burst in."

"Bravo, my indomitable Miss Mandeville. Is it wise of me to call on you tomorrow? I would like to."

"Why not?"

"Your mother is aware of this venture, you said?"

"Oh, yes." What an age ago that seemed, and yet it had only been this morning. "I don't think she'll batter you with a stool. After all, we will be home again before nightfall." No need for him to know that she'd confessed to more than that.

"And I do want to know your cousin's story. Are you sure — ?"

"Absolutely. There will be no scandal out of this. I'll make sure of that."

"I was the one who insisted on coming," she said.

"We couldn't have expected Crofton's interruption. Without that, everything would have been smooth."

As they talked, she saw farewell in his eyes and felt it in her heart. She had a visit to look forward to tomorrow, but then this journey was over.

Too soon, a rumble told of the approaching coach. His longing for one last kiss must be as desperate as hers, but who knew who watched? Even these precious, lingering moments had been foolish.

The coach rumbled in, and ostlers leaped to change the horses. Cressida had only a moment to look at Tris, then she hurried to present her ticket and be allowed to climb on. By the time she'd squeezed into the middle of a seat, all was ready and she had to let it take her away without even a wave.

A wave seemed entirely inadequate for the end of this part of her life. The end of the Travels of Cressida Mandeville.

She had not found dragons, serpents, and cockadrills, but she'd encountered equally fantastical beasts — dukes, whores, and highwaymen. And there among them she had found and lost the most precious treasure of all.

Jean-Marie Bourreau stood in thought, watching from a window as first the laden stage left, then his cousin in his most excellent curricle drawn by most excellent horses.

Thus the adventure ended, and it seemed he would gain what he had come for — the fulfillment of his vow to his mother, and the means to live the life of a gentleman artist in France. It was his right. It was less than his father had promised.

And yet, he felt a pang. In his cousin, whom he had expected to hate, he had found someone he could like very much. He shrugged. He would fix that if he could, but not at the price of his necessities.

He turned from the window and began to finish the work on the easel. He had a few commissions to complete — all decorous portraits. Then London and settlement with his cousin. Then, thank the good God, a boat for France. France, where he could report at his mother's grave that he had made the Duke of St. Raven pay. France, where he could return to a civilized life.

Why on earth Napoleon had ever wanted to invade England, he could not imagine.

He had just finished the work when the door opened and a woman walked in. She wore an elegant blue outfit, but he recognized her.

He bowed. "Madame Coop."

She closed the door. "You stole something from me, sir."

Now here was a delightful surprise, both the lady and the fact that she spoke in tolerable French. "Did I?"

The deep blue matched her lovely, knowing eyes. "If you did, monsieur, you would find me very generous in payment. . . ."

She slowly, expertly, ran a tongue around her lips, lips that were doubtless reddened, but so subtly that she could still appear a lady.

Jean-Marie sighed with pleasure and walked toward her. "Payment from you, madame, would be more precious to me than gold and rubies. But alas, I fear I have nothing to sell."

A brow rose. "No?"

"You behold a fool. In a fit of most abject folly, I have just returned that statue to its rightful owner."

"The rightful owner of that statue is me, sir!"

"Alas, no. It is a gentleman called Mandeville."

Her arched brows twitched into a puzzled frown. "The nabob who lost everything to Crofton? What madness made you do that? If they were anybody's, they were Crofton's." She swirled to pace the small room, magnificently angry. "Devil take you, sir, you had no right to do that. That statue was mine!"

"What can it matter to you, my most beautiful lady? A statue worth perhaps thirty pounds. Of course," he said, suddenly thoughtful, "so many seemed to want it. . . ."

She paused to look at him. "What? Who?"

Jean-Marie considered possible danger to his cousin and the interesting Miss Mandeville, but he was careless by nature. "The Duke of St. Raven was here. He also wanted it. For a little houri, he said. He has arranged to purchase it from the Mandevilles."

"Damn the man, he's gammoned me!" But then she shrugged, a wry smile on her lips. "It seems I have dragged myself from my bed at dawn and hurtled about the country for no purpose at all."

"For no purpose?" Jean-Marie strolled to her and took her hand. "I have a bed, beautiful lady, if you need to make up for lost time."

She eyed him as a duchess might eye a peasant. "I doubt you can afford me, monsieur."

He tugged on her hand. "Perhaps we can discuss it, madame. In bed."

She resisted. "That is not the way I do business."

She had not, however, pulled free, and her eyes were amused, intrigued, perhaps even aroused. He had grown up in the company of whores, and he knew many retained the gift to allow themselves true pleasure in the right times.

"Then perhaps, this is not business. I am not entirely the highwayman, my lovely Miranda. Surely you are not entirely the whore? Can we not sometimes do just as we please, without thought of commerce?"

He raised his hands and pushed off her charming, elegant hat, and still, she did not resist.

Chapter Twenty-six

Cressida arrived home in a hackney carriage, and her mother opened the door, a thousand anxieties in her eyes.

As soon as she was in the house, Cressida fell into her arms. "It worked!" she exclaimed, burying the tragic aspects deep. "I have them."

She pulled free and led her mother up to her bedroom. She shut the door, then dug in her pocket, and pulled out the handful of jewels to pour them, shining, into her mother's hands.

Her mother looked down at them. "So few, but they are beautiful. . . . Surely there must be enough here to pay our way." But then she looked up. "And you, dearest?"

Cressida put on her brightest smile. "I'm home before I could be wicked, you see." But she busied herself in taking off her dull bonnet and the cap with the curls before turning back. "And it's for the best, Mama. He doesn't care for me. Not in the right way."

She lied because it was a lie she had to believe.

"The duke does want to call here tomorrow, if you don't object. To ensure that I am all right, and to explain one part of the adventure."

Her mother stared for a moment, but then looked at the jewels. "I can hardly object, can I?"

"He's arranged for the return of a lot of Father's Indian ornaments from Stokeley, as well."

"How?"

"It's a long story. . . ."

And yet it took such a short time to relate the events in Hatfield.

"Oh, dear," her mother said. "There will be talk."

"Talk?" How could her mother guess about the orgy and the houri?

"Your being there unchaperoned and encountering drunken men. It will seem a little rash, dear."

Once she, too, would have quailed at that, but now it seemed a mere nothing. "I don't think it will ruin me, Mama."

"True, and no one need know that you traveled part of the way with the duke. That was foolish, dear, and I should never have permitted it. Heaven knows what would happen if they ever learned of such a thing in Matlock."

True, true. "I know it, Mama, but don't worry. I'm done with wildness now."

Her mother embraced her. "I knew I could trust to your good sense. Come along, and we'll see what effect this treasure has on your poor father."

Cressida followed her mother down the corridor to her parents' room, unable to stop thinking that her "poor father" was the author of all their problems.

And yet, he had caused her adventures, too. Impossible to imagine returning to Matlock without ever having known Tris as more than the

Duke of St. Raven, glimpsed across glittering rooms.

Sir Arthur lay in the bed in the same state as before, eyes fixed on nothing, limp, looking eerily not there. Her mother hurried over. "See, dear, here's Cressida with your lost property. Your jewels."

Nothing.

Her mother took his limp hand and put the jewels into it, closing his hand over them. Did his brows twitch?

Cressida sat on the other side of the bed, trying to think of the right words. "I took them back from Crofton, Father. A couple of gentlemen helped me. We have all the statues back, and most of the smaller items from Stokeley. Not the bronze Buddha, I'm afraid. Hard to carry that on a horse."

Was that movement of his lips a weak smile?

What else to say? Surely he'd like to hear of Crofton's defeat.

"Crofton was furious. Almost raging. I thought he might fall to the ground and froth at the mouth! And . . ." — dangerous, but necessary — "one of the gentlemen who helped me was the Duke of St. Raven. He squashed Crofton with a look."

"Crofton . . ." It came out hoarse, as from a person with a sore throat, but it was a word, and her father blinked. He turned his head slowly to look at Cressida, then at her mother. "Louisa?"

Tears escaped down her mother's cheeks. "Yes, love. And see, here are the jewels. There is enough, here, isn't there, for a decent life?"

Her father began to tremble, perhaps with life returning to his limbs. "Praise God, praise God. Oh, Louisa, love, I've been such a fool."

Cressida's mother gathered him into her arms. "I know, dear. And if you are ever so stupid again, I will part your hair with a chair! I know what you've been up to, escaping into this state so that I couldn't give you all the many angry pieces of my mind that I have wanted to. . . ."

Biting her lip, Cressida tiptoed out of the room. She didn't think her parents noticed. Though touched, she wondered at her mother's complete forgiveness.

Yet her father might never change his nature, and the marriage vows did include "for better, for worse." That made her think of Tris, who had suggested that her father was addicted to adventure, to risk, and had arranged his entire life to provide it. They said the best thief-takers were thieves. Had Tris recognized a nature similar to his own?

That was another reason to lock him away in the forbidden part of her mind. She was not like her mother, and would never tolerate such impossible behavior, especially if it involved other women!

Her mother's nature, however, meant that she, too, could not be relied on for security. She would bend to her husband's persuasions.

A trust fund, Cressida thought, heading briskly back to her room. She didn't know exactly how that worked, but she knew that once a trust was set up for a woman, it was hers to manage. A husband or father could not misuse it.

And jewelry. This time she would allow her father to give her as much fine jewelry as he could afford. She would not be forced into desperate need again, into desperate ventures to exotic lands. She was returning to Matlock and common sense for the rest of her life.

Tris arrived home intent on privacy. Since he'd not taken a servant he had to drive to the mews and enter his house through the kitchens. His servants were not unaccustomed to this, but giving them careless smiles was a strain.

He reached the hall as the knocker rapped. The footman there hurried to answer it before Tris could stop him, so when it opened he was pinned in view of his oldest cousin, Cornelia, Countess of Tremaine. She had always been heavy and sour, but now in her forties, she was developing a mustache and jowls.

Whatever the footman was trying to say, Cornelia plodded by him, reinforced by her own footman and maid. "St. Raven. I need to speak with you."

He almost had her thrown out, but duty required a minimum of courtesy to relatives.

"Of course, cousin. Please come up to the drawing room." He even found a smile for the miserable footman. "Tea, Richard."

He had not changed the drawing room from his uncle's day, and that seemed to find his cousin's approval. Even so, as she thumped down on a sofa, she said, "You need a wife."

He looked around. "To dust?"

"To procreate."

He couldn't resist. "Not a strict necessity, cousin."

Insane to think it would fluster her.

"For an heir, it is. Since you lack parent or guardian, it is my duty to bring you to awareness of your duties to the name."

He felt his jaw ache with tension. "Cousin Cornelia, this is not a good time —"

"Hungover, are you? Probably never a time when you're not."

"Of course there is." He bit it off before he started to explain himself to her, and by a blessing the tea arrived.

All his cousins except the youngest, Claretta, were older than he and had married before he moved to St. Raven's Mount. He hardly knew them, but they all, and especially Cornelia, believed they had the right to manage him.

He ignored the cup of tea she poured for him.

"I am perfectly aware of my duties, cousin, including my duty to set up my nursery. I have only been back in England a few months, however."

"You've had a season, met all the possibles. What point in delay?"

He was not mad enough to speak of love. Cornelia had, after all, married Tremaine, a singularly unpleasant man, doubtless for his rank as one of England's senior earls.

"Marriage is not a matter to rush into."

"Nonsense. You think it will cut up your pleasure. Choose the right girl, and she won't deign to notice your wild parties at Nun's Chase, or your mistresses."

"I do not have even one mistress."

"That's likely the problem. Set one up, marry, and settle down."

This view of "settling down" almost struck him as funny, but then it became depressing. It was the way of their world, and it was doubtless his future, but he couldn't contemplate it just now.

Unless Cressida . . .

No. Once he had entertained the idea, but now it would not do. He could never put her in a position of less than perfect honor.

"Well?" his cousin demanded. "What do you have to say?"

He made a sudden decision. "That I will marry before the year's end. I do know my duty, but I am perhaps spoiled for choice."

She nodded, a feather on her maroon turban nodding, stirring crazy thoughts in Tris of sultans and highwaymen. "I recommend the Swinamer chit. She's beautiful enough to please and will behave exactly as she ought. Her mother's a friend of mine and has raised her properly. So many girls these days have harum-scarum ideas and throw tantrums if their husband doesn't sit by the hearth every night."

She held out a hand, and he had to go and heave her to her feet. "I'll think about it," he said.

"I'll arrange a house party including her. When are you free. Next weekend?"

"I have an engagement next weekend."

"Cancel it. I'll invite —"

"*No.* I will not be forced, cousin."

She scowled at him, looking distressingly like a bulldog. "Willful. Shame you weren't raised at the Mount. You'd have had it beaten out of you."

"I doubt it." He took her arm and steered her toward the door. "I will inform you when it's convenient, cousin."

She halted at the door. "I don't forget your word."

"Nor do I." Tris opened the door and nearly thrust her into the hands of her attendants. "Thank you for your concern, cousin."

He watched to be sure she left, then sought the sanctuary of his own room. As soon as he made it there, he dropped into a chair to sink his head in his hands.

What had he done to have such a hell of a life?

He was a fatalist. He'd learned that lesson young when his parents had ceased to exist one sunny day, taking his entire life with them. Life was uncertain. Live for the moment. Seize fragile joy.

He'd shrugged off the fact that his only blood relatives rejected him, and been grateful for the Peckworths, who had filled that void. He'd never expected much of marriage except good manners and a few healthy children, some male.

For a moment now and then over the past few days he'd seen another way. Marriage to a friend, a helpmeet, a companion in laughter and adventure, but it wasn't how it was done. Such pleasures faded, and it really wouldn't be fair to Cressida to plunge her into a position for which she was completely untrained. Cornelia would eat her for breakfast.

He stood and poured himself some brandy. The Duke of St. Raven would marry, not poor romantic Tris Tregallows.

He contemplated the amber liquid. He was a fatalist there, too. Nothing but death could save him from being duke, and suicide had seemed a drastic solution. Since he was the duke, no point in spending his life kicking against it like a spoiled child.

He was applying himself to his duties, and that included marriage. Had he nurtured hopes of making the sort of marriage his parents had? He drank a mouthful, letting the warmth and spice of the spirit swirl from his tongue to his mind.

A folly. What did a twelve-year-old know, anyway? They could have fought most of the time and appeared in harmony for him.

The door opened, and he turned to repulse whoever dared invade. But it was Cary, who was allowed.

And who knew him well. "I'm sorry."

He turned to go, but Tris said, "No, stay. Brandy?"

"Thank you." Cary came forward. "It didn't go well?"

"It went perfectly. Miss Mandeville has her jewels. As a bonus, she has all the other statues along with some other Indian gewgaws from Stokeley."

"And — ?" Cary asked, who did indeed know him well.

Tris laughed and gave his friend a swift account of the adventure.

"Gads. Crofton will talk?"

"Not directly, but he'll feed the word. I'm not sure how to stop him short of murder."

"Call him out?"

"Killing him in a duel could drop me in hot water, but it won't serve, anyway. Unless he comes out with some direct slander about Cressida, a challenge would be assumed to be about secret things. Disastrous. At least I established a right to defend her reputation, so it should curb him a bit. For now, we need to get the true picture out before he and his cronies start to talk."

"The true one?"

"That dreary Miss Mandeville, daughter of the nabob who threw away a fortune at cards, was attempting to sell some of her father's possessions when Crofton and his cronies, drunk, burst in and embarrassed her."

"Ah. Very good."

"It wouldn't hurt to wonder, just wonder, about Crofton's skill at cards."

Cary's eyes lit and he toasted him. "*Very* good. We go now?"

"Yes." Tris put down his glass, but then said, "What can we expect from marriage? My uncle's was cold, and the Arrans' is merely practical."

Cary finished his brandy. "My parents seem content. My sister looks at her husband as if the sun shone out his arse."

"But how does he look at her?"

Cary's lips twitched. "As if the sun shone out of somewhere else. They've only been married a twelve-month, though."

"Newlyweds are often ecstatic, but does it last? Have I done Anne Peckworth a favor in helping her to a rash love match?"

"Probably not, but at least she'll have the brief ecstasy."

Tris pressed his fingers to his head for a moment. "I've promised Cousin Cornelia that I'll marry before the year's end."

"Why, for hell's sake?"

"For hell's sake, perhaps." He shrugged. "It'll stop this pointless dithering."

"Miss Mandeville being out of reach."

Tris worked at not showing anything. "That would have been a mistake." He plucked Cary's glass from his hand. "On to the clubs to ensure her safety, however."

But would she find a husband who would appreciate her free-spirited nature, who would play all the bed-games she could imagine and then more?

No, she'd end up dressed in the sort of dull, abominable clothes she'd worn today, being a worthy wife to a stodgy professional man, saying and doing the right things, and devoting her energy to the worthy poor.

Lucky beggars.

He stopped at the door. "Oh, Lord. The Minnows."

"Who?"

"Little fish caught in my net. The Pike will take care of them."

"What?"

Tris laughed at Cary's worried expression. "I'm not fit for Bedlam yet. Not quite, at least. Come on."

As he went downstairs, however, he knew he'd have to do something about the Minnows. Something far away. He couldn't be tripping over them all the time, constant reminder.

"Did you really promise to marry within the year?" Cary asked as they waited for their hats, gloves, and canes.

"Why not? I'm thinking of making Phoebe Swinamer deliriously happy. 'If it were done when 'tis done, then 'twere well/It were done quickly.' "

"But can you say a marriage is done when 'tis done? The trouble with a marriage is that it goes on, and on, and on."

"And thus produces lots of little Tregallows, which is the purpose of the exercise."

Cary glanced around and then said quietly, "Haven't you described her as a china doll with little brain and no heart?"

Tris smiled. "But that's what makes her perfect. She won't care if I spend most of my time elsewhere and with others. She informed me at one ball that a lady is blind to her husband's behavior outside the home and lives to serve his wishes within it. What more could a man wish for?"

"A wife rather than a slave?"

The footman approached then, and Tris took his things. "How quaint," he said, and led the way outdoors.

Chapter Twenty-seven

Cressida awoke to a new day resolved on a practical future. How soon could they remove to Matlock?

Her father was out of his stupor. He was physically weak, and inclined to tears over his folly. Cressida didn't think those tears were false, but she didn't think those tears were truly repentant, either. He was already talking of ways to make a new fortune, a distinct gleam in his eye.

Yes, his wits were returning, which meant he'd soon want a coherent explanation for the return of the jewels. She'd better come up with one. Her mother had agreed to keep the truth about her first absence a secret, so it shouldn't be too hard.

She'd like to keep Tris's name out of it as much as possible. Her father had always fancied a grand husband for her. Heaven knows what he'd do if he thought he could pressure a duke into marriage.

She sat bolt upright. Tris had promised to call today! Almost, she wished he wouldn't. After all, surgeons tried to perform amputations as quickly as possible. And yet perhaps this would provide the opportunity for a better farewell, one that wouldn't leave such a bleeding wound.

The clock said nine. Hours yet before a fashionable call. Time to prepare, so she wouldn't embarrass him or herself.

She knew his behavior yesterday had been acting, presenting the right impression to those disgusting men, but even so it had etched her mind. Those men had believed that she was not the sort of woman the Duke of St. Raven could be interested in. She was conventional, proper, and had always behaved as she ought. Having experienced an impropriety, she had not developed a taste for it.

Or not for its public aspects. To which he was an experienced guide.

He might change. . . .

She rejected that folly. Tris was like her father — perilously charming, but addicted to excitement, to the wild places. If it came to a choice between them and her, he would choose them. And she was not her mother, to bear it with tranquility.

This was a short, sharp pain. Marriage to a man like Tris would be a lifetime of it.

She hugged her knees, resting her chin on the top of them. During the season she'd observed some fashionably arid marriages where husband and wife were hardly ever seen in each other's company. The husband had his mistress, and once the wife had provided a couple of boys who seemed likely to survive, she took lovers.

Discreetly, always discreetly, but still it was known. At house parties, husband and wife were given separate rooms, and their lovers, if available, were housed nearby. It must at times be a great puzzle for the hostess.

Cressida's night of passion made her more sympathetic to the wanton wives, but all the same, adultery disgusted her. When she married, she would be faithful, and she'd expect the same of her husband. Which Tris, no doubt, would think ridiculous.

She climbed out of bed to splash cold water on her face.

As she pulled on her stockings, she realized that once news of her father's recovery spread, his City friends would call. They must hire extra servants. Cook should be told to prepare cakes and other delicacies.

In fact, she thought as she shrugged into an easy corset, at least one of those gems would have to be translated into money to cover their immediate needs. She wondered exactly what they were worth. She must find out because those jewels might have to support them forever.

She was hooking the front of the corset when she realized she was dressing in Matlock fashion. Should she ring for Sally and put on a London gown? No. Better to say farewell to Tris this way. It would make it easier for him.

"A fine husband I'd look to be dressed by the best and driving this rig but with my wife in servant's clothes."

She chose a pale green dress with a beige stripe and a trim of narrow white lace. She remembered liking it when she'd ordered it in the spring of last year, but now she saw that it was stodgily prim and dull.

". . . that outfit and hat cry out a lack of funds."

She shrugged and put it on, fastening the apron front.

Tris, undoing the back of her gown . . .

She unplaited her hair and brushed it the required one hundred times, blocking, blocking, blocking the memory of him brushing her hair. Then she plaited it again and coiled it on the top of her head.

Not low down on her neck.

She squeezed her eyes shut as if that could kill the clear memories. If this carried on, she'd have her hair all cut off!

She sat a curl-trimmed cap on top and tied the laces, thinking that one benefit of a return to Matlock was that she could do without this idiocy soon.

Her hands stilled.

Perhaps not.

Would it not be an essential part of her disguise? If she encountered one of the gentlemen from the orgy, if there was any talk at all, any speculation, would her curl-less face look too like Roxelana's?

She studied her appearance. With the curls and without the darkened brows and reddened lips, surely she looked different. The color of the gown did nothing for her complexion, something she had not recognized before. She picked up her spectacles and added them, pursing her lips a little, like Mrs. Wemworthy. . . .

Oh, don't think of that!

But anyone would laugh at the mere idea that the woman in the mirror could have been a shameless houri at an orgy. In truth, it was hard for her to believe it herself.

She was with her father and had just finished her careful explanation of Hatfield when Sally came, all agog, to say that the Duke of St. Raven was below, asking to see her.

She rose, praying that her fluttering heart didn't show. "Tell him I'll be with him directly, Sally. And inform my mother."

Her mother was in the kitchens, helping to prepare for exactly this, as well as the expected visits from her father's friends. Her father was on the chaise rather than the bed, but still weak.

"Do you wish to speak to him, Father?"

"No, no. A wild sprig as I remember, though. But he seems to have behaved well in Hatfield."

"Yes, and we must thank him."

There was something in her father's look that made her tense, but he only picked a jewel from the little hoard in his lap — a ruby as big as a robin's egg. "Do you know what this is worth, Cressy?"

"Enough, I hope."

He turned it, sparkling in the sunlight. "Enough for what? In a good market, it should bring more than ten thousand pounds."

Cressida gaped. "But there are ten!"

"A couple of these might buy you a duke if you want one. I know St. Raven needs money. His uncle drained and mismanaged the estates." He looked at her. "Do you want him?"

She could laugh wildly at the thought, but her

father didn't know that he was being as tempting as Satan.

"No, Father," she said as calmly and firmly as she could. "Thank you, but really, can you imagine me as a duchess? And as you say, he's wild. I heard . . . I heard him mention holding wicked parties at his house."

He pulled a face. "Aye, they've been the talk of the town, and I can see you'd not be one to turn a blind eye to that. Ah well, it'll be exactly as you wish. There's wealth enough here to ensure whatever future you want, Cressy."

Cressida managed to thank him, then escaped. In the corridor, she leaned against the wall for a moment, fighting tears. Most problems could be solved by money, but not hers. Not hers.

She stopped in her room to press a cold cloth to her eyes and to be sure she was neat, then went quickly to the drawing room.

Tris was alone.

Was her mother being tactful by staying away? Cressida wished she hadn't, then was glad she had.

She closed the door. No one inside this house was going to be scrutinizing the proprieties.

"You've been crying," he said.

"Not quite. And it was to do with my father." That was not a complete lie.

"He is still unwell?"

She shook her head and unglued herself from the door. She went to a chair and sat in it, waving him to the sofa. "No, he's recovering, thank God. The jewels did the trick. He now has to regain his strength and deal with his guilt, but he's of a positive nature. He is already turning his mind toward making more money."

"Not at the tables, I hope."

"Definitely not."

Ah, but there was a poignant pleasure here that she had not expected. The pain hovered, and once he left for good it would strike, but there was such joy, such comfort, to see him, to be with him, to talk to him in such an ordinary situation.

"As you suggested," she said, as lightly as she could, "his sickness seems to have been boredom. Now that he has the challenge of building a new fortune, he is in high spirits again."

"And his venturesome daughter?"

She knew what image she must present. "Wants only security. Security and a quiet life."

"I see. Then you will have it."

She had to look down for a moment. "Thank you." When she could, she met his eyes again. "Now, tell me your cousin's story. Are you really going to give him some of your wealth?"

She remembered her father's comments about the ducal finances. And her father would know.

Tris crossed his legs, not apparently in distress. "Prepare yourself for an outrageous saga. I explained about my uncle's desperation for a son, and the bitter rivalry between him and my father. It seems that it pushed the duke to extremes.

"He traveled frequently to France — this was before the Revolution, of course — and kept a string of mistresses there. On one visit, he met a pretty country widow with two sons — Jeanine Bourreau. Jean-Marie insists that his mother was virtuous, but I suspect she was looking for a rich protector. Be that as it may, she conceived another child, and the duke came up with a plan. My mother had just announced that she was with child. It seems to have been the last straw for him.

"Perhaps my uncle was remembering the supposed origins of James the Second's son — that he was smuggled into the birthing chamber in a warming pan to substitute for a dead child. He apparently promised Jeanine Bourreau that if her child by him was a son, he would be duke. His duchess would announce that she, too, expected another child. Later in the pregnancy, Jeanine would travel to England, and when her child was born, it would be made to seem the duchess's."

"Heaven's above! Did the duchess agree?"

"Apparently. Remember, she was desperate to be the mother of the next duke, and to please her husband."

"So what went wrong? The child was another daughter?"

"The child was Jean-Marie. Unfortunately, a minor inconvenience occurred — the Revolution. Marie's travel to England was blocked, and Jean-Marie arrived before she could leave. She managed to get a letter to the duke, but now that his plan was thwarted, he rejected her."

"Poor lady."

"True enough. She survived by being mistress to a succession of men, and I gather from Jean-Marie that she raised him and his brothers well enough, and even arranged his training as an artist. She doesn't seem to have planned any action until Napoleon was beaten — the first time, in 1814. Then she and a lover came up with a wild plot."

"What? Jean-Marie couldn't still be a substitute for a daughter."

"No, but during the Revolution a great many records were destroyed. So they forged the record of her first marriage to show not marriage to Albert Bourreau but to Hugh Tregallows, then holding the heir's title of Earl of Marston."

Cressida stared at him. "Making Jean-Marie the true heir? Good heavens . . . But what of the older brothers?"

"They, alas, were dead by then. One of illness, and one in the war. Perhaps this helped turn the woman's wits, or perhaps it simply cleared the way. For you see, her cunning intent was not to wait until the duke died to present this evidence, but to persuade him to endorse it."

Cressida's mind raced. "He wouldn't. He *couldn't!*"

"Would he not? We'll never know, but my money says he'd have seized on it."

"But that would have made his true marriage invalid, his daughters bastards."

"To claim the ultimate victory — a son to inherit? To cut out his brother's son, me? I think he'd have done it. The irony is, I would have been delighted."

Cressida had her hand over her mouth. "What happened?"

"What happened? Oh, another twist of history. When Jean-Marie and his mother were preparing to travel to England, Napoleon escaped from

Elba, and we were at war again. Jean-Marie was fully engaged in staying out of the army, and then his mother took a sudden fever and died. Not, however, before exacting a vow that he would pursue the plan. I told you it was good enough for a play."

"And then?"

"And then Waterloo brought peace again, and Jean-Marie eventually made his way to Mount St. Raven — to arrive only days after my uncle's funeral. To add to his frustration, I had gone abroad, to France among other places."

Cressida bit her lip. "Is it wrong to feel a little sorry for him?"

"Not wrong, no, but unnecessary. His stay here has given him a deep dislike of England, especially our climate and our food. He now realizes that he wants to be an English duke even less than I do."

"That's hard to imagine." She realized that they were sharing private jokes and it was dangerous, but she'd drink poison if it tasted as sweet as this. "So he settled to wait for you to return, earning his living as an artist. But why Le Corbeau?"

"Sheer deviltry, but he has his mother's cunning streak. He balanced knocking on my door and presenting me with the evidence against making me come to him, and preferred the latter."

"But you said he didn't want the dukedom."

"True, and his vow to his mother was only to make the duke pay. What he wants now is enough money to live graciously in France, to be a gentleman artist, moving in the best circles. I have agreed to give him that."

"Why? You could call his bluff. It would take years to try to prove his claim, and his case is thin without his father's support."

He smiled. "I love to see you on your high horse. . . ." Then the smile faded as he looked down. *Love,* the forbidden word.

He looked up again, smiling. "I suspect he's a coolheaded gambler. If I'd refused, he might have dragged it through the courts, and I have no taste for the scandal or the cost. And," he added, "there is right and justice to consider. He is owed something. He is my cousin. I believe that. He was created as part of a dastardly plot, and his mother was shamefully used. I have agreed to give him twenty thousand pounds."

Not a huge sum to a dukedom, but to this dukedom now? She moved to the sofa beside him. She couldn't help it. "Can you afford that?"

"My dear, I am the Duke of St. Raven."

"Whose estate was reduced by your uncle's extravagances, and by his diversion of all possible property to his daughters so it wouldn't fall into your hated hands."

His lips tightened. "How do you know that?"

"My father is a businessman. The men of the City of London know all about such things."

"The devil they do. I hope they'll still lend me money." He took her hand. "You are not to worry about this, Cressida. This would all have happened if I hadn't held up Crofton's coach, if you hadn't agreed to his bargain, if your father hadn't gambled at all."

"I worry because I'm your friend, Tris. We are friends, aren't we?"

He raised her hand and kissed it, with no humor on his face at all. "We are lovers, Cressida, blighted though we be. Don't deny that. But, yes, we are also friends. I curse myself hourly for bringing about this disaster."

"None of this is your fault."

"I should never have taken you to the orgy."

"I should never have gone. It appears to be our *qismet*. See, I benefited from your book about Araby."

He rose, bringing her to her feet, too. "Logic tells me that such a brief acquaintance cannot have etched deep into our hearts. . . . Don't smile like that, love."

"Why not? I refuse to be sour-faced all my life. I want happiness for you, Tris Tregallows."

"And I for you. But let me say it once before we part. At this moment, Cressida Mandeville, I love you, I desire you, and I wish there were some way I could ask you to be my wife."

His honesty demanded her own. It was as perilous as plunging a dagger into her own heart, but she said, "And at this moment, Tris Tregallows, I might even be mad enough to say yes. But it wouldn't work, love. You know it wouldn't."

"Do I?"

She felt rooted. She did not want to take the next step, but the woman should be strong for both. She tugged one hand free, led him to the door and opened it. There she freed the other.

"Bon voyage, mon ami," she said.

He caught her hand and raised it to his lips, to kiss it, eyes intent on hers, as she'd once seen him kiss a lady's hand at the theater. As she'd dreamed of . . .

But she'd always known that dream was not for her.

"Bon voyage, ma chère aventurière."

Then he let himself out, and she could, in careful silence, weep.

Chapter Twenty-eight

After that, Cressida threw herself into the preparations for removal to Matlock, wishing they could leave immediately, as if such a short distance would put her in another world.

To her frustration, her parents were in no great hurry. They entertained their friends, and within days were venturing out to be entertained. Many of the City gentlemen owned country properties near London, often on the river, and Cressida spent impatient afternoons traveling by boat down the wide waterway to a villa.

The lingering time gave her opportunity to see if she could do something about young whores, but it brought more frustration than result. Most important people were out of town, and the few she spoke to were appalled. Not at the whores, but at the idea of a lady having anything directly to do with them.

"Soot always leaves a mark," as one woman said, urging her to prevent such things by even greater support of the foundling hospitals.

A man might be able to do more. A man like the Duke of St. Raven.

There was little chance of meeting him, however, and she had to be glad.

Shortly after their parting, she read that he was

at Lea Park for a ball announcing the betrothals of two of the duke's daughters, Lady Anne and Lady Marianne. The paper announced Lady Anne's groom to be Mr. Racecombe de Vere of Derbyshire.

Matlock was in Derbyshire!

She spent an entire day in a fret imagining Tris visiting his foster sister, riding around the county, visiting the spas. Suddenly Matlock was no safe refuge at all. She was trying to think of arguments for her family to move to a safer spot — the Welsh hills, perhaps, or the Scottish Highlands — when her friend Lavinia Harbison paid a visit.

"A warm day for once!" Lavinia declared. "Do let's walk in the park."

Lavinia was stout, kind, funny, and practical and contentedly engaged to marry a Captain Killigrew. She was Cressida's counterbalance to wicked dukes.

Captain Killigrew was a merchant captain currently sailing the world to make his fortune, and Lavinia seemed perfectly content to wait. Cressida often thought that this match would be much like her parents'. She didn't understand it, but she enjoyed Lavinia's company very much.

Walking in Green Park was an excellent idea, too. It brought her back to earth. Tris would be wise enough to avoid Matlock. The Mandevilles did not move in the same orbit of Derbyshire society as the Duke of St. Raven and a daughter of the Duke of Arran. Tris would probably stay at Chatsworth, grand home of the Duke of

Devonshire. Cressida had visited the house once, on an open day.

"Still no plan for the move?" Lavinia asked. "Of course, I don't wish you to ever leave London, but I know you long for home."

"What is home?" Cressida said without thinking.

Lavinia stared at her. "Not Matlock?"

Cressida laughed. "Pay no attention. I'm blue-deviled. But, Lavinia, when you marry Captain Killigrew, where will you make your home?"

"On board his ship for a while."

"On board his ship? But then why aren't you there now?"

"This trip is to be a riskier one with a lot of hard sailing in order to make a bigger profit so we can marry. After this, Giles plans some simpler trading routes in order to show me some of the world. I can't wait."

"Aren't you afraid for him?"

The bright smile dimmed a little. "A little, but what good does it do? And he's a very skillful captain. And he promised me faithfully to return."

Cressida took her friend's hand and squeezed. What a lot of secret emotions ran beneath social relationships.

Suddenly she felt impelled to say, "I've fallen in love with the Duke of St. Raven. A little . . ."

She'd told Lavinia about Hatfield. The public version, at least. She'd had to since the story was known.

Lavinia didn't show shock. "I'm not surprised. I remember seeing him at the theater and thinking how wonderful it must be to be Lady Anne Peckworth. I saw in the paper that she's to marry another, though. Is he brokenhearted?"

"No." Too late, Cressida knew she should have said she didn't know. "I mean, he gives no sign of it. But then, why would he with us almost strangers? . . ." She was babbling. "It's as well we'll never meet again, or I'd doubtless make a complete fool of myself, and in time I'm sure I'll meet someone as wonderful as your Giles."

Lavinia squeezed her hand. "I do hope so. But come on. There's nothing like a very brisk walk to blow away nonsense."

The brisk walk and cheerful talk did work to blow away nonsense — such as Cressida's urge to impress upon her friend that she meant she really *loved* the Duke of St. Raven, and why, and what they'd done together.

They stopped at Montel's for cakes, and as they took their seats, Lavinia bounced up. "Winnie! What are you doing in town?"

In moments Cressida found herself seated at another table with two other women, a young, fashionable, rather uneasy young woman and a full-bosomed matron, her mother.

They proved to be Mrs. Scardon, and her daughter Winifred — Lady Pugh.

Cressida had to work not to stare at the young woman not much older than herself who was stuck with the odious Pugh. Did she know what her husband got up to?

Apparently Lavinia and Winifred had been friends before Winnie had married. Lady Scardon made a rather slighting reference to the delay in Lavinia's marriage, which made Cressida want to kick her.

Lavinia and Winnie seemed genuinely fond of one another, and it turned out that mother and daughter were in town to buy clothing suitable for Lady Pugh's increasing condition.

Of course she must have been intimate with the odious Pugh, but the proof made Cressida feel slightly sick. She also thought it disgusting that Pugh had been at Stokeley when his wife was expecting their first child.

"Pugh is in Scotland," Mrs. Scardon said, making Cressida wonder if her thoughts had been so obvious. "Grouse, you know. I'm sure there are some gentlemen most inconvenienced by the Arran wedding."

"Oh, Lady Anne and Lady Marianne," Lavinia said. "I saw the announcement. The wedding is already?"

"A scrambling sort of affair." Mrs. Scardon could be said to smirk. "One must wonder . . ."

"Wonder what?" asked Cressida with malicious blankness.

Lady Scardon cast her a dismissive look. "Hasty weddings are always suspect, Miss Mandeville. Oh," she added, false as a wooden guinea, "you're the young lady who had that unfortunate encounter in Hatfield. I believe my daughter's husband came to your assistance. He did wonder at the wisdom of you being there alone."

Was that his story? So tempting to tell the truth, but it would hurt herself and Lady Pugh and hardly touch him at all. "There were a number of gentlemen," Cressida said accurately.

"I believe Lord Pugh was one of them. But the Duke of St. Raven was my principal protector. He was very kind."

"So he should be, after turning up drunk with Lord Crofton and others. After attendance at a wild party, I gather."

Cressida was almost shocked into arguing the truth, but how could she know exactly who was who? "The duke was sober, Mrs. Scardon. I assure you of that."

"Such men hold their drink very well, dear. A young lady like yourself would not understand that."

"As I understand it, he was visiting his cousin. He wasn't with Lord Crofton at all."

"No? Yet it's common gossip that he was at Crofton's party."

So was Lord Pugh. The words burned to be spoken. Cressida drank her tea instead. "I wouldn't know about that."

Mrs. Scardon's smile agreed, and somehow made it an insult instead of praise. Lord save her from the company of women like this. She flashed Lavinia a glance, and in moments they took their leave.

"I'm sorry," said Lavinia as they walked down the street. "She's a cold woman, but Winnie used to be great fun. I don't think her marriage agrees with her."

Cressida had to tell someone. "Lord Pugh was one of Crofton's drunken party."

"Oh, dear. It was good of you not to say."

"I doubt I'd have been believed."

"Oh, no," said Lavinia, "I'm sure they know."

Cressida realized her friend was correct. "Poor Lady Pugh."

"Yes. She was encouraged into it for the title. I don't know whether she feels she had a fair bargain for her father's money, but I wouldn't reckon it so."

Cressida wondered if Lavinia would expect Giles to be faithful, but couldn't think of a way to ask. Surely she must. Or were her own expectations absurd?

"I note that St. Raven was at Crofton's affair," Lavinia said with an air of the casual comment. "Not surprising. He's known for such. According to Matt, his recent choice of pleasure is the house of a woman called Violet Vane."

The Queen of the Night. Fighting La Coop. Cressida smothered pain under a blank look. "Oh?"

"I think it's a bordello. Matt is vague, which almost certainly means it's a bordello."

"I don't think your brother should tell you these things."

"How else am I to know? Would you rather not know, Cressida?"

Cressida sighed. So Lavinia was telling her on purpose. "No. I mean, it's better to know. Is there anything else?"

"Just that Violet Vane seems to specialize in very young whores and Matt saw St. Raven there with three of the youngest. Even he thought it was a bit much. There's something of a movement at the moment against that sort of thing, as there should be."

"Definitely."

If St. Raven had not been with her, would he have been groping those girls at Crofton's? Was that his real taste? And she'd wanted to recruit him against the trade! What a fool she was.

Cressida was trying so hard not to show what she felt that she probably looked like a wax head. And Lavinia would know, as she'd known that Lady Pugh knew about her husband, so it was all for nothing except to preserve foolish pride.

"The Crofton affair at Stokeley was pretty disgusting, too, according to Matt. I hate to admit it, but he was there. He came home quite sick — noxious brews and oriental peculiarities — and was upset because it had been your home."

"Not home."

"Thank heavens." After a moment, Lavinia said, "I just thought you should know."

Cressida stopped and turned to her. "And I thank you. The duke's handsome and can be charming. He could easily steal a woman's heart. But I am not so foolish as that, I assure you."

"Oh, good. I'd hate to see you end up like Winnie."

Cressida found a laugh. "There was never any question of marriage."

"Of course not. Duchess Cressida. Imagine it! But," she sighed, "I wish I'd been rescued by him. I've never so much as spoken to a duke."

"They say 'Good day,' and 'Dreadful weather, isn't it?' just like other men."

Lavinia laughed. "Oh, surely not. What a disappointment." She eyed Cressida. "Shall I confess something?"

"Please do. I will be able to hold it over your head forever more."

"I don't think it's quite so terrible as that. But when Matt was talking about the horrible orgy, with half-naked people and impropriety everywhere, I wished I could have been a fly on the wall. I would like to see true wickedness once in my life."

Cressida burst out laughing, and had to lean against some railings to recover.

Laughter was healing, and she returned home in a lighter mood, but now completely determined on an early return to Matlock. Matlock had become like her corset. Only when properly encased in it would she feel safe from her own weak folly, and now she knew just how deep her folly was.

When their new footman said her father wished to speak to her, she saw an excellent opportunity. Her father seemed to be dragging his feet about Matlock, and it was time to push. No point talking to her mother, who would only do as her father wished.

She hurried to her room to remove her bonnet and tidy herself, then went to her father's study planning the best approach.

He was at his desk, happily surrounded by ledgers and documents, but on her arrival he picked up a folded sheet of paper. "Here's a letter from St. Raven, Cressy, asking to buy the rest of those statues. What do you say to that?"

Cressida stared at the letter as if it were a snake about to strike. "The statues?" They were the only words she could think of.

"The naughty ones. He's that sort of man, of course. What do you say? Do we sell 'em to him? Your mother doesn't care for 'em."

He unfolded the crested notepaper and held it out to her. She had to take it, to look at the strong, flowing writing, and the slashed signature. St. Raven. In her imagination she could smell sandalwood.

Dear sir,

You are undoubtedly aware that I had the honor to make your daughter's acquaintance and be of some assistance to her. In the process I became aware of a set of statues in your possession, carved in ivory. I purchased one from your daughter and would appreciate the opportunity to acquire the rest. I would be much obliged if you would inform me whether the same price is appropriate. It could well be that the set is more valuable.

I also have in my possession a dagger that I believe is called a wisdom sword. I acquired it at Stokeley Manor, thus I assume it to be yours. I will return it if you wish, but would like to purchase it, also.

I understand you are recovered from your incapacity and congratulate you upon it. I hope Miss Mandeville is similarly recovered from her encounter with some who, though considered members of our higher orders, behaved little better than ruffians. I assure you she need fear no repercussions from that encounter.

Please direct your reply to me at St. Raven's Mount, Cornwall.

He signed with that flourish, but it was all in his own handwriting.

He was in Cornwall. Hundreds of miles away. It was both relief and agony. Had he realized that she would see this letter, touch this letter? Had he intended it as pleasure or torture? What did he *want?*

"Cressida?"

She pulled herself together. "I think we should give them to him, Father. He did help me, and they're not worth a great deal, are they?"

"Not now they're all empty." He was eyeing her all too shrewdly. "Very well. What about the wisdom sword? Now that's a piece of some value, and this is all your inheritance in the end."

If you don't throw it away again next time you're bored.

"If he had it from Crofton, it is legally his. I don't think we should take advantage of his honest nature."

His bushy brows shot up. "Honest nature? A duke?"

Cressida didn't care what she revealed. "Honest nature. Is his offer not proof of it?"

"It could just be proof of cunning. He doubtless thinks I'll give it to him in hope of favors. As if I cared for a duke's favors." But he looked at her from under his bushy brows, tapping a restless finger. "Very well. If you want him to have it, so be it. Write a reply to him, won't you? Write it from yourself."

Cressida froze. "That would be improper, Father."

"Tush. I've no patience with such things. You're not going to compromise yourself with a business letter, are you?"

"But . . ." Cressida feared that more protest might cause more trouble. If he even suspected her feelings or her wickedness . . . A lifetime in India made him inclined to ride roughshod toward his goals.

"Very well, Father." She dropped a curtsy and retreated to her bedroom, the precious letter clutched in one hand. She suppressed a sigh as she pulled out a sheet of her paper and trimmed up her pen.

How to do this?

Very formally.

To His Grace the Duke of St. Raven,
St. Raven's Mount,
Cornwall

My Lord Duke,

With respect to your gracious communication with regards to the ivory statues in my father's possession, in view of the assistance you so kindly provided me, it is my father's wish that you kindly accept the statues as an expression of our gratitude.

As for the wisdom sword, it was acquired from Lord Crofton while he was in legal possession of it, so my father can see no justification for accepting payment. He urges you to consider it rightly and justly yours, and is assured that you will be a proper custodian of such a treasure.

For you are in need of wisdom, Tris Tregallows, she thought sadly as she wiped her pen.

She dipped it again, weakly unwilling to leave it there.

Please permit me to again express my thanks for your gracious assistance in my recent difficulties. Thanks to you, instead of distress and even injury, I now have an enlightening adventure to remember.

I have the honor to remain, Your Grace,

Your most obedient servant.

She signed it, blotted it, then returned with it to the study. "Do you wish to read it, Father?"

He looked up from another letter. "What? No, no. I'm sure you've covered matters appropriately. Fold it, seal it, and get it on its way."

She was pressing her father's seal into the melted wax when he cleared his throat. She looked up to find him leaning back in his chair, regarding her.

"Cressy, there's something I need to talk to you about."

Oh, Lord — did he know? Did he guess?

She raised the seal with care and returned it to its stand. "Yes, Father?"

He worked his mouth for a moment, a sure sign he was uncomfortable with what was to come. "The thing is that your mother and I . . . well, we are thinking of going abroad."

She felt as if the floor had dropped beneath her feet. "Abroad? But what about Matlock?"

"We know that's your home, my dear, and perhaps we can find a way for you to stay there, but we would like you to come with us to India if you feel able."

"To *India!* Father, you can't! Mother wants to return to Matlock."

"I'm not dragging her away by force, Cressy! She wants to come, and I've had a bellyful of England. I miss sunshine and spices."

Oh, this was the outside of enough! She leaned forward on the desk. "Mama *hated* India — you know that. If she goes with you, it will be from duty and affection. It is so unfair to drag her away from her home and friends because you have wanderlust!"

She expected a sharp response to such impudence, but he only shook his head. "I told her she should have told you the truth years ago."

She straightened. "The truth? What truth? You tell me. Now."

He sighed. "You were a delicate child, Cressy. You failed in the heat. You caught infections. You nearly died twice. You had to come home, and your mother chose to come with you. I — I elected to stay awhile, to make my fortune. Year after year, I told myself I would return soon, but then I'd suffer a reversal. . . ."

Thoughts raced through Cressida's head. Tris had been right about her father, but who could have guessed about her mother?

"Mother was waiting for me to marry before joining you."

"Perhaps, or I was to come home. It was never written of directly. . . ."

Cressida put a hand to her spinning head. "Dear heaven, have I been a burden all my life?"

He rose. "No, no. Don't think like that. Our marriage was never a grand love, and the years haven't been unpleasant for either of us. But now, well, perhaps now we've found a fondness beyond us when younger, and we're ready to go adventuring together. But we'd like you to come with us."

He leaned forward. "You're not delicate any longer, and there's enough of me in you to savor the wonders of it all. You can dress in sarees and ride on elephants. Eat fruit and spices such as you've never imagined, see temples studded with diamonds, be rubbed with precious oils . . ."

Oils. Oh, God!

But, why not? India would be a world away from temptation. She would never have to fear turning a corner one day and bumping into Tris, or weakening and running into his wicked, careless arms.

"And there's always plenty of men over there eager for an English bride. We'll have you married off in no time."

Cressida looked down at the letter, now crushed in her anger and made her decision.

"It does sound exciting, Father. I think I would like to go with you very much."

Chapter Twenty-nine

Tris was in his study in Mount St. Raven, re-reading the business letter that was not a business letter, drinking brandy that wasn't wise, and ignoring a pile of work that Leatherhulme's new assistant had delivered, when a footman tapped and entered.

"Your Grace, a Monsieur Bourreau has arrived and requests a moment of your time."

Gads, if Jean-Marie wanted more money, he could dance on clouds for it. But Tris said, "Bring him up."

He put down the letter and topped up his glass. He was drinking too much, but what the hell else was there to do when he was merely passing the days until the house party here at which he would propose to Phoebe Swinamer.

Cornelia was cock-a-hoop to be planning a party here in her old home. She'd be here in a week. Then a week later the various guests would arrive, including the Swinamers. Then there would be a grand masquerade. He'd insisted on a masquerade, despite Cornelia's objections. She thought such events vulgar. So they were, but he was going out in grand style.

And thus, Cressida would be safe.

He had confirmed that the Marquess of Arden

had indeed married a governess. Tris had fabricated an excuse to visit their charming small house and confirmed that Beth Arden was an ordinary woman, and even something of a bluestocking reformer. Not a pattern-card duchess at all.

Of course, Arden was not duke yet, and probably wouldn't be for decades, lucky man, but all the same, the heavens had not cracked. Their small baby had been brought into company and left with the parents without an attendant, and Arden — Arden! — had even cradled the infant with apparent confidence and pleasure.

He couldn't imagine Miss Swinamer encouraging such outrageous behavior.

Tris had left after an hour, aware of wanting unworthy things, but not having the power to grasp them.

Lady Arden had been poor and middle-class, but there had been no taint of scandal there. And even so, the marriage was still talked of, her suitability still questioned. She had the sharp confidence to deal with that. He wasn't sure Cressida did.

What's more, Cressida knew what she wanted — a quiet, orderly, obscure life — and there was no way he could give her that.

Jean-Marie came in smiling. *"Cousin,"* he said in French, bowing.

Tris inclined his head. "To what do I owe this dubious honor?"

Jean-Marie's brows rose. "To goodwill. I beg you to believe that."

"I thought you already in France."

"I had commissions. I am a man of honor, so I must complete them. I also have friends to take farewell of."

"Miranda," Tris said.

He had been surprised by that relationship, especially as La Coop appeared to have taken herself out of circulation for a while.

"Ah, no. Miranda, she comes with me."

Tris allowed his surprise to show. "Did you come all this way to give me this happy news?"

Jean-Marie strolled around the room and paused to inspect a painting. "No, I came all this way to offer you some assistance." He turned. "I encountered your Miss Mandeville recently."

Tris contemplated the brandy in his glass. "And?"

"And me, I am observant. Miranda is with me — we are at a linen draper's considering fabrics, you see — and Miss Mandeville, she recognizes her. She hides it quickly, but she does. When I ask Miranda, she tells me of Crofton's party, and of your presence, and of your companion, and of your interest in the statues. Things snap together. Tell me, cousin, what was in those statues?"

Tris considered him, then told the truth. "A fortune in gemstones."

Jean-Marie swore, but then shrugged. "I do not repine. I have enough. There is wisdom in knowing when enough is enough, is there not?"

"There is, indeed. But wisdom often comes with blade and fire." Tris contemplated the wisdom sword, which was mounted on the wall where he could not help but see it from the desk. "What do you want, Jean-Marie?"

"I want you to hold an orgy at Nun's Chase."

Tris demonstrated that he'd improved upon his tutor's French in some low places. He concluded with, "Anyway, the place is on the market."

"So I understand. A farewell celebration." He threw up a hand to block protest. "Attend. What if this would gain you Miss Mandeville, along with — one has to acknowledge the benefit — a portion of her father's wealth and hope of all the rest one day?"

Tris couldn't fight off a weakening stir of hope, but he kept his voice cool. "What mischief are you up to now?"

Jean-Marie strolled over and plucked the glass from Tris's hand. "Do you know that the Mandevilles are going to India?"

"What?"

The sense of loss was sharp as a death. In Matlock Cressida would be still in his world. There was nothing to say the Duke of St. Raven couldn't visit Matlock, couldn't use their small acquaintance to call. . . .

"Why would they do that?"

"Mr. Mandeville, he is a wanderer. It appears his wife is willing to go with him, and that their daughter will go, too. I do not think her heart will be in it."

Tris grabbed him by the cravat. "What the devil do you know about her heart?"

Jean-Marie broke free and put wary distance between them.

Tris exhaled. "She's curious as a cat and loves to get into trouble. She and India deserve each other."

"Cousin, cousin! Unless my guesses are completely wrong, Miss Mandeville loves you as much as you love her. Do not deny it! She will go to protect her heart, but also in order to protect yours, to free you to make the marriage you must. Ah, it is a grand romance in the best tradition!"

Tris swore at him again, collapsed into his chair, and sank his head into his hands. One thought pounded there. He couldn't let Cressida go half a world away.

What did this make of the house party and Phoebe? To hell with them both. He looked up. "What good will holding an orgy at Nun's Chase do? I have no taste for that sort of thing anymore."

"Except with one lady, eh? Love is beautiful. And in that cause, Miranda offers her professional skills."

Tris stared at him. "No, thank you."

"Her skills," said Jean-Marie, "in portraying a certain houri . . ."

Hope, painful in its shock, made Tris dizzy. "Go on."

"You are ahead of me, no? The reason you cannot offer marriage to Miss Mandeville is that too close connection with you will make men remember the houri. Already there is talk because of Hatfield. But it is brushed aside. Miss Mandeville, she is so ordinary, so boring. Ah, you Englishmen. You have no soul!"

"Some Englishmen." But Tris was remembering that he hadn't noticed her before that night. Incredible.

"By the way, cousin, what have you done with the so disagreeable Crofton?"

Tris smiled. "Nothing directly, but I understand he has found it necessary to leave England. A matter of a girl from good family enticed from home. Thank God I had Violet Vane in a vise by then and could save the child."

"Thank God, indeed. Crofton was trading in such wares?"

"Violet was handling the girls for him but swears they were all willing. Judging from the ones I encountered at her house, that was true. Losing their virginity to Crofton was no treat, but he paid well. But I heard rumors of some who had been unwilling and then Mary Atherton turned up. By that time I had Violet scared out of her wits, so she came straight to me full of shock and horror. The men who'd snatched Mary confessed that they'd been paid by Crofton. I put it together in a nice little package and advised Crofton to leave England."

"You did not think your courts would convict him?"

"They might, but a viscount is a viscount. It would go before the House of Lords. The peers of the realm don't like to expose each other to common inspection. Faced with court, the kidnappers and Violet Vane might have tried to tell another story, and of course, whatever happened, poor Mary Atherton would have been ruined at thirteen. So I let him run."

Jean-Marie leaned against a table. "I understand your reasoning, my friend, but it has stirred other problems. Perhaps enraged, he left behind more open accusations. What had he then to lose? There are men who were at Stokeley who are now convinced that Miss Mandeville was there with you, and that she was also my mistress. It is not possible to kill them all."

"Damnation. Is it talked of openly?"

"No, but sooner or later it will leak out of the men's clubs to their wives. . . ."

"Perhaps she'll be better off in India."

"India is not far enough."

When scandal flew, nowhere was far enough. Part of him was appalled, but part of him thought that this made marriage, even a tainted marriage, essential. For weeks he'd fought off his need for Cressida as wife, but now it surged in him like a torrent.

"You mentioned an orgy. At Nun's Chase. Miranda playing the houri. But it won't serve. It could still be Cressida."

"In one week," said Jean-Marie, "the Mandevilles host a ball to mark the end of their stay in London and the beginning of their journey to Plymouth, where they will take ship. Most of the guests will be of the merchant class, but there will be some of the higher orders. Certainly, it will be a notable event, and recorded in the papers.

"On the same night, you host a party at Nun's Chase, which you attend with your houri. That will not be reported in the papers, but the whole world will know of it. . . ."

"And there will no longer be the slightest chance that Cressida could have been my companion at Stokeley." Tris surged to his feet. "My

God, why did I not think of such a device myself?"

"Because you are a dull Englishman, rather than a Frenchman of brilliant invention."

Tris threw a mock blow.

Jean-Marie laughed. "And this Frenchman hopes that perhaps by doing this service he will open a way to friendship between two who could be close as brothers?"

"After extorting twenty thousand pounds from me, you scoundrel?"

Another shrug. "What would you? I swore it to my mother on her deathbed. And it is right. And, I admit, I want it."

Tris rubbed his hands over his face, trying to decide whether this was brandy-madness or a real chance. Trying to analyze what this would mean to Cressida. Surely it could be managed so she was free of scandal. All other problems shrank away.

"And consider," said Jean-Marie cheerfully. "Though unwittingly, I gave Miss Mandeville that fortune in jewels. By arranging that you can marry, I pass some of it on to you. And thus, our accounts are balanced."

"Your gall is incredible!"

"But true. I am a genius."

Tris took a turn around the room. "I'll have to invite some men I'd hoped never to consort with again. . . ."

"And draw attention to Miss Mandeville being in London. I can do that."

"And perhaps add a suggestion that Crofton had a grudge against Miss Mandeville — because he'd offered for her before her father's disaster and been turned down. He never was a popular man. It'll be believed. But how will it look when I woo her?"

Jean-Marie considered. "You were smitten at Hatfield. Slain by her courage under fire, entranced by her dignity and virtue. Women always want to believe that men are entranced by dignity and virtue."

Tris laughed. "In this case, it happens to be true." But then he considered, and added, "After a fashion."

He realized then that he'd never believed that Cressida's true milieu was Matlockian propriety. She'd shown too much wicked interest in the orgy for that. No, she belonged somewhere on the borders, and he could make a place for her there.

Jean-Marie was observing him. "Perhaps your friend Mr. Lyne can spread the story of your lurking admiration. And thus, spurred by her intolerable imminent departure, you come to your senses, fling yourself on your knees before her and win her hand and heart. Ah, I should have been a playwright, me."

But Tris was wakening to problems. "Lord, Cornelia . . ."

Jean-Marie looked a question.

"My oldest cousin, Lady Tremaine. I have asked her to hold a house party here, including Miss Phoebe Swinamer, whose hand and fictional heart I was to win."

"A madness from which you are now recovered. You planned for tragedy, but now you have a happy ending. Cancel it."

"You don't know Cornelia. She'll come here anyway, sure she can bludgeon events to her choosing."

"Forbid her."

"Bar her from her old home? No, I'll have to let her continue. I've not said anything to the Swinamers, thank heavens, though I'm sure Cornelia's hinted." He thought for a moment and smiled. "I'll invite Cressida and her family. We're close enough to Plymouth. I'll announce our betrothal at the masquerade, but she will not, of course, be in a houri costume."

"Alas. I would have liked to see it. You are very confident, my friend."

Tris looked at him in surprise. "Nothing now stands in our way."

"She might have come to her senses."

It was clearly a tease. "Hell, I know better than any what a poor bargain I am, but I can make it worth it to her. I can't give her Matlock, but I'll make Nun's Chase into a home, a refuge. Or if she doesn't want that, I'll buy somewhere new. We never need to go to London unless she wishes to, and there will be compensations. We are right for each other, Jean-Marie. Two halves. I've known it almost since we met. Without her, I'm half a man. It is the same for her."

"I hope so, cousin." Jean-Marie raised the glass he'd taken from him. "To perfect women and perfect love."

Cressida prepared for the farewell ball with no expectation of pleasure. She'd argued against it, but her father had been adamant. He and her mother bubbled with excitement and delight, but she was more in the mood for a wake.

Tonight marked the end of her life in England, and she was discovering daily how much she would miss it. Spices held no lure for her — she didn't even like mulligatawny soup. The sarees her father had brought home with him were pretty, but she preferred a sensible cotton dress. Temples of gold and diamonds only made her think of naughty statues, which made her think of orgies, which led her straight to Tris, and pain.

It was not a pain that would be assuaged by distance. In fact, she was realizing that India would be full of such painful memories.

It was done, however. The house in Matlock had been sold, and farewells taken of friends there. She had promised long letters, but planned a cleaner break. Letters from India would mean letters to India. Unfortunately, her supposedly brief brush with the great already made everyone assume she wanted to hear every scrap of news about the Duke of St. Raven.

He had returned from Cornwall to dance at his foster sisters' weddings. He had attended a house party in Bedfordshire. He had won an impromptu horse race at Epsom for a purse of a thousand guineas. Invitations had gone out for a masquerade party at Mount St. Raven, presumably one suitable for polite society. Rumor said he might announce his choice of bride then, and even that it might be Phoebe Swinamer.

Cressida discounted that. They would not suit, but Miss Swinamer and her mother were quite capable of spreading such a rumor themselves in an attempt to force his hand. She knew Tris would not be maneuvered by a stratagem like that.

At least he would not be here tonight. Her father had insisted on sending an invitation, but they had received a polite regret. She told herself that made her very, very happy.

She glared in the mirror and adjusted the turban her maid had placed on her carefully arranged hair. Deliberately, she was wearing the outfit she'd worn when she'd set off with Crofton — the Nile green silk dress and the striped turban. A suitable end, and after this event she would give it all to the maid.

This time, however, the curls were real — well, with tedious help from a curling iron. Since the curls were part of what made it impossible that she be St. Raven's houri, she'd gritted her teeth and had her front hair cropped and daily endured the curling iron.

One attraction of India was that in time she'd be able to let her hair grow again. And surely once she was so far away, weak wistfulness about a certain rakish duke would fade.

She opened her jewel box, now full of expensive pieces. It was weeks since her adventure, and scandal had not crashed on her head, but this would be the first large gathering since Crofton's orgy, the first with ton people present.

Including, surely, some of the men at Stokeley Manor.

She had to create the right impression.

She knew gossip hummed through the men's

clubs. Lavinia had passed on more stories from Matthew. Crofton had fled the country — something to do with attempted rape of a child, which disgusted even the most rakish of the ton. His wild attack on her in Hatfield had somehow been woven in there, however. The stories said nothing to her discredit, Lavinia assured her, but as had been pointed out, any brush with soot left marks.

Recently, there had been an increase in speculation — formless, but damaging and moving beyond masculine circles to feminine. Cressida had received some strange looks from the ladies and could imagine what was behind them.

What exactly had Miss Mandeville been doing in Hatfield, unchaperoned? No matter what the necessity, should a lady be attempting to sell a risqué statue to a foreigner, especially one who had spent some days in jail under suspicion of being a highwayman?

Of course, the Frenchman was an acknowledged connection of the Duke of St. Raven, but all the same — she was sure the mamas were saying to the daughters — only see what happens when a young lady forgets correct behavior.

As far as she knew, no one was talking openly of her having been at Crofton's party dressed as a harem girl and in the company of St. Raven, but the idea must lurk in the minds of some of the men. It could be her imagination, but she'd thought in the past few days that some visiting gentlemen had looked at her in a searching way.

She'd been pursing her lips and wearing her

spectacles. Tonight she must confirm the impossibility.

She'd had the bodice of her dress raised high, and the dowdy effect would be helped by the fact that the gown hung loose. She seemed to have no appetite these days. She put down an emerald necklace and took out her old string of small pearls. Her father would think it strange, but so be it.

She eyed herself in the mirror. A pity she couldn't wear her spectacles, but no one did so to a ball. Such a peculiarity might raise suspicions.

A pity her lips were so pink. Easy enough to redden pale lips, but how did one create pallor? She pursed them. There, that was better. She tried a pursed-lip smile and achieved a horrible smirk. Better still. Thoughts tended to show on the face, so she must act all evening as if saying the word *breeches* would give her a fit of the vapors, not to mention *codpiece* or *aphrodisiac*.

Drat, that made her blush, and blushing became her. She concentrated on sermons, cold porridge, and Mrs. Wemworthy as she stood to let the maid drape a diaphanous shawl across her elbows. Then, tight-lipped and stiff-spined, she went to join her parents.

The ball was being held at Almack's Assembly Rooms, rented for the occasion. Soon she and her parents were receiving their guests there. The earliest arrivals were the City families — the merchants and professional men, as well as some friends from Sir Arthur's India days. All of those seemed to envy him his planned return. Cressida told herself that she might enjoy the adventure.

Then came the fashionable guests, lighter, more brittle. These were the dangerous ones, teased by tedium to a lust for scandal. Cressida didn't recognize any of the men — until Lord and Lady Pugh were announced.

Fat-faced Lord Pugh looked comical in fashionable wear that was unforgiving of huge stomach and swelling thighs, but the way he peered at her was not funny at all. Had he come precisely to check out his suspicions?

Wemworthy, Cressida thought, smirking at him.

Poor Lady Pugh was looking gratified by his presence at her side. There was something very wrong with a marriage when the wife was delighted by such crumbs.

After a moment of staring, Lord Pugh shook his head, muttered something about a waste of time, and headed off for the card room. Lavinia took Lady Pugh under her wing and led her away. What a sad way to be, and marriage was for life.

When the dancing began, Cressida gave her hand to Mr. Halfstock, eldest son of a rich silk merchant who was pretending tragic hurt at her departure. She chose to be amused, though she could easily have screamed at him. What did he know of broken hearts?

By the end of the first dance, she realized that she had abandoned Wemworthy. She loved to dance, and was smiling at Tim Halfstock's airs. So be it. She seemed to have satisfied Pugh, and surely her reputation had to act to her advantage. Except for her curiosity about how the world worked, she'd always been held to be the sort of young lady who did just as she ought. An interest in water supply, metals, and the shaping of bonnets hardly marked her out for hell.

So she gave her hand to Sir William Danby for the cotillion and lost herself in the steps, pushing aside all other matters, including the fact that she did not want to leave England. That she had been right oh so long ago, when she had decided that she enjoyed small adventures, but had no interest in the exotic or the wild.

Except, perhaps, in a man . . .

Naked.

Glistening with exotic oils.

Heavy-lidded with sated desire . . .

Hoping her red face was taken for exertion, she blocked those thoughts and focused on her steps.

Chapter Thirty

Tris strolled around Nun's Chase with a smile on his mustachioed face and a houri on his arm, disgusted by the mess and disorder all around him. For his purpose, he'd had to invite some of the men who'd been at Stokeley, and some of them had arrived already drunk.

It was of interest to hear what they said about Crofton. Some washed their hands of him, but some doubted the truth of the stories.

"Liked a little rosebud, Croffy did," Billy Ffytch said, "but no need to snatch one from a good family."

"Some predators," said Tris, "don't like tame prey."

Ffytch nodded. "Aye, that could be it. Shame, though. He could stir wild times, Croffy could." The man's bleary eyes slid to Tris. "Some say you had a hand in it, St. Raven. Had it in for him over that Hatfield affair."

"Hatfield?" Tris allowed a momentary hesitation, as if it had slipped to the back of his mind. "Oh, yes, when he raved at that poor Miss Mandeville. I do fear the man was unbalanced. To imagine I was trysting *her,* and at such a minor hostelry when this place was not far away. I believe he offered for her hand and was refused, which might explain his bile. Before her father lost all his money, of course."

Ffytch was clearly having trouble following the switches of focus. "Got it all back," he said at last.

"I believe Mandeville had a reserve of gemstones. We must rejoice for him."

"Aye. Almost makes the daughter worth going after. If I wasn't married, of course." He took a frowning swig of rum punch. "Croffy had more than that on his mind, you know. Kept saying your Turkish delight was Miss Mandeville." He swayed forward to study the houri on Tris's arm. "You're right, St. Raven. The man was mad."

Ffytch lurched off toward a group including some welcoming nymphs of the night, and for effect, Tris gathered Miranda to his side and kissed her through her veil. "You are performing the part beautifully. Thank you."

She had the build and was wearing a long wig, but he was surprised by how cleverly she was reproducing Cressida's manner, half bold, half uncertain. No one would guess this was La Coop.

"Amusing to act the innocent," she said. "But you really wish to marry Miss Mandeville? A woman like that will clip your wings."

"If you mean curtail events like this, then I will be delighted."

She chuckled. "It's perhaps as well I'm off to France. Tragic, positively tragic, to see such a wild fire tabbied inside a hearth."

"No constraints for you? Or for Jean-Marie? He is to go with any woman who catches his eye?"

Her eyes narrowed, and then she laughed. "You're a devil. But at least neither of us is conventional."

Tris just smiled, but then Miranda said, "I remember that houri. . . . Perhaps you're not so foolish as you seem."

He didn't respond to that. "I think everyone is relaxed and sozzled enough for the next move of this game."

He clapped his hands to gain the attention of those around. "As bloom on ripe fruit, so is novelty to love — and to lust, my friends. For your novel pleasure tonight, I give you — country dancing!"

The men looked at each other, puzzled. At a gesture from Tris, a curtain was drawn back to reveal a trio of musicians, all blind. They were well known in London for both normal and outrageous affairs.

They began to play, and Tris clapped his hands again. Ten whores came into the room, specially chosen by Miranda for their ability to look like pretty, innocent young ladies. They were dressed almost as if attending Almack's, the *almost* being that their fashionable dresses were of sheerest gauze and they wore nothing beneath but the scarlet dye on their nipples, and striped stockings held up by scarlet garters. Their jewels were maidenly pearls — artificial, but convincing — and virginal white roses wreathed their hair.

Coyly, they each chose a man and led him into the dance.

Tris watched, amused by just how well the ploy worked. He'd arranged this to make a tight connection between a ball in London and this event, but he'd clearly hit on an erotic novelty. The men were glassy-eyed at the sight of these wicked simulacra of the virtuous young ladies they must not touch unless they had marriage in mind.

The men seemed happy just to dance for now, exactly as if they were at Almack's. Tris paraded around the room, making sure he and his houri were in view; then, as the set ended and new men rushed to partner the whores, he led her into the long dance. Her jewel-like garments flared amid the flimsy pale dresses.

These men would never doubt or forget that they'd seen St. Raven with his houri at the same time Miss Mandeville was on display at her own ball in London.

He looked around for his cousin, who had the next part to play. The sooner this was settled, the sooner he could move away from center stage. The party could riot on without him, and tomorrow he could go to London. As soon as decently possible, he'd call on Cressida. Decently possible meant, damn it, after noon, but he'd see her, scandal scotched.

Then he had a conventional though speedy courtship in mind. He'd love to do a Lochinvar and once again ride off with her, but nothing must stir extra talk. The world would talk anyway when ordinary Miss Mandeville caught the Duke of St. Raven, but there must be no breath of scandal. Embers would still smolder among the ashes, and a breath would be enough to stir them to flame.

It was inconvenient that the Mandevilles were

about to leave London, but once he had status as suitor, he could travel with them. Plymouth was not far from the Mount, so they could conclude with a short visit there. Because of her parents' travel, the wedding would be hasty.

In nine days, she would be his. Everything else could fall into place from there.

The music ended, and Jean-Marie stepped onto the dance floor. "I have just realized! Ze oh so stupid Crofton mistook poor Miss Mandeville for zis delight! Behold, my friends, and marvel!"

He took Miranda's hand and twirled her.

Lord Blayne was lolling on a sofa with a whore, but he staggered to his feet. "Croffy must need spectacles as much as she does!" He lurched over to leer at Miranda. "To imagine that pallid porridge was this spicy dish."

Miranda wriggled and blew him a kiss.

Something Cressida would never have done. *Be careful, Miranda.*

"I understand," Jean-Marie continued, "zat ze Mandevilles are hosting a ball tonight at Almack's before leaving for India. Miss Porridge dances zere like our so lovely demoiselles, while St. Raven enjoys zis spicy dish. And some fool linked his name with hers! Lunacy!"

"Aye!" shouted Jolly Roger. "Shiver me timbers, that's fit for Bedlam."

"St. Raven wouldn't waste time on a dull piece like that," chortled another.

Tris gritted his teeth behind his smile and started a new ball rolling. "Except for her dowry. Her father has wealth again, and she's his sole heir. Makes a man think."

The world was going to believe that he'd married her for her money, but Cressida would know the truth. And in time everyone would see that love had grown.

"Bugger me, it does," said Tiverton, who was single. "Seems a shame to let such a rich prize sail off to India!"

"She'll be snapped up in no time there," Lord Peterbrook said. "All those men starved of a bit of white tit."

Intolerable disgust spurred Tris into action. He flicked Jean-Marie a look and called out, "My cousin challenges me to a wager!"

He had their attention. These men cared for little, but they all cared for and remembered a wager.

"He bets a thousand I can't make it from the arms of my Turkish delight to the arms of Miss Porridge before midnight."

Jean-Marie's eyes flashed amused alarm, but the men cheered and started to make side bets.

"On one horse, St. Raven?" one man asked.

"By curricle, and I keep horses on the London road."

The odds instantly switched to his favor.

"You going to try for her?" Tiverton asked. "Bloody unfair. I was thinking of having a go."

Useful. "Then race with me, Tiverton. You have your rig here, don't you? You'll have your chance, too."

"Against a duke!"

"I have the impression that Miss Mandeville wants nothing to do with high rank. Are you game?" He looked at all the men. "Lay your bets whether I, Tiverton, or none shall win the lady's hand before she leaves England."

Someone demanded a book to record the bets. Tris left Jean-Marie and Cary to deal with it, and ran up to change into evening clothes. Not suitable for driving, but a double-change might take too much time.

Tiverton didn't have evening clothes, so he'd have to do a change in London, and he howled at the unfairness even as he raced to his curricle. Let him have the lead. Tris ran downstairs and climbed into his own vehicle.

Jean-Marie had come out to see him off.

"Wish me luck," Tris said.

"When a thousand rides on it? I think not, my friend, though it is clever to take a witness to it all."

"Good fortune dropped that into my hands."

"Then good luck, cousin. In love, at least."

Tris caught up to Tiverton near Ware, but didn't try to overtake. Jolly Roger would have to change. The real danger was an accident, but there was enough moon to show the road, and it was in good condition.

They should have slowed when they hit the streets of London, but Tiverton took wild risks trying to build a lead, and Tris had to drive like a madman to keep close or Tiverton might suspect a sham. Time was short, but that wager didn't matter.

Tiverton yelled back a curse as he veered off toward his rooms, knowing the race was lost. But he'd follow to try his luck with Cressida. Poor man.

Tris arrived at the doors of Almack's at a quarter to midnight, slightly out of breath, but wild with the thrill of the race and the awareness that Cressida was close. He tossed his reins to a startled footman, dusted himself off, and strode into the building.

A footman tried to demand an invitation, but Tris gave his name and a ducal stare, and the man bowed out of the way. He paused in the arch to the ballroom, thinking of the times he'd come here expecting nothing but tedium broken by the irritation of women acting like hounds on the hunt.

But now the world was different, because Cressida was here.

She was dancing, circling with a rotund gentleman, and glowing with delight. She obviously loved to dance, and he hadn't known that. She was beautiful, but he'd known that for eons.

He reminded himself to look bored and bowed to Sir Arthur Mandeville, who was hurrying over.

"Your Grace, we are honored you could attend after all."

Was there something sharp in the man's eyes? No matter.

"I found a previous engagement cut short, and wished to take farewell of you and your family. You were most generous in the matter of the statues."

"Oh, that was Cressida's wish," the man said with ingenuous innocence, turning to look at where the dance was ending. "You must come and thank her yourself."

Tris had spoken for the people around, who

were paying attention. They all now had a reason for his arrival, and her father had provided a reason for him to go and speak to Cressida.

Heaven was on his side.

"St. Raven!" He turned to see Lord Harry Monke approaching with his pretty wife. "What the devil are you doing here? Oh, yes — you met Miss Mandeville in Hatfield."

Tris kissed pretty Lady Harry's hand. "I was able to do her a small service."

"I heard Crofton's hopped abroad. Good riddance."

"A horrid man," Lady Harry agreed, then smiled at Cressida's father. "So delightful that you recovered from your encounter with him, Sir Arthur. Now, St. Raven," she said, tucking her hand on his arm, "save me from being provincial and clinging to my husband and dance with me."

Trapped, he could not refuse, and perhaps it would be better not to go straight to Cressida. He glanced over and met her startled eyes. More than startled, stunned! Praying she wouldn't ruin everything now, he gave her a slight bow and turned back to Lady Harry's chatter.

He led her into the next dance. There were two lines, but he made sure they joined the one where Cressida danced. As they progressed, they would meet, touch, turn together. Crumbs to a starving man, but something. He was having trouble paying attention to Lady Harry's light chatter.

"How do you come to know the Mandevilles?" he asked.

"The Ladies' Committee for Support of the Foundling Hospital. Unlike many, the Mandeville ladies are genuinely concerned in charitable works, rather than amusing themselves, or seeking to rub shoulders with their betters."

Their betters. He was insanely tempted to ask what that meant, how anyone could be *better* than Cressida.

"How provincial," he drawled.

She surprised him with a disapproving look. "Poverty and suffering exist everywhere, St. Raven. I have been meaning to squeeze you for both money and patronage."

The music started, and they moved into their places, facing each other, to begin. Tris was honestly surprised by her response. Perhaps there were more goodhearted people among the highest ranks than he'd thought.

So Cressida might not be so out of place.

He glanced down the line to where she was beginning the steps opposite a young man in military uniform. She was smiling brilliantly at him, damn it. He found himself calculating just how long it would be before they progressed along the lines and encountered each other.

Cressida fixed her smiling attention on Lieutenant Grossthorp, but her mind was hooked onto St. Raven. What was he *doing* here? Was he going to ruin everything at the last moment by revealing their connection? She'd seen him with her father and feared they were coming to her, but then he'd asked Lady Harry to dance.

She almost missed a move and pulled her mind back to the dance. But, oh, Lord — she and Grossthorp were progressing up the line, and Tris and Lady Harry were progressing down. In moments, they would be together. She'd have to link arms and swing with him. She would be supposed to look into his eyes and smile. . . .

She looked back at her own partner and smiled and saw a startled look in his eyes along with his own smile. What message was she sending?

Damn Tris Tregallows.

Tris kept his attention off Cressida, but he was aware of her as if she were an extra instrument in the music, or a bright light at the corner of his eye. Coming closer, ever closer.

Then he noticed that the lady he turned with now was goggle-eyed, and he dragged his mind back to the moment. His meeting with Cressida would come, and in the meantime to dance with a duke would be an unforgettable thrill for many of these ladies, even for a sensible middle-aged mother like this.

He smiled at her and exchanged a comment. When he moved on to a starry-eyed young miss, he paid her a light compliment and sent a message with his eyes that had she but been older . . . With a frisky grandmother he said outright that had she but been younger . . .

She chuckled and called him a wicked rascal.

Then it was Cressida, and all words escaped him. They linked arms and turned, eye-to-eye, then reversed. Soon this moment would be over, and he hadn't said a blasted thing.

The clock struck, and he found a word. "Midnight."

Was that the best he could do?

She stared, as well she might. "What are you *doing* here?"

"Dancing with you." On that inanity, their encounter ended.

He wanted to howl with laughter or tears. He hadn't been such a tongue-tied blockhead at sixteen!

"Midnight," said Lady Harry as they stepped together. "You're lucky this isn't one of the assemblies or even you would not have gained admittance this late. And you're not in knee-breeches, either."

"If this had been an assembly, I'd have come earlier and correctly dressed."

"True. Apparently Sir Arthur was set on this ball and this location because his wife and daughter could never get vouchers. Said that before they left London, they would dance at Almack's."

Her expression was not unkind, but she recognized as he did that Sir Arthur had missed the point. Dancing at Almack's meant not this place, for hire to anyone, but the exclusive weekly assemblies held during the season.

Tris did not care deeply for the ways of the elite, but he realized how natural they were to him and his sort. Could Cressida learn the strange and at times incomprehensible customs and values?

She must. She would. He would be her experienced guide.

As the dance was ending, he saw Tiverton enter, scanning the room for his prey. Tris strolled over to the man and passed Lady Harry on. She wouldn't mind as long as she gained a young, handsome dance partner.

Tris turned back and saw Cressida surrounded by four men vying to be her partner. Damnation. She couldn't know that he was in process of clearing the risk of scandal, so if he asked her to dance she might reject him.

He sought out Sir Arthur. "Alas, sir, your daughter is surrounded by would-be partners. Perhaps you can pave my way."

"Your way is paved with strawberry leaves, Duke," said the man, causing a chuckle among the people nearby, for strawberry leaves decorated the ducal coronet. "But if you want a father's blessing . . ."

That caused some looks. So, Tris thought, Cressida's father had ideas, and was not opposed to the match.

Sir Arthur broke into the little group vying for Cressida's hand. "You can all go away. Here's St. Raven demanding a dance, and a duke's a duke, after all."

The men dispersed, grumbling. Tris bowed to her, unable to stop a smiling look. "If you are completely opposed to the idea, Miss Mandeville . . ."

"She wouldn't be so silly. One dance with you, and she's made — here and in India."

Cressida looked into his eyes, her round cheeks flushed. Everyone would take that for excitement, but was she angry?

She lowered her lids and curtsied. "How can I refuse, Your Grace?"

Her father left them alone together, but in a crowd. A crowd that would be watching every movement, every expression, simply because of who he was. He put her hand on his arm and turned to stroll as they waited for the next dance to start.

"This is the first time we've been together in society," he said, looking ahead as if they spoke nothings.

"Yes." She was doubtless doing the same thing. She would handle this correctly, his intrepid Miss Mandeville. "Why are you here? It's so dangerous."

"No. Trust me. I . . ." He almost spilled his proposal then and there, but he had a scrap of sanity left. "Crofton has fled the country," he said.

"Oh. Good." But the glance she flashed him showed worry. "I fear he has left his poison behind."

"Not after tonight —"

The music broke in, signaling the dance.

"Trust me, Cressida," he said softly as they moved into the lines.

It was a waltz, which meant they would be together throughout the dance, and would have moments turning in one another's arms. Many still thought it scandalous, and now he saw why. It turned him dizzy with delight.

Soon, soon, she would be in his arms as his wife.

In Tris's arms for the first waltz turns, Cressida felt as if she danced on sword blades, but with delight. As the dance progressed and no one screamed out in shock, she began to dream.

If they could dance, perhaps they could meet. Perhaps drive in the park, stroll through a garden? All the ordinary things men and women did . . .

But then she remembered that such pleasures would be pointless torment. This wickedly entrancing man was a rake. Like her father, he was addicted to the wild places. Even after professing his love for her, he'd been drawn to Violet Vane's establishment.

He could change, hope whispered.

Men never change, insisted sense.

But he was here. It had to mean something. And he felt something for her. She saw it, shielded for safety, in his eyes. She felt it in his touch.

Love could change people, and perhaps with Crofton gone the risk of scandal was small. Perhaps marriage was possible.

Tris was here. It *had* to mean something.

Her dazed eye caught Lavinia tapping her furled fan against her lips. She recognized a signal. Lavinia had something she needed to talk about, in the ladies' withdrawing room, now.

Oh, Lord. It was something about St. Raven. After all, Matt Harbison was here. She saw from Lavinia's expression that it was something bad. She longed to turn away and ignore the summons, but she'd rather know.

With a word, she escaped and followed her friend. As soon as she entered the room, Lavinia dragged her to a sofa. Cressida looked around, but there was no one there except the maids. She'd be careful what she said, knowing how servants' gossip could fly.

"How delightful to have the duke turn up,"

Lavinia said brightly, perhaps also with the maids in mind. "And he is just as handsome up close as from a distance!"

"Yes. What do you have to tell me, Lavinia?"

Her friend's bright manner dropped. "I'm sorry. . . . It's just that I remember you saying you had warm feelings for him. . . ."

Cressida knew she was blushing. "Do you fear my heart will break over a dance?"

"No, but . . . The thing is, Cressida, Matt says he's only here because of a wager."

"A *wager?* Gentlemen wager over anything."

"Yes, but . . ."

"Please, just say it!"

Lavinia bit her lip, then dropped her voice to a whisper. "Sir Roger Tiverton came here with the duke, and Matt knows him quite well, so he has the whole story. St. Raven was holding a wild party at his house in Hertfordshire. They were pretending it was an Almack's Assembly, if you can imagine anything so silly. And then someone wagered that the duke couldn't go from dancing with a whore there to dancing with you here before midnight. And that," she ended miserably, "is the only reason he's here. I thought you should know. . . ."

It hurt to breathe, though Cressida couldn't imagine why. She'd never held any illusions about what he was. He'd never promised to reform. She'd never expected that he would, not really.

But another orgy, and a wager. A wager about *her.* When she had thought that at least he cared for her reputation.

She pinned on a bright smile and rose. "Most

people here won't know, so his attendance and his dancing with me will be a small feather in my cap. In India I'll be able to drop my dance with the Duke of St. Raven into conversation to great benefit."

Lavinia stood. "I'm so relieved. I didn't want you hurt."

Cressida even managed a laugh. "Of course I'm not hurt. When I talked of loving St. Raven, it was a lighthearted kind of love. A game. Like our starry-eyed adoration of the actor, Kean."

Lavinia relaxed, smiling with her. "And only see how silly everyone is being over him tonight. Even my mother is as flustered as a schoolgirl! People are storing up the way he says 'good evening' to report back to their less fortunate friends, and Deb Westforth was so overwhelmed by one flattering comment that she's lying down in an anteroom with a vinegar cloth on her head."

"Poor man," Cressida said, meaning it.

Lavinia linked arms. "He probably loves it. Come on. If I stick by you, perhaps he'll ask me to dance and toss me a flattering comment or two. That will be something to tell my grandchildren."

Cressida would rather flee home, but that would throw the fat on the fire. As soon as she returned to the ballroom she saw him, as if he were the only real person amid a room of waxworks. He came toward her, and she couldn't escape. She told herself that she was bound by Lavinia's wish to meet him, but she wasn't sure her feet would move. And anyway, from a look in his eye she suspected that he would pursue.

What did he *want?*

He'd presumably won his wager, and though he'd put her reputation at risk, they seemed to have avoided disaster. Or was the wager that he achieve something more. A kiss? More than that?

He was so handsome, though, in his dark evening clothes and perfect linen. She'd never seen him dressed that way before. He was so dear to her, too, because her foolish mind seemed trapped in those few days when his butterfly attention was all on her, when he'd created that illusion of closeness, of more than closeness, that had carried her into deepest folly.

She smiled at him, chatted for a moment, then virtually commanded him to ask Lavinia to dance. She saw his brow twitch, but good manners allowed him no escape.

She was then approached by her mother offering Sir Roger Tiverton as a partner. Good manners left her equally without escape, but he behaved correctly and even apologized for his behavior in Hatfield.

"Want you to know, Miss Mandeville, that no one pays any notice to Lord Crofton's ravings. Especially not now. The man was clearly mad."

"Then I must feel sorry for him. A shame, perhaps, that he is not receiving appropriate care."

"Indeed." He led her toward the forming lines. "Now, Miss Mandeville, do say you will drive out with me tomorrow."

What start was this? Was the wager more widespread? Damn them all. She gave him a cool smile. "I'm sorry, Sir Roger, I will be far too busy. We set off for Plymouth the day after next."

"Plymouth, hey? I have an interest in things nautical, Miss Mandeville. Might take a little jaunt down there myself!"

Cressida gritted her teeth and prayed that something prevent that, but it was the least of her troubles. She watched where Tris took Lavinia and made sure to join the other line, but her heart still beat deeply in dread of what would happen next.

Dread, or dreadful desire. Despite all logic a part of her swooned to be weak, to be played with again, to be wicked.

Tris watched Cressida in the dance, but was careful now not to give too much away. A little attention would set the right tone. Any glimpse of his raging passion would not.

He longed to stay, to capture her companionship over supper, to linger till the dying chord of the last dance, his attention all on her. It would get him nowhere of significance, however, and open up too much chance of disaster.

She was safe from scandal now. Tiverton had agreed that there was absolutely no chance that this Miss Mandeville led a secret life, attending orgies in outrageous costumes. He'd agreed that Crofton must have made up the whole story out of spite over being rejected. Tris had encountered Pugh and led him to the same declaration.

Tiverton was set on his courtship, of course, which was a nuisance, but of little concern. The stage was set, and the way to play this now was in complete formality. Tomorrow he would write to

Sir Arthur, requesting permission to court his daughter, and therefore permission to travel with them to the West Country.

From the world's point of view, it would be a hasty wooing, but not outrageous, and by the time it was formally announced at Mount St. Raven, no one would be shocked.

With all set, he might as well leave. Dancing with other women gave no pleasure.

Cressida watched Tris leave, wryly amused. Wager complete and off he went. Useful, really, to have it clear how little she meant to him. And that — his straight back and broad shoulders disappearing through an archway — was the last she would ever see of him.

She didn't deny her broken heart, but she knew it would mend. And if it didn't, it was a preferable pain to living day by day like Lady Pugh, grateful for the crumbs of his occasional attention and pretending to the world that she did not know about his whoring amusements.

In her room with dawn breaking, she let her maid prepare her for bed. Weariness weakened her, and her memory scrolled out the last time she'd taken off the Nile green dress.

Struggling with the fastenings and corset.

Tris's hands on her back.

That first kiss. *"You really should go. . . ."*

He'd always been so *honest* about himself that she really couldn't blame him. He'd never forced her into anything. That night of passion had been her doing, not his. She remembered how careful he'd been to ensure that she understood that it meant nothing for the future.

How unfair to blame him for not being the sort of conventional Matlockian gentleman she could marry. How ridiculous to presume that he'd be happier with a different way of life. She didn't want his life, so why should he want hers?

She dismissed the maid and went to bed, determined to think only of what needed to be done on the morrow to ensure a smooth journey to Plymouth.

Her mind would not behave, however, and despite exhaustion she could not escape into sleep. In the end she stirred a dose of Dr. Willy's Elixir of Morpheus into a glass of water and drank it all. She lay back down again, fought for mental control again, then knew nothing more until her maid woke her in the morning.

Chapter Thirty-one

Opiates always left Cressida feeling drained. She considered spending the rest of the day in bed, but people would call, and there was much to be done.

She breakfasted in her room going over lists, but then received a summons to her father's study. Oh, dear, what now? He was anxious to get on his way back to India, and wanted to be in Plymouth in plenty of time to supervise the arrangement for his cargo. Surely he wouldn't try to put off their departure.

He looked up from his desk with a frown. "Sit down, Cressy. You're a shadow of yourself. You didn't used to look so ragged after a night's dancing!"

"There's been so much to do, Father."

He nodded. "And you've been a marvel. If you'd been a man, you'd have been a fair hand at business." He picked up a letter. "See here. After last night it's not so big a surprise, but here I have the Duke of St. Raven asking for leave to court you."

Cressida stared, stunned. "By *letter?*" she asked. It seemed the most ridiculous thing of all.

"Nothing wrong with that. Good old-fashioned way of doing things. Well? What do you want me to say? With us on our way tomorrow, he suggests he travel with us. He makes no secret of the fact that he'll want a grand dowry, but he claims to have formed a high regard for your character and good sense. Which shows he has more good sense than I expected. Well?"

Cressida wanted to drag her hands through her carefully arranged hair.

"I confess I'll miss you," her father went on, "but I'll not hold you back from your course. You can hardly be indifferent to a man like that, and you'll be a duchess, no less."

"Oh, Father, that's the last thing I want to be!" Tris wanted to marry her? It struck at the foundations of her strength, but she tried to cling to sense.

Her father huffed out a breath. "Lookee here, Cressy, don't play me for a fool. You went haring off to Hatfield, and there was the duke. There's more to that story than's in the open. I made inquiries about him. He's a bold rascal, but he treats people decently, pays his debts, even to his tradesmen — and that's a rarity among his sort. He's even spoken with sense a time or two in Parliament."

Cressida looked down at her tangled hands. "He's a rake, Father. He came to our ball from a wild party. On a wager, and dragged my name into it."

He grimaced. "I heard. Heard some other stories last night I'd not heard before."

Cressida knew she was red. "Some people have nothing better to do than gossip, and for some reason Lord Crofton held a grudge."

"Now there's a man I wish I'd never met. But what of St. Raven? What shall I reply? Or do you want to?"

"No!" She steadied herself. Could this possibly be an extension of that wager?

No, even he wouldn't bind himself for life on a bet. He probably did want to marry her in his reckless way, but it wouldn't work for her.

"Say no, Father. As politely as possible, say no." She looked at him. "Could we leave today? As soon as possible. Most arrangements are made."

He pulled a face. "Like that, is it? I'll not say you're wrong, my dear. The world would call you a fool to throw away the chance to be a duchess, but you're not the sort to put great store in rank and coronet. And as you say, he's a rake. I've known plenty, and they rarely change. It's in their blood, the way it's in my blood to go adventuring. Some wives are happy enough with a wandering husband, but I doubt you would be. Especially if you cared."

She didn't say anything to that. There was no need. "So can we leave today, Father? And can you perhaps delay your reply?"

"There's nothing to stop him racing after us."

"I know, but perhaps he'll realize there's no point."

Tris read Sir Arthur's formal regrets with icy disbelief.

"Not a happy reply, I gather."

He looked up at Cary. "Did he perhaps not ask her?"

Cary raised his brows and looked down.

Tris was amazed to find how physically painful this was. Jaw, throat, chest, all ached. "She must have misunderstood. . . ."

"Possible," Cary obligingly agreed.

Tris stood, carefully folding the letter and putting it aside. "I won't believe it until I hear it from her own lips. I know the problems, but surely there's enough between us . . . I can arrange things. I'll protect her. . . ."

Cary had risen, too. "By all means, let's go and see if she'll receive you."

"She'll receive me."

Tris didn't realize how grim his tone had been until Cary said, "Oh, dear. I've mislaid the battering ram and siege engines. . . ."

That broke a laugh. "Dammit, I know Cressida. She'd never refuse to at least see me. This has to all be a misunderstanding. Tiverton, damn him, babbled all over about the wager last night. Perhaps she's miffed about that. Come on."

But when he arrived at her house in Otley Street the knocker was off the door. When his thundering brought a servant, he was told that the Mandevilles had left town over an hour ago, that their lease of the house was over.

Tris stood in front of the house, stunned and furious. "He sent that letter as they drove away. She can't have been told!"

He moved toward the curricle, but Cary grasped his arm. "Why would he withhold it?"

"He wants her to go to India. He's a selfish brute. He's not going to get away with this." Tris ripped free and climbed into the curricle and set the horses off at a race toward the Newington Gate.

Cary stood in the road and cursed, then turned to run to the nearest stables where he could hire a horse.

The sight of a curricle overtaking them was not a huge shock to Cressida. She'd prepared for the journey in a white-hot frenzy, but once in the coach she'd had nothing to do but think.

Tris would follow. Sitting as she was with her back to the horses, she saw him coming, riding the light carriage in a way that was painfully familiar, his prime horses eating the ground.

She should have written the letter herself. He might have accepted it then. She had written a stern note to Sir Roger Tiverton and he was nowhere to be seen.

The coach drew up.

"What?" said her father, looking up from a book.

"It must be an accident," said her mother, peering out.

"It's St. Raven," Cressida said.

Her parents looked at her, and she saw that neither of them were surprised, that they perhaps thought her rejection foolish, that she'd come to her senses.

"He'd make a terrible husband!" she exclaimed.

He swung open the door, all fire and icy dignity. "Miss Mandeville, may I have a moment of your time?"

She swallowed through a painfully tight throat, but climbed out of the coach without taking his outstretched hand. He flushed and stepped back.

His curricle sat at an angle across the road, blocking the coach. Their groom had control of his steaming horses. Behind, their luggage coach was drawing up, the servants peering out, goggle-eyed. The road was quiet at the moment, but another vehicle could come by at any time and wonder. People might stop to ask if they could help.

More gossip.

She couldn't bear it.

She walked six paces away from the coach and spoke quickly. "You probably think my father didn't show me your letter, Your Grace, or something equally extreme. He did. And though I am suitably aware of the honor you pay me, I regret that I could never become your wife."

His face had been set, but now it turned white. "Why?"

"I thought gentlemen were never supposed to ask that."

"Probably, but I'm a duke. Explain. I . . . had the strong impression that you felt a connection to me, Miss Mandeville."

The emotions beating out of him reminded her of their first encounter, of her terror. She was surely safe now.

She looked away from him, across peaceful, golden fields. A reasonable crop here, while in many areas the poor summer meant a thin harvest. "I do not deny your many virtues, Your Grace —"

"Yes, you do, but I am willing to improve."

"I mean, I do not deny your many qualities, but our characters are not harmonious." She looked back, begging him to understand. "It seems impossible that I might hurt you, but I think I am. It will only sting for a little while, but if we marry the pain will be for life! You are following a whim. You are used to having what you want, and right now you want me. Good Lord, it's the challenge, isn't it? My running away only added to that. But if we were to marry, that would all end, don't you see? I'll bore you" — she swept on over a protest — "and you'll turn back to a more exciting life, and I will *not* smile sweetly over it."

She spread her hands. "You'll turn me into a shrew, and I'll turn you into a monstrous husband, and I never wanted to be a duchess. You can find a better wife than I."

He seemed puzzled as much as anything. "You really don't think much of me, do you?"

Her whole face ached with stopped-up tears. "I said you had many qualities."

"But no virtues."

"That was you, not me."

She saw him suck in a breath. "Cressida, I can be the man you want me to be. This is more than some whim, dammit!"

"Don't swear at me!"

"Once you didn't care."

She looked around, alarmed that someone might hear. "That was a brief madness. It was not me. It was not you."

"I love you. I told you that before, and I haven't changed."

She met his eyes. "Precisely."

They hung in frozen silence, his eyes dark. She felt the beat of his violent will, but this time he surely couldn't seize her, carry her off from amid her family and servants —

The pounding wasn't only her heart.

Hooves.

A rider charged up, leaped off his horse.

Mr. Lyne, hatless, disordered. He looked between them, then bowed. "Miss Mandeville."

"Late as usual, Cary," said Tris, in a tone both light and ice. "Miss Mandeville has finally convinced me that there was no misunderstanding." He stepped back and bowed, fully. "Bon voyage."

With that he turned on his heel and strode back to his curricle, climbed in, and drove off at speed.

Cressida watched him go, fighting not to cry.

"If he said anything to offend, Miss Mandeville, you must excuse him. He really does care."

She could not get into an argument with this man, too. "I hope you will follow, Mr. Lyne. He drives well, but . . ."

His expression was rueful and kind. "Don't worry. I'll pick up the pieces. Bon voyage, Miss Mandeville, but I hope you are very sure of your proper destination."

He swung into the saddle and rode off. After a moment, she turned and climbed back into the coach.

Her mother was biting her lower lip and looking upset. Her father looked put out.

Cressida jolted as the coach moved off again. "If you wanted me to marry the duke, you might have told me. I could have saved you both some distress. But that should be an end of it."

"That's for sure," her father grunted. "I just hope you know what you're doing."

" 'Can the Ethiopian change his skin,' " she quoted, " 'or the leopard his spots?' "

Her father snorted and returned to his book; her mother sighed and returned to her knitting.

To herself, for strength, Cressida recited the rest of that passage from Jeremiah. ". . . *I have seen thine adulteries, and thy neighings, the lewdness of thy whoredom, and thine abominations* . . ."

One day she would look back on this and know it was right.

Cary came up with Tris walking his horses in the approach to Camberley. "Are we for the Mount, then?"

"Of course. There's a masquerade to prepare for."

Cary bit the inside of his cheek. This was not the moment to argue about Miss Swinamer. Give Tris a day or two to cool off.

In Camberley he arranged to return his horse to the livery in London, and sent a message requesting both his and Tris's belongings be sent down to Mount St. Raven.

He didn't have long. Once a change of horses was in place, Tris was ready to be off. He didn't have to explain that he wanted to be well ahead of the Mandevilles.

Which was as well, as he said not a word in the five hours it took to reach Amesbury, which was certainly beyond any possible stopping place of

Cressida Mandeville and her family.

Breaking with his custom, Tris commanded two separate bedrooms, went into his, and shut the door. The innkeeper, a kindly-looking woman, said, "What will His Grace want for dinner?"

"If he wants to eat, he'll tell you. As for me," Cary said with a smile, "spread the best table you can, Mrs. Wheeling. I'm empty as a dry sack. And I'll have a flagon of ale to be going on with."

He went into his room and collapsed into a chair, leaning back to think, though it didn't help. Miss Mandeville was not playing coy games. She didn't want to marry St. Raven, and it wasn't altogether surprising. He wasn't an easy person, they had little in common, and being a duke or a duchess was the very devil unless you had a taste for playing God.

All the same, at heart, Tris Tregallows was one of the best men Cary knew, and he deserved a good wife and a chance at a happy life.

Chapter Thirty-two

Broken hearts did not precisely mend, but they grew scar tissue. In the six leisurely days it took to reach Plymouth, Cressida achieved a certain peace with her destiny. Perhaps close observance of her parents helped.

Her father was like Tris in so many ways, even if his weakness was adventure through travel rather than through wild indulgence. The sparkle in his eye, his anticipation and enthusiasm for the future, were all new to Cressida.

With Tris it had been the reverse. She'd first met the real man. The social gentleman was the incomplete version, a part he played because he must.

Over days of thought she decided that St. Raven had assumed that she was like him, that the woman she'd been at first was the real one, the propriety an act. Yes, she'd thrilled for a while in her exploration of the wild places, but in the end she'd been desperate to return home — to ordinary ways and propriety. She had absolutely no desire to return to rakes and orgies.

What's more, she was not like her mother. Since learning why her mother had left India, Cressida had tried to understand, but in the end she was defeated. Her mother seemed to have a blessed ability to be content with her fate, whatever it might be. Admirable, but perhaps overcompliant.

She had learned that her parents' marriage had been one of fondness rather than passion, so perhaps it hadn't been hard for Louisa to leave her husband. Cressida's mother claimed to have enjoyed the venture to India, but also not to have suffered over the decision to return home.

"Your health was the most important thing," she said as if that explained all, "and I knew your father could manage without me."

"But didn't you think of joining him at some time?"

"Perhaps when you'd married."

It was said without reproach, but Cressida felt guilt again over her carelessness. She could have married years ago if she'd known.

Cressida couldn't cling to the idea that her mother was being dragged abroad against her will. When not knitting, she was reading books about India and having her husband teach her useful phrases. Cressida dutifully learned phrases, too, but when she caught sight of the ships in Plymouth harbor, it was only the thought of having to face the Duke of St. Raven again that prevented her from backing out.

The King's Arms was a comfortable hostelry, and they had a spacious suite of rooms. Their ship, the *Sally Rose*, was already in port, carrying their possessions from London as well as goods her father had purchased for trade. Her father busied himself with checking it all and loading up yet more. Her mother bustled about, buying comforts and necessities for the journey.

Cressida could have done her part, but she spent her time in long walks. It wasn't exactly wise since it gave her too much time to think, but she reasoned that she had only so much longing in her, and the quicker she worked through it, the quicker it would be gone.

Longing for England as well as for a man. Or for one face of a many-faceted man. . . .

Then one day, as she walked back toward the inn, she saw a familiar figure approaching. Her heart halted for a moment, but then she realized that it was not Tris, but his French cousin.

"Monsieur Bourreau," she said in French.

He bowed. "Miss Mandeville."

"What on earth are you doing in Plymouth?"

"So close to the ends of the earth, is it not? But I am on my way back from Mount St. Raven, where I took farewell of my cousin."

Was she supposed to ask how he was? She waited in silence.

He was carrying a small, leather-bound notebook and opened it. If it was another letter from Tris, she was going to scream.

It was not a notebook, but a kind of portfolio. He took out a sheet and offered it. "For you, Miss Mandeville."

One glance showed her Tris, brilliantly executed in pencil, lounging, a glass of something in his hand, in disorder, shirt open at the neck.

"Why would you think I would want that?"

"Ah! Almost exactly his words when I offered him its partner. Interesting, is it not?"

She gave him an icy look. "When offered an

unwanted item, what else is a person to say? It would seem that you are meddling in matters that have nothing to do with you, Mr. Bourreau."

She walked on, but he kept pace.

"Am I? Miss Mandeville, I came to England bent on revenge, and on squeezing as much as possible out of the wicked Duke of St. Raven. But alas, I discover a friend. More than a friend, one who could be a brother if circumstances were different. We must part. We will likely not see a great deal of each other. But I cannot be uninvolved. I have discovered my lovely Miranda. I wish no less for my cousin."

This was startling enough to make Cressida stop and stare. "Do you mean Miranda Coop?"

"Exactly!" he said with a brilliant smile. "A queen among women. In France, she will become my wife, and respectable. Perhaps one day you will be able to visit our house in perfect propriety."

"You forget. I am about to sail for India."

He looked out at the forest of masts. "Ah yes. India. Do you truly think you can be happy there?"

"I am willing to try."

"But not to try other adventures? What if I tell you that St. Raven is most unhappy?"

"I will be full of regrets, sir, but without power to assist him."

"And if I tell you that tonight at a masquerade ball he will ask the icy Miss Swinamer to be his duchess? Not his wife. She is, in my opinion, unable to be his wife. His friend Cary and I talk. We decide that it must not be. I come here."

He whipped out another picture and held it before her.

Phoebe Swinamer, to the inch. The beauty might think it an excellent portrayal, for it captured all her fine looks and even a slight smile. But in some subtle way it also captured her complete lack of heart. A china doll would have more feeling for the world beyond her own selfish interests.

Cressida turned away. "What do you expect me to *do?*"

"Marry him."

She swung back. "Sacrifice myself to make him happy. No, I will not! Why should I?"

"Sacrifice!" He almost spat it. "You are scared of the different, so you dig a hole and bury yourself in it. All very well. You are safe there. But you are also in a hole! What sort of life is that? Life offers excitement, spice, and exquisite pleasures, but only for those willing to venture out of their safe little holes."

Cressida found she could not express herself in French and switched to English. "It would kill me to have him unfaithful."

"So you would rather not have him at all?"

"Yes."

"Does that make sense?"

"Yes!"

He shrugged. "As well say zat for fear of poisoning, one must never eat. But if zat is your price, demand it. Demand zat he vow faithfulness."

"It is in the marriage vows, Mr. Bourreau, but

many of his sort seem to ignore it."

"His sort? What do you know of *his sort?* Do you link him with Crofton, Pugh, and such others?"

"You can know a person by the company he keeps."

Good Lord, now she sounded like Mrs. Wemworthy.

"Zese days he keeps his own company. What does zat tell you? Nun's Chase, it is now suitable for ze nuns, zough he plans to sell it. He lives like a nun — or rather, like a monk."

"A week of chastity will hardly kill him. He came to my ball from an orgy, on a wager."

He stared at her, and broke into French so rapid she had to struggle to understand.

"My God, he did not tell you? Idiot!" And some other word she did not know.

He calmed. "Miss Mandeville, that orgy was arranged precisely to clear your name. Miranda portrayed the houri before all those men who had seen you in that part. Since you were on full view in London at the same time, all suspicion would be blown away."

Cressida felt as if the pounding waves were shaking the earth beneath her feet. "And the wager?"

"A last-moment touch, perhaps foolish. But a wager, it is remembered, when a dance might not be. Tiverton took it up as a race, which strengthened the effect. Of course you should never have known any of this."

"There are gossips in every circle. . . ." Agonizing to open herself again to hope, but Cressida couldn't help it. "What of Violet Vane? I heard he had become a frequenter of her house."

He spat more words that she didn't understand. "My apologies, please! But I am enraged by our stupidity. Of course such things are known!"

"So you see —"

"No, no! *You* must see. I pray you will believe me. My cousin, he was only there to put an end to all that. At Stokeley Manor, he grew suspicious about the age of some of the nymphs. There was a connection to La Violette, and so he pursued. Alas, the trade is not stamped out, but that road is blocked."

It could all be lies, but something about it, and about Bourreau's manner, argued that it might be truth. Besides, it had been hard — almost impossible — to think that of Tris.

"I can tell you also," he said, "though it is only my belief, that he has not been in any woman's bed since I met him in Hatfield."

She turned again to look at the sea, aware of being at the most crucial moment of her life. Monsieur Bourreau was right about the hole, but call it burrow. A comfort place, a safe place. It offered only minor pleasures, but it protected against tormenting pains.

Demand fidelity? As she'd said, it was in the wedding vows, but perhaps that ritual deafened people to their full meaning. If she asked Tris to promise fidelity and he agreed, she suddenly knew, with clarity, that he would honor that vow.

"How far is it from here to Mount St. Raven?" she whispered, afraid to put it into clear words.

"Three hours or so. You will come?"

She turned to him. "You will take me?"

"But, of course. There is no time for delay. Lyne will try to stop him, but you know my cousin cannot be entirely stopped. Once he asks Miss Swinamer, it will be too late. That, too, will be a vow he will not break."

She felt frantically as if it were happening *now.* "When does it start?"

"At nine."

"It is four. We must go!"

"I have a vehicle waiting."

She began hurrying toward the inn. "I must tell my mother."

"She will let you go?"

"I'll go anyway, but I must tell her."

She sped, tempted to run, but knowing she'd end up breathless halfway. Sensible to the end, Cressida! Pray that you don't have to pay the price for it. She was breathing hard by the time she reached the inn and paused there at the door.

"What if he no longer wants me?"

Bourreau was unsympathetic. "That is a doubt you have brought on yourself." But he offered the picture and this time she took it, tears starting. It was Tris, not the duke, relaxed, ordinary except for his looks. And he was unhappy, alone, without hope.

"You have great skill."

"But, of course."

"Is it true?"

"Exactly. I gave him a picture of you. He did not reject it."

"Thank you for that, for hope. I won't be a moment."

She hurried up to their rooms, and found her mother knitting. She looked up, then stood. "Cressida? What is it, dear?"

"I've made a terrible mistake, Mama. I need to go to Mount St. Raven."

To her astonishment, her mother bloomed with delight. "Oh, my dear, I'm so glad you've realized! Your father said we must let you have your way. You are so sensible and clearheaded, and he does worry a bit about the duke's wildness. But you should follow your heart, even into danger. And we will follow, as soon as we can. We can't have it looking as if you've been running around wildly again."

Cressida shook her head, dashed over to give her mother a fierce hug, then ran out of the room and down, to find Bourreau with a curricle.

"This looks like Tris's," she said as she climbed in.

"It is. Pray that I do not overturn."

They were off, and she clutched the rail. "Are you not a good whip?"

"Not particularly," he shouted cheerfully, urging the horses to speed.

Cressida clutched harder but didn't ask him to slow.

He didn't have Tris's skill, and the roads became rougher. Sometimes he had to let the horses walk.

It was close to nine, and the sun had set by the time they approached the large pale house on a hill, where windows blazed, but not with an illusion of hell's flames.

To Cressida it was heaven, as long as she arrived in time.

Carriages were pouring toward it. The event had begun.

Jean-Marie — they had arrived at first name terms on the journey — turned away.

"Where are we going?" she cried.

"We cannot take you in the front way, but I know a road to the stables. From there you can enter the house. If Tris has joined his guests, you will need a costume."

They turned into a narrow lane, and Cressida prayed. She prayed that Tris still be in his room, that he had not proposed to Miss Swinamer before the event.

As soon as they arrived in the busy stables, she jumped out of the curricle. Jean-Marie joined her and they hurried into the house.

He led her to narrow servants' stairs, and up to a wide, carpeted corridor. They entered a grand bedchamber hung with red velvet that was embroidered in gold with some heraldic device.

Tris's room. Cressida knew it by its grandeur, but also by sandalwood and every other sense.

And Tris wasn't here.

They explored the whole of the grand suite, but Tris wasn't here!

Jean-Marie swore again. "Stay here!" he said, and disappeared.

Cressida paced the bedchamber wringing her hands, almost running out into the house a dozen times. But she would look like a madwoman. Servants would probably throw her out.

Then Jean-Marie was back with a nun. A nun, complete with winged wimple. A nun who pulled off her complicated headdress, then began to strip.

"Go away," Miranda Coop commanded her lover. "Go and make sure Tris doesn't do anything stupid."

Cressida didn't need to be told. She began to tear off her gown, grateful she didn't need help. And that this time she didn't need to take off drawers, shift, or corset.

"That's a quite decorous nun's habit," she said.

"I'm reformed," said Miranda with a grin. "Here."

She tossed the long black gown, and Cressida struggled into it, aware with some amazement that being in the company of a former whore, both of them in underwear, was not shocking her.

As she knotted a rope round her waist she noted that Miranda's drawers were pink silk, and her corset was embroidered with pink roses and laced with scarlet ribbons. Her flesh-colored stockings had vines embroidered up them to flower near the black garters. She suspected Tris might like underwear like that.

She draped the white yoke around her neck, and Miranda tied it, then the half-mask over her face. Then Miranda pushed her into a chair and settled the headdress on, tucking away curls and fixing it with hairpins.

"There," she said. "Go!"

Cressida shot to her feet but paused. "What's he wearing?"

"Jean-Marie's Crow outfit. But there's half a dozen here."

"Heavens! What's Miss Swinamer wearing?"

Miranda grinned. "She's a shepherdess. All pink ruffles. Go! Turn left, follow the corridor, the ballroom is at the other end of the house, but he might be anywhere."

Cressida shot into the corridor and ran left, but then a door opened and she slammed to a halt. A couple in medieval clothes emerged chattering, inclined their heads to her, and went on their way.

Damnation, now she had to progress at the same stately pace as they or look peculiar. What was the price of looking peculiar? At this point, she didn't care. She pushed past and ran, despite exclamations of affront.

Two turns in the corridor, one of which took her across a landing above the main entrance. She stopped to hang over and search the crowd. This was a masquerade, so the host wouldn't be receiving his guests. Even so, a fat woman in a long velvet robe and a diadem was doing just that.

She saw three big hats with sweeping plumes, but none were Tris. Two shepherdesses, but she didn't think either was Miss Swinamer.

Please let Jean-Marie have found Tris in time to stop him from committing himself. Or let Mr. Lyne have him in control.

She went on, walking now, since people were all around, wishing she were taller and could see over the growing crowd. Wishing she didn't have the stupid horns that kept bumping into things.

She came to the ballroom. Music played, but not yet for dancing. Four chandeliers cast light along with lamps on the walls. Cressida paused to breathe, to calm, to collect her wits.

A Puritan, complete to steeple hat, stopped by her side. "Jean-Marie's with him, but he's looking for Miss Swinamer."

"Mr. Lyne." Extreme urgency popped, letting in doubts. "Perhaps she's what he wants."

"Since driving away from your coach, he hasn't allowed his wants to show. If you're looking for guarantees," he added with puritanical sternness, "there are none. You may have hurt him too much."

She bit her lip. "He might have explained."

"You might have trusted him."

He'd asked her to trust him, but she wasn't a person for blind trust. "Only help me find him. Where should I start?"

"I left him as he entered this room. I don't know where the Swinamers are."

Cressida couldn't see farther than the people nearby. She looked up and saw small, curtained balconies in each corner. "I could go up there and search."

He followed her gaze. "I'll go, and I'll direct you." He smiled. "At least those starched horns make you easy to spot."

She spent the waiting time maneuvering through the guests, fending off the occasional flirtation. As was the custom, people were acting in part, which made it easy for her to reject advances.

Then she saw Mr. Lyne's head, minus hat,

poke around the corner of the curtain. He scanned the room, then pointed urgently to her left.

Relief washed over her like . . . like perfumed oil. She pushed left as fast as she could, but her headdress made navigation difficult, especially in an encounter with a medieval lady in a steeple cap.

She emerged from that, shoved her headdress straight again and glanced at the balcony. The Puritan was frantically pointing down below him. Cressida switched directions and headed that way, keeping more of an eye on her guide.

She bumped into someone.

A shepherdess.

And this time it was Phoebe Swinamer, with only the tiniest of masks to conceal her beauty.

"Be careful, do!" Miss Swinamer snapped, twitching her ruffled elbow-cuffs back into line. She turned back to a woman who wore only a domino cloak over her gown, and an equally small mask. Phoebe's mother.

"I quite expected St. Raven to speak before this event, Mama. It is such a crush."

"His first major entertainment here, dear. Of course everyone attends."

"Mostly country bumpkins." The beauty made no attempt to speak quietly.

"Now, now, dear, mind your manners. These people will soon be your dependents, and it will be a grand audience for the announcement."

"I do hope St. Raven will not wish to spend too much time in Cornwall. It is so far from anywhere. Traveling here took days."

Cressida had been so fixed on this conversation that she'd forgotten to watch her guide. She looked up to see him making a frantic gesture that she couldn't interpret.

But then she realized he meant that Tris was coming her way and would encounter the Swinamers first!

With a muttered excuse, she pushed past them. Phoebe spat another complaint, but Cressida watched her guide. A Le Corbeau blocked her way and she grabbed him.

He looked down, startled. He was a stranger.

"Tripped!" she gasped, and escaped, headdress slipping over one eye.

Then she came face-to-face with Tris, in black, masked, but without the beard and mustache. It made her smile. Clearly his heart hadn't been in any of this. "Miranda? Jean-Marie was here a moment ago." He glanced around.

Should she be offended that he couldn't tell the difference? Carried on a wave of mischief and relief, Cressida stepped forward and walked her fingers up his jacket.

He caught her hand. "You disappoint me."

He really was disappointed, angry even. Because he thought his cousin's love was unfaithful.

Cressida looked into his masked eyes. "It's not Miranda."

He froze. "I'm brandy-mad."

She realized then that he'd been drinking. He wasn't staggering drunk, but there was a slight slur in his voice and a slackness in his features.

What to say? The Swinamers could be close behind. What had she imagined would happen now? Him asking her again, giving her another chance?

"St. Raven!"

Lady Swinamer's piercing voice. They were coming.

She raised her other hand, so she held his with both. "You're not mad. My name is Cressida Mandeville, and you asked me to marry you." Desperately she added, "You asked me first!"

He frowned, and for a dreadful moment she was sure he had changed his mind. It had been a whim, now passed.

"St. Raven!" Lady Swinamer again, nearer, almost here.

He changed their grip and turning, pulled her away, away from that demanding voice, out of the ballroom, through an arch, along a corridor, and down a curving stairwell. He stopped suddenly, on the curve with no sight of top above or bottom below.

"Cressida?"

They'd passed a flickering lamp, and it provided some light, but chancy here, around the bend. She couldn't see him clearly, but his voice told her what she needed to know.

By planning or accident, he'd stopped with her one step higher so she could easily cradle his face. "I want to change my answer, if you'll let me. But I have a boon to request."

His hands covered hers. His eyes seemed entirely black. "What?"

"I don't have the right to ask. I've been a fool. I heard you were at Violet Vane's and assumed the worst. I heard you'd come to my ball from an

orgy, on a wager, and I believed it."
"Cressida —"
She sealed his lips with her thumbs. "But for both our sakes I ask you now. Please, Tris, can you swear to be faithful to me, all the days that we live? If you swear that, I'll never doubt you again."
He held her thumbs against his lips, and she felt his words as well as heard them. "I do so swear. I can't imagine wanting anyone but you."
An explosion of happiness struck her dumb, and then she said, "I ate a cake with pink icing."
Why that? At a moment like this? He'd think her an idiot.
But he smiled. "Why not? If we eat oysters, eating insects is not so strange. And honey, after all, is insect food. . . . I'm somewhat drunk, my love. Forgive me."
"Only if you kiss me." She leaned to him, but one of her horns collided with the wall, knocking the wimple all over her face, and the other pushed off his hat.
Laughing, they freed her, sliding down to sit on the stairs. He tossed his hat and her headdress to roll down the stairs. She pushed his mask up and off his beloved face. He untied hers, cleverly loosening her hair so she felt it tumble down her back as he kissed her as she'd hungered to be kissed over long weeks of separation.
It wasn't enough. Desire built in her — physical desire, but more than that. A burning need to be his, and to claim him as hers. Even as they kissed, she climbed onto him, slid her hands beneath his jacket. She needed more. Skin. She

began to tug his shirt loose —

He moved back, captured her hands. "Cressida, love . . ."

But then his eyes met hers and she saw practicalities explode into dust. He rose with her still latched around him with arms and legs and climbed the stairs up to the light. In the corridor, he put her down, but her protest was brief. He swept her into his arms and carried her away — away from the music and chatter of the ballroom, up stairs, along a corridor. . . .

Cressida wasn't paying attention to anything but him. She'd undone his cravat and was stroking his neck, his jaw, tangling her fingers in his hair. Drawing his head down.

He stopped. They kissed again, passion building so fiercely that Cressida could imagine she'd drunk Crofton's brew, could imagine surrendering to Tris, here, in a corridor.

She heard something and opened her eyes, then pulled back from the kiss. A maidservant was passing, carrying a pile of cloths, watching them with high eyebrows and a crooked-tooth grin. Once Cressida would have been appalled, but now she grinned back.

Tris looked at the maid, not quite grinning, but not straight-faced either. "My duchess," he said. "You'll be seeing a lot of this."

The woman chuckled as she bobbed a curtsy. "Many blessings on you, zur," she said in a heavy Cornish burr, and hurried away.

"She'll tell everyone," Cressida said.

"We'll tell everyone. Soon."

They weren't kissing. They were talking coherently, but that seemed close to a miracle. Cressida wanted only one thing.

Shyly, in a whisper, she said, "I want . . . I want to be closer to you, Tris, than I've been to anyone since I slid messily from my mother's womb. Now."

She saw her words hit him, and then he moved quickly, carrying her along the corridor, opening a door, then kicking it shut behind him.

She was in his bedroom.

He walked to the huge bed and slid her to her feet beside it. She immediately turned so he could untie her yoke. "Just one little knot this time," she said, unable to manage more than a whisper.

His touch at her nape sent ripples of desire through her, and she could feel the unsteadiness of his hands.

"Which almost defeats me," he said. His voice was hoarse. "But there."

It came loose. She turned back, holding the yoke, then letting it fall. Eyes on his, she unknotted the rope belt as he tore off his jacket.

Cressida dragged the black gown over her head and flung it away, then she recognized the same old problem. "My corset."

Gloriously naked down to his breeches, he laughed, but walked to his washstand and picked up his razor. For a second she thought of protesting, but urgency beat in her, too. She turned her back and felt the blade slice right down the laces.

She tossed the corset on the black gown and stripped the drawers and stockings off beneath her shift, back to him. An awkward shyness was creeping over her now.

"Miranda has scarlet ribbons on her corset and flowers on her stockings."

Hands grasped her shift and pulled it up over her head. He turned her toward him. "And you'll look splendid in such things, too. But now is a time for nakedness, my dearest love."

He was naked. Magnificently naked, rampant with desire.

Cressida sucked in a huge breath of satisfaction.

"Tris, my love." She placed her hands on his chest, and now everything seemed perfectly natural, perfectly . . . perfect. "Make me yours. Now."

He went to the bed and dragged the rich covers back, exposing white linen, as he had once before, on that special night. All the feelings he'd summoned that night rushed back over her so she walked to join him on unsteady legs and leaned on him for support. He swung her up and laid her gently on the bed, then lay beside her, big, strong, hot. . . .

Hers.

Cressida slid a hand from strong thigh to broad chest, trembling. "I keep thinking perhaps I'm dreaming."

"I've dreamed of this," he said, and kissed her again, his leg moving over hers, between hers as his knowing hand stroked. This time she opened her thighs eagerly, arching at his lightest touch, as if long into this game.

She heard him laugh softly, but it was almost a

groan, then his clever mouth was on her breasts and she began to tumble off that cliff.

"Tris!" she cried, wrapping herself around him, afraid he'd let her fall alone again. But his hot weight came over her, stretching her wider, as wide as she longed to be. Hardness pressed.

"Yes, yes!" She could hear herself as if from a distance.

"Oh, yes . . ."

The pain was sharp and startling, but didn't seem to matter because now, at last, they were joined fully, deeply, one, complete. She'd never felt anything so glorious in her life.

Until he started to move.

"Oh, my. Oh, my. Oh, *yes!*"

She thought she kept saying it, but she wasn't sure for her mind seemed far from her seething body. This wasn't like throwing herself off a cliff into mist. It was like spiraling in fire, like becoming one with his strength, his heat, his potency.

She arched, gripping him tight, feeling him arch against her as fierce, burning ecstasy consumed them both.

A thumb brushed her cheek. "I hope those tears aren't regret, love." He didn't sound at all unsure of himself, and confirmed it by his next words. "Because you're mine now."

She knew she was smiling as she opened her eyes. "And you are mine," she said, cradling his face. "I'm so sorry for almost plunging us into disaster with my doubts."

He shook his head, brushed a kiss on her thumb. "I'm sorry my sad career was food for those doubts."

"Without that sad career, would you be able to give me so much pleasure?"

He laughed, moving off her a little. "You are, as I once observed, a minx at heart, Cressida Mandeville." One hand rested on her hip, sweet possession. "Cressida St. Raven, soon. How soon? I'm not sure I can bear one more night without you in my bed."

She felt heat in her cheeks, but it was heat of pleasure at his frank desire. Tris Tregallows, the wonderful Duke of St. Raven, burned with desire for *her*.

"Soon," she said, unable to stop looking down as if bashful. It was simply too much, too overwhelming at this moment. "My parents are due to sail shortly."

"Blessed parents."

"And they're on their way here. They might be here. . . ."

"Excellent." He tilted her chin up so she had to look at him. "My dear Miss Mandeville, will you do me the honor of becoming my wife and my duchess? Tomorrow."

"Tomorrow? Can it be done so fast?"

"Your parents will be here, and if a duke cannot obtain a license in short order, what use is he? You haven't said yes, yet, you know."

She relaxed into a laugh. "Yes, yes, a thousand times yes! Oh, Tris, I've been so miserable without you. I've felt half alive."

He cinched her into a tight hug. "And I feel like a man sentenced to hang who is suddenly reprieved. Not just reprieved, but given a glorious reward."

He swept her long hair forward, then kissed her breasts through it with a hum of pleasure that made her feel faint.

"I never thought to ask," he mumbled. "How did you get here? On angel's wings?"

She gathered enough of her wits to pull his head up so she could form sentences, then told the story.

He worried about his horses, but seemed more interested in her navel.

She admitted that his cousin did not drive as well as he, trying to wriggle out of reach. She knew they both wanted to stay here, to make love again, to twine together and talk all night, but . . .

"You have an entertainment going on, Tris! You must return."

"Nag." He was too strong for her. "The Swinamers are there. Let's hide."

"You can't."

"I'm a duke. I can do what I damn well please."

At the word, their eyes met and they laughed together.

She put her hand over his lips. "Seriously, Tris. You must return to your guests. And what of Phoebe Swinamer? I feel a little sorry for her."

He captured her hand and began to kiss the tip of each finger. "Don't. She wouldn't feel sorry for you if your positions were reversed."

Since she lay nakedly half over him, this made her laugh. "Hard to imagine."

"Quite. I must have been mad. You admitted it was all your fault. You tell her."

"Oh, no!"

He left off his games and rubbed his knuckle down her cheek. "At this moment I want the whole world to be happy, but I fear the best we can do for poor Phoebe is make the announcement and let her preserve her dignity. Nothing has been said."

"I know. And I've seen so many instances of her petty cruelties that my heart cannot ache."

Still, he made no move. Perhaps this was one of those situations where the woman must be strong. Cressida pulled herself away from him and climbed out of the bed. "We need to get dressed."

He sat up, watching her in a way she'd never dreamed of being watched by a man. "You've lost your horns. There should be a risqué joke in that somewhere."

"Not one suitable for a lady's ear, I'm sure."

"Oh, you never know." But he rolled out of bed.

His beautiful naked body had Cressida leaning against a chair for support. Perhaps they could stay here. . . .

She saw the same thought in him, but he put on a gold and scarlet banjan that weakened her even further. Perhaps it would be easier for Miss Swinamer if nothing happened tonight. . . .

He smiled at her in a way not at all steadying. "Stay here. I'll send someone for our headgear. As you say, all the servants will know by now." Then he went into the adjoining room, closing the door.

Cressida simply stood, taking in the disordered bed with a smear of blood on the sheets. Inhaling the sweet musky smell of their lovemaking. A proper young lady of Matlock should surely be riven by shame — or at least doubts — at this moment. She would know she should have waited until her wedding night.

Cressida felt that her world was finally exactly as it should be.

Smiling — when would she stop smiling? — she washed herself, then dressed again. It was a good thing this costume did not need a corset. In a pointless attempt at discretion, she tucked the useless garment in one of his drawers.

Dressed as best she could be, she sat at his dressing table and tried to pin her hair up. Her hands would hardly work. Perhaps it was love-making. Perhaps it was the aftereffect of the mad dash here. Perhaps it was because she hadn't known how deeply, how entirely, she'd needed Tris until now. She hadn't been able to let herself know, or she couldn't have gone on.

He came back, with his hat and her horns.

"What's the matter?"

She heard the cold edge of fear and turned quickly. "Nothing! Only that I realized how close I had come to losing you forever."

She held out her hands and he came to take them, to kiss them. "I wish you didn't have to be a duchess for me, Cressida."

She met his serious eyes and teased him. "Oh, no, sir. You don't get out of it like that now you've had your wicked way with me!"

He laughed and kissed her, then helped her pin up her hair with what few pins they could find.

Cressida settled her horns in place, happily watching him dress. She'd rather he stay naked, but she enjoyed watching him, no matter what he was doing.

It was real. He was hers. Life stretched before her like a universe of delights to discover. There would be hazards and discomforts, as there must be on any journey, but the pleasures would definitely be worth the pains.

He put his hat on and came to take her hand, a ring in his other. "Not the traditional betrothal ring, which is old-fashioned and which I have let Jean-Marie keep, but a modern version of it."

He slid the ring onto her finger — a star sapphire in a lovely, delicate setting. Tears threatened, and she bit her lip to control them.

She noticed that it fit perfectly, which made her think. "This would have been loose on Miss Swinamer's thin finger."

He frowned. "You're right. Poor Phoebe. I never truly gave up hope, and never would have done. She's well out of this, though she may not believe it yet." He kissed the ring. "I sent a message to Cary, asking him to forewarn her. He probably wants to shoot me."

Cressida wouldn't have believed that she could be more moved. "Tris Tregallows, you are a very good man."

"Cressida Mandeville, I will be a better one with you at my side." He took her hand and led her to the door. "Alas, now I must plunge you into the land of serpents and dragons."

Cressida laughed. "Dragons, serpents, and cockadrills are nothing to a Mandeville! Especially, Your Grace, when she has such a very experienced guide."

About the Author

Jo Beverley is widely regarded as one of the most talented romance writers today. She is a five-time winner of Romance Writers of America's cherished RITA Award and one of only a handful of members of the RWA Hall of Fame. She has also received the *Romantic Times* Career Achievement Award. Born in England, she has two grown sons and lives with her husband in Victoria, British Columbia, just a ferry ride away from Seattle.